Praise for award-winning author Anne Bishop

Daughter of the Blood

"A terrific writer. . . . The more I read, the more excited I became because of the freshness of [her] take on the usual high fantasy setting, the assurance of [her] language, all the lovely touches of characterization that [she slips] in so effortlessly."   —Charles de Lint

"Darkly mesmerizing . . . [a] fascinating, dark world."   —*Locus*

"Vividly painted . . . dramatic, erotic, hope-filled."   —Lynn Flewelling

"Lavishly sensual . . . a richly detailed world based on a reversal of standard genre cliches."   —*Library Journal*

"Intense . . . erotic, violent, and imaginative. This one is white-hot."   —Nancy Kress

"A fabulous new talent . . . a uniquely realized fantasy filled with vibrant colors and rich textures. A wonderful new voice, Ms. Bishop holds us spellbound from the very first page."   —*Romantic Times* (4½ stars)

"Anne Bishop has scored a hit. . . . Her poignant storytelling skills are surpassed only by her flair for the dramatic and her deft characterization. . . . A talented author."   —*Affaire de Coeur*

"Mystical, sensual, glittering with dark magic, Anne Bishop's debut novel brings a strong new voice to the fantasy field."
    —Terri Windling, coeditor of *The Year's Best Fantasy and Horror*

"Dark, intricate, and disturbing."
    —Josepha Sherman, author of *Forging the Runes*

"Has immense appeal for fans of dark fantasy or horror. Most highly recommended."   —*Hypatia's Hoard*

"A high-voltage ride through a new realm. Bishop draws her characters with acute emotion [and] leaves the reader lusting for her next novel."
    —Lois H. Gresh, coauthor of *The Termination Node*

continued . . .

"Dark, morbid, sinister, and yet it holds you completely fascinated and spellbound by its beauty. Once I'd begun reading . . . I couldn't bring myself to put down the book and leave the world that Anne Bishop had magically spun around me. . . . Rich in both positive and negative emotions, and intense in its portrayal of human behavior and human desires . . . one of the most original and readable books in the fantasy genre."

—The 11th Hour

Heir to the Shadows

"Daemon, Lucivar, and Saetan ooze more sex appeal than any three fictional characters created in a very long time."   —*The Romance Reader*

"Heir to the Shadows isn't as dark as its predecessor. . . . All the other elements that made the first book such a gripping read are present: vivid and sympathetic characters, a fascinating and fully realized magical system . . . lavish and sensuous descriptions, and interesting world building that turns traditional gender roles and concepts of dominance and submission on their heads. . . . It's a terrific read, and I highly recommend both it and *Daughter of the Blood*."   —SF Site

"Bishop seems to delight in turning fantasy conventions on their heads. . . . Still darkly opulent, often exotic."   —*Locus*

"The fabulous talent of Anne Bishop is showcased in *Heir to the Shadows*. . . . Ms. Bishop's striking magical concepts and powerful images are wonderfully leavened with unexpected dash and humor, creating an irresistible treat for fantasy fans."   —*Romantic Times*

Queen of the Darkness

"As engaging, as strongly characterized, and as fully conceived as its predecessors . . . a perfect—and very moving—conclusion."   —SF Site

"A storyteller of stunning intensity, Ms. Bishop has a knack for appealing but complex characterization realized in a richly drawn, imaginative ambiance."   —*Romantic Times*

"A powerful finale for this fascinating, uniquely dark trilogy."   —*Locus*

Dreams Made Flesh

"Fans of Bishop's *Black Jewels Trilogy* won't want to miss this new collection."　　　　　　　　　　　　　　　　　　　　　　　　*—Locus*

"[Full of] sensual richness."　　　　　　　　　　　　　*—Library Journal*

"Will delight [Bishop's] fans . . . carefully written with lovely language and great characterization and humor."　　　　　　　　　　　*—SFRevu*

"Exciting, entertaining, and exotic tales . . . absolutely riveting romantic fantasy . . . a great character study . . . beautiful."　*—Midwest Book Review*

The Invisible Ring

"Plenty of adventure, romance, dazzling wizardly pyrotechnics, and [a] unique and fascinating hierarchical magic system. . . . Darkly macabre with spine-tingling emotional intensity, mesmerizing magic, lush sensuality, and exciting action, all set in a thoroughly detailed invented world of cultures in conflict . . . *The Invisible Ring* will serve as an enticement, whetting the appetite to explore more of the realms in *The Black Jewels Trilogy*. It and its predecessors are genuine gems of fantasy much to be prized."　*—SF Site*

"[An] entertaining otherworld fantasy adventure with battles and dangers and chases. Fresh and interesting."　　　　　　　　　*—Chronicle*

"A weird but highly diverting and oddly heartwarming mix."　*—Locus*

"A formidable talent, Ms. Bishop weaves another intense emotional tale that sparkles with powerful and imaginative magic."　*—Romantic Times*

Sebastian

"Erotic, fervently romantic, superbly entertaining, *Sebastian* satisfies."　　　　　　　　　　　　　　　　　　　　　　　　*—Booklist*

"Bishop's talents lie both in her ability to craft a story filled with intriguing characters and in her flair for smoldering sensuality that recommends her to fans of Tanith Lee, Storm Constantine, and Anne Rice. Highly recommended."　　　　　　　　　　　　　　　　　　*—Library Journal*

"Pure originality and lyrical prose. . . . Tender romances and friendships will delight fantasy readers tired of gore and lust."　*—Publishers Weekly*

ALSO BY ANNE BISHOP

THE EPHEMERA SERIES
Sebastian
Belladonna

THE BLACK JEWELS SERIES
Heir to the Shadows
Queen of the Darkness
The Invisible Ring
Dreams Made Flesh

THE TIR ALAINN TRILOGY
Pillars of the World
Shadows and Light
The House of Gaian

ANNE BISHOP

DAUGHTER
OF THE
BLOOD

Book 1 of
The Black Jewels Trilogy

A ROC BOOK

ROC

Published by New American Library, a division of
Penguin Group (USA) Inc., 375 Hudson Street,
New York, New York 10014, USA
Penguin Group (Canada), 90 Eglinton Avenue East, Suite 700, Toronto,
Ontario M4P 2Y3, Canada (a division of Pearson Penguin Canada Inc.)
Penguin Books Ltd., 80 Strand, London WC2R 0RL, England
Penguin Ireland, 25 St. Stephen's Green, Dublin 2,
Ireland (a division of Penguin Books Ltd.)
Penguin Group (Australia), 250 Camberwell Road, Camberwell, Victoria 3124,
Australia (a division of Pearson Australia Group Pty. Ltd.)
Penguin Books India Pvt. Ltd., 11 Community Centre, Panchsheel Park,
New Delhi – 110 017, India
Penguin Group (NZ), 67 Apollo Drive, Rosedale, North Share,
Auckland 1311, New Zealand (a division of Pearson New Zealand Ltd.)
Penguin Books (South Africa) (Pty.) Ltd., 24 Sturdee Avenue,
Rosebank, Johannesburg 2196, South Africa

Penguin Books Ltd., Registered Offices:
80 Strand, London WC2R 0RL, England

Published by Roc, an imprint of New American Library, a division of Penguin Group (USA) Inc.
Previously published in a Roc mass market edition and as part of the Roc trade paperback omnibus edition of
The Black Jewels Trilogy.

First Roc Trade Paperback Printing, June 2007
1 3 5 7 9 10 8 6 4 2

For
Blair Boone
and
Charles de Lint

Acknowledgments

Every creative endeavor, especially the creative endeavor we call Life, is a journey of many. My thanks to the friends and neighbors who make that endeavor a joyous one, and to the members of Spin-a-Story Tellers for the stories shared in performance and around the table. A special thanks to Kathy and Blair Boone, Nadine and Mike Fallacaro, Pat and Bill Feidner, Neil Schmitz, Grace Tongue, Ellen Datlow, Charles de Lint, Nancy Kress, Pat York, Laura Anne Gilman, Jennifer Jackson—and you who have picked up this book to share in the wonder of Story.

Jewels

White
Yellow
Tiger Eye
Rose
Summer-sky
Purple Dusk
Opal★
Green
Sapphire
Red
Gray
Ebon-gray
Black

★Opal is the dividing line between lighter and darker Jewels because it can be either.

When making the Offering to the Darkness, a person can descend a maximum of three ranks from his/her Birthright Jewel.

Example: Birthright White could descend to Rose.

AUTHOR'S NOTE

The "Sc" in the names Scelt, Sceval, and Sceron is pronounced "Sh."

Blood Hierarchy/Castes

MALES:

landen—non-Blood of any race

Blood male—a general term for all males of the Blood; also refers to any Blood male who doesn't wear Jewels

Warlord—a Jeweled male equal in status to a witch

Prince—a Jeweled male equal in status to a Priestess or a Healer

Warlord Prince—a dangerous, extremely aggressive Jeweled male; in status, slightly lower than a Queen

FEMALES:

landen—non-Blood of any race

Blood female—a general term for all females of the Blood; mostly refers to any Blood female who doesn't wear Jewels

witch—a Blood female who wears Jewels but isn't one of the other hierarchical levels; also refers to any Jeweled female.

Healer—a witch who heals physical wounds and illnesses; equal in status to a Priestess and a Prince

Priestess—a witch who cares for altars, Sanctuaries, and Dark Altars; witnesses handfasts and marriages; performs offerings; equal in status to a Healer and a Prince

Black Widow—a witch who heals the mind; weaves the tangled webs of dreams and visions; is trained in illusions and poisons

Queen—a witch who rules the Blood; is considered to be the land's heart and the Blood's moral center; as such, she is the focal point of their society

PROLOGUE

Terreille

I am Tersa the Weaver, Tersa the Liar, Tersa the Fool.

When the Blood-Jeweled Lords and Ladies hold a banquet, I'm the entertainment that comes after the musicians have played and the lithesome girls and boys have danced and the Lords have drunk too much wine and demand to have their fortunes told. "Tell us a story, Weaver," they yell as their hands pass over the serving girls' rumps and their Ladies eye the young men and decide who will have the painful pleasure of serving in the bed that night.

I was one of them once, Blood as they are Blood.

No, that's not true. I *wasn't* Blood as they are Blood. That's why I was broken on a Warlord's spear and became shattered glass that only reflects what might have been.

It's hard to break a Blood-Jeweled male, but a witch's life hangs by the hymenal thread, and what happens on her Virgin Night determines whether she is whole to practice the Craft or becomes a broken vessel, forever aching for the part of her that's lost. Oh, some magic always remains, enough for day-to-day living and parlor tricks, but not the Craft, not the lifeblood of our kind.

But the Craft can be reclaimed—if one is willing to pay the price.

When I was younger, I fought against that final slide into the Twisted Kingdom. Better to be broken and sane than broken and mad. Better to see the world and know a tree for a tree, a flower for a flower rather than to look through gauze at gray and ghostly shapes and see clearly only the shards of one's self.

So I thought then.

As I shuffle to the low stool, I struggle to stay at the edge of the Twisted Kingdom and see the physical world clearly one last time. I carefully place the wooden frame that holds my tangled web, the web of dreams and visions, on the small table near the stool.

The Lords and Ladies expect me to tell their fortunes, and I always have, not by magic but by keeping my eyes and ears open and then telling them what they want to hear.

Simple. No magic to it.

But not tonight.

For days now I have heard a strange kind of thunder, a distant calling. Last night I surrendered to madness in order to reclaim my Craft as a Black Widow, a witch of the Hourglass covens. Last night I wove a tangled web to see the dreams and visions.

Tonight there will be no fortunes. I have the strength to say this only once. I must be sure that those who must hear it are in the room before I speak.

I wait. They don't notice. Glasses are filled and refilled as I fight to stay on the edge of the Twisted Kingdom.

Ah, there he is. Daemon Sadi, from the Territory called Hayll. He's beautiful, bitter, cruel. He has a seducer's smile and a body women want to touch and be caressed by, but he's filled with a cold, unquenchable rage. When the Ladies talk about his bedroom skills, the words they whisper are "excruciating pleasure." I don't doubt he's enough of a sadist to mix pain and pleasure in equal portions, but he's always been kind to me, and it's a small bone of hope that I throw out to him tonight. Still, it's more than anyone else has given him.

The Lords and Ladies grow restless. I usually don't take this long to begin my pronouncements. Agitation and annoyance build, but I wait. After tonight, it will make no difference.

There's the other one, in the opposite corner of the room. Lucivar Yaslana, the Eyrien half-breed from the Territory called Askavi.

Hayll has no love for Askavi, nor Askavi for Hayll, but Daemon and Lucivar are drawn to one another without understanding why, so wound into each other's lives they cannot separate. Uneasy friends, they have fought legendary battles, have destroyed so many courts the Blood are afraid to have them together for any length of time.

I raise my hands, let them fall into my lap. Daemon watches me. Nothing about him has changed, but I know he's waiting, listening. And because he's listening, Lucivar listens too.

"She is coming."

At first they don't realize I've spoken. Then the angry murmurs begin when the words are understood.

"Stupid bitch," someone yells. "Tell me who I'll love tonight."

"What does it matter?" I answer. "She is coming. The Realm of Terreille will be torn apart by its own foolish greed. Those who survive will serve, but few will survive."

I'm slipping farther from the edge. Tears of frustration spill down my cheeks. Not yet. Sweet Darkness, not yet. I must say this.

Daemon kneels beside me, his hands covering mine. I speak to him, only to him, and through him, to Lucivar.

"The Blood in Terreille whore the old ways and make a mockery of everything we are." I wave my hand to indicate the ones who now rule. "They twist things to suit themselves. They dress up and pretend. They wear Blood Jewels but don't understand what it means to be Blood. They talk of honoring the Darkness, but it's a lie. They honor nothing but their own ambitions. The Blood were created to be the caretakers of the Realms. That's why we were given our power. That's why we come from, yet are apart from, the people in every Territory. The perversion of what we are can't go on. The day is coming when the debt will be called in, and the Blood will have to answer for what they've become."

"They're the Blood who rule, Tersa," Daemon says sadly. "Who is left to call in this debt? Bastard slaves like me?"

I'm slipping fast. My nails dig into his hands, drawing blood, but he doesn't pull away. I lower my voice. He strains to hear me. "The Darkness has had a Prince for a long, long time. Now the Queen is coming. It may take decades, even centuries, but she is coming." I point with my chin at the Lords and Ladies sitting at the tables. "They will be dust by then, but you and the Eyrien will be here to serve."

Frustration fills his golden eyes. "What Queen? Who is coming?"

"The living myth," I whisper. "Dreams made flesh."

His shock is replaced instantly by a fierce hunger. "You're sure?"

The room is a swirling mist. He's the only thing still in sharp focus. He's the only thing I need. "I saw her in the tangled web, Daemon. I saw her."

I'm too tired to hang on to the real world, but I stubbornly cling to his hands to tell him one last thing. "The Eyrien, Daemon."

He glances at Lucivar. "What about him?"

"He's your brother. You are your father's sons."

I can't hold on anymore and plunge into the madness that's called the Twisted Kingdom. I fall and fall among the shards of myself. The world spins and shatters. In its fragments, I see my once-Sisters pouring around the tables, frightened and intent, and Daemon's hand casually reaching out, as if by accident, destroying the fragile spidersilk of my tangled web.

It's impossible to reconstruct a tangled web. Terreille's Black Widows may spend year upon frightened year trying, but in the end it will be in vain. It will not be the same web, and they will not see what I saw.

In the gray world above, I hear myself howling with laughter. Far below me, in the psychic abyss that is part of the Darkness, I hear another howling, one full of joy and pain, rage and celebration.

Not just another witch coming, my foolish Sisters, but Witch.

PART 1

CHAPTER ONE

1 / Terreille

Lucivar Yaslana, the Eyrien half-breed, watched the guards drag the sobbing man to the boat. He felt no sympathy for the condemned man who had led the aborted slave revolt. In the Territory called Pruul, sympathy was a luxury no slave could afford.

He had refused to participate in the revolt. The ringleaders were good men, but they didn't have the strength, the backbone, or the balls to do what was needed. They didn't enjoy seeing blood run.

He had not participated. Zuultah, the Queen of Pruul, had punished him anyway.

The heavy shackles around his neck and wrists had already rubbed his skin raw, and his back was a throbbing ache from the lash. He spread his dark, membranous wings, trying to ease the ache in his back.

A guard immediately prodded him with a club, then retreated, skittish, at his soft hiss of anger.

Unlike the other slaves who couldn't contain their misery or fear, there was no expression in Lucivar's gold eyes, no psychic scent of emotions for the guards to play with as they put the sobbing man into the old, one-man boat. No longer seaworthy, the boat showed gaping holes in its rotten wood, holes that only added to its value now.

The condemned man was small and half-starved. It still took six guards to put him into the boat. Five guards held the man's head, arms, and legs. The last guard smeared bacon grease on the man's genitals before sliding a wooden cover into place. It fit snugly over the boat, with holes cut out for the head and hands. Once the man's hands were tied to iron rings on the outside of the boat, the cover was locked into place so that no one but the guards could remove it.

One guard studied the imprisoned man and shook his head in mock dismay. Turning to the others, he said, "He should have a last meal before being put to sea."

The guards laughed. The man cried for help.

One by one, the guards carefully shoved food into the man's mouth before herding the other slaves to the stables where they were quartered.

"You'll be entertained tonight, boys," a guard yelled, laughing. "Remember it the next time you decide to leave Lady Zuultah's service."

Lucivar looked over his shoulder, then looked away.

Drawn by the smell of food, the rats slipped into the gaping holes in the boat.

The man in the boat screamed.

Clouds scudded across the moon, gray shrouds hiding its light. The man in the boat didn't move. His knees were open sores, bloody from kicking the top of the boat in his effort to keep the rats away. His vocal cords were destroyed from screaming.

Lucivar knelt behind the boat, moving carefully to muffle the sound of the chains.

"I didn't tell them, Yasi," the man said hoarsely. "They tried to make me tell, but I didn't. I had that much honor left."

Lucivar held a cup to the man's lips. "Drink this," he said, his voice a deep murmur, a part of the night.

"No," the man moaned. "No." He began to cry, a harsh, guttural sound pulled from his ruined throat.

"Hush, now. Hush. It will help." Supporting the man's head, Lucivar eased the cup between the swollen lips. After two swallows, Lucivar put the cup aside and stroked the man's head with gentle fingertips. "It will help," he crooned.

"I'm a Warlord of the Blood." When Lucivar offered the cup again, the man took another sip. As his voice got stronger, the words began to slur. "You're a Warlord Prince. Why do they do this to us, Yasi?"

"Because they have no honor. Because they don't remember what it means to be Blood. The High Priestess of Hayll's influence is a plague that has been spreading across the Realm for centuries, slowly consuming every Territory it touches."

"Maybe the landens are right, then. Maybe the Blood are evil."

Lucivar continued stroking the man's forehead and temples. "No. We are what we are. Nothing more, nothing less. There is good and evil among every kind of people. It's the evil among us who rule now."

"And where are the good among us?" the man asked sleepily.

Lucivar kissed the top of the man's head. "They've been destroyed or enslaved." He offered the cup. "Finish it, little Brother, and it will be finished."

After the man took the last swallow, Lucivar used Craft to vanish the cup.

The man in the boat laughed. "I feel very brave, Yasi."

"You are very brave."

"The rats . . . My balls are gone."

"I know."

"I cried, Yasi. Before all of them, I cried."

"It doesn't matter."

"I'm a Warlord. I shouldn't have cried."

"You didn't tell. You had courage when you needed it."

"Zuultah killed the others anyway."

"She'll pay for it, little Brother. Someday she and the others like her will pay for it all." Lucivar gently massaged the man's neck.

"Yasi, I—"

The movement was sudden, the sound sharp.

Lucivar carefully let the lolling head fall backward and slowly rose to his feet. He could have told them the plan wouldn't work, that the Ring of Obedience could be fine-tuned sufficiently to alert its owner to an inner drawing of strength and purpose. He could have told them the malignant tendrils that kept them enslaved had spread too far, and it would take a sweeter savagery than a man was capable of to free them. He could have told them there were crueler weapons than the Ring to keep a man obedient, that their concern for each other would destroy them, that the only way to escape, for even a little while, was to care for no one, to be alone.

He could have told them.

And yet, when they had approached him, timidly, cautiously, eager to ask a man who had broken free again and again over the centuries but was still enslaved, all he had said was, "Sacrifice everything." They had gone away, disappointed, unable to understand he had meant what he'd said. Sacrifice everything. And there was one thing he couldn't—wouldn't—sacrifice.

How many times after he'd surrendered and been tethered again by that cruel ring of gold around his organ had Daemon found him and pinned him against a wall, snarling with rage, calling him a fool and a coward to give in?

Liar. Silky, court-trained liar.

Once, Dorothea SaDiablo had searched desperately for Daemon Sadi after he'd vanished from a court without a trace. It had taken a hundred years to find him, and two thousand Warlords had died trying to recapture him. He could have used that small, savage Territory he had held and conquered half the Realm of Terreille, could have become a tangible threat to Hayll's encroachment and absorption of every people it touched. Instead, he had read a letter Dorothea sent through a messenger. Read it and surrendered.

The letter had simply said: "Surrender by the new moon. Every day you are gone thereafter, I will take a piece of your brother's body in payment for your arrogance."

Lucivar shook himself, trying to dislodge the unwelcome thoughts. In some ways, memories were worse than the lash, for they led to thoughts of Askavi, with its mountains rising to cut the sky and its valleys filled with towns, farms, and forests. Not that Askavi was that fertile anymore, having been raped for too many centuries by those who took but never gave anything back. Still, it was home, and centuries of enslaved exile had left him aching for the smell of clean mountain air, the taste of a sweet, cold stream, the silence of the woods, and, most of all, the mountains where the Eyrien race soared.

But he was in Pruul, that hot, scrubby desert wasteland, serving that bitch Zuultah because he couldn't hide his disgust for Prythian, Askavi's High Priestess, couldn't leash his temper enough to serve witches he despised.

Among the Blood, males were meant to serve, not to rule. He had never challenged that, despite the number of witches he'd killed over the centuries. He had killed them because it was an insult to serve them, because he was an Eyrien Warlord Prince who wore Ebon-gray Jewels and refused to believe that serving and groveling meant the same thing. Because he was a half-breed bastard, he had no hope of attaining a position of authority within a court, despite the rank of his Jewels. Because he was a trained Eyrien warrior and had a temper that was explosive even for a Warlord Prince, he had even less hope of being allowed to live outside the social chains of a court.

And he was caught, as all Blood males were caught. There was something bred into them that made them crave service, that compelled them to bond in some way with a Blood-Jeweled female.

Lucivar twitched his shoulder and sucked air through his teeth as a lash wound reopened. When he gingerly touched the wound, his hand came away wet with fresh blood.

He bared his teeth in a bitter smile. What was that old saying? A wish, offered with blood, is a prayer to the Darkness.

He closed his eyes, raised his hand toward the night sky, and turned inward, descending into the psychic abyss to the depth of his Ebon-gray Jewels so that this wish would remain private, so that no one in Zuultah's court could hear the sending of this thought.

Just once, I'd like to serve a Queen I could respect, someone I could truly believe in. A strong Queen who wouldn't fear my strength. A Queen I could also call a friend.

Dryly amused by his own foolishness, Lucivar wiped his hand on his baggy cotton pants and sighed. It was a shame that the pronouncement Tersa had made seven hundred years ago had been nothing more than a mad delusion. For a while, it had given him hope. It had taken him a long time to realize that hope was a bitter thing.

Hello?

Lucivar looked toward the stables where the slaves were quartered. The guards would make their nightly check soon. He'd take another minute to savor the night air, even if it smelled hot and dusty, before returning to the filthy cell with its bed of dirty, bug-infested straw, before returning to the stink of fear, unwashed bodies, and human waste.

Hello?

Lucivar turned in a slow circle, his physical senses alert, his mind probing for the source of that thought. Psychic communication could be broadcast to everyone in an area—like shouting in a crowded room—or narrowed to a single Jewel rank or gender, or narrowed even further to a single mind. That thought seemed aimed directly at him.

There was nothing out there except the expected. Whatever it was, it was gone.

Lucivar shook his head. He was getting as skittish as the landens, the non-Blood of each race, with their superstitions about evil stalking in the night.

"Hello?"

Lucivar spun around, his dark wings flaring for balance as he set his feet in a fighting stance.

He felt like a fool when he saw the girl staring at him, wide-eyed.

She was a scrawny little thing, about seven years old. Calling her plain would have been kind. But, even in the moonlight, she had the most extraordinary eyes. They reminded him of a twilight sky or a deep mountain lake. Her clothes were of good quality, certainly better than a beggar child would wear. Her gold hair was done up in sausage curls that indicated care even if they looked ridiculous around her pointed little face.

"What are you doing here?" he asked roughly.

She laced her fingers and hunched her shoulders. "I-I heard you. Y-you wanted a friend."

"You *heard* me?" Lucivar stared at her. How in the name of Hell had she heard him? True, he had sent that wish out, but on an Ebon-gray thread. He was the only Ebon-gray in the Realm of Terreille. The only Jewel darker than his was the Black, and the only person who wore *that* was Daemon Sadi. Unless . . .

No. She couldn't be.

At that moment, the girl's eyes flicked from him to the dead man in the boat, then back to him.

"I have to go," she whispered, backing away from him.

"No, you don't." He came toward her, soft-footed, a hunter stalking his prey.

She bolted.

He caught her within seconds, heedless of the noise the chains made. Looping a chain over her, he wrapped an arm around her waist and lifted her off her feet, grunting when her heel banged his knee. He ignored her attempts to scratch, and her kicks, while bruising, weren't the same kind of deterrent one good kick in the right place would have been. When she started shrieking, he clamped a hand over her mouth.

She promptly sank her teeth into his finger.

Lucivar bit back a howl and swore under his breath. He dropped to his knees, pulling her with him. "Hush," he whispered fiercely. "Do you want to bring the guards down on us?" She probably did, and he expected her to struggle even harder, knowing there was help nearby.

Instead, she froze.

Lucivar laid his cheek against her head and sucked air. "You're a spitting little cat," he said quietly, fighting to keep the laughter out of his voice.

"Why did you kill him?"

Did he imagine it, or did her voice change? She still sounded like a young girl, but thunder, caverns, and midnight skies were in that voice. "He was suffering."

"Couldn't you take him to a Healer?"

"Healers don't bother with slaves," he snapped. "Besides, the rats didn't leave enough of him to heal." He pulled her tighter against his chest, hoping physical warmth would make her stop shuddering. She looked so pale against his light-brown skin, and he knew it wasn't simply because she was fair-skinned. "I'm sorry. That was cruel."

When she started struggling against his hold, he raised his arms so that she could slip under the chain between his wrists. She scrambled out of reach, spun around, and dropped to her knees.

They studied each other.

"What's your name?" she finally asked.

"I'm called Yasi." He laughed when she wrinkled her nose. "Don't blame me. I didn't choose it."

"It's a silly word for someone like you. What's your real name?"

Lucivar hesitated. Eyriens were one of the long-lived races. He'd had 1,700 years to gain a reputation for being vicious and violent. If she'd heard any of the stories about him . . .

He took a deep breath and released it slowly. "Lucivar Yaslana."

No reaction except a shy smile of approval.

"What's your name, Cat?"

"Jaenelle."

He grinned. "Nice name, but I think Cat suits you just as well."

She snarled.

"See?" He hesitated, but he had to ask. Zuultah's guessing he'd killed that slave and knowing for sure would make a difference when he was stretched between the whipping posts. "Is your family visiting Lady Zuultah?"

Jaenelle frowned. "Who?"

Really, she did look like a kitten trying to figure out how to pounce on a large, hoppy bug. "Zuultah. The Queen of Pruul."

"What's Pruul?"

"This is Pruul." Lucivar waved a hand to indicate the land around them and then swore in Eyrien when the chains rattled. He swallowed the last curse when he noticed the intense, interested look on her face. "Since you're not from Pruul and your family isn't visiting, where are you from?" When she hesitated, he tipped his head toward the boat. "I can keep a secret."

"I'm from Chaillot."

"Chai—" Lucivar bit back another curse. "Do you understand Eyrien?"

"No." Jaenelle grinned at him. "But now I know some Eyrien words."

Should he laugh or strangle her? "How did you get here?"

She fluffed her hair and frowned at the rocky ground between them. Finally she shrugged. "Same way I get to other places."

"You ride the Winds?" he yelped.

She raised a finger to test the air.

"Not breezes or puffs of air." Lucivar ground his teeth. "The Winds. The Webs. The psychic roads in the Darkness."

Jaenelle perked up. "Is that what they are?"

He managed to stop in mid-curse.

Jaenelle leaned forward. "Are you always this prickly?"

"Most people think I'm a prick, yes."

"What's that mean?"

"Never mind." He chose a sharp stone and drew a circle on the ground between them. "This is the Realm of Terreille." He placed a round stone in the circle. "This is the Black Mountain, Ebon Askavi, where the Winds meet." He drew straight lines from the round stone to the circumference of the circle. "These are tether lines." He drew smaller circles within the circle. "These are radial lines. The Winds are like a spiderweb. You can travel on the tether or the radial lines, changing direction where they intersect. There's a Web for each rank of the Blood Jewels. The darker the Web, the more tether and radial lines there are and the faster the Wind is. You can ride a Web that's your rank or lighter. You can't ride a Web darker than your Jewel rank unless you're traveling inside a Coach being driven by someone strong enough to ride that Web or you're being shielded by someone who can ride that Web. If you try, you probably won't survive. Understand?"

Jaenelle chewed on her lower lip and pointed to a space between the strands. "What if I want to go there?"

Lucivar shook his head. "You'd have to drop from the Web back into the Realm at the nearest point and travel some other way."

"That's not how I got here," she protested.

Lucivar shuddered. There wasn't a strand of any Web around Zuultah's compound. Her court was deliberately in one of those blank spaces. The only way to get here directly from the Winds was by leaving the Web and gliding blind through the Darkness, which, even for the strongest and the best, was a chancy thing to do. Unless . . .

"Come here, Cat," he said gently. When she dropped in front of him, he rested his hands on her thin shoulders. "Do you often go wandering?"

Jaenelle nodded slowly. "People call me. Like you did."

Like he did. Mother Night! "Cat, listen to me. Children are vulnerable to many dangers."

There was a strange expression in her eyes. "Yes, I know."

"Sometimes an enemy can wear the mask of a friend until it's too late to escape."

"Yes," she whispered.

Lucivar shook her gently, forcing her to look at him. "Terreille is a dangerous place for little cats. Please, go home and don't go wandering anymore. Don't . . . don't answer the people who call you."

"But then I won't see you anymore."

Lucivar closed his gold eyes. A knife in the heart would hurt less. "I know. But we'll always be friends. And it's not forever. When you're grown up, I'll come find you or you'll come find me."

Jaenelle nibbled her lip. "How old is grown up?"

Yesterday. Tomorrow. "Let's say seventeen. It sounds like forever, I know, but it's really not that long." Even Sadi couldn't have spun a better lie than that. "Will you promise not to go wandering?"

Jaenelle sighed. "I promise not to go wandering in Terreille."

Lucivar hauled her to her feet and spun her around. "There's one thing I want to teach you before you go. This will work if a man ever tries to grab you from behind."

When they'd gone through the demonstration enough times that he was sure she knew what to do, Lucivar kissed her forehead and stepped back. "Get out of here. The guards will be making the rounds any minute now. And remember—a Queen never breaks a promise made to a Warlord Prince."

"I'll remember." She hesitated. "Lucivar? I won't look the same when I'm grown up. How will you know me?"

Lucivar smiled. Ten years or a hundred, it would make no difference. He'd always recognize those extraordinary sapphire eyes. "I'll know. Good-bye, Cat. May the Darkness embrace you."

She smiled at him and vanished.

Lucivar stared at that empty space. Was that a foolish thing to say to her? Probably.

A gate rattling caught his attention. He swiftly rubbed out the drawing of the Winds and slipped from shadow to shadow until he reached the stables. He passed through the outside wall and had just settled into his cell when the guard opened the barred window in the door.

Zuultah was arrogant enough to believe her holding spells kept her slaves from using Craft to pass through the cell walls. It was uncomfortable to pass through a spelled wall but not impossible for him.

Let the bitch wonder. When the guards found the slave in the boat, she'd suspect him of breaking the man's neck. She suspected him when *anything* went wrong in her court—with good reason.

Maybe he would offer a little resistance when the guards tried to tie him to the whipping posts. A vicious brawl would keep Zuultah distracted, and the violent emotions would cover up any lingering psychic scent from the girl.

Oh, yes, he could keep Lady Zuultah so distracted, she would *never* realize that Witch now walked the Realm.

2 / Terreille

Lady Maris turned her head toward the large, freestanding mirror. "You may go now."

Daemon Sadi slipped out of bed and began dressing slowly, tauntingly, fully aware that she watched him in the mirror. She always watched the mirror when he serviced her. A bit of self-voyeurism perhaps? Did she pretend the man in the mirror actually cared about her, that her climax aroused him?

Stupid bitch.

Maris stretched and sighed with pleasure. "You remind me of a wild cat, all silky skin and rippling muscles."

Daemon slipped into the white silk shirt. A savage predator? That was a fair enough description. If she ever annoyed him beyond his limited tolerance for the distaff gender, he would be happy to show her his claws. One little one in particular.

Maris sighed again. "You're so beautiful."

Yes, he was. His face was a gift of his mysterious heritage, aristocratic and too beautifully shaped to be called merely handsome. He was tall and broad-shouldered. He kept his body well toned and muscular enough to please. His voice was deep and cultured, with a husky, seductive edge to it that made women go all misty-eyed. His gold eyes and thick black hair were typical of all three of Terreille's long-lived races, but his warm, golden-brown skin was a little lighter than the Hayllian aristos—more like the Dhemlan race.

His body was a weapon, and he kept his weapons well honed.

Daemon shrugged into his black jacket. The clothes, too, were weapons, from the skimpy underwear to the perfectly tailored suits. Nectar to seduce the unwary to their doom.

Fanning herself with her hand, Maris looked directly at him. "Even in this weather, you didn't work up a sweat."

It sounded like the complaint it was.

Daemon smiled mockingly. "Why should I?"

Maris sat up, pulling at the sheet to cover herself. "You're a cruel, unfeeling bastard."

Daemon raised one finely shaped eyebrow. "You think I'm cruel? You're quite right, of course. I'm a connoisseur of cruelty."

"And you're proud of it, aren't you?" Maris blinked back tears. Her face tightened, showing all the petulant age lines. "Everything they said about you is true. Even that." She waved a hand toward his groin.

"That?" he asked, knowing perfectly well what she meant. She, and every woman like her, would forgive every vicious thing he did if she could coax him into an erection.

"You're not a true man. You never were."

"Ah. In that, too, you're quite right." Daemon slipped his hands into his trouser pockets. "Personally, I've always thought it's the discomfort of the Ring of Obedience that's caused the problem." The cold, mocking smile returned. "Perhaps if you removed it . . ."

Maris became so pale he wondered if she was going to faint. He doubted Maris wanted to test his theory badly enough that she would actually remove that gold circle around his organ. Just as well. She wouldn't survive one minute after he was free.

Most of the witches he'd served hadn't survived anyway.

Daemon smiled that cold, familiar, brutal smile and settled next to her on the bed. "So you think I'm cruel." Her eyes were already glazing from the psychic seduction tendrils he was weaving around her.

"Yes," Maris whispered, watching his lips.

Daemon leaned forward, amused at how quickly she opened her mouth for a kiss. Her tongue flirted hungrily with his, and when he finally raised his head, she tried to pull him down on top of her. "Do you really want to know why I don't work up a sweat?" he asked too gently.

She hesitated, lust warring with curiosity. "Why?"

Daemon smiled. "Because, my darling Lady Maris, your so-called intelligence bores me to tears and that body you think so fine and flaunt whenever and wherever possible isn't fit to be crowbait."

Maris's lower lip quivered. "Y-you're a sadistic brute."

Daemon slipped off the bed. "How do you know?" he asked pleasantly. "The game hasn't even begun."

"Get out. GET OUT!"

He quickly left the bedroom, but waited a moment outside the door. Her wail of anguish was perfect counterpoint to his mocking laughter.

A light breeze ruffled Daemon's hair as he followed a gravel path through the back gardens. Unbuttoning his shirt, he smiled with pleasure as the breeze caressed his bare skin. He pulled a thin black cigarette from its gold case, lit it, and sighed as the smoke drifted slowly out of his mouth and nostrils, burning away Maris's stench.

The light in Maris's bedroom went out.

Stupid bitch. She didn't understand the game she played. No—she didn't understand the game *he* played. He was 1,700 years old and just coming into his prime. He'd worn a Ring of Obedience controlled by

Dorothea SaDiablo, Hayll's High Priestess, for as long as he could remember. He had been raised in her court as her cousin's bastard son, had been educated and trained to serve Hayll's Black Widows. That is, taught enough of the Craft to serve those witch-bitches as they wanted to be served. He'd been whoring in courts long turned to dust while Maris's people were just beginning to build cities. He'd destroyed better witches than her, and he could destroy her, too. He'd brought down courts, laid waste to cities, brought about minor wars as vengeance for bedroom games.

Dorothea punished him, hurt him, sold him into service in court after court, but in the end, Maris and her kind were expendable. He was not. It had cost Dorothea and Hayll's other Black Widows dearly to create him, and whatever they had done, they couldn't do again.

Hayll's Blood was failing. In his generation, there were very few who wore the darker Jewels—not surprising since Dorothea had been so thorough about purging the stronger witches who might have challenged her rule after she became High Priestess, leaving her followers within Hayll's Hundred Families, lighter-Jeweled witches who had no social standing, and Blood females who had little power as the only ones capable of mating with a Blood male and producing healthy Blood children.

Now she needed a dark bloodline to mate with her Black Widow Sisters. So while she gladly humiliated and tortured him, she wouldn't destroy him because, if there was any possibility at all, she wanted his willing seed in her Sisters' bodies, and she would use fools like Maris to wear him down until he was ready to submit.

He would never submit.

Seven hundred years ago, Tersa had told him the living myth was coming. Seven hundred years of waiting, watching, searching, hoping. Seven hundred heartbreaking, exhausting years. He refused to give up, refused to wonder if she'd been mistaken, refused because his heart yearned too much for that strange, wonderful, terrifying creature called Witch.

In his soul, he knew her. In his dreams, he saw her. He never envisioned a face. It always blurred if he tried to focus on it. But he could see her dressed in a robe made of dark, transparent spidersilk, a robe that slid from her shoulders as she moved, a robe that opened and closed as she walked, revealing bare, night-cool skin. And there would be a scent in the room that was her, a scent he would wake to, burying his face in her pillow after she was up and attending her own concerns.

It wasn't lust—the body's fire paled in comparison to the embrace of mind to mind—although physical pleasure was part of it. He wanted to touch her, feel the texture of her skin, taste the warmth of her. He wanted to caress her until they both burned. He wanted to weave his life into hers until there was no telling where one began and the other ended. He wanted to put his arms around her, strong and protecting, and find himself protected; possess her and be possessed; dominate her and be dominated. He wanted that Other, that shadow across his life, who made him ache with every breath while he stumbled among these feeble women who meant nothing to him and never could.

Simply, he believed that he had been born to be her lover.

Daemon lit another cigarette and flexed the ring finger of his right hand. The snake tooth slid smoothly out of its channel and rested on the underside of his long, black-tinted fingernail. He smiled. Maris wondered if he had claws? Well, this little darling would impress her. Not for very long, though, since the venom in the sac beneath his fingernail was extremely potent.

He was lucky that he'd reached sexual maturity a little later than most Hayllians. The snake tooth had come along with the rest of the physical changes, a shocking surprise, for he'd thought it was impossible for a male to be a natural Black Widow. During that time, he'd been serving in a court where it was fashionable for men to wear their nails long and tint them, so no one had thought it strange when he assumed the fashion, and no one had ever questioned why he continued to wear them that way.

Not even Dorothea. Since the witches of the Hourglass covens specialized in poisons and the darker aspects of the Craft, as well as dreams and visions, he'd always thought it strange that Dorothea had never guessed what he was. If she had, no doubt she would have tried to maim him beyond recognition. She might have succeeded before he had made the Offering to the Darkness to determine his mature strength, when he had still worn the Red Jewel that had come to him at his Birthright Ceremony. If she tried now, even with her coven backing her, it would cost her dearly. Even Ringed, a Black-Jeweled Warlord Prince would be a formidable enemy for a Red-Jeweled Priestess.

Which is why their paths seldom crossed anymore, why she kept him away from Hayll and her own court. She had one trump card to keep him submissive, and they both knew it. Without Lucivar's life in the balance, even the pain inflicted by the Ring of Obedience wouldn't hold him anymore. Lucivar . . . and the wild card that Tersa had added to the game of submission and control. The wild card Dorothea didn't know about. The wild card that would end her domination of Terreille.

Once, the Blood had ruled honorably and well. The Blood villages within a District would look after, and treat fairly, the landen villages that were bound to them. The District Queens would serve in the Province Queen's court. The Province Queens, in their turn, would serve the Territory Queen, who was chosen by the majority of the darker-Jeweled Blood, both male and female, because she was the strongest and the best.

Back then, there was no need for slavery to control the strong males. They followed their hearts to the Queen who was right for them. They handed over their lives willingly. They served freely.

Back then, the Blood's complicated triangle of status hadn't leaned so heavily on social rank. Jewel rank and caste had weighed just as heavily in the balance, if not more. That meant control of their society was a fluid dance, with the lead constantly changing depending on the dancers. But in the center of that dance, always, was a Queen.

That had been the genius and the flaw in Dorothea's purges. Without any strong Queens to challenge her rise to power, she had expected the males to surrender to her, a Priestess, the same way they surrendered to a Queen. They didn't. So a different kind of purge began, and by the time it was done, Dorothea had the sharpest weapons of all—frightened males who stripped any weaker female of her power in order to feel strong and frightened females who Ringed potentially strong males before they could become a threat.

The result was a spiraling perversion of their society, with Dorothea at its center as both the instrument of destruction and the only safe haven.

And then it spread outward, into the other Territories. He had seen those other lands and people slowly crumble, crushed beneath Hayll's relentless, whispered perversion of the ways of the Blood. He had seen the strong Queens, bedded much too young, rise from their Virgin Night broken and useless.

He had seen it and grieved over it, furious and frustrated that he could do so little to stop it. A bastard had no social standing. A slave had even less, no matter what caste he was born to or what Jewels he wore. So while Dorothea played out her game of power, he played out his. She destroyed the Blood who opposed her. He destroyed the Blood who followed her.

In the end, she would win. He knew that. There were very few Territories that didn't live in Hayll's shadow now. Askavi had spread its legs for Hayll centuries ago. Dhemlan was the only Territory in the eastern part of the Realm that was still fighting with its last breaths to stay free of Dorothea's influence. And there were a handful of small Territories in the far west that weren't completely ensnared yet.

In another century, two at the most, Dorothea would achieve her ambition. Hayll's shadow would cover the entire Realm and she would be *the* High Priestess, the absolute ruler of Terreille, which had once been called the Realm of Light.

Daemon vanished the cigarette and buttoned his shirt. He still had to attend to Marissa, Maris's daughter, before he could get some sleep.

He'd only gone a few steps when a mind brushed against his, demanding his attention. He turned away from the house and followed the mental tug. There was no mistaking that psychic sent, those tangled thoughts and disjointed images.

What was she doing here?

The tugging stopped when he reached the small woods at the far end of the gardens.

"Tersa?" he called softly.

The bushes beside him rustled and a bony hand closed on his wrist. "This way," Tersa said, tugging him down a path. "The web is fragile."

"Tersa—" Daemon half-dodged a low-hanging branch that slapped him in the face and got his arm yanked for the effort. "Tersa—"

"Hush, boy," she said fiercely, dragging him along.

He concentrated on dodging branches and avoiding roots that tried to trip him. Gritting his teeth, he forced himself to ignore the tattered dress that clothed her half-starved body. As a child of the Twisted Kingdom, Tersa was half wild, seeing the world as ghostly grays through the shards of what she had been. Experience had taught him that when Tersa was intent upon her visions, it was useless talking to her about mundane things like food and clothes and safe, warm beds.

They reached an opening in the woods where a flat slab of stone rested above two others. Daemon wondered if it was natural, or if Tersa had built it as a miniature altar.

The slab was empty except for a wooden frame that held a Black Widow's tangled web.

Uneasy, Daemon rubbed his wrist and waited.

"Watch," Tersa commanded. She snapped the thumbnail of her left hand against the forefinger nail. The forefinger nail changed to a sharp point. She pricked the middle finger of her right hand, and let one drop of blood fall on each of the four tether lines that held the web to the frame. The blood ran down the top lines and up the bottom ones. When they met in the middle, the web's spidersilk threads glowed.

A swirling mist appeared in front of the frame and changed into a crystal chalice.

The chalice was simple. Most men would have called it plain. Daemon thought it was elegant and beautiful. But it was what the chalice held that pulled him toward the makeshift altar.

The lightning-streaked black mist in the chalice contained power that slithered along his nerves, snaked around his spine, and sought its release in the sudden fire in his loins. It was a molten force, catastrophic in intensity, savage beyond a man's comprehension . . . and he wanted it with all his being.

"Look," Tersa said, pointing to the chalice's lip.

A hairline crack ran from a chip in the chalice's lip to the base. As Daemon watched, a deeper crack appeared.

The mist swirled inside the chalice. A tendril passed through the glass at the bottom into the stem.

Too fragile, he thought as more and more cracks appeared. The chalice was too fragile to hold that kind of power.

Then he looked closer.

The cracks were starting from the outside and going in, not starting from the inside and going out. So it was threatened by something beyond itself.

He shivered as he watched more of the mist flow into the stem. It was a vision. There was nothing he could do to change a vision. But everything he was screamed at him to *do* something, to wrap his strength around it and cherish it, protect it, keep it safe.

Knowing it would change nothing that happened here and now, he still reached for the chalice.

It shattered before he touched it, spraying crystal shards over the makeshift altar.

Tersa held up what was left of the shattered chalice. A little of mist still swirled inside the jagged-edged bottom of the cup. Most of it was trapped inside the stem.

She looked at him sadly. "The inner web can be broken without shattering the chalice. The chalice can be shattered without breaking the inner web. They cannot reach the inner web, but the chalice . . ."

Daemon licked his lips. He couldn't stop shivering. "I know the inner web is another name for our core, the Self that can tap the power within us. But I don't know what the chalice stands for."

Her hand shook a little. "Tersa is a shattered chalice."

Daemon closed his eyes. A shattered chalice. A shattered mind. She was talking about madness.

"Give me your hand," Tersa said.

Too unnerved to question her, Daemon held out his left hand.

Tersa grabbed it, pulled it forward, and slashed his wrist with the chalice's jagged edge.

Daemon clamped his hand over his wrist and stared at her, stunned.

"So that you never forget this night," Tersa said, her voice trembling. "That scar will never leave you."

Daemon knotted his handkerchief around his wrist. "Why is a scar important?"

"I told you. So you won't forget." Tersa cut the strands of the tangled web with the shattered chalice. When the last thread broke, the chalice and web vanished. "I don't know if this will be or if it may be. Many strands in the web weren't visible to me. May the Darkness give you courage if you need it, when you need it."

"The courage for what?"

Tersa walked away.

"Tersa!"

Tersa looked back at him, said three words, and vanished.

Daemon's legs buckled. He huddled on the ground, gasping for air, shuddering from the fear that clawed at his belly.

What had the one to do with the other? Nothing. *Nothing!* He would be there, a protector, a shield. He *would!*

But where?

Daemon forced himself to breathe evenly. That was the question. Where.

Certainly not in Maris's court.

It was late morning before he returned to the house, aching and dirty. His wrist throbbed and his head pounded mercilessly. He had just reached the terrace when Maris's daughter, Marissa, flounced out of the garden room and planted herself in front of him, hands on her hips, her expression a mixture of irritation and hunger.

"You were supposed to come to my room last night and you didn't. Where have you been? You're filthy." She rolled her shoulder, looking at him from beneath her lashes. "You've been naughty. You'll have to come up to my room and explain."

Daemon pushed past her. "I'm tired. I'm going to bed."

"You'll do as I say!" Marissa thrust her hand between his legs.

Daemon's hand tightened on Marissa's wrist so fast and so hard that she was on her knees whimpering in pain before she realized what happened. He continued squeezing her wrist until the bones threatened to shatter. Daemon smiled at her then, that cold, familiar, brutal smile.

"I'm not 'naughty.' Little boys are naughty." He pushed her away from him, stepping over her where she lay sprawled on the flagstones. "And if you ever touch me like that again, I'll rip your hand off."

He walked through the corridors to his room, aware that the servants skittered away from him, that an aftertaste of violence hung in the air around him.

He didn't care. He went to his room, stripped off his clothes, lay down on his bed, and stared at the ceiling, terrified to close his eyes because every time he did he saw a shattered crystal chalice.

Three words.

She has come.

3 / Hell

Once, he'd been the Seducer, the Executioner, the High Priest of the Hourglass, the Prince of the Darkness, the High Lord of Hell.

Once, he'd been Consort to Cassandra, the great Black-Jeweled, Black Widow Queen, the last Witch to walk the Realms.

Once, he'd been the only Black-Jeweled Warlord Prince in the history of the Blood, feared for his temper and the power he wielded.

Once, he'd been the only male who was a Black Widow.

Once, he'd ruled the Dhemlan Territory in the Realm of Terreille and her sister Territory in Kaeleer, the Shadow Realm. He'd been the only male ever to rule without answering to a Queen and, except for Witch, the only member of the Blood to rule Territories in two Realms.

Once, he'd been married to Hekatah, an aristo Black Widow Priestess from one of Hayll's Hundred Families.

Once, he'd raised two sons, Mephis and Peyton. He'd played games with them, told them stories, read to them, healed their skinned knees and broken hearts, taught them Craft and Blood Law, showered them with his love of the land as well as music, art, and literature, encouraged them to look with eager eyes upon all that the Realms had to offer—not to conquer but to learn. He'd taught them to dance for a social occasion and to dance for the glory of Witch. He'd taught them how to be Blood.

But that was a long, long time ago.

Saetan, the High Lord of Hell, sat quietly by the fire, a hearth rug wrapped around his legs, turning the pages of a book he had no interest in reading. He sipped a glass of yarbarah, the blood wine, taking no pleasure in its taste or warmth.

For the past decade, he'd been a quiet invalid who never left his private study deep beneath the Hall. For more than fifty thousand years before that, he'd been the ruler and caretaker of the Dark Realm, the undisputed High Lord.

He no longer cared about Hell. He no longer cared about the demon-dead family and friends who were still with him, or the other demon-dead and ghostly citizens of this Realm, the Blood who were still too strong to return to the Darkness even after their bodies had died.

He was tired and old, and the loneliness he'd carried inside him all his life had become too heavy to bear. He no longer wanted to be a Guardian, one of the living dead. He no longer wanted the half-life a handful of the Blood had chosen in order to extend their lifetimes into years beyond imagining. He wanted peace, wanted to quietly fade back into the Darkness.

The only thing that kept him from actively seeking that release was his promise to Cassandra.

Saetan steepled his long, black-tinted nails and rested his golden eyes on the portrait hanging on the far wall between two bookcases.

She'd made him promise to become a Guardian so that the extended half-life would allow him to walk among the living when his daughter was born. Not the daughter of his loins, but the daughter of his soul. The daughter she'd seen in a tangled web.

He'd promised because what she'd said had made his nerves twang like tether lines in a storm, because that was her price for training him to be a Black Widow, because, even then, the Darkness sang to him in a way it didn't sing to other Blood males.

He had kept his promise. But the daughter never came.

The insistent knocking on the door of his private study finally pulled him from his thoughts.

"Come," he said, his deep voice a tired whisper, a ghost of what it once had been.

Mephis SaDiablo entered and stood beside the chair, silent.

"What do you want, Mephis?" Saetan asked his eldest son, demon-dead since that long-ago war between Terreille and Kaeleer.

Mephis hesitated. "Something strange is going on."

Saetan's gaze drifted back to the fire. "Someone else can look into it, if anyone so desires. Your mother can look into it. Hekatah always wanted power without my interference."

"No," Mephis said uneasily.

Saetan studied his son's face and found that he had a hard time swallowing. "Your . . . brothers?" he finally asked, unable to hide the pain that the question caused him. He'd been a flattered fool to cast the spell that temporarily gave him back the seed of life. He couldn't regret Daemon's and Lucivar's existence, but he'd tortured himself for centuries with reports of what had been done to them.

Mephis shook his head and stared at the dark-red marble mantel. "On the *cildru dyathe*'s island."

Saetan shuddered. He'd never feared anything in Hell, but he'd always felt an aching despair for the *cildru dyathe,* the demon-dead children. In Hell, the dead retained the form of their last living hour. This cold, blasted Realm had never been a kind place, but to look upon those children, to see what had been done to them by another's hand, for there to be no escape from those blatant wounds. . . . It was too much to bear. They kept to their island, unwilling to have any contact with adults. He never intruded on them, having Char, their chosen leader, come to him once in a while to bring back the books, games, and whatever else he could find that might engage their young minds and help while away the unrelenting years.

"The *cildru dyathe* take care of themselves," Saetan said, fussing with the hearth rug. "You know that."

"But . . . every so often, for the past few weeks, there's another presence there. Never for very long, but I've felt it. So has Prothvar when he's flown over the island."

"Leave them alone," Saetan snapped, his temper returning some strength to his voice. "Perhaps they've found an orphaned Hound pup."

Mephis took a deep breath. "Hekatah has already had an altercation with Char over this. The children are hiding from everyone who approaches because of it. If she had any authority to—"

Before Saetan could respond to the sharp rap on the study door, it swung open. Andulvar Yaslana, once the Eyrien Warlord Prince of Askavi, strode into the room. His grandson, Prothvar, followed him, carrying a large globe covered with a black cloth.

"SaDiablo, there's something you should see," Andulvar said. "Prothvar brought this from the *cildru dyathe*'s island."

Saetan assumed an expression of polite interest. As young men, he and Andulvar had become unlikely friends and had served together in a number of courts. Even Hekatah hadn't severed that friendship when she'd strutted around, gleefully carrying a child that wasn't his—Andulvar's child. It didn't turn him against the only man he'd ever called a friend—who could blame a man for getting tangled up in one of Hekatah's schemes?—but it had ended his stormy marriage.

Saetan looked at each man in turn and saw the same uneasiness in three pairs of gold eyes. Mephis was a Gray-Jeweled Warlord Prince and almost unshakable. Prothvar was a Red-Jeweled Eyrien Warlord, a warrior bred and trained. Andulvar was an Eyrien Warlord Prince who wore the Ebon-gray, the second darkest Jewel. They were all strong men who didn't frighten easily—but now they *were* frightened.

Saetan leaned forward, their fear pricking the bubble of indifference he'd sealed himself in a decade ago. His body was weak and he needed a cane to walk, but his mind was still sharp, the Black Jewels still vibrant, his skill in the Craft still honed.

Suddenly, he knew he would need all that strength and skill to deal with whatever was happening on the *cildru dyathe*'s island.

Andulvar pulled the cloth off the globe. Saetan just stared, his face full of wonder and disbelief.

A butterfly. No, not just a butterfly. This was a huge fantasy creature that gently beat its wings within the confines of the globe. But it was the colors that stunned Saetan. Hell was a Realm of forever-twilight, a Realm that muted colors until there was almost no color at all. There was nothing muted about the creature in the globe. Its body was pumpkin orange, its wings an unlikely blend of sky blue, sun yellow, and spring-grass green. As he stared, the butterfly lost its shape, and the colors bled together like a chalk painting in the rain.

Someone on the *cildru dyathe*'s island had created that glorious piece of magic, had been able to hold the colors of the living Realms in a place that bleached away the vitality, the vibrancy of life.

"Prothvar threw a shielded globe around this one," Andulvar said.

"They dissolve almost immediately," Prothvar said apologetically, pulling his dark, membranous wings tight to his body.

Saetan straightened in his chair. "Bring Char to me, Lord Yaslana." His voice was soft thunder, caressing, commanding.

"He won't come willingly," Prothvar said.

Saetan stared at the demon-dead Warlord. "Bring Char to me."

"Yes, High Lord."

The High Lord of Hell sat quietly by the fire, his slender fingers loosely steepled, the long nails a glistening black. The Black-Jeweled ring on his right hand glittered with an inner fire.

The boy sat opposite him, staring at the floor, trying hard not to be frightened.

Saetan watched him through half-closed eyes. For a thousand years now, Char had been the leader of the *cildru dyathe*. He'd been twelve, maybe thirteen, when someone had staked him and set him on fire. The will to survive had been stronger than the body, and he'd tumbled through one of the Gates to end up in the Dark Realm. His body was so burned it was impossible to tell what race he had come from. Yet this young demon boy had gathered the other maimed children and created a haven for them, the *cildru dyathe*'s island.

He would have been a good Warlord if he'd been allowed to come of age, Saetan thought idly.

Andulvar, Mephis, and Prothvar stood behind Char's chair in a half circle, effectively cutting off any means of escape.

"Who makes the butterflies, Char?" Saetan asked too quietly.

There were winds that came down from the north screaming over miles of ice, picking up moisture as they tore over the cooling sea until, when they finally touched a man, the cold, knife-sharp damp seeped into his bones and chilled him in places the hottest fire couldn't warm. Saetan, when he was this calm, this still, was like those winds.

"Who makes the butterflies?" he asked again.

Char stared at the floor, his hands clenched, his face twisted with the emotions raging within him. "She's ours." The words burst from him. "She belongs to us."

Saetan sat very still, cold with the fury rising in him. Until he had an answer, he had no time for gentleness.

Char stared back, frightened but willing to fight.

All of Hell's citizens knew the subtle nuances of death, that there was dead and there was *dead*. All of Hell's citizens knew the one person capable of obliterating them with a thought was their High Lord. Still, Char openly challenged him, and waited.

Suddenly, something else was in the room. A soft touch. A question running on a psychic thread. Char hung his head, defeated. "She wants to meet you."

"Then bring her here, Char."

Char squared his shoulders. "Tomorrow. I'll bring her tomorrow."

Saetan studied the trembling pride in the boy's eyes. "Very well, War-lord, you may escort her here . . . tomorrow."

4 / Hell

Saetan stood at the reading lectern, the candle-lights spilling a soft glow around him as he leafed through an old Craft text. He didn't turn at the quiet knock on his study door. A swift psychic probe told him who was there.

"Come." He continued to leaf through the book, trying to rein in his temper before dealing with that impudent little demon. Finally, he closed the book and turned.

Char stood near the doorway, his shoulders proudly pulled back.

"Language is a curious thing, Warlord," Saetan said with deceptive mildness. "When you said 'tomorrow,' I didn't expect five days to pass."

Fear crept into Char's eyes. His shoulders wilted. He turned toward the doorway, and a strange blend of tenderness, irritation, and resignation swept over his face.

The girl slipped through the doorway, her attention immediately caught by the stark Dujae painting, *Descent into Hell,* hanging over the fireplace. Her summer-sky blue eyes flitted over the large blackwood desk, politely skipped over him, lit up when she saw the floor-to-ceiling bookcases that covered most of one wall, and lingered on Cassandra's portrait.

Saetan gripped his silver-headed cane, fighting to keep his balance while impressions crashed over him like heavy surf. He'd expected a gifted *cildru dyathe.* This girl was *alive!* Because of the skill needed to make those butterflies, he'd expected her to be closer to adolescence. She couldn't be more than seven years old. He'd expected intelligence. The expression in her eyes was sweet and disappointingly dull-witted. And what was a living child doing in Hell?

Then she turned and looked at him. As he watched the summer-sky blue eyes change to sapphire, the surf swept him away.

Ancient eyes. Maelstrom eyes. Haunted, knowing, *seeing* eyes.

An icy finger whispered down his spine at the same moment he was filled with an intense, unsettling hunger. Instinct told him what she was. It took a little longer for him to find the courage to accept it.

Not the daughter of his loins, but the daughter of his soul. Not just a gifted witch, but Witch.

She lowered her eyes and fluffed her sausage-curled golden hair, apparently no longer sure of her welcome.

He stomped down the desire to brush out those ridiculous curls.

"Are you the Priest?" she asked shyly, lacing her fingers. "The High Priest of the Hourglass?"

One black eyebrow lifted slightly, and a faint, dry smile touched his lips. "No one's called me that in a long time, but, yes, I'm the Priest. I am Saetan Daemon SaDiablo, the High Lord of Hell."

"Saetan," she said, as if trying out the name. "Saetan." It was a warm caress, a sensuous, lovely caress. "It suits you."

Saetan bit back a laugh. There had been many reactions to his name in the past, but never this. No, never this. "And you are?"

"Jaenelle."

He waited for the rest, but she offered no family name. As the silence lengthened, a sudden wariness tinged the room, as if she expected some kind of trap. With a smile and a dismissive shrug to indicate it was of no importance, Saetan gestured toward the chairs by the fire. "Will you sit and talk with me, witch-child? My leg can't tolerate standing for very long."

Jaenelle went to the chair nearest the door, with Char in close, possessive attendance.

Saetan's gold eyes flashed with annoyance. Hell's fire! He'd forgotten about the boy. "Thank you, Warlord. You may go."

Char sputtered a protest. Before Saetan could respond, Jaenelle touched Char's arm. No words were spoken, and he couldn't feel a psychic thread. Whatever passed between the two children was very subtle, and there was no question who ruled. Char bowed politely and left the study, closing the door behind him.

As soon as they were settled by the fire, Jaenelle pinned Saetan to his chair with those intense sapphire eyes. "Can you teach me Craft? Cassandra said you might if I asked."

Saetan's world was destroyed and rebuilt in the space of a heartbeat. He allowed nothing to show on his face. There would be time for that later. "Teach you Craft? I don't see why not. Where is Cassandra staying now? We've lost touch over the years."

"At her Altar. In Terreille."

"I see. Come here, witch-child."

Jaenelle rose obediently and stood by his chair.

Saetan raised one hand, fingers curled inward, and gently stroked her cheek. Anger instantly skimmed her eyes, and there was a sudden pulse in the Black, within him. He held her eyes, letting his fingers travel slowly along her jaw and brush against her lips, all the way around and back. He didn't try to hide his curiosity, interest, or the tenderness he felt for most females.

When he was done, he steepled his fingers and waited. A moment later, the pulse was gone, and his thoughts were his own again. Just as well, because he couldn't stop wondering why being touched made her so angry. "I'll make you two promises," he said. "I want one in return."

Jaenelle eyed him warily. "What promise?"

"I promise, by the Jewels that I wear and all that I am, that I'll teach you whatever you ask to the best of my ability. And I promise I'll never lie to you."

Jaenelle thought this over. "What do I have to promise?"

"That you'll keep me informed of any Craft lessons you learn from others. Craft requires dedication to learn it well and discipline to handle the responsibilities that come with that kind of power. I want the assurance that anything you learn has been taught correctly. Do you understand, witch-child?"

"Then you'll teach me?"

"Everything I know." Saetan let her think this over. "Agreed?"

"Yes."

"Very well. Give me your hands." He took the small, fair hands in his light-brown ones. "I'm going to touch your mind." The anger again. "I won't hurt you, witch-child."

Saetan carefully reached with his mind until he stood before her inner barriers. They were the shields that protected the Blood from their own kind. Like rings within rings, the more barriers that were passed, the more personal the mental link. The first barrier protected everyday thoughts. The last barrier protected the core of the Self, the essence of a being, the inner web.

Saetan waited. As much as he wanted answers, he wouldn't open her by force. Too much now depended on trust.

The barriers opened, and he went in.

He didn't rummage through her thoughts or descend deeper than was necessary, despite his curiosity. That would have been a shocking betrayal of the Blood's code of honor. And there was a strange, deep blankness to her mind that troubled him, a soft neutrality that he was sure hid something very different. He quickly found what he was looking for—the psychic thread that would vibrate in sympathy with a plucked, same-rank thread and would tell him what Jewels she wore, or would wear after her Birthright Ceremony. He began with the White, the lightest rank, and worked his way down, listening for the answering hum.

Hell's fire! Nothing. He hadn't expected anything until he'd reached the Red, but he'd expected a response at that depth. She had to wear Birthright Red in order to wear the Black after she made the Offering to the Darkness. Witch always wore the Black.

Without thinking, Saetan plucked the Black thread.

The hum came from below him.

Saetan released her hands, amazed that his own weren't shaking. He swallowed to get his heart out of his throat. "Have you had the Birthright Ceremony yet?"

Jaenelle drooped.

He gently lifted her chin. "Witch-child?"

Misery filled her sapphire eyes. A tear rolled down her cheek. "I f-failed the t-test. Does that mean I have to give the Jewels back?"

"Failed the— What Jewels?"

Jaenelle slipped her hand into the folds of her blue dress and pulled out a velvet bag. She upended it on the low table beside his chair with a proud but watery smile.

Saetan closed his eyes, leaned his head against the back of the chair, and sincerely hoped the room would stop spinning. He didn't need to look at them to know what they were: twelve uncut Jewels. White, Yellow, Tiger Eye, Rose, Summer-sky, Purple Dusk, Blood Opal, Green, Sapphire, Red, Gray, and Ebon-gray.

No one knew where the Jewels had come from. If one was destined to wear a Jewel, it simply appeared on the Altar after the Birthright Ceremony or the Offering to the Darkness. Even when he was young, receiving an uncut Jewel—a Jewel that had never been worn by another of the Blood—was rare. His Birthright Red Jewel had been uncut. When he'd been gifted with the Black, it, too, had been uncut. But to receive an entire set of uncut Jewels . . .

Saetan leaned over and tapped the Yellow Jewel with the tip of his nail. It flared, the fire in the center warning him off. He frowned, puzzled. The Jewel already identified itself as female, as being bonded to a witch and not a Blood male, but there was the faintest hint of maleness in it too.

Jaenelle wiped the tears from her cheeks and sniffed. "The lighter Jewels are for practice and everyday stuff until I'm ready to set these." She upended another velvet bag.

The room spun in every direction. Saetan's nails pierced the leather arms of his chair.

Hell's fire, Mother Night, and may the Darkness be merciful!

Thirteen uncut Black Jewels, Jewels that already glittered with the inner fire of a psychic bond. Having a child bond with one Black Jewel without having her mind pulled into its depths was disturbing enough, but the inner strength required to bond and hold *thirteen* of them . . .

Fear skittered up his spine, raced through his veins.

Too much power. Too much. Even the Blood weren't meant to wield this much power. Even Witch had never controlled this much power.

This one did. This young Queen. This daughter of his soul.

With effort, Saetan steadied his breathing. He could accept her. He could love her. Or he could fear her. The decision was his, and whatever he decided here, now, he would have to live with.

The Black Jewels glowed. The Black Jewel in his ring glowed in answer. His blood throbbed in his veins, making his head ache. The power in those Jewels pulled at him, demanding recognition.

And he discovered the decision was an easy one after all—he had actually made it a long, long time ago.

"Where did you get these, witch-child?" he asked hoarsely.

Jaenelle hunched her shoulders. "From Lorn."

"L-Lorn?" *Lorn?* That was a name from the Blood's most ancient legends. Lorn was the last Prince of the Dragons, the founding race who had created the Blood. "How . . . where did you meet Lorn?"

Jaenelle withdrew further into herself.

Saetan stifled the urge to shake the answer out of her and let out a theatrical sigh. "A secret between friends, yes?"

Jaenelle nodded.

He sighed again. "In that case, pretend I never asked." He gently rapped her nose with his finger. "But that means you can't go telling him *our* secrets."

Jaenelle looked at him, wide-eyed. "Do we have any?"

"Not yet," he grumped, "but I'll make one up just so we do."

She let out a silvery, velvet-coated laugh, an extraordinary sound that hinted at the voice she'd have in a few years. Rather like her face, which was too exotic and awkward for her now, but, sweet Darkness, when she grew into that face!

"All right, witch-child, down to business. Put those away. You won't need them for this."

"Business?" she asked, scooping up the Jewels and tucking the bags into the folds of her dress.

"Your first lesson in basic Craft."

Jaenelle drooped and perked up at the same time.

Saetan twitched a finger. A rectangular paperweight rose off the black-wood desk and glided through the air until it settled on the low table. The paperweight was a polished stone taken from the same quarry as the stones he'd used to build the Hall in this Realm.

Saetan positioned Jaenelle in front of the table. "I want you to point one finger at the paperweight . . . like this . . . and move it as far across the table as you can."

Jaenelle hesitated, licked her lips, and pointed her finger.

Saetan felt the surge of raw power through his Black Jewel.

The paperweight didn't move.

"Try again, witch-child. In the other direction."

Again there was that surge, but the paperweight didn't move.

Saetan rubbed his chin, confused. This was simple Craft, something she shouldn't have any trouble with whatsoever.

Jaenelle wilted. "I try," she said in a broken voice. "I try and try, but I never get it right."

Saetan hugged her, feeling a bittersweet ache in his heart when her arms wrapped around his neck. "Never mind, witch-child. It takes time to learn Craft."

"Why can't I do it? All my friends can do it."

Reluctant to let her go, Saetan forced himself to hold her at arm's length. "Perhaps we should start with something personal. That's usually easier. Is there anything you have trouble with?"

Jaenelle fluffed her hair and frowned. "I always have trouble finding my shoes."

"Good enough." Saetan reached for his cane. "Put one shoe in front of the desk and then stand over there."

He limped to the far side of the room and stood with his back to Cassandra's portrait, grimly amused at giving his new Queen her first Craft lesson under the watchful but unknowing eyes of his last Queen.

When Jaenelle joined him, he said, "A lot of Craftwork requires translating physical action into mental action. I want you to imagine—by the way, how *is* your imagination?" Saetan faltered. Why did she look so bruised? He'd only meant to tease a little since he'd already seen that butterfly. "I want you to imagine picking up the shoe and bringing it over here. Reach forward, grasp, and bring it in."

Jaenelle stretched her arm as far as it would go, clenched her hand, and yanked.

Everything happened at once.

The leather chairs by the fire zipped toward him. He countered Craft with Craft and had a moment to feel shocked when nothing happened before one of the chairs knocked him off his feet. He fell into the other one and had just enough time to curl into a ball before the chair behind the blackwood desk slammed into the back of the chair he was in and came down on top of it, caging him. He heard leather-bound books whiz around the room like crazed birds before hitting the floor with a thump. His shoes pattered frantically, trying to escape his feet. And over all of it was Jaenelle wailing, "Stop stop stop!"

Seconds later, there was silence.

Jaenelle peered into the space between the chair arms. "Saetan?" she said in a small, quivery voice. "Saetan, are you all right?"

Using Craft, Saetan sent the top chair back to the blackwood desk. "I'm fine, witch-child." He stuffed his feet into his shoes and gingerly stood up. "That's the most excitement I've had in centuries."

"Really?"

He straightened his black tunic-jacket and smoothed back his hair. "Yes, really." And Guardian or not, a man his age shouldn't *have* his heart gallop around his rib cage like this.

Saetan looked around the study and stifled a groan. The book that had been on the lectern hung in the air, upside down. The rest of the books formed drifts on the study floor. In fact, the only leather object that hadn't answered that summons was Jaenelle's shoe.

"I'm sorry, Saetan."

Saetan clenched his teeth. "It takes time, witch-child." He sank into the chair. So much raw power but still so vulnerable until she learned how to use it. A thought shivered across his mind. "Does anyone else know about the Jewels Lorn gave you?"

"No." Her voice was a midnight whisper. Fear and pain filled her sapphire eyes, and something else, too, that was stronger than those surface feelings. Something that chilled him to the core.

But he was chilled even more by the fear and pain in her eyes.

Even a strong child, a powerful child, would be dependent on the adults around her. If her strength could unnerve *him,* how would her people, her family, react if they ever discovered what was contained inside that small husk? Would they accept the child who already was the strongest Queen in the history of the Blood, or would they fear the power? And if they feared the power, would they try to cut her off from it by breaking her?

A Virgin Night performed with malevolent skill could strip her of her power while leaving the rest intact. But, since her inner web was so deep in the abyss, she might be able to withdraw far enough to withstand the physical violation—unless the male was able to descend deep enough into the abyss to threaten her even there.

Was there a male strong enough, dark enough, vicious enough?

There was . . . one.

Saetan closed his eyes. He could send for Marjong, let the Executioner do what was needed. No, not yet. Not to that one. Not until there was a reason.

"Saetan?"

He reluctantly opened his eyes and watched, at first stupidly and then with a growing sense of shock, as she pushed up her sleeve and offered her wrist to him.

"There's no need for a blood price," he snapped.

She didn't drop her wrist. "It will make you better."

Those ancient eyes seared him, stripped him of his flesh until he shivered, naked before her. He tried to refuse, but the words wouldn't come. He could smell the fresh blood in her, the life force pumping through her veins in counter-rhythm to his own pounding heart.

"Not that way," he said huskily, drawing her to him. "Not with me." With a lover's gentleness, he unbuttoned her dress and nicked the silky skin of her throat with his nail. The blood flowed, hot and sweet. He closed his mouth over the wound.

Her power rose beneath him, a slow, black tidal wave skillfully controlled, a tidal wave that washed over him, cleansed him, healed him even as his mind shuddered to find itself engulfed by a mind so powerful and yet so gentle.

He counted her heartbeats. When he reached five, he raised his head. She didn't look shocked or frightened, the usual emotions the living felt when required to give blood directly from the vein.

She brushed a trembling finger against his lips. "If you had more, would it make you completely well?"

Saetan called in a bowl of warm water and washed the blood off her throat with a square of clean linen. He wasn't about to explain to a child what those two mouthfuls of blood were already doing to him. He ignored the question, hoping she wouldn't press for an answer, and concentrated on the Craft needed to heal the wound.

"Would it?" she asked as soon as he vanished the linen and bowl.

Saetan hesitated. He'd given his word he wouldn't lie. "It would be better for the healing to take place a little at a time." That, at least, was true enough. "Another lesson tomorrow?"

Jaenelle quickly looked away.

Saetan tensed. *Had* she been frightened by what he'd done?

"I . . . I already promised Morghann I'd see her tomorrow and Gabrielle the day after that."

Relief made him giddy. "In three days, then?"

She studied his face. "You don't mind? You're not angry?"

Yes, he minded, but that was a Warlord Prince's instinctive possessiveness talking. Besides, he had a lot to do before he saw her next. "I don't think your friends would care much for your new mentor if he took up all your time, do you?"

She grinned. "Probably not." The grin vanished. The bruised look was back in her eyes. "I have to go."

Yes, he had a great deal to do before he saw her next.

She opened the door and stopped. "Do you believe in unicorns?"

Saetan smiled. "I knew them once, a long time ago."

The smile she gave him before disappearing down the corridor lit the room, lit the darkest corners of his heart.

"Hell's fire! What happened, SaDiablo?"

Saetan waggled Jaenelle's abandoned shoe at Andulvar and smiled dryly. "A Craft lesson."

"What?"

"I met the butterfly maker."

Andulvar stared at the mess. "She did this? Why?"

"It wasn't intentional, just uncontrolled. She isn't *cildru dyathe* either. She's a living child, a Queen, and she's Witch."

Andulvar's jaw dropped. "Witch? Like Cassandra was Witch?"

Saetan choked back a snarl. "Not like Cassandra but, yes, Witch."

"Hell's fire! Witch." Andulvar shook his head and smiled.

Saetan stared at the shoe. "Andulvar, my friend, I hope you've still got all that brass under your belt that you used to brag about, because we're in deep trouble."

"Why?" Andulvar asked suspiciously.

"Because you're going to help me train a seven-year-old Witch who's got the raw power right now to turn us both into dust and yet"—he dropped the shoe onto the chair—"is abysmal at basic Craft."

Mephis knocked briskly and entered the study, tripping on a pile of books. "A demon just told me the strangest thing."

Saetan adjusted the folds of his cape and reached for his cane. "Be brief, Mephis. I'm going to an appointment that's long overdue."

"He said he saw the Hall shift a couple of inches. The whole thing. And a moment later, it shifted back."

Saetan stood very still. "Did anyone else see this?"

"I don't think so, but—"

"Then tell him to hold his tongue if he doesn't want to lose it."

Saetan swept past Mephis, leaving the study that had been his home for the past decade, leaving his worried demon-dead son behind.

CHAPTER TWO

1 / Terreille

In the autumn twilight, Saetan studied the Sanctuary, a forgotten place of crumbling stone, alive with small vermin and memories. Yet within this broken place was a Dark Altar, one of the thirteen Gates that linked the Realms of Terreille, Kaeleer, and Hell.

Cassandra's Altar.

Cloaked in a sight shield and a Black psychic shield, Saetan limped through the barren outer rooms, skirting pools of water left by an afternoon storm. A mouse, searching for food among the fallen stones, never sensed his presence as he passed by. The Witch living in this labyrinth of rooms wouldn't sense him either. Even though they both wore the Black Jewels, his strength was just a little darker, just a little deeper than hers.

Saetan paused at a bedroom door. The covers on the bed looked fairly new. So did the heavy curtains pulled across the window. She would need those when she rested during the daylight hours.

At the beginning of the half-life, Guardians' bodies retained most of the abilities of the living. They ate food like the living, drank blood like the demon-dead, and could walk in the daylight, though they preferred the twilight and the night. As centuries passed, the need for sustenance diminished until only yarbarah, the blood wine, was required. Preference for darkness became necessity as daylight produced strength-draining, physical pain.

He found her in the kitchen, humming off-key as she took a wineglass out of the cupboard. Her shapeless, mud-colored gown was streaked with dirt. Her long braided hair, faded now to a dusty red, was veiled with cobwebs. When she turned toward the door, still unaware of his presence, the firelight smoothed most of the lines from her face, lines he knew were there because they were in the portrait that hung in his private study, the portrait he knew so well. She had aged since the death that wasn't a death.

But so had he.

He dropped the sight shield and psychic shield.

The wineglass shattered on the floor.

"Practicing hearth-Craft, Cassandra?" he asked mildly, struggling to tamp down an overwhelming sense of betrayal.

She backed away from him. "I should have realized she'd tell you."

"Yes, you should have. You also should have known I'd come." He tossed his cape over a wooden chair, grimly amused at the way her emerald eyes widened when she noticed how heavily he leaned on the cane. "I'm old, Lady. Quite harmless."

"You were never harmless," she said tartly.

"True, but you never minded that when you had a use for me." He looked away when she didn't answer. "Did you hate me so much?"

Cassandra reached toward him. "I never hated you, Saetan. I—"

—*was afraid of you.*

The words hung between them, unspoken.

Cassandra vanished the broken wineglass. "Would you like some wine? There's no yarbarah, but I've got some decent red."

Saetan settled into a chair beside the pine table. "Why aren't you drinking yarbarah?"

Cassandra brought a bottle and two wineglasses to the table. "It's hard to come by here."

"I'll send some to you."

They drank the first glass of wine in silence.

"Why?" he finally asked.

Cassandra toyed with her wineglass. "Black-Jeweled Queens are few and far between. There was no one to help me when I became Witch, no one to talk to, no one to help me prepare for the drastic changes in my life after I made the Offering." She laughed without humor. "I had no idea what being Witch would mean. I didn't want the next one to go through the same thing."

"You could have told me you intended to become a Guardian instead of faking the final death."

"And have you stay around as the loyal, faithful Consort to a Queen who no longer needed one?"

Saetan refilled the glasses. "I could have been a friend. Or you could have dismissed me from your court if that's what you wanted."

"Dismiss you? *You?* You were . . . are . . . Saetan, the Prince of the Darkness, High Lord of Hell. No one dismisses you. Not even Witch."

Saetan stared at her. "Damn you," he said bitterly.

Cassandra wearily brushed a stray hair from her face. "It's done, Saetan. It was lifetimes ago. There's the child to think about now."

Saetan watched the fire burning in the hearth. She was entitled to her own life, and certainly wasn't responsible for his, but she didn't understand—or didn't want to understand—what that friendship might have meant to him. Even if he'd never seen her again, knowing she still existed would have eased some of the emptiness. Would he have married Hekatah if he hadn't been so desperately lonely?

Cassandra laced her fingers around her glass. "You've seen her?"

Saetan thought of his study and snorted. "Yes, I've seen her."

"She's going to be Witch. I'm sure of it."

"Going to be?" Saetan's golden eyes narrowed. "What do you mean, 'going to be'? Are we talking about the same child? Jaenelle?"

"Of course we're talking about Jaenelle," she snapped.

"She isn't 'going to be' Witch, Cassandra. She already *is* Witch."

Cassandra shook her head vigorously. "Not possible. Witch always wear the Black Jewels."

"So does the daughter of my soul," Saetan replied too quietly.

It took her a moment to understand him. When she did, she lifted the wineglass with shaking hands and drained it. "H-how do you . . ."

"She showed me the Jewels she was gifted with. A full uncut set of the 'lighter' Jewels—and that was the first time I'd ever heard *anyone* refer to the Ebon-gray as a lighter Jewel—and thirteen uncut Blacks."

Cassandra's face turned gray. Saetan gently chafed her ice-cold hands, concerned by the shock in her eyes. She was the one who'd first seen the child in her tangled web. She was the one who'd told him about it. Had she only seen Witch but not understood what was coming?

Saetan put a warming spell on his cape and wrapped it around her, then warmed another glass of wine over a little tongue of witchfire. When her teeth stopped chattering, he returned to his own chair.

Her emerald eyes asked the question she couldn't put into words.

"Lorn," he said quietly. "She got the Jewels from Lorn."

Cassandra shuddered. "Mother Night." She shook her head. "It's not supposed to be like this, Saetan. How will we control her?"

His hand jerked as he refilled his glass. Wine splashed on the table. "We don't control her. We don't even try."

Cassandra smacked her palm on the table. "She's a child! Too young to understand that much power and not emotionally ready to accept the responsibilities that come with it. At her age, she's too open to influence."

He almost asked her whose influence she feared, but Hekatah's face popped into his mind. Pretty, charming, scheming, vicious Hekatah, who had married him because she'd thought he would make her the High Priestess of Terreille at least or, possibly, the dominant female influence in all three Realms. When he'd refused to bend to her wishes, she'd tried on her own and had caused the war between Terreille and Kaeleer, a war that had left Terreille devastated for centuries and had been the reason why many of Kaeleer's races had closed their lands to outsiders and were never seen or heard from again.

If Hekatah got her claws into Jaenelle and molded the girl into her own greedy, ambitious image . . .

"You have to control her, Saetan," Cassandra said, watching him.

Saetan shook his head. "Even if I were willing, I don't think I could. There's a soft fog around her, a sweet, cold, black mist. I'm not sure, even young as she is, that I'd like to find out what lies beneath it without her invitation." Annoyed by the way Cassandra kept glaring at him, Saetan looked around the kitchen and noticed a primitive drawing tacked on the wall. "Where did you get that?"

"What? Oh, Jaenelle dropped it off a few days ago and asked me to keep it. Seems she was playing at a friend's house and didn't want to take the picture home." Cassandra tucked stray hairs back into her braid. "Saetan, you said there's a soft fog around her. There's a mist around Beldon Mor, too."

Saetan frowned at her. What did he care about some city's weather? That picture held an answer if he could just figure it out.

"A psychic mist," Cassandra said, rapping her knuckles on the table, "that keeps demons and Guardians out."

Saetan snapped to attention. "Where's Beldon Mor?"

"On Chaillot. That's an island just west of here. You can see it from the hill behind the Sanctuary. Beldon Mor is the capital. I think Jaenelle lives there. I tried to find a way into—"

Now she had his full attention. "Are you mad?" He combed his fingers through his thick black hair. "If she went to that much effort to retain her privacy, why are you trying to invade it?"

"Because of what she is," Cassandra said through clenched teeth. "I thought that would be obvious."

"Don't invade her privacy, Cassandra. Don't give her a reason to distrust you. And the reason for *that* should be obvious, too."

Minutes passed in tense silence.

Saetan's attention drifted back to the picture. A creative use of vivid colors, even if he couldn't quite figure out what it was supposed to be. How could a child capable of creating butterflies, moving a structure the size of the Hall, and constructing a psychic shield that only kept specific kinds of beings out be so hopeless at basic Craft?

"It's clumsy," Saetan whispered as his eyes widened.

Cassandra looked up wearily. "She's a child, Saetan. You can't expect her to have the training or the motor control—"

She squeaked when he grabbed her arm. "But that's just it! For Jaenelle, doing things that require tremendous expenditures of psychic energy is like giving her a large piece of paper and color-sticks she can wrap her fist around. Small things, the basic things we usually start with because they don't require a lot of strength, are like asking her to use a single-haired brush. She doesn't have the physical or mental control yet to do them." He sprawled in the chair, exultant.

"Wonderful," Cassandra said sarcastically. "So she can't move furniture around a room, but she can destroy an entire continent."

"She'll never do that. It's not in her temperament."

"How can you be sure? How will you control her?"

They were back to that.

He took his cape back and settled it over his shoulders. "I'm not going to control her, Cassandra. She's Witch. No male has the right to control Witch."

Cassandra studied him. "Then what are you going to do?"

Saetan picked up his cane. "Love her. That will have to be enough."

"And if it's not?"

"It will have to be." He paused at the kitchen door. "May I see you from time to time?"

Her smile didn't quite reach her eyes. "Friends do."

He left the Sanctuary feeling exhilarated and bruised. He'd loved Cassandra dearly once, but he had no right to ask anything of her except what Protocol dictated a Warlord Prince could ask of a Queen.

Besides, Cassandra was his past. Jaenelle, may the Darkness help him, was his future.

2 / Hell

Dropping from the Black Wind, Saetan appeared in an outer courtyard that held one of the Keep's official landing webs, which was etched in the stone with a clear Jewel at its center. The clear Jewels acted as beacons for those who rode the Winds—a kind of welcoming candle in the window—and every landing web had a piece of one. It was the only use that had ever been found for them.

Leaning heavily on his cane, Saetan limped across the empty courtyard to the huge, open-metal doors embedded into the mountain itself, rang the bell, and waited to enter the Keep, the Black Mountain, Ebon Askavi, where the Winds meet. It was the repository for the Blood's history as well as a sanctuary for the darkest-Jeweled Blood. It was also the private lair of Witch.

The doors opened silently. Geoffrey, the Keep's historian/librarian, waited for him on the other side. "High Lord." Geoffrey bowed slightly in greeting.

Saetan returned the bow. "Geoffrey."

"It's been a while since you've visited the Keep. Your absence has been noted."

Saetan snorted softly, his lips curving into a faint, dry smile. "In other words, I haven't been useful lately."

"In other words," Geoffrey agreed, smiling. As he walked beside Saetan, his black eyes glanced once at the cane. "So you're here."

"I need your help." Saetan looked at the Guardian's pale face, a stark, unsettling white when combined with the black eyes, feathery black eyebrows, black hair with a pronounced widow's peak, the black tunic and trousers, and the most sensuous blood-red lips Saetan had ever seen on anyone, man or woman. Geoffrey was the last of his race, a race gone to dust so long ago that no one remembered who they were. He was ancient when Saetan first came to the Keep as Cassandra's Consort. Then, as now, he was the Keep's historian and librarian. "I need to look up some of the ancient legends."

"Lorn, for example?"

Saetan jerked to a stop.

Geoffrey turned, his black eyes carefully neutral.

"You've seen her," Saetan said, a hint of jealousy in his voice.

"We've seen her."

"Draca, too?" Saetan's chest tightened at the thought of Jaenelle confronting the Keep's Seneschal. Draca had been caretaker and overseer of Ebon Askavi long, long before Geoffrey had ever come. She still served the Keep itself, looking after the comfort of the scholars who came to study, of the Queens who needed a dark place to rest. She was reserved to the point of coldness, using it as a defense against those who shuddered to look upon a human figure with unmistakably reptilian ancestry. Coldness as a defense for the heart was something Saetan understood all too well.

"They're great friends," Geoffrey said as they walked through the twisting corridors. "Draca's given her a guest room until the Queen's apartment is finished." He opened the library door. "Saetan, you are going to train her, aren't you?"

Hearing something odd in Geoffrey's voice, Saetan turned with much of his old grace. "Do you object?" He immediately choked back the snarl in his voice when he saw the uneasiness in Geoffrey's eyes.

"No," Geoffrey whispered, "I don't object. I'm . . . relieved." He pointed to the books neatly stacked at one end of the blackwood table. "I pulled those out anticipating your visit, but there are some other volumes, some very ancient texts, that I'll pull out for you next time. I think you'll need them."

Saetan settled into a leather chair beside the large blackwood table and gratefully accepted the glass of yarbarah Geoffrey offered. His leg ached. He wasn't up to this much walking.

He pulled the top book off the stack and opened it at the first marker. Lorn. "You did anticipate."

Geoffrey sat at the other end of the table, checking other books. "Some. Certainly not all." They exchanged a look. "Anything else I can check for you?"

Saetan quickly swallowed the yarbarah. "Yes. I need information about two witches named Morghann and Gabrielle." He started reading the entry about Lorn.

"If they wear Jewels, they'll be in the Keep's registry."

"It's a safe bet you'll find them in the darker ranks," Saetan said, not looking up.

Geoffrey pushed his chair back. "What Territories?"

"Hmm? I've no idea. Jaenelle's from Chaillot, so start with Territories around there where those names are common."

"Saetan," Geoffrey said with annoyed humor, "sometimes you're as useful as a bucket with a hole in the bottom. Can you give me a little more of a starting point?"

Pulled away from his third attempt to read the same paragraph, Saetan snapped, "Between the ages of six and eight. Now will you let me read?"

Geoffrey replied in a language Saetan didn't understand, but translation wasn't required. "I'll have to check the registry at Terreille's Keep, so this may take a while even if any of your information is remotely accurate. Help yourself to more yarbarah."

The hours melted away. Saetan read the last entry Geoffrey had marked, carefully closed the book, and rubbed his eyes. When he finally looked up, he found Geoffrey studying him. A strange look was in the librarian's black eyes. Two registers lay on the table.

Saetan rested his steepled fingers on his chin. "So?"

"You got the names and the age range right," Geoffrey said softly.

That icy finger whispered down Saetan's spine. "Meaning?"

Geoffrey slowly, almost reluctantly, opened the first book at the page marker. "Morghann. A Queen who wears Birthright Purple Dusk. Almost seven years old. Lives in the village of Maghre on the Isle of Scelt in the Realm of Kaeleer."

"*Kaeleer!*" Saetan tried to jump up. His leg buckled immediately. "How in the name of Hell did she get into the Shadow Realm?"

"Probably the same way she got into the Dark Realm." Geoffrey opened the second register and hesitated. "Saetan, you will train her well, won't you?" He didn't wait for an answer. "Gabrielle. A Queen who wears Birthright Opal. Seven years old. Strong possibility she's a natural Black Widow. Lives in the Realm of Kaeleer in the Territory of the Dea al Mon."

Saetan pillowed his head in his arms and moaned. The Children of the Wood. She'd seen the Children of the Wood, the fiercest, most private race ever spawned in Kaeleer. "It's not possible," he said, bracing his arms on the table. "You've made a mistake."

"I've made no mistake, Saetan."

"She lives in Terreille, not Kaeleer. You've made a mistake."

"I've made no mistake."

Ice whispered down his spine, freezing nerves, turning into a cold dagger in his belly. "It's not possible," Saetan said, spacing out the words. "The Dea al Mon have never allowed anyone into their Territory."

"It appears they've made an exception."

Saetan shook his head. "It's not possible."

"Neither is finding Lorn," Geoffrey replied sharply. "Neither is walking with impunity through the length and breadth of Hell. Yes, we know about that. The last time she visited here, Char came with her."

"The little bastard," Saetan muttered.

"You asked me to find Morghann and Gabrielle. I found them. Now what are you going to do?"

Saetan stared at the high ceiling. "What would you have me do, Geoffrey? Shall we take her away from her home? Confine her in the Keep until she comes of age?" He let out a strained laugh. "As if we could. The only way to confine her would be to convince her she couldn't get out, to brutalize her instincts until she wasn't sure of anything anymore. Do you want to be the bastard responsible for that emotional butchering? Because I won't do it. By the Darkness, Geoffrey, the living myth has come, and this is the price required to have her walk among us."

Geoffrey carefully closed the registers. "You're right, of course, but . . . is there nothing you can do?"

Saetan closed his eyes. "I will teach her. I will serve her. I will love her. That will have to be enough."

3 / Terreille

Surreal swung through the front door of Deje's Red Moon house in Beldon Mor, flashed a smile at the brawny red-coated doorman, and continued through the plant-strewn, marble-floored entryway until she reached the reception desk. Once there, she smacked the little brass bell on the desk enough times to annoy the most docile temper.

A door marked "Private" snapped open, and a voluptuous middle-aged woman hurried out. When she saw Surreal, her scowl vanished and her eyes widened with delighted surprise.

"So, you've come again at last." Deje reached under the desk, pulled out a thick stack of small papers, and waved them at Surreal. "Requests. All willing to pay your asking price—and everyone knows what a thief you are—and all wanting a full night."

Without taking them, Surreal riffled the stack with her fingertip. "If I accommodated them all, I could end up being here for months."

Deje tilted her head. "Would that be so bad?"

Surreal grinned, but there was something sharp and predatory in her gold-green eyes. "I'd never get my asking price if my"—she twiddled her fingers at the papers—"friends thought I'd always be around. That would cut into your profit margin, too."

"Too true," Deje said, laughing.

"Besides," Surreal continued, hooking her black hair behind her delicately pointed ears, "I'll only be here for a few weeks, and I'm not looking for a heavy schedule. I'll work enough days to pay for room and board and spend the rest of the time sightseeing."

"How many ceilings do you want to see? That's all you'll look at in this business."

"Why, Deje!" Surreal fanned herself. "That's not at all true. Sometimes I get to see the patterns in the silk sheets."

"You could always take up horseback riding." Deje stuffed the papers under the desk. "I hear there are some pretty trails just outside the city proper."

"No thanks. When the work's done, I'm not interested in mounting anything else. You want me to start tonight?"

Deje patted her dark, richly dressed hair. "I'm sure there's someone who made a reservation tonight who'll rise to the occasion."

They grinned at each other.

Deje called in a slim leather folder and removed a piece of expensive parchment. "Hmm. A full house. And there's always one or two who'll show up sure that they're too important to need a reservation."

Surreal propped her elbows on the desk, her face in her hands. "You've got an excellent chef. Maybe they're just here for dinner."

Deje smiled wickedly. "I try to accommodate all kinds of hunger."

"And if the special's taken, the main entrées are still delicious."

Deje laughed, her shaking bosom threatening to shimmy out of her low-cut gown. "Well put. Here." She pointed to a name on the list. "I remember you saying you don't mind him. He'll probably be half-starved, but he appreciates appetizers as well as the main course."

Surreal nodded. "Yes, he'll do nicely. One of the garden rooms?"

"Of course. I've done a little redecorating since you were last here. I think you'll like it. You have a true appreciation for such things." Deje reached into one of the little cubbyholes in the wall behind the desk and pulled out a key. "This one will suit."

Surreal palmed the key. "Dinner in the room, I think. Is there a menu there? Good. I'll order ahead."

"How do you remember all their likes and dislikes, particularly from so many places, so many different customs?"

Surreal looked mockingly offended. "Deje. You used to play the rooms before you got ambitious. You know perfectly well that's what little black books are for."

Deje shooed Surreal from the desk. "Away with you. I have work to do, and so do you."

Surreal walked down the wide corridor, her sharp eyes taking in the rooms on either side. It was true. Deje was ambitious. Starting out with a packet of gifts from satisfied clients, she had bought a mansion and converted it into the best Red Moon house in the district. And unlike the other houses, at Deje's a man could find more than just a warm body in a bed. There was a small private dining room that served excellent food all night; a reception room, where those with an artistic temperament made a habit of gathering to debate each other while they ate the tidbits and drank good wine; a billiards room, where the politically ambitious met to plan their next move; a library filled with good books and thick leather chairs; private rooms, where a man could get away from his everyday life and be catered to, receiving nothing more than a good dinner, an expert massage, and peace; and, finally, the rooms and the women who would satisfy the carnal appetites.

Surreal found her room, locked the door, and took a long look around, nodding in approval. Soft, thick rugs; white walls with tasteful watercolor paintings; dark furniture; an oversized, gauze-enveloped poster bed; music spheres and the ornate brass stand to hold them; sliding glass doors that led out into a walled private garden with a small fountain and petite willow trees as well as a variety of night-blooming flowers; and a bathroom with a shower and a large walk-up sunken tub that was positioned in front of the glass window overlooking the garden.

"Very good, Deje," Surreal said quietly. "Very, very good."

She quickly settled into the room, calling in her work clothes and carefully hanging them in the wardrobe. She never carried much, just enough variety to satisfy the different appetites in whatever Territory she was in. Most of her things were scattered in a dozen hideaways throughout Terreille.

Surreal suppressed a shudder. It was better not to think of those hideaways. Certainly better not to wonder about *him*.

Opening the glass doors so she could listen to the fountain, Surreal settled into a chair, her legs tucked beneath her. Two black leather books appeared, floating before her. She took one, leafed through to the last written page, called in a pen, and made a notation.

That contract was finished. It hadn't taken the fool as long to die as she would have liked, but the pain had been exquisite. And the money had been very, very good.

She vanished the book and opened the other one, checked the entry she needed, wrote out her menu, and with a flick of her wrist sent it to the kitchen. Vanishing the second book, she got up and stretched. Another flick of her wrist and there was the familiar weight of the knife's handle, its stiletto blade a shining comfort. Turning her wrist the other way, she vanished the knife and smacked her hands together. One was all she'd need tonight. He never gave her any trouble. Besides—she smiled at the memory—she was the one who had taught him, how long ago? Twelve, fourteen years?

She took a quick shower, dressed her long black hair so it could be easily unpinned, made up her face, and slipped into a sheer gold-green dress that hid as much as it revealed. Finally, clenching her teeth against the inevitable, she walked over to the freestanding mirror and looked at the face, at the body, she had hated all her life.

It was a finely sculpted face with high cheekbones, a thin nose, and slightly oversized gold-green eyes that saw everything and revealed nothing. Her slender, well-shaped body looked deceptively delicate but had strong muscles that she had hardened over the years to ensure she was always in peak condition for her chosen profession. But it was the sunkissed, light-brown skin that made her snarl. Hayllian skin. Her father's skin. She could easily pass for Hayllian if she wore her hair down and wore tinted glasses to hide the color of her eyes. The eyes would mark her as a half-breed. The ears with the tips curving to a delicate point . . . those were Titian's ears.

Titian, who came from no race Surreal had met in all her travels through Terreille. Titian, who had been broken on Kartane SaDiablo's spear. Titian, who had escaped and whored for her keep so Kartane couldn't find her and destroy the child she carried. Titian, who was found one day with her throat slit and was buried in an unmarked grave.

All the assassinations, all those men going to their planned deaths, were dress rehearsals for patricide. Someday she would find Kartane in the right place at the right time, and she would pay him back for Titian.

Surreal turned away from the mirror and forced the memories aside. When she heard the quiet knock on the door, she positioned herself in the center of the room so her guest would see her when he first walked in. And she would see him and plan the evening accordingly.

Using Craft, she opened the door before he turned the handle, and let the seduction tendrils flow from her like some exotic perfume. She opened her arms and smiled as the door locked behind him.

He came at her in a rush, need flowing out of him, the Gray Jewel around his neck blazing with his fire. She put her hands on his chest, stopping him and caressing him with one smooth stroke. Breathing hard, he clenched and unclenched his hands, but he didn't touch her.

Satisfied, Surreal glided to the small dining table near the glass doors and sent a thought to the kitchen. A moment later, two chilled glasses and a bottle of wine appeared. She poured the wine, gave him a glass, and raised hers in a salute. "Philip."

"Surreal." His voice was husky, aching.

She sipped her wine. "Doesn't the wine please you?"

Philip consumed half the glass in a swallow.

Surreal hid her smile. Whom did he really hunger for that he couldn't have? Who did he pretend she was when he closed the curtains and turned off all the lights so he could satisfy his lust while clinging to his illusions?

She kept the meal to a leisurely pace, letting him consume her with his eyes as he drank the wine and ate the delicacies. As he always did, he talked to her in a meandering, obscure fashion, telling her more than he realized or intended.

Philip Alexander. Gray-Jeweled Prince. A handsome man with sandy hair and honest, troubled gray eyes. Half brother to Robert Benedict, a premiere political player since he had tied himself to Hayll, to . . . Kartane. Robert only wore the Yellow, and barely that, but he was the legitimate son, entitled to his father's estate and wealth. Philip, a couple of years younger and never formally acknowledged, was raised as his brother's accessory. Tired of playing the grateful bastard, he broke with his family and became an escort/consort for Alexandra Angelline, the Queen of Chaillot.

Subtle cultural poisoning over a couple of generations had allowed Chaillot's Blood males to twist matriarchal rule into something unnatural and wrest control of the Territory from the Queens, so Alexandra was nothing more than a figurehead, but she was still the Queen of Chaillot and wore an Opal Jewel. A little strange, too. Well, unusual. It was rumored that she still had dealings with the Hourglass covens even though Black Widows had been outlawed by the Blood males in power. She had one daughter, Leland, who was Robert Benedict's wife.

And they all lived together at the Angelline estate in Beldon Mor.

She played dinner as long as she could before beginning to play the bed. A Gray-Jeweled Prince who had gone without pleasure for a long time could be an unintentionally rough companion, but he didn't worry her. She, too, wore the Gray, but never for this job. She always wore her Birthright Green, or no Jewel at all, allowing her clients to feel in control. Still, tonight he wouldn't mind a little rough handling, and he was one of the few men she knew in her second profession who actually wanted to give as well as receive pleasure.

Yes, Philip was a good way to begin this stay.

Surreal dimmed the candle-lights, turning the room to smoke, to dusk. He didn't rush now. He touched, tasted, savored. And she, subtly guiding, let him do what he had come here to do.

★　★　★

It was dawn before Philip dressed and kissed her good-bye.

Surreal stared at the gauze canopy. He'd gotten his money's worth and more. And he'd been a pleasant distraction from the memories that had been crowding her lately, that were the reason she'd come to Chaillot. Memories of Titian, of Tersa . . . of the Sadist.

Surreal was ten years old when Titian brought Tersa home one afternoon and tucked the bedraggled witch into her own bed. During the few days the mad Black Widow stayed with them, Titian spent hours listening to Tersa's gibberish interspersed with strange jokes and cryptic sayings.

A week after Tersa left them, she returned with the coldest, handsomest man Surreal had ever seen. The first Warlord Prince she had ever seen. He said nothing, letting Tersa babble while he watched Titian, while his gaze burned the child trembling beside her mother.

Finally Tersa stopped talking and tugged at the man's sleeve. "The child is Blood and should be trained in the Craft. She has the right to wear the Jewels if she's strong enough. Daemon, please."

His golden eyes narrowed as he came to a decision. Reaching into the inner pocket of his jacket, he removed several gold hundred-mark notes from a billfold and laid them carefully on the table. He called in a piece of paper and a pen, wrote a few words, and left the paper and a key on top of the notes.

"The place isn't elegant, but it's warm and clean." His deep, seductive voice sent a delightful shiver through Surreal. "It's a few blocks from here, in a neighborhood where no one asks questions. There are the names of a couple of potential tutors for the girl. They're good men who got on the wrong side of the ones who have power. You're welcome to use the flat as long as you want."

"And the price?" Titian's soft voice was full of ice.

"That you don't deny Tersa access to the place whenever she's in this part of the Realm. I won't make use of it while you're there, but Tersa must be able to use the refuge I originally acquired for her."

So it was agreed, and a few days later Surreal and Titian were in the first decent place the girl had ever known. The landlord, with a little tremor of fear in his voice, told them the rent was paid. The hundred-mark notes went for decent food and warm clothes, and Titian gratefully no longer had to allow any man to step over her threshold.

The next spring, after Surreal had begun making some progress with her tutors, Tersa returned and took Surreal to the nearest Sanctuary for her Birthright Ceremony. Surreal returned, proudly holding an uncut Green. With tears in her eyes, Titian carefully wrapped the Jewel in soft cloth and stored it in a strangely carved wooden box.

"An uncut Jewel is a rare thing, little Sister," Titian said, removing something from the box. "Wait until you know who you are before you have it set. Then it will be more than a receptacle for the power your body can't hold; it will be a statement of what you are. In the meantime"—she slipped a silver chain over Surreal's head—"this will help you begin. It was mine, once. You're not a moon child; gold would suit you better. But it's the first step down a long road."

Surreal looked at the Green Jewel. The silver mounting was carved into two stags curved around the Jewel, their antlers interlocking at the top, hiding the ring where the chain was fastened. As she studied it, her blood sang in her veins, a faint summoning she couldn't trace.

Titian watched her. "If ever you meet my people, they will know you by that Jewel."

"Why can't we go to see them?"

Titian shook her head and turned away.

Those two years were good ones for Surreal. She spent her days with her tutors, one teaching her Craft, the other all the basic subjects for a general education. At night, Titian taught her other things. Even broken, Titian was expert with a knife, and there was a growing uneasiness in her, as if she were waiting for something that made her relentless in the drills and exercises.

One day, when Surreal was twelve, she returned home to find the apartment door half open and Titian lying in the front room with her throat slit, her horn-handle dagger nearby. The walls pulsed with violence and rage . . . and the warning to run, run, run.

Surreal hesitated a moment before racing into Titian's bedroom and removing the carved box with her Jewel from its hiding place. At a stumbling run, she swept the dagger up from the floor and vanished it and the box as she'd been taught to do. Then she ran in earnest, leaving Titian and whoever had been hunting them behind.

Titian had just turned twenty-five.

Less than a week after her mother's death, Surreal was speared for the first time. As she fought without hope, she saw herself falling down a long, dark tunnel, her thread in the abyss. At the level of the Green was a shimmering web that stretched across the tunnel. As she fell toward it, out of control, as the pain of being broken into washed the walls with red, Surreal remembered Tersa, remembered Titian. If she hit her inner web while out of control, she would break it and return to the real world as a shadow of her self, forever aware and grieving the loss of her Craft and what she might have been.

Remembering Titian gave her the inner strength to fight the pounding that seemed to go on forever, each thrust driving her closer to her inner web. She hung on, fighting with all her heart. When the thrusts stopped . . . when it was finally over . . . she was barely a hand's span away from destruction.

Her mind cowered there, exhausted. When the man left, she forced herself to ascend. The physical pain was staggering, and the sheets were soaked with her blood, but she was still intact in the most important way. She still wore the Jewels. She was still a witch.

Within a month, she made her first kill.

He was like all the others, taking her to a seedy room, using her body and paying her with a copper mark that would barely buy her enough food to stagger through the next day. Her hatred for the men who used her, and Titian before her, turned to ice. So when his thrusts became stronger, when he arched his back and his chest rose above her, she called in the horn-handle dagger and stabbed him in the heart. His life force pumped into her while his life's blood spilled out.

Using Craft, Surreal pushed his heavy body off hers. This one wouldn't hit her or refuse to pay. It was exhilarating.

For three years she roamed the streets, her child's body and unusual looks a beacon to the most sordid. But her skill with a knife was not unknown, and it became common knowledge in the streets that a wise man paid Surreal in advance.

Three years. Then one day as she was slipping down an alley she'd already probed to be sure it was empty, she felt someone behind her. Whirling around, dagger in hand, she could only stare at Daemon Sadi as he leaned against the wall, watching her. Without thinking, she ran up the alley to get away from him, and hit a psychic shield that held her captive until his hand locked on her wrist. He said nothing. He simply caught the

Winds and pulled her with him. Never having ridden one of those psychic Webs, Surreal clung to him, disoriented.

An hour later, she was sitting at a kitchen table in a furnished loft in another part of the Realm. Tersa hovered over her, encouraging her to eat, while Daemon watched her as he drank his wine.

Too nervous to eat, Surreal threw the words at him. "I'm a whore."

"Not a very good one," Daemon replied calmly.

Incensed, Surreal hurled every gutter word she knew at him.

"Do you see my point?" he asked, laughing, when she finally sputtered into silence.

"I'll be what I am."

"You're a child of mixed blood. Part Hayllian blood." He toyed with his glass. "Your mother's people live—what—a hundred, two hundred years? You may see two thousand or more. Do you want to spend those years eating scraps dumped in alleys and sleeping in filthy rooms? There are other ways of doing what you do—for better rooms, better food, better pay. You'd have to start as an apprentice, of course, but I know a place where they'd take you and train you well."

Daemon spent several minutes making out a list. When he was done, he pushed it in front of Surreal. "A woman with an education may be able to spend more time sitting in a chair instead of lying on her back. A sound advantage, I should think."

Surreal stared at the list, uneasy. There were the expected subjects—literature, languages, history—and then, at the bottom of the page, a list of skills more suited to the knife than to paid sex.

As Tersa cleared the table, Daemon rose from his chair and leaned over Surreal, his chest brushing her back, his warm breath tickling her pointed ear. "Subtlety, Surreal," he whispered. "Subtlety is a great weapon. There are other ways to slit a man's throat than to wash the walls with his blood. If you continue down that road, they'll find you, sooner or later. There are so many ways for a man to die." He chuckled, but there was an underlying viciousness in the sound. "Some men die for lack of love . . . some die because of it. Think about it."

Surreal went to the Red Moon house. The matron and the other women taught her the bedroom arts. The rest she learned quietly on her own. Within ten years, she was the highest-paid whore in the house—and men began to bargain for her other skills as well.

She traveled throughout Terreille, offering her skills to the best Red Moon house in whatever city she was in and carefully accepting contracts for her other profession, the one she found more challenging—and more pleasurable. She carried a set of keys to town houses, suites, lofts—some in the most expensive parts of town, others in quiet, backwater streets where people asked no questions. Sometimes she met Tersa and gave her whatever care she could.

And sometimes she found herself sharing a place with Sadi when he slipped away from whatever court he was serving in for a quiet evening. Those were good times for Surreal. Daemon's knowledge was expansive when he felt like talking, and when she chattered, his golden eyes always held the controlled amusement of an older brother.

For almost three hundred years they came and went comfortably with each other. Until the night when, already a little drunk, she consumed a bottle of wine while watching him read a book. He was comfortably slouched in a chair, shirt half unbuttoned, bare feet on a hassock, his black hair uncharacteristically tousled.

"I was wondering," Surreal said, giving him a tipsy smile.

Daemon looked up from his book, one eyebrow rising as a smile began to tweak the corners of his mouth. "You were wondering?"

"Professional curiosity, you understand. They talk about you in the Red Moon houses, you know."

"Do they?"

She didn't notice the chill in the room or the golden eyes glazing to a hard yellow. She didn't recognize the dangerous softness in his voice. She just smiled at him. "Come on, Sadi, it would be a real feather in my cap, career-wise. There isn't a whore in the Realm who knows firsthand what it's like to be pleasured by Hayll's—"

"Be careful what you ask for. You may get it."

She laughed and arched her back, her nipples showing through the thin fabric of her blouse. It wasn't until he uncoiled from his chair with predatory speed and had her pressed against him with her hands locked behind her back that she realized the danger of taunting him. Pulling her hair hard enough to bring tears to her eyes, he forced her head up. His hand tightened on her wrists until she whimpered from the pain. Then he kissed her.

She expected a brutal kiss, so the tenderness, the softness of his lips nuzzling hers frightened her far more. She didn't know what to think, what to feel with his hands deliberately hurting her while his mouth was so giving, so persuasive. When he finally coaxed her mouth open, each easy stroke of his tongue produced a fiery tug between her legs. When she could no longer stand, he took her to the bedroom.

He undressed her with maddening slowness, his long nails whispering over her shivering skin as he kissed and licked and peeled the fabric away. It was sweet torture.

When she was finally naked, he coaxed her to the bed. Psychic ropes tightened around her wrists and pulled her arms over her head. Ropes around her ankles held her legs apart. As he stood by the bed, Surreal became aware of the cold, unrelenting anger coiling around her . . . and a soft, controlled breeze, a spring wind still edged with winter, running over her body, caressing her breasts, her belly, riffling the black hair between her legs before splitting to run along the inside of her thighs, circling her feet, traveling up the outside of her thighs, past her ribs to circle around her neck and begin again.

It went on and on until she couldn't stand the teasing, until she was desperate for some kind of touch that would give her release.

"Please," she moaned, trying to shake off the relentless caress.

"Please what?" He slowly stripped off his clothes.

She watched him hungrily, her eyes glazing as she waited to see the proof of his pleasure. The shock of seeing the Ring of Obedience on a totally flaccid organ made her realize the anger swirling around her had changed. His smile had changed.

As he stretched out beside her, his warm body cool compared to the heat inside her, as his living hand began to play the same game the phantom one had, she finally understood what was in the air, in his smile, in his eyes.

Contempt.

He played with deadly seriousness. Each time his hands or his tongue gave her some release, the gauze veils of sensuality were ripped from her mind and she was forced to drink cup after cup of his contempt. When he brought her up the final time, she thrust her hips toward him while pleading for him to stop. His cold, biting laughter tightened around her ribs until she couldn't breathe. Just as she started sliding into a sweet, unfeeling release, it stopped.

Everything stopped.

As her head cleared, she heard water running in the bathroom. A few minutes later, Daemon reappeared, fully dressed, wiping his face with a towel. There was a throbbing need between her legs to be filled, just once. She begged him for some small comfort.

Daemon smiled that cold, cruel smile. "Now you know what it's like to get into bed with Hayll's Whore."

She began to cry.

Daemon tossed the towel onto a chair. "I wouldn't try using a dildo if I were you," he said pleasantly. "Not for a couple of days anyway. It won't help, and it might even make things much, much worse." He smiled at her again and walked out of the apartment.

She didn't know how long he'd been gone when the ropes around her wrists and ankles finally disappeared and she was able to roll over, her knees tucked tight to her chest, and cry out her shame and rage.

She became afraid of him, dreaded to feel his presence when she opened a door. When they met, he was coldly civil and seldom spoke—and never again looked at her with any warmth.

Surreal stared at the gauze canopy. That was fifty years ago, and he had never forgiven her. Now . . . She shuddered. Now, if the rumors were true, there was something terribly wrong with him. There hadn't been a court anywhere that could keep him for more than a few weeks. And too many of the Blood disappeared and were never heard from again whenever his temper frayed.

He had been right. There were many, many ways for a man to die. Even as good as she was, she still had to make some effort to dispose of a body. The Sadist, however, never left the smallest trace.

Surreal stumbled into the shower and sighed as her tight muscles relaxed under the pounding hot water. At least there didn't seem to be any danger of stumbling upon him while she stayed in Beldon Mor.

4 / Hell

Even the fierce pounding on his study door couldn't compete with Prothvar's unrestrained cursing and Jaenelle's shrieks of outrage.

Saetan closed the book on the lectern. There was a time, and not that long ago, when no one wanted to open that door, let alone pummel it into kindling. Easing himself onto a corner of the blackwood desk, he crossed his arms and waited.

Andulvar burst into the room, his expression an unsettling blend of fear and fury. Prothvar came in right behind him, dragging Jaenelle by the back of her dress. When she tried to break his grip, he grabbed her from behind and lifted her off her feet.

"Put me down, Prothvar!" Jaenelle cocked her knee and pistoned her leg back into Prothvar's groin.

Prothvar howled and dropped her.

Instead of falling, Jaenelle executed a neat roll in the air before springing to her feet, still a foot above the floor, and unleashing a string of profanities in more languages than Saetan could identify.

Saetan forced himself to look authoritatively neutral and decided, reluctantly, that this wasn't the best time to discuss Language Appropriate for Young Ladies. "Witch-child, kicking a man in the balls may be an effective way to get his attention, but it's not something a child should do." He winced when she turned all her attention on him.

"Why not?" she demanded. "A friend told me that's what I should do if a male ever grabbed me from behind. He made me promise."

Saetan raised an eyebrow. "This friend is male?" How interesting.

Before he could pursue it further, Andulvar rumbled ominously, "That's not the problem, SaDiablo."

"Then what is the problem?" Not that he really wanted to know.

Prothvar pointed at Jaenelle. "That little . . . she . . . tell him!"

Jaenelle clenched her hands and glared at Prothvar. "It was your fault. You laughed and wouldn't teach me. *You* knocked me down."

Saetan raised one hand. "Slow down. Teach you what?"

"He wouldn't teach me to fly," Jaenelle said accusingly.

"You don't have wings!" Prothvar snapped.

"I can fly as well as you can!"

"You haven't got the training!"

"Because you wouldn't teach me!"

"And I'm damn well not going to!"

Jaenelle flung out an Eyrien curse that made Prothvar's eyes pop.

Andulvar's face turned an alarming shade of purple before he pointed to the door and roared, "OUT!"

Jaenelle flounced out of the study with Prothvar limping after her.

Saetan clamped a hand over his mouth. He wanted to laugh. Sweet Darkness, how he wanted to laugh, but the look in Andulvar's eyes warned him that if he so much as chuckled, they were going to engage in a no-holds-barred brawl.

"You find this amusing," Andulvar rumbled, rustling his wings.

Saetan cleared his throat several times. "I suppose it's difficult for Prothvar to find himself on the losing end of a scrap with a seven-year-old girl. I didn't realize a warrior's ego bruises so easily."

Andulvar's grim expression didn't change.

Saetan became annoyed. "Be reasonable, Andulvar. So she wants to learn to fly. You saw how well she balances on air."

"I saw a lot more than that," Andulvar snapped.

Saetan ground his teeth and counted to ten. Twice. "So tell me."

Andulvar crossed his muscular arms and stared at the ceiling. "The waif's friend Katrine is showing her how to fly, but Katrine flies like a butterfly and Jaenelle wants to fly like a hawk, like an Eyrien. So she asked Prothvar to teach her. And he laughed, which, I admit, wasn't a wise thing to do, and she—"

"Got her back up."

"—jumped off the high tower of the Hall."

There was a moment of silence before Saetan exploded. *"What?"*

"You know the high tower, SaDiablo. You built this damned place. She climbed onto the top of the wall and jumped off. Do you still find it amusing?"

Saetan clamped his hands on the desk. His whole body shook. "So Prothvar caught her when she fell."

Andulvar snorted. "He almost killed her. When she jumped off, he dove over the side after her. Unfortunately, she was standing, *on the air,* less than ten feet below the ledge. When he went over the side, he barreled into her and took them both down almost three quarters of the way before he came out of the dive."

"Mother Night," Saetan muttered.

"And may the Darkness be merciful. So what are you going to *do?*"

"Talk to her," Saetan replied grimly as he flicked a thought at the door and watched it open smoothly and swiftly. "Witch-child."

Jaenelle approached him, her anger now cooled to the unyielding determination he'd come to recognize all too well.

Fighting to control his temper, Saetan studied her for a moment. "Andulvar told me what happened. Have you anything to say?"

"Prothvar didn't have to laugh at me. I don't laugh at him."

"Flying usually requires wings, witch-child."

"You don't need wings to ride the Winds. It's not that different. And even Eyriens need a little Craft to fly. Prothvar said so."

He didn't know which was worse: Jaenelle doing something outrageous or Jaenelle being reasonable.

Sighing, Saetan closed his hands over her small, frail-looking ones. "You frightened him. How was he to know you wouldn't just plummet to the ground?"

"I would have told him," she replied, somewhat chastened.

Saetan closed his eyes for a moment, thinking furiously. "All right. Andulvar and Prothvar will teach you the Eyrien way of flying. You, in turn, most promise to follow their instructions and *take the training in the proper order.* No diving off the tower, no surprising leaps from cliffs . . ." Her guilty look made his heart pound in a very peculiar rhythm. He finished in a strangled voice, ". . . no testing on the Blood Run . . . or any other Run until they feel you're ready."

Andulvar turned away, muttering a string of curses.

"Agreed?" Saetan asked, holding his breath.

Jaenelle nodded, unhappy but resigned.

Like the Gates, the Runs existed in all three Realms. Unlike the Gates, they only existed in the Territory of Askavi. In Terreille, they were the Eyrien warriors' testing grounds, canyons where winds and Winds collided in a dangerous, grueling test of mental and physical strength. The Blood Run held the threads of the lighter Winds, from White to Opal. The other . . .

Saetan swallowed hard. "Have you tried the Blood Run?"

Jaenelle's face lit up. "Oh, yes. Saetan, it's such fun." Her enthusiasm wavered as he stared at her.

Remember how to breathe, SaDiablo. "And the Khaldharon?"

Jaenelle stared at the floor.

Andulvar spun her around and shook her. "Only a handful of the best Eyrien warriors each year dare try the Khaldharon Run. It's the absolute test of strength and skill, not a playground for girls who want to flit from place to place."

"I don't flit!"

"Witch-child," Saetan warned.

"I only tried it a little," she muttered. "And only in Hell."

Andulvar's jaw dropped.

Saetan closed his eyes, wishing the sudden stabbing pain in his temples would go away. It would have been bad enough if she'd tried the Khaldharon Run in Terreille, the Realm farthest from the Darkness and the full strength of the Winds, but to make the Run in Hell . . . "You will not make the Runs until Andulvar says you're ready!"

Startled by his vehemence, Jaenelle studied him. "I scared you."

Saetan circled the room, looking for something he could safely shred. "You're damn right you scared me."

She fluffed her hair and watched him. When he returned to the desk, she performed a respectful, feminine curtsy. "My apologies, High Lord. My apologies, Prince Yaslana."

Andulvar grunted. "If I'm going to teach you to fly, I might as well teach you how to use the sticks, bow, and knife."

Jaenelle's eyes sparkled. "Sceron is teaching me the crossbow, and Chaosti is showing me how to use a knife," she volunteered.

"All the more reason you should learn Eyrien weapons as well," Andulvar said, smiling grimly.

When she was gone, Saetan looked at Andulvar with concern. "I trust you'll take into account her age and gender."

"I'm going to work her ass off, SaDiablo. If I'm going to train her, and it seems I have no choice, I'll train her as an Eyrien warrior should be trained." He grinned maliciously. "Besides, Prothvar will love being her opponent when she learns the sticks."

Once Andulvar was gone, Saetan settled into his chair behind the blackwood desk, unlocked one of the drawers, and pulled out a sheet of expensive white parchment half filled with his elegant script. He added three names to the growing list: Katrine, Sceron, Chaosti.

With the parchment safely locked away again, Saetan leaned back in his chair and rubbed his temples. That list disturbed him because he didn't know what it meant. Children, yes. Friends, certainly. But all from Kaeleer. She must be gone for hours at a time in order to travel those distances, even on the Black Wind. What did her family think about her disappearances? What did they say? She never talked about Chaillot, her home, her family. She evaded every question he asked, no matter how he phrased it. What was she afraid of?

Saetan stared at nothing for a long time. Then he sent a thought on an Ebon-gray spear thread, male to male. *Teach her well, Andulvar. Teach her well.*

5 / Hell

Saetan left the small apartment adjoining his private study, vigorously toweling his hair. His nostrils immediately flared and the line between his eyebrows deepened as he stared at the study door.

Harpies had a distinctive psychic scent, and this one, patiently waiting for him to acknowledge her presence, made him uneasy.

Returning to the bedroom, he dressed swiftly but carefully. When he was seated behind the blackwood desk, he released the physical and psychic locks on the door and waited.

Her silent, gliding walk brought her swiftly to the desk. She was a slender woman with fair skin, oversized blue eyes, delicately pointed ears, and long, fine, silver-blond hair. She was dressed in a forest-green tunic and pants with a brown leather belt and soft, calf-high boots. Attached to the belt was an empty sheath. She wore no Jewels, and the wound across her throat was testimony to how she had died. She studied him, as he studied her.

The tension built in the room.

Harpies were witches who had died by a male's hand. No matter what race they originally came from, they were more volatile and more cunning than other demon-dead witches, and seldom left their territory, a territory that even demon-dead males didn't dare venture into. Yet she was here, by her own choice. A Dea al Mon Black Widow and Queen.

"Please be seated, Lady," Saetan said, nodding to the chair before the desk. Without taking her eyes off him, she sank gracefully into the chair. "How may I help you?"

When she spoke, her voice was a sighing wind across a glade. But there was lightning in that voice, too. "Do you serve her?"

Saetan tried to suppress the shiver her words produced, but she sensed it and smiled. That smile brought his anger boiling to the surface. "I'm the High Lord, witch. I serve no one."

Her face didn't change, but her eyes became icy. "Hell's High Priestess is asking questions. That isn't good. So I ask you again, *High Lord,* do you serve her?"

"Hell has no High Priestess."

She laughed grimly. "Then no one has informed Hekatah of that small detail. If you don't serve, are you friend or enemy?"

Saetan's lip curled into a snarl. "I don't serve Hekatah, and while we were married once, I doubt she considers me a friend."

The Harpy looked at him in disgust. "She's important only because she threatens to interfere. The child, High Lord. Do you serve the child? Are you friend or enemy?"

"What child?" An icy dagger pricked his stomach.

The Harpy exploded from the chair and took a swift turn around the room. When she returned to the desk, her right hand kept rubbing the sheath as if searching for the knife that wasn't there.

"Sit down." When she didn't move, the thunder rolled in his voice. "Sit down." Hekatah was suspicious of recent activities, and rumors of a strange witch appearing and disappearing from the Dark Realm had sharpened her interest. But he had no control of where Jaenelle went or whom she saw. If the Harpies knew of her, then who else knew? How long would it be before Jaenelle followed a psychic thread that would lead her straight into Hekatah's waiting arms? And was this Harpy a friend or an enemy? "The child is known to the Dea al Mon," he said carefully.

The Harpy nodded. "She is friends with my kinswoman Gabrielle."

"And Chaosti."

A cruel, pleased smile brushed her lips. "And Chaosti. He, too, is a kinsman."

"And you are?"

The smile faded. Cold hatred burned in her eyes. "Titian." She swept her eyes over his body and then leaned back in the chair. "The one who broke me . . . he carries your family name but not your bloodline. I was barely twelve when I was betrayed and taken from Kaeleer. He took me for his amusement and broke me on his spear. But everything has a price. I left him a legacy, the only seed of his that will ever come to flower. In the end, he'll pay the debt to her. And when the time comes, she'll serve the young Queen."

Saetan exhaled slowly. "How many others know about the child?"

"Too many . . . or not enough. It depends upon the game."

"This isn't a game!" He became very still. "Let me in."

Loathing twisted Titian's face.

Saetan leaned forward. "I understand why being touched by a male disgusts you. I don't ask this lightly . . . or for myself."

Titian bit her lip. Her hands dug into the chair. "Very well."

Focusing his eyes on the fire, Saetan made the psychic reach, touched the first inner barrier, and felt her recoil. He patiently waited until she felt ready to open the barriers for him. Once inside, he drifted gently, a well-mannered guest. It didn't take long to find what he was looking for, and he broke the link, relieved.

They didn't know. Titian wondered, guessed too close. But no one outside his confidence knew for sure. A strange child. An eccentric child. A mysterious, puzzling child. That would do. His wise, cautious child. But he couldn't help wondering what experience had made her so cautious so young.

He turned back to Titian. "I'm teaching her Craft. And I serve."

Titian looked around the room. "From here?"

Saetan smiled dryly. "Your point's well taken. I've grown tired of this room. Perhaps it's time to remind Hell who rules."

"You mean who rules in proxy," Titian said with a predatory smile. She let the words linger for a moment. "It's good you're concerned, High Lord," she acknowledged reluctantly. "It's good she has so strong a protector. She's fearless, our Sister. It's wise to teach her caution. But don't be deceived. The children know what she is. She's as much their secret as their friend. Blood sings to Blood, and all of Kaeleer is slowly turning to embrace a single dark star."

"How do you know about the children?" Saetan asked suspiciously.

"I told you. I'm Gabrielle's kinswoman."

"You're dead, Titian. The demon-dead don't mingle with the living. They don't interfere with the concerns of the living Realms."

"Don't they, High Lord? You and your family still rule Dhemlan in Kaeleer." She shrugged. "Besides, the Dea al Mon aren't squeamish about dealing with those who live in the forever-twilight of the Dark Realm." Hesitating, she added, "And our young Sister doesn't seem to understand the difference between the living and the dead."

Saetan stiffened. "You think knowing me has confused her?"

Titian shook her head. "No, the confusion was there before she ever knew of Hell or met a Guardian. She walks a strange road, High Lord. How long before she begins to walk the borders of the Twisted Kingdom?"

"There's no reason to assume she will," Saetan replied tightly.

"No? She will follow that strange road wherever it leads her. What makes you think a child who sees no difference between the living and the dead will see a difference between sanity and the Twisted Kingdom?"

"NO!" Saetan leaped out of his chair and went to stand before the fire. He tried to suppress the thought of Jaenelle sliding into madness, unable to cope with what she was, but the anxiety rolled from him in waves. No one else in the history of the Blood had worn the Black as a Birthright Jewel. No one else had had to shoulder the responsibility—and the isolation—that was part of the price of wearing so dark a Jewel at so young an age.

And he knew she had already seen things a child shouldn't see. He had seen the secrets and shadows in her eyes.

"Is there no one in Terreille you can trust to watch over her?"

Saetan let out a pained laugh. "Who would you trust, Titian?"

Titian rubbed her hands nervously on her trousers.

She was barely a woman when she died, he thought with tender sadness. So frail beneath all that strength. As they all are.

Titian licked her lips. "I know a Black-Jeweled Warlord Prince who sometimes looks after those who need help. If approached, he might—"

"No," he said harshly, pride warring with fear. How ironic that Titian considered Daemon a suitable protector. "He's owned by Hekatah's puppet, Dorothea. He can be made to comply."

"I don't believe he'd harm a child."

Saetan returned to his desk. "Perhaps not willingly, but pain can make a man do things he wouldn't willingly do."

Titian's eyes widened with understanding. "You don't trust him." She thought it over and shook her head. "You're wrong. He's—"

"A mirror." Saetan smiled as she drew in a hissing breath. "Yes, Titian. He's blood of my blood, seed of my loins. I know him well . . . and not at all. He's a double-edged sword capable of cutting the hand that holds him as easily as he cuts the enemy." He led her to the door. "I thank you for your counsel and your concern. If you hear any news, I would appreciate being informed."

She turned at the doorway and studied him. "What if she sings to his blood as strongly as she sings to yours?"

"Lady." Saetan quietly closed the door on her and locked it. Returning to his desk, he poured a glass of yarbarah and watched the small tongue of fire dance above the desktop, warming the blood wine.

Daemon was a good Warlord Prince, which meant he was a dangerous Warlord Prince.

Saetan drained the glass. He and Daemon were a matched pair. Did he really believe his namesake was a threat to Jaenelle or was it jealousy over having to yield to a potential lover, especially when that lover was also his son? Because he honestly couldn't answer that question, he hesitated to give the order for Daemon's execution.

As yet there was no reason to send for Marjong the Executioner. Daemon was nowhere near Chaillot and, for some reason, Jaenelle didn't wander around Terreille as she did Kaeleer. Perhaps Titian was right about Daemon, but he couldn't take the chance. His namesake had the cunning to ensnare a child and the strength to destroy her.

But if Daemon had to be executed to protect Jaenelle, it wouldn't be a stranger's hand that put him in his grave.

He owed his son that much.

PART II

CHAPTER THREE

1 / Kaeleer

Saetan smiled dryly at his reflection. His full head of black hair was more silvered at the temples than it had been five years ago, but the lines left in his face by illness and despair had softened while the laugh lines had deepened.

Turning from the mirror, he strolled the length of the second-floor gallery. His bad leg still stiffened if he walked too long, but he no longer needed that damned cane. He laughed softly. Jaenelle was a bracing tonic in more ways than one.

As he descended the staircase that ended in the informal reception room, he noticed the tall, slim woman watching him through narrowed eyes. He also noticed the ring of keys attached to her belt and felt relieved that finding the current housekeeper had been so easy.

"Good afternoon," he said pleasantly. "Are you Helene?"

"And what if I am?" She crossed her arms and tapped her foot.

Well, he hadn't expected an open-armed welcome, but still . . . He smiled at her. "For a staff who's had no one to serve for so long and so little incentive, you've kept the place quite well."

Helene's shoulders snapped back and her eyes glinted with anger. "We care for the Hall because it's the Hall." Her eyes narrowed even further. "And who are you?" she demanded.

He raised an eyebrow. "Who do you think I am?"

"An interloper, that's what I think," Helene snapped, placing her hands on her hips. "One of those who sneaks in here from time to time to gawk and 'soak up the atmosphere.' "

Saetan laughed. "They'd do well not to soak up too much of the atmosphere of this place. Although it was always calmer than its Terreille counterpart. I suppose after so many years away, I am an interloper of sorts, but . . ." He raised his right hand. As the Black Jewel in the ring flashed, there was an answering rumble from the stones of SaDiablo Hall.

Helene paled and stared at him.

He smiled. "You see, my dear, it still answers my call. And I'm afraid I'm about to wreak havoc with your routine."

Helen fumbled a low curtsy. "High Lord?" she stammered.

He bowed. "I'm opening the Hall."

"But . . ."

Saetan stiffened. "There's a problem with that?"

There was a gleam in Helene's gold eyes as she briskly wiped her hands on her large white apron. "A thorough cleaning will help, to be sure, but"—she looked pointedly at the drapes—"some refurbishing would help even more."

The tension drained out of him. "And give you something to be proud of instead of having to make do with an empty title?"

Helene blushed and chewed her lip.

Hiding a smile, Saetan vanished the drop cloths and studied the room. "New drapes and sheers definitely. With a good polishing, the wood pieces will still do, providing the preservation spells have held and they're structurally sound. New sofas and chairs. Plants by the windows. A few new paintings for the walls as well. New wallpaper or paint? What do you think?"

It took Helene a moment to find her voice. "How many rooms are you thinking of restoring?"

"This one, the formal receiving room across the hall, the dining room, my public study, my suite, a handful of guest rooms—and a special suite for my Lady."

"Then perhaps your Lady would like to oversee the redecorating."

Saetan looked at her with horrified amusement. "No doubt she would. However, my Lady will be twelve in four months, and I'd much prefer that she live in a suite I've decorated on her behalf than that I live in a Hall decorated with her somewhat . . . eclectic . . . tastes."

Helene stared at him for a moment but refrained from asking the question he saw in her eyes. "I could have some swatch books brought up to the Hall for you to choose from."

"An excellent idea, my dear. Do you think you can have this place presentable in four months?"

"The staff is rather small, High Lord," Helene said hesitantly.

"Then hire the help you need." Saetan strolled to the door that opened onto the great hall. "I'll meet you again at the end of the week. Is that sufficient time?"

"Yes, High Lord." She curtsied again.

Having been born in the slums of Draega, Hayll's capital, as the son of an indifferent whore, he'd never expected or wanted servants to grovel in his presence. He didn't mention this to Helene because, if he read her right, that was the last curtsy he would ever receive.

At the end of the great hall, he hesitated before opening the door of his public study. He walked around the room, lightly touching the covered furniture, grimacing slightly at his dusty fingertips.

He'd once ruled Dhemlan Kaeleer from this room. Still ruled, he reminded himself. He'd given Dhemlan Terreille to Mephis when he became a Guardian, but not her sister land in the Shadow Realm.

Ah, Kaeleer. It had always been a sweet wine for him, with its deeper magic and its mysteries. Now those mysteries were coming out of the mist once more, and the magic was still strong. Strand by strand, Jaenelle was rebuilding the web, calling them all to the dance.

He hoped she'd be pleased to have the use of this place. He hoped he'd be invited when she established her own court. He wanted to see who she selected for her First Circle, wanted to see the faces attached to that list of names. Did they know about each other? Or him?

Saetan shook his head and smiled.

Whether she'd intended to or not, his fair-haired daughter of the soul had certainly thrown him back among the living.

2 / Terreille

Surreal switched the basket of groceries from one hand to the other and fished her keys out of her trouser pocket as she climbed the stairs to her third-floor apartment. When she reached the landing and saw the dark shape curled up against her door, the keys vanished, replaced by her favorite stiletto.

The woman pushed the matted black hair from her face and staggered to her feet.

"Tersa," Surreal whispered, vanishing the stiletto as she leaped toward the swaying woman.

"You must tell him," Tersa muttered.

Surreal dropped the basket and wrapped her arm around Tersa's waist. After calling in her keys and unlocking the door, she half-carried the muttering woman to the sofa, swearing under her breath at the condition Tersa was in.

She retrieved the basket and locked the door before returning to the sofa with a small glass of brandy.

"You must tell him," Tersa muttered, weakly batting at the glass.

"Drink this. You'll feel better," Surreal said sternly. "I haven't seen him in months. He doesn't have much use for me anymore."

Tersa grabbed Surreal's wrist and said fiercely, "Tell him to beware of the High Priest of the Hourglass. He's not a forgiving man when someone threatens what is his. Tell him to beware of the Priest."

Sighing, Surreal pulled Tersa to her feet and helped the older woman shuffle to the bathroom.

Tell him? She didn't want to get anywhere *near* him.

And what was she going to do with Tersa? There were only two beds in the place. She knew better than to give up her own, so Tersa would have to use Sadi's. But Hell's fire, he'd become so sensitive about having a woman in his room, he could tell if there had been a different cleaning woman, even if she came only once. Shit. He wasn't likely to show up— sweet Darkness, please don't let him show up—but if he did and he objected to Tersa's using his bed, *he* could throw her out.

Surreal stripped off Tersa's tattered clothing. "Come on, Tersa. You need a hot bath, a decent meal, and a good night's sleep."

"You must tell him."

Surreal closed her eyes. She owed him. She never forgot that she owed him. "I'll tell him. Somehow, I'll tell him."

3 / Terreille

After several minutes of uncomfortable silence, Philip Alexander shifted on the couch and faced his niece. He reached for her limp hand. She pulled away from his touch.

Frustrated, Philip raked his fingers through his hair and tried, once more, to be reasonable.

"Jaenelle, we're not doing this to be cruel. You're a sick little girl, and we want to help you get better."

"I'm not sick," Jaenelle said softly, staring straight ahead.

"Yes, you are." Philip kept his voice firm but gentle. "You can't tell the difference between make-believe and the real world."

"I know the difference."

"No, you don't," Philip insisted. He rubbed his forehead. "These friends, these places you visit . . . they aren't real. They were *never* real. The only reason you see them is because you're not well."

Pain, confusion, and doubt filled her summer-sky blue eyes. "But they feel so real," she whispered.

Philip pulled her close to him, grateful that she didn't push him away. He hugged her as if that would cure what years of treatment hadn't. "I know they feel real to you, sweetheart. That's the problem, don't you see? Dr. Carvay is the leading healer for—"

Jaenelle twisted out of his arms. "Carvay is *not* a healer, he's—"

"Jaenelle!" Philip took a deep breath. "That's exactly what we're talking about. Making up vicious stories about Dr. Carvay isn't going to help you. Making up stories about magical creatures—"

"I don't talk about them anymore."

Philip sighed, frustrated. That was true. She'd been cured or had outgrown those fantasies, but the stories she made up now were a different coat cut from the same cloth. A much more dangerous coat.

Philip rose and straightened his jacket. "Maybe . . . maybe if you work hard and let Dr. Carvay help you, you'll be cured this time and will be able to come home for good. In time for your birthday."

Jaenelle gave him a look he couldn't decipher.

Philip guided her to the door. "The carriage is outside. Your father and grandmother will go with you, help you get settled."

As he watched the carriage disappear down the long drive, Philip sincerely hoped that this time would be the last time.

4 / Kaeleer

Saetan sat behind the blackwood desk in his public study, a half-empty wineglass in his hand, and looked around the refurbished room.

Helene had worked her hearth-Craft well. Not only were the rooms he had requested to be refurbished done, but most of the public rooms and an entire wing of the living quarters as well. That she'd hired practically the whole village of Halaway to accomplish it . . . Well, they all needed a purpose. Even him. Especially him.

A sharp rapping on the door finally drew his attention. "Come," he said, draining the wineglass.

Helene gave the room a satisfied look before approaching the desk and squaring her shoulders. "Mrs. Beale wants to know how much longer she should hold dinner."

"An excellent meal such as Mrs. Beale has prepared shouldn't be wasted. Why don't you and the others enjoy her efforts?"

"Then your guest isn't coming?"

"Apparently not."

Helene put her hands on her hips. "A hoyden, that's what she is, not to have the manners at least to send her regrets when—"

"You forget yourself, madam," Saetan snarled softly. There was no mistaking the anger in his words, or the threat.

Helene shrank from the desk. "I . . . I beg your pardon, High Lord."

Somewhat mollified, Saetan took a deep breath and exhaled slowly. "If she couldn't come, she had her reasons. Don't judge her, Helene. If she's here and you have some complaint about serving her, then come to me and I'll do what I can to alleviate the problem. But don't judge." He slowly walked to the door. "Keep sufficient staff on hand to serve any guests who may arrive. And keep a record of who comes and goes—especially anyone who inquires about the Lady. No one enters here without identifying themselves beforehand. Is that clear?"

"Yes, High Lord," Helene answered.

"Enjoy your dinner, my dear." Then he was gone.

Saetan walked the long stone corridor toward his private study deep beneath the Hall in the Dark Realm. He had abandoned the small apartment adjoining it, having returned to his suite several floors above, but as the days and weeks had passed, he found himself returning, and staying. Just in case.

A slight figure stepped away from the shadows near the study door. Anxiety rolled out of the boy in waves as Saetan unhurriedly unlocked the door and beckoned him in. A glance at the candle-lights produced a soft glow, blurring the room's edges and relieving the feeling of immense power that filled the room he'd occupied for so long.

"Would you join me in a glass of yarbarah, Char?" Without waiting for an answer, Saetan poured a glass from the decanter on his desk and warmed it with a little tongue of fire. He handed the glass to Char.

The boy's hand shook as he took the glass, and his eyes were filled with fear.

Uneasy, Saetan warmed a glass for himself before settling into the other chair by the fire.

Char drank quickly, a momentary smile on his lips as he savored the last mouthful. He glanced at the High Lord, at the face that seldom betrayed any flicker of emotion, and looked away. He tried to speak, but no sound came out. Clearing his throat, he tried again. "Have you seen her?" he asked in a cracked whisper.

Saetan sipped the blood wine before answering. "No, Char, I haven't seen her in three months. And you?"

Char shook his head. "No, but . . . something's been happening on the island. Others have come."

Saetan leaned forward. "Others? Not children?"

"Children, yes, but . . . something happens when they come. They don't come through the Gates, or find the island by riding the Winds. They come . . ." Char shook his head, stumbling for the words.

Saetan dropped his voice into a deep, soothing croon. "Will you let me in, Char? Will you let me see?" Char's relief was so intense, it made Saetan more uneasy. Leaning back in his chair, he reached for the boy's mind, found the barriers already opened, and followed Char to the memory of what he had seen that had troubled him so much.

Saetan expelled his breath in a hiss of recognition and severed the link as quickly as he could without harming the boy.

When had Jaenelle learned to do *that*?

"What is it?" Char asked.

"A bridge," Saetan answered. He drained his glass and poured another, surprised that his hand was steady, since his insides were shaking apart. "It's called a bridge."

"It's very powerful."

"No, the bridge itself has no power." He met Char's troubled look and allowed the boy to see the turmoil he felt. "However, the one who made the bridge *is* very powerful." He put the glass down and leaned forward, elbows resting on his knees, his steepled fingers brushing his chin. "Where do these children come from? Do they say?"

Char licked his lips. "From a place called Briarwood. They won't say if it's a village or a town or a Territory. They say a friend told them about the island, showed them the road." He hesitated, suddenly shy. "Would you come and see? Maybe . . . you'd understand."

"Shall we go now?" Saetan rose, tugging on his jacket's sleeves.

Char stared at the floor. "It must be an awful place, this Briarwood." He looked up at Saetan, his troubled eyes pleading for some comfort. "Why would she go to such an awful place?"

Pulling Char to his feet, Saetan put an arm around the boy's thin shoulders, more troubled than he wanted to admit when Char leaned into him, needing the caress. Locking the study door, he kept his pace slow and steady as he fed the boy drop after psychic drop of strength and the feeling of safety. When Char's shoulders began to straighten again, Saetan let his arm casually drop away.

Three months. There had been no word from her for three months. Now children were traveling over a bridge to the *cildru dyathe*'s island.

Jaenelle's new skill would have intrigued him more if Char's question hadn't been pounding in his blood, throbbing in his temples.

Why would she go to such an awful place? Why, why, why?

And where?

5 / Terreille

"Briarwood?" Cassandra warmed two glasses of yarbarah. "No, I've never heard of Briarwood. Where is it?" She handed a glass to Saetan.

"In Terreille, so it's probably on Chaillot somewhere." He sipped the blood wine. "Maybe a small town or village near Beldon Mor. You wouldn't have a map of that damned island, would you?"

Cassandra blushed. "Well, yes. I went to Chaillot. Not to Beldon Mor," she added hurriedly. "Saetan, I had to go because . . . well, something strange has been happening. Every once in a while, there's a sensation on the Webs, almost as if . . ." She made a frustrated sound.

"Someone was plucking them and then braiding the vibrations," Saetan finished dryly. He and Geoffrey had spent hours poring over Craft books in the Keep's library in order to figure out that much, but they still couldn't figure out *how* Jaenelle had done it.

"Exactly," Cassandra said.

Saetan watched her call in a map and spread it on the kitchen table. "What you've been sensing is a bridge that Jaenelle built." He deftly caught the glass of yarbarah as it fell from her hand. Setting both glasses on the table, he led her to a bench by the hearth and held her, stroking her hair and crooning singsong words. After a while, she stopped shaking and found her voice.

"That's not how a bridge is built," she said tightly.

"Not how you or I would—or could—build one, no."

"Only Blood at the peak of their Craft can build a bridge that spans any distance worth the effort. I doubt there's anyone left in Terreille who has the training to do it." She pushed at him, then snarled when he didn't let her go. "You'll have to talk to her about this, Saetan. You really will. She's too young for this kind of Craft. And why is she building a bridge when she can ride the Winds?"

Saetan continued to stroke her hair, holding her head against his shoulder. Five years of knowing Jaenelle and she still didn't understand what they were dealing with, still didn't understand that Jaenelle wasn't a young Queen who would become Witch but already *was* Witch. But, right now, he wasn't sure he understood either. "She's not traveling on the bridge, Cassandra," he said carefully. "She's sending others over. Those who wouldn't be able to come otherwise."

Would the truth frighten her as much as it had frightened him? Probably not. She hadn't seen those children.

"Where are they coming from?" she asked uneasily.

"From Briarwood, wherever that is."

"And going to?"

Saetan took a deep breath. "The *cildru dyathe*'s island."

Cassandra pushed him away and stumbled to the table. She grabbed the edge to hold herself upright.

Saetan watched her, relieved to see that, although she was frightened, she wasn't beyond reason. He waited until she'd regained her composure, saw the moment when she stopped to consider, and appreciate, the Craft required.

"She's building a bridge from here *into Hell?*"

"Yes."

Cassandra pushed a stray lock of hair from her face, the vertical line between her eyebrows deepening as she thought. She shook her head. "The Realms can't be spanned that way."

Saetan retrieved his glass of yarbarah and drained it. "Obviously, with that kind of bridge, they *can*." He studied the map, beginning at the south end of the island and working north toward Beldon Mor, section by section. He rapped the table with his long nails. "Not listed. If it's a small village near Beldon Mor, it might not be deemed significant enough to identify."

"If it's a village at all," Cassandra murmured.

Saetan froze. "What did you say?"

"What if it's just a place? There are a lot of places that are named, Saetan."

"Yes," he crooned, a faraway look in his eyes. But what kind of place would do that to children? He snarled in frustration. "She's hiding something behind that damned mist. That's why she doesn't want anyone from the Dark Realm in that city. Who is she protecting?"

"Saetan." Cassandra tentatively placed a hand on his arm. "Perhaps she's trying to protect herself."

Saetan's golden eyes instantly turned hard yellow. He pulled his arm from beneath her hand and paced around the room. "I'd never harm her. She knows me well enough to know that."

"I believe she knows you wouldn't deliberately harm her."

Saetan spun on the balls of his feet, a graceful dancer's move. "Say what you're going to say, Cassandra, and be done with it." His voice, although quiet, was full of thunder and a rising fury.

Cassandra moved around the room, gradually putting the table between them. Not that it would stop him. "It's not just you, Saetan. Don't you understand?" She opened her arms, pleading. "It's me and Andulvar and Prothvar and Mephis, too."

"They wouldn't harm her," he said coldly. "I won't speak for you."

"You're insulting," she snapped, and then took a deep breath to regain control. "All right. Say you show up on her family's doorstep tonight. Then what? It's unlikely they know about you, about any of us. Have you considered what kind of shock it will be to them to find out about your association with her? What if they desert her?"

"She can live with me," he snarled.

"Saetan, be reasonable! Do you want her to grow up in Hell, playing with dead children until she forgets what it feels like to walk among the living? Why would you inflict that on her?"

"We could live in Kaeleer."

"For how long? Remember who you are, Saetan. How eager will those little friends be to come to the house of the High Lord of Hell?"

"Bitch," he whispered, his voice shaking with pain. He splashed yarbarah into his glass, drank it cold, and grimaced at the taste.

Cassandra dropped into a chair by the table, too weary to stand. "Bitch I may be, but your love is a luxury she may not be able to afford. She has deliberately kept all of us out, and she doesn't come around anymore. Doesn't that tell you something? You haven't seen her, no one's seen her for the past three months." She gave him a wavering smile. "Maybe we were just a phase she was going through."

A muscle twitched in Saetan's jaw. There was a queer, sleepy look in his eyes. When he finally spoke, his words were soft and venomous. "I'm not a phase, Lady. I'm her anchor, her sword, and her shield."

"You sound as though you serve her."

"I *do* serve her, Cassandra. I served you once, and I served you well, but no longer. I'm a Warlord Prince. I understand the Blood Laws that apply when my kind serve, and the first law is not to serve, it's to protect."

"And if she doesn't want your protection?"

Saetan sat down opposite her, his hands tightly clasped. "When she forms her own court, she can toss me out on my ass if that's what she wants. Until then . . ." The words trailed away.

"There may be another reason to let her go." Cassandra took a deep breath. "Hekatah came to see me a few days ago." She flinched at Saetan's hiss of anger but continued in a sassy voice, "On the surface, she came to see your newest amusement."

Saetan stared at her. She was inviting him to make light of it, to dismiss Hekatah's appearance as if it meant nothing! No, she understood the danger. She just didn't want to deal with his rage.

"Go on," he said too softly. That blend of fear and wariness in her eyes was too familiar. He'd seen that look in every woman he'd ever bedded after he began wearing the Black. Even Hekatah, although she had hidden it well for her own purposes. But Cassandra was Witch. She wore the Black. At that moment he hated her for being afraid of him. "Go on," he said again.

"I don't think she was very impressed," Cassandra said hurriedly, "and I doubt she knew who I was. But she was disconcerted when she realized I was a Guardian. Anyway, she seemed more interested in finding out if I knew of a child that might be of interest to you, a 'young feast,' as she put it."

Saetan swore viciously.

Cassandra flinched. "She went out of her way to tell me about your interest in young flesh, hoping, I suppose, to create sufficient jealousy to make me an ally."

"And what did you tell her?"

"That your interest here was the restoration of the Dark Altar that was named in honor of the Queen you once served, and while I was flattered that she thought you might find me amusing, it was, unfortunately, not true."

"Perhaps I should rectify that impression."

Cassandra gave him a saucy smile, but there was panic in her eyes. "I don't tumble with just anyone, Prince. What are your credentials?"

Out of spite, Saetan walked around the table, drew Cassandra to her feet, and gave her a gentle, lingering kiss. "My credentials are the best, Lady," he whispered when he finally lifted his lips from hers. He released her, stepped away, and settled his cape over his shoulders. "Unfortunately, I'm required elsewhere."

"How long are you going to wait for her?"

How long? Dark witches, strong witches, powerful witches. Always willing to take what he offered, in bed and out, but they had never liked him, never trusted him, always feared him. And then there was Jaenelle. How long would he wait?

"Until she returns."

6 / Hell

It tingled his nerves, persistent and grating.

Growling in his sleep, Saetan rolled over and pulled the bedcovers up around his shoulders.

The tingling continued. A calling. A summons.

Along the Black.

Saetan opened his eyes to the night-dark room, listening with inner as well as outer senses.

A shrill cry of fury and despair flooded his mind.

"Jaenelle," he whispered, shivering as his bare feet touched the cold floor. Pulling on a dressing robe, he hurried into the corridor, then stopped, unsure where to go. Gathering himself, he sent one thunderous summons along the Black. *Jaenelle!*

No answer. Just that tingling laced with fear, despair, and fury.

She was still in Terreille. The thought spun through his head as he raced through the twisting corridors of the Hall. No time to wonder how she'd sent that thought-burst between the Realms. No time for anything. His Lady was in trouble and out of easy reach.

He ran into the great hall, ignoring the burning pain in his bad leg. A thought ripped the double front doors off the Hall. He raced down the broad steps and around the side of the Hall to the separate building where the Dark Altar stood.

Gasping, he tore the iron gate off its hinges and entered the large room. His hands shook as he centered the four-branched silver candelabra on the smooth black stone. Taking a deep breath to steady himself, he lit the three black candles that represented the Realms in the proper order to open a Gate between Hell and Terreille. He lit the candle in the center of the triangle made by the other three, the candle that represented the Self, and summoned the power of the Gate, waiting impatiently as the wall behind the Altar slowly changed from stone to mist and became a Gate between the Realms.

Saetan walked into the mist. His fourth step took him out of the mist and into the ruin that housed this Dark Altar in Terreille. As he passed the Altar, he noticed the black candle stubs in the tarnished candelabra and wondered why this Altar was getting so much use. Then he was outside the building, and there was no more time to wonder.

He gathered the strength of the Black Jewels and set a thought along a tight psychic thread. *Jaenelle!* He waited for a response, fighting the urge to catch the Black Web and fly to Chaillot. If he was on the Winds, he'd be out of reach for several hours. By then it might be too late. *Jaenelle!*

Saetan? Saetan! From the other side of the Realm, her voice came to him as a broken whisper.

Witch-child! He poured his strength into that tenuous link.

Saetan, please, I have to . . . I need . . .

Fight, witch-child, fight! You have the strength!

I need . . . don't know how to . . . Saetan, please.

Even the Black had limits. Grinding his teeth, Saetan swore as his long nails cut his palms and drew blood. If he lost her now . . . No. He *wouldn't* lose her! No matter what he had to do, he'd find a way to send her what she needed.

But this link between them was spun out so fine that anything might snap it, and most of her attention was focused elsewhere. If the link broke, he wouldn't be able to span the Realm and find her again. Holding his end of it was draining the Black Jewel at a tremendous rate. He didn't want to think about what it had cost her to reach him in Hell. If he could use someone as a transfer point, if he could braid his strength with an-other's for a minute . . . Cassandra? Too far. If he diverted any of his strength to search, he might lose Jaenelle altogether.

But he needed another's strength!

And it was there. Wary, angry, intent. Another mind on the Black psy-chic thread, turned toward the west, toward Chaillot.

Another male.

Saetan froze. Only one other male wore the Black Jewels.

Who are you? It was a deep, rich, cultured voice with a rough, se-ductive edge to it. A dangerous voice.

What could he say? What did he *dare* say to this son he'd loved for a few short years before he'd been forced to walk away from him? There was no time to settle things between them. Not now. So he chose the title that hadn't been used in Terreille in 1,700 years. *I'm the High Priest of the Hourglass.*

A quiver passed between them. A kind of wary recognition that wasn't quite recognition. Which meant Daemon had heard the title somewhere but couldn't name the man who held it.

Saetan took a deep breath. *I need your strength to hold this link.*

A long silence. *Why?*

Saetan ground his teeth, not daring to let his thoughts stray. *I can't give her the knowledge she needs without amplifying the link, and if she doesn't get the knowledge, she may be destroyed.* Even without a full link between them, he felt Daemon weighing his words.

Suddenly a stream of raw, barely controlled Black power rushed toward him as Daemon said, *Take what you need.*

Saetan tapped into Daemon's strength, ruthlessly draining it as he sent a knife-sharp thought toward Chaillot. *Lady!*

Help . . . Such desperation in that word.

Take what you need. Words of Protocol, of service, of surrender.

Saetan threw open his inner barriers, giving her access to everything he knew, everything he was. He sank to his knees and grabbed his head, sure his skull would shatter from the pain as Jaenelle slammed into him and rummaged through his mind as if she were opening cupboards and flinging their contents onto the floor until she found what she wanted. It only took a moment. It felt like forever. Then she withdrew, and the link with her faded.

Thank you. A faint whisper, almost gone. *Thank you.*

The second "thank you" wasn't directed at him.

It seemed like hours, not minutes, before his hands dropped to his thighs and he tilted his head back to look at the false-dawn sky. It took a minute more to realize he wasn't alone, that another mind still lightly touched his with something more than wariness.

Saetan swiftly closed his inner barriers. *You did well, Prince. I thank you . . . for her sake.* He cautiously began to back away from the link between them, not sure he could win a confrontation with Daemon.

But Daemon, too, backed away, exhausted.

As the link faded, just before Saetan was once more alone within himself, Daemon's voice came to him faintly, the words a silky threat.

Don't get in my way, Priest.

Grabbing one of the posts of the four-poster bed, Daemon hauled himself to his feet just as the door burst open and six guards cautiously entered the room.

Normally they had good reason to fear him, but not tonight. Even if he hadn't drained his strength to the point of exhaustion, he wouldn't have fought them. Tonight, whatever happened to him, he was buying time because she, wherever she was, needed a chance to recover.

The guards circled him and led him to the brightly lit outer courtyard. When he saw the two posts with the leather straps secured at the base and top, he hesitated for the briefest moment.

Lady Cornelia, the latest pet Queen who had bought his services from Dorothea SaDiablo, stood near the posts. Her eyes sparkled. Her voice dripped with excitement. "Strip him."

Daemon angrily shrugged off the guards' hands and began undressing when a bolt of pain from the Ring of Obedience made him catch his breath. He looked at Cornelia and lowered his hands to his sides.

"Strip him," she said.

Rough hands pulled his clothes off and dragged him to the posts. The guards lashed his ankles and wrists to the posts, tightening the leather straps until he was stretched taut.

Cornelia smiled at him. "A slave is forbidden to use the Jewels. A slave is forbidden to do anything but basic Craft, as you well know."

Yes, he knew. Just as he'd known that Cornelia would sense the unleashing of that much dark power and punish him for it. For most males, the threat of pain—especially the pain that could be produced by the Ring of Obedience—was enough to keep them submissive. But he'd learned to embrace agony like a sweet lover and used it to fuel his hatred for Dorothea and everything and everyone connected with her.

"The punishment for this kind of disobedience is fifty strokes," Cornelia said. "*You* will do the counting. If you miss a stroke, it will be repeated until you give the count. If you lose your place, the counting will begin again."

Daemon forced his voice to remain neutral. "What will Lady SaDiablo say about your treatment of her property?"

"Under the circumstances, I don't think Lady SaDiablo will mind," Cornelia replied sweetly. Then her voice became a whip crack. "Begin!"

Daemon heard the lash whistle before it struck. For a brief moment, a strange shiver of pleasure ran through him before his body recognized the pain. He drew in a ragged breath. "One."

Everything has a price. "Two." A Blood Law, or part of a code of honor? "Three." He'd never heard of the High Priest of the Hourglass until he'd found one of Surreal's warnings, but there was something vaguely familiar about that other mind. "Four." Who *was* the Priest? "Five." A Warlord Prince . . . "Six." . . . like himself . . . "Seven." . . . who wore the Black Jewels. "Eight." Everything has a price. "Nine." Who had taught him that? "Ten." Older. More experienced. "Eleven." To the east of him. "Twelve." And she was to the west. "Thirteen." He didn't know who she was, but he *did* know *what* she was. "Fourteen. Fifteen."

Everything has a price.

The guards dragged him back to his room and locked the door.

Daemon fell heavily onto his hands and knees. Pressing his forehead to the floor, he tried to dull the burning pain in his back, buttocks, and legs long enough to get to his feet. Fifty strokes, each one slicing through his flesh. Fifty strokes. But no more. He hadn't missed the count once, despite the bursts of pain that Cornelia had sent through the Ring of Obedience to distract him.

Slowly gathering his feet under him, he pushed himself to an almost upright position and shuffled to the bathroom, unable to stifle the moaning sob that accompanied each step.

When he finally reached the bathroom, he braced one trembling hand against the wall and turned the water taps to fill the bath with warm water. His vision kept blurring, and his body shook with pain and exhaustion. It took three tries to call in the small leather case that held his stash of healing supplies. Once he had it open, it took a minute for his vision to clear sufficiently to find the jar he wanted.

When combined with water, the powdered herbs cleansed wounds, numbed pain, and allowed the healing process to begin—*if* he could keep his mind fixed enough, and *if* he could withdraw far enough into himself to gather the power, the Craft he would need to heal the torn flesh.

Daemon's lips twisted in a grim smile as he turned off the water. If he sent a summons along the Black, if he asked the Priest for help, would he get it? Unlikely. Not an enemy. Not yet. But Surreal had done well to leave those notes warning him about the Priest.

Daemon let out a cry as the jar slipped from his hands and shattered on the bathroom floor. He sank to his knees, hissing as a piece of glass sliced him, and stared at the powder, tears of pain and frustration welling in his eyes. Without the powder to help heal the wounds, he might still be able to heal them to some extent, still be able to stop the bleeding . . . but he would scar. And he didn't need a mirror to know what he would look like.

No! He wasn't aware of sending. He was only trying to relieve the frustration.

A minute later, as he knelt on the bathroom floor, shaking, trying not to vent the sobs building in him, a hand touched his shoulder.

Daemon twisted around, his teeth bared, his eyes wild.

There was no one in the room. The touch was gone. But there was a presence in the bathroom. Alien . . . and not.

Daemon probed the room and found nothing. But it was still there, like something seen out of the corner of the eye that vanishes when you turn to look at it. Breathing hard, Daemon waited.

The touch, when it came again, was hesitant, cautious. He shivered as it gently probed his back. Shivered because along with exhaustion and dismay, that gentle touch was filled with a cold, cold anger.

The powdered herbs and broken glass vanished. A moment later a brass ball, perforated like a tea ball, appeared above the bath and sank into the water. Small phantom hands, gentle yet strong, helped him into the bath.

Daemon gasped when the open wounds touched the water, but the hands pushed him down, down, down until he was stretched out on his back, the water covering him. After a moment he couldn't feel the hands. Dismayed that the link might be broken, he struggled to rise to a sitting position only to find himself held down. He relaxed and slowly realized that his skin felt numb from his chin down, that he no longer felt the pain. Sighing with gratitude, Daemon leaned his head against the bath and closed his eyes.

A sweet, strange darkness rolled through him. He moaned, but it was a moan of pleasure.

Strange how the mind could wander. He could almost smell the sea, feel the power of the surf. Then there was the rich smell of fresh-turned earth after a warm spring rain. And the luscious warmth of sunlight on a soft summer afternoon. The sensual pleasure of slipping naked between clean sheets.

When he reluctantly opened his eyes, her psychic scent still lingered, but he knew she was gone. He moved his foot through the now-cold water. The brass ball was gone too.

Daemon carefully got out of the bath, opened the drain, and swayed on his feet, unsure what to do. Reaching for a towel, he patted the front of his body to absorb most of the water, but he was reluctant to touch the back. Gritting his teeth, he turned his back to the mirror and looked over his shoulder. Best to know how bad the damage was.

Daemon stared.

There were fifty white lines, like chalk lines on his golden-brown skin. The lines looked fragile, and it would take days of being careful before the wounds were truly, strongly knit, but he was healed. If he didn't reopen the wounds, those lines would fade. No scars.

Daemon carefully walked to the bed and lay face down, inching his arms upward until they were under the pillow, supporting his head. It was hard to stay awake, hard not to think about how a meadow looks so silvery in the moonlight. Hard . . .

Someone had been touching his back for some time before he was aware of it. Daemon resisted the urge to open his eyes. There would be nothing to see, and if she knew he was awake, she might pull away.

Her touch was firm, gentle, knowing. It traveled in slow, circular lines down his back. Cool, soothing, comforting.

Where was she? Not nearby, so how was she able to make the reach? He didn't know. He didn't care. He surrendered to the pleasure of that phantom touch, a hand that someday he would hold in the flesh.

When she was gone again, Daemon slowly eased one arm around and gingerly touched his back. He stared at the thick salve on his fingers and then wiped them on the sheet. His eyes closed. There was no point in fighting the sleep he so desperately needed.

But just before he surrendered to need, he thought once more about the kind of witch who would come to a stranger's aid, already exhausted from her own ordeal, and heal his wounds. "Don't get in my way, Priest," he muttered, and fell asleep.

CHAPTER FOUR

1 / Hell

Saetan slammed the book down on the desk and shook with rage.

A month since that plea for knowledge. A month of waiting for some word, *some* indication that she was all right. He'd tried to enter Beldon Mor, but Cassandra had been right. The psychic mist surrounding the city was a barrier that only the dead could feel, a barrier that kept them all out. Jaenelle was taking no chances with whatever secret lay behind the mist, and her lack of trust was a blade between his ribs.

Embroiled in his own thoughts, he didn't realize someone else was in the study until he heard his name called a second time.

"Saetan?" Such pain and pleading in that small, weary voice. "Please don't be angry with me."

His vision blurred. His nails dug into the blackwood desk, gouging its stone-hard wood. He wanted to vent all the fear and anger that had been growing in him since he'd last seen her, months ago. He wanted to shake her for daring to ask him to swallow his anger. Instead he took a deep breath, smoothed his face into as neutral a mask as he could create, and turned toward her.

The sight of her made him ill.

She was a skeleton with skin. Her sapphire eyes were sunk into her skull, almost lost in the dark circles beneath them. The golden hair he loved to touch hung limp and dull around her bruised face. There were rope burns and dried blood on her ankles and wrists.

"Come here," he said, all emotion drained from his voice. When she didn't move, he took a step toward her. She flinched and stepped back. His voice became soft thunder. "Jaenelle, come here."

One step. Two. Three. She stared at his feet, shaking.

He didn't touch her. He didn't trust himself to control the jealousy and spite that seared him as he looked at her. She preferred staying with her family and being treated like this over being with him, who loved her with all his being but wasn't entrusted with her care because he was a Guardian, because he was the High Lord of Hell.

Better that she play with the dead than become one of them, he thought bitterly. She wasn't strong enough right now to fight him. He would keep her here for a few days and let her heal. Then he would bring that bastard of a father to his knees and force him to relinquish all paternal rights. He would—

"I can't leave them, Saetan." Jaenelle looked up at him.

The tears sliding down her bruised face twisted his heart, but his face was stone-carved, and he waited in silence.

"There's no one else. Don't you see?"

"No, I don't see." His voice, although controlled and quiet, rumbled through the room. "Or perhaps I do." His cold glance raked her shaking body. "You prefer enduring this and remaining with your family to living with me and what I have to offer."

Jaenelle blinked in surprise. Her eyes lost some of their haunted look, and she became thoughtful. "Live with you? Do you mean it?"

Saetan watched her, puzzled.

Slowly, regretfully, she shook her head. "I can't. I'd like to, but I can't. Not yet. Rose can't do it by herself."

Saetan dropped to one knee and took her frail, almost transparent hands in his. She flinched at his touch but didn't pull away. "It wouldn't have to be in Hell, witch-child," he said soothingly. "I've opened the Hall in Kaeleer. You could live there, maybe attend the same school as your friends."

Jaenelle giggled, her eyes momentarily dancing with amusement. "Schools, High Lord. They live in many places."

He smiled tenderly and bowed his head. "Schools, then. Or private tutors. Anything you wish. I *can* arrange it, witch-child."

Jaenelle's eyes filled with tears as she shook her head. "It would be lovely, it truly would, but . . . not yet. I can't leave them yet."

Saetan bit back the arguments and sighed. She had come to him for comfort, not a fight. And since he couldn't officially serve her until she established a court, he had no right to stand between her and her family, no matter what he felt. "All right. But please remember, you have a place to come to. You don't have to stay with them. But . . . I'd be willing to make the appropriate arrangements for your family to visit or live with you, under my supervision, if that's what you wish."

Jaenelle's eyes widened. "Under your supervision?" she said weakly. She let out a gurgle of laughter and then tried to look stern. "You wouldn't make my sister learn sticks with Prothvar, would you?"

Saetan's voice shook with amusement and unshed tears. "No, I wouldn't make her learn sticks with Prothvar." He carefully drew her into his arms and hugged her frail body. Tears spilled from his closed eyes when her arms circled his neck and tightened. He held her, warmed her, comforted her. When she finally pulled away from him, he stood quickly, wiping the tears from his face.

Jaenelle looked away. "I'll come back as soon as I can."

Nodding, Saetan turned toward the desk, unable to speak. He never heard her move, never heard the door open, but when he turned back to say good-bye, she was already gone.

2 / Terreille

Surreal lay beneath the sweating, grunting man, thrusting her hips in the proper rhythm and moaning sensuously whenever a fat hand squeezed her breasts. She stared at the ceiling while her hands roamed up and down the sweaty back in not-quite-feigned urgency.

Stupid pig, she thought as a slobbering kiss wet her neck. She should have charged more for the contract—and would have if she'd known how unpleasant he would be in bed. But he only had the one shot, and he was almost at his peak.

The spell now. Ah, to weave the spell.

She turned her mind inward, slipped from the calm depths of the Green to the stiller, deeper, more silent Gray, and quickly wove her death spell around him, tying it to the rhythms of the bed, to the quickened heartbeat and raspy breathing.

Practice had made her adept at her Craft.

The last link of the spell was a delay. Not tomorrow, but the day after, or the one after that. Then, whether it was anger or lust that made the heart pound, the spell would burst a vessel in his heart, sear his brain with the strength of the Gray, shatter his Jewel, and leave nothing but carrion behind.

It was an offhand remark Sadi had made once that convinced Surreal to be thorough in her kills. Daemon entertained the possibility that the Blood, being more than flesh, could continue to wear the Jewels after the body's death—and remember who had helped them down the misty road to Hell. He'd said, "No matter what you do with the flesh, finish the kill. After all, who wants to turn a corner one day and meet up with one of the demon-dead who would like to return the favor?"

So she always finished the kill. There would be nothing traceable, nothing that could lead them to her. The Healers that practiced in Terreille now, such as they were, would assume he had burned out his mind and his Jewels trying to save his body from the physical death.

Surreal came out of her reverie as the grunts and thrusts increased for a moment. Then he sagged. She turned her head, trying not to breathe the enhanced odor of his unwashed body.

When he finally lay on his back, snoring, Surreal slipped out of bed, pulled on a silk robe, and wrinkled her nose. The robe would have to be cleaned before she could wear it again. Hooking her hair behind her ears, she went to the window and pulled the curtain aside.

She had to decide where to go now that this contract was done. She should have made the decision days ago, but she'd kept hesitating because of the recurring dreams that washed over her mind like surf over a beach. Dreams about Titian and Titian's Jewel. Dreams about needing to be someplace, about being *needed* someplace.

Except Titian couldn't tell her where.

Maybe there were just too many lights in this old, decrepit city. Maybe she couldn't decide because she couldn't see the stars.

Stars. And the sea. Someplace clean, where she could take a light schedule and spend her days reading or walking by the sea.

Surreal smiled. It had been three years since she'd last spent time with Deje. Chaillot had some beautiful, quiet beaches on the east side. On a clear day, you could even see Tacea Island. And there was a Sanctuary nearby, wasn't there? Or some kind of ancient ruin. Picnic lunches, long solitary walks. Deje would be happy to see her, wouldn't push to fill every night.

Yes. Chaillot.

Surreal turned from the window when the man grunted and thrashed onto his side. The Sadist was right. There were so many ways to efficiently kill a man other than splattering his blood over the walls.

It was too bad they didn't give her as much pleasure.

3 / Terreille

Lucivar Yaslana listened to the embroidered half-truths Zuultah was spewing about him to a circle of nervous, wide-eyed witches and wondered if snapping a few female necks would add color to the stories. Reluctantly putting aside that pleasant fantasy, he scanned the crowded room for some diversion.

Daemon Sadi glided past him.

Lucivar sucked in his breath, suppressed a grin, and turned back to Zuultah's circle. The last time the Queens had gotten careless about keeping them separated, he and Daemon had destroyed a court during a fight that escalated from a disagreement over whether the wine being served was just mediocre or was really colored horse piss.

Forty years ago. Enough time among the short-lived races for the randy young Queens to convince themselves that they could control him and Daemon or, even better, that they were the Queens strong-willed enough and wonderful enough to tame two dark-Jeweled Warlord Princes. Well, this Eyrien Warlord Prince wasn't tamable—at least, not for another five years. As for the Sadist . . . Any man who referred to his bedroom skills as poisoned honey wasn't likely to be tamed or controlled unless he chose to be.

It was late in the evening before Lucivar got the chance to slip out to the back garden. Daemon had gone out a few minutes before, after an abrupt, snarling disagreement with Lady Cornelia.

Moving with a hunter's caution, Lucivar followed the ribbon of chilled air left by Daemon's passing. He turned a corner and stopped.

Daemon stood in the middle of the gravel path, his face raised to the night sky while the delicate breeze riffled his black hair.

The gravel under Lucivar's feet shifted slightly.

Daemon turned toward the sound.

Lucivar hesitated. He knew what that sleepy, glazed look in Daemon's eyes meant, remembered only too well what had happened in courts when that tender, murderous smile had lasted for more than a brief second. Nothing, and no one, was safe when Daemon was in this mood. But, Hell's fire, that's what made dancing with the Sadist fun.

Smiling his own lazy, arrogant smile, Lucivar stepped forward and slowly stretched his dark wings their full span before tucking them tight to his body. "Hello, Bastard."

Daemon's smile thawed. "Hello, Prick. It's been a long time."

"So it has. Drunk any good wines lately?"

"None that you'd appreciate." Daemon studied Lucivar's clothes and raised an eyebrow. "You've decided to be a good boy?"

Lucivar snorted. "I decided I wanted decent food and a decent bed for a change and a few days out of Pruul, and all I have to do is lick the bottom of Zuultah's boots when she returns from the stable."

"Maybe that's your trouble, Prick. You're not supposed to lick her boots, you're supposed to kiss her ass." He turned and glided down the path.

Remembering why he'd wanted to talk to Daemon, Lucivar followed reluctantly until they reached a gazebo tucked in one corner of the garden where they couldn't be seen from the mansion. Daemon smiled that cold, sweet smile and stepped aside to let him enter first.

Never let a predator smell fear.

Annoyed by his own uneasiness, Lucivar turned to study the luminescent leaves of the firebush nearby. He stiffened when Daemon came up behind him, when the long nails whispered over his shoulders, teasing his skin in a loverlike fashion.

"Do you want me?" Daemon whispered, brushing his lips against Lucivar's neck.

Lucivar snorted and tried to pull away, but the caressing hand instantly became a vise. "No," he said flatly. "I endured enough of that in Eyrien hunting camps." With a teeth-baring grin, he turned around. "Do you really think your touch makes my pulse race?"

"Doesn't it?" Daemon whispered, a strange look in his eyes.

Lucivar stared. Daemon's voice was too crooning, too silky, too dangerously sleepy. Hell's fire, Lucivar thought desperately as Daemon's lips brushed his, what was *wrong* with him? This wasn't his kind of game.

Lucivar jerked back. Daemon's nails dug into the back of his neck. The sharp thumbnails pricked his throat. Keeping his fists pressed against his thighs, Lucivar closed his eyes and submitted to the kiss.

No reason to feel humiliation and shame. His body was responding to stimulation the same way it would to cold or hunger. Physical response had nothing to do with feelings or desire. Nothing.

But, Mother Night, Daemon could set a stone on fire!

"Why are you doing this?" Lucivar gasped. "At least tell me why."

"Why not?" Daemon replied bitterly. "I have to whore for everyone else, why not you?"

"Because I don't want you to. Because you don't want to. Daemon, this is madness! Why are you doing this?"

Daemon pressed his forehead against Lucivar's. "Since you already know the answer, why ask me?" He kneaded Lucivar's shoulders. "I can't stand being touched by them anymore. Ever since . . . I can't stand the feel of them, the smell of them, the taste of them. They've raped everything I am until there's nothing clean left to offer."

Lucivar wrapped his hands around Daemon's wrists. The shame and bitterness saturating Daemon's psychic scent scraped a nerve he had refused to probe over the past five years. Once she was old enough to understand what it meant, *would* that sapphire-eyed little cat despise them for the way they'd been forced to serve? It wouldn't matter. He would fight with everything in him for the chance to serve her. And so would Daemon. "Daemon." He took a deep breath. "Daemon, she's come."

Daemon pulled away. "I know. I've felt her." He stuffed his shaking hands into his trouser pockets. "There's trouble around her—"

"What trouble?" Lucivar asked sharply.

"—and I keep wondering if he can—if he *will*—protect her."

"Who? *Daemon!*"

Daemon dropped to the floor, clutching his groin and moaning.

Swearing under his breath, Lucivar wrapped his arms around Daemon and waited. Nothing else could be done for a man enduring a bolt of pain sent through the Ring of Obedience.

By the time it was over and Daemon got to his feet, his beautiful, aristocratic face had hardened into a cold, pain-glazed mask and his voice was empty of emotion. "It seems Lady Cornelia requires my presence." He flicked a twig off his jacket sleeve. "You'd think she would know better by now." He hesitated before he left the gazebo. "Take care, Prick."

Lucivar leaned against the gazebo long after Daemon's footsteps had faded away. What had happened between Daemon and the girl? And what did "Take care, Prick" mean? A warm farewell . . . or a warning?

"Daemon?" Lucivar whispered, remembering another place and another court. "Daemon, no." He ran toward the mansion. *"Daemon!"*

Lucivar charged through the open glass doors and shoved his way through gossiping knots of women, briefly aware of Zuultah's angry face in front of him. He was halfway up the stairs leading to the guest rooms when a bolt of pain from the Ring of Obedience brought him to his knees. Zuultah stood beside him, her face twisted with fury. Lucivar tried to get to his feet, but another surge from the Ring bent him over so far his forehead pressed against the stairs.

"Let me go, Zuultah." His voice cracked from the pain.

"I'll teach you some manners, you arrogant—"

Lucivar twisted around to face her. "Let me go, you stupid bitch," he hissed. "Let me go before it's too late."

It took her a long minute to understand she wasn't what he feared, and another long minute before he could get to his feet.

With one hand pressed to his groin, Lucivar hauled himself up the stairs and pushed himself into a stumbling run toward the guest wing. There was no time to think about the crowd growing behind him, no time to think about anything except reaching Cornelia's room before . . .

Daemon opened Cornelia's door, closed it behind him, calmly tugged his shirt cuffs into place, and then smashed his fist into the wall.

Lucivar felt the mansion shudder as the power of the Black Jewel surged into the wall.

Cracks appeared in the wall, running in every direction, opening wider and wider.

"Daemon?"

Daemon tugged his shirt cuffs down once more. When he finally looked at Lucivar, his eyes were as cold and glazed as a murky gemstone— and no more human.

Daemon smiled.

Lucivar shivered.

"Run," Daemon crooned. Seeing the crowd filling the hall behind Lucivar, he calmly turned and walked the other way.

The mansion continued to shudder. Something crashed nearby.

Licking his lips, Lucivar opened Cornelia's door. He stared at the bed, at what was on the bed, and fought to control his heaving guts. He turned away from the open door and stood there, too numb to move.

He smelled smoke, heard the roar of flames consuming a room. People screamed. The mansion walls rumbled as they split farther and farther. He looked around, confused, until part of the ceiling crashed a few feet away from him.

Fear cleared his head, and he did the only sensible thing.

He ran.

4 / Terreille

Dorothea SaDiablo, the High Priestess of Hayll, paced the length of her sitting room, the floor-length cocoon she wore over a simple dark dress billowing out behind her. She tapped her fingertips together, over and over, absently noting that her cousin Hepsabah grew more agitated as the silence and pacing continued.

Hepsabah squirmed in her chair. "You're not really bringing him back *here?*" Her voice squeaked with her growing panic. She tried to keep her hands still because Dorothea found her nervous gestures annoying, but the hands were like wing-clipped birds fluttering hopelessly in her lap.

Dorothea shot a dagger glance in Hepsabah's direction and continued pacing. "Where else can I send him?" she snapped. "It may be *years* before anyone is willing to sign a contract for him. And with the stories flying, I may not be able to even make a present of the bastard. With so much of that place burned beyond recognition ... and Cornelia's room untouched. Too many people saw what was in that bed. There's been too much talk."

"But ... he's not there, and he's not here. Where is he?"

"Hell's fire, how should I know. Nearby. Skulking somewhere. Maybe twisting a few other witches into shattered bones and pulped flesh."

"You could summon him with the Ring."

Dorothea stopped pacing and stared at her cousin through narrowed eyes. Their mothers had been sisters. The bloodline was good on that side. And the consort who'd sired Hepsabah had shown potential. How could two of Hayll's Hundred Families have produced such a simpering idiot? Unless her dear aunt had seeded herself with a piece of gutter trash. To think Hepsabah was the best she had to work with to try to keep some rein on him. That had been a mistake. Maybe she should have let that mad Dhemlan bitch keep him. No. There were other problems with that. The Dark Priestess had warned her. As much good as it did.

Dorothea smiled at Hepsabah, pleased to see her cousin shrink farther into the chair. "So you think I should summon him? Use the Ring when the debris in that place is barely cooled? Are *you* willing to be the one to welcome him home if I bring him back that way?"

Hepsabah's smooth, carefully painted face crumpled with fear. "Me?" she wailed. "You wouldn't make me do that. You *can't* make me do that. He doesn't *like* me."

"But you're his *mother,* dear," Dorothea purred.

"But you know . . . you know . . ."

"Yes, I know." Dorothea continued pacing, but slower. "So. He's in Hayll. He signed in this morning at one of the posting stations. He'll be here soon enough. Let him have a day or two to vent his rage on someone else. In the meantime, I'll have to arrange a bit of educational entertainment. And I'll have to think about what to do with him. The Hayllian trash and the landens don't understand what he is. They *like* him. They think that pittance generosity he shows them is the way he is. I should have preserved the image of Cornelia's bedroom in a spelled crystal and shown them what he's really like. No matter. He won't stay long. I'll find *someone* foolish enough to take him."

Hepsabah got to her feet, smoothed her gold dress over her padded, well-curved body, and patted her coiled black hair. "Well. I should go and see that his room is ready." She let out a tittering laugh behind her hand. "That's a mother's duty."

"Don't rub against his bedpost too much, dear. You know how he hates the scent of a woman's musk."

Hepsabah blinked, swallowed hard. "I never," she sputtered indignantly, and instantly began to pout. "It's just not fair."

Dorothea tucked a stray hair back into Hepsabah's elegant coils. "When you start getting thoughts like that, dear, remember Cornelia."

Hepsabah's brown skin turned gray. "Yes," she murmured as Dorothea led her to the door. "Yes, I'll remember."

5 / Terreille

Daemon glided down the crowded sidewalk, his ground-eating stride never breaking as people around him skittered out of his way, filling back in as he passed. He didn't see them, didn't hear the murmuring voices. With his hands in his trouser pockets, he glided through the crowds and the noise, unaware and uncaring.

He was in Draega, Hayll's capital city.

He was home.

He'd never liked Draega, never liked the tall stone buildings that shouldered against one another, blocking out the sun, never liked the concrete roads and the concrete sidewalks with the stunted, dusty trees growing out of circular patches of earth cut out of the concrete. Oh, there were a thousand things to do here: theaters, music halls, museums, places to dine. All the things a long-lived, arrogant, useless people needed to fill the empty hours. But Draega . . . If he could be sure that two particular witches would lie crushed and buried in the rubble, he would tear the city apart without a second thought.

He swung into the street, weaving his way between the carriages that came to a stuttering halt, oblivious of their irate drivers. One or two passengers thrust their heads through a side window to shout at him, but when they saw his face and realized who he was, they hastily pulled their heads back in, hoping he hadn't noticed them.

Since he'd arrived that morning, he'd been following a psychic thread that tugged him toward an unknown destination. He wasn't troubled by the pull. Its chaotic meandering told him who was at the other end. He didn't know why she was in Draega of all places, but her need to see him was strong enough to pull him toward her.

Daemon entered the large park in the center of the city, veered to the footpath leading to the southern end, and slowed his pace. Here among the trees and grass, with the street sounds muted, he breathed a little easier. He crossed a footbridge that spanned a trickling creek, hesitated for a moment, then took the right-hand fork in the path that led farther into the park.

Finally he came to a small oval of grass. A lacy iron bench filled the back of the oval. A half-circle of lady's tears formed a backdrop, the small, white-throated blue flowers filling the bushes. Two old, tall trees stood at either end of the oval, their branches intertwining high above, letting a dappling of sunlight reach the ground.

The tugging stopped.

Daemon stood in the oval of grass, slowly turning full circle. He started to turn away when a low giggle came from the bushes.

"How many sides does a triangle have?" a woman's husky voice asked.

Daemon sighed and shook his head. It was going to be riddles.

"How many sides does a triangle have?" the voice asked again.

"Three," Daemon answered.

The bushes parted. Tersa shook the leaves from her tattered coat and pushed her tangled black hair from her face. "Foolish boy, did they teach you nothing?"

Daemon's smile was gentle and amused. "Apparently not."

"Give Tersa a kiss."

Resting his hands on her thin shoulders, Daemon lightly kissed her cheek. He wondered when she'd eaten last but decided not to ask. She seldom knew or cared, and asking would only make her unhappy.

"How many sides does a triangle have?"

Daemon sighed, resigned. "Darling, a triangle has three sides."

Tersa scowled. "Stupid boy. Give me your hand."

Daemon obediently held out his right hand. Tersa grasped the long, slender fingers with her own frail-looking sticks and turned his hand palm up. With the forefinger nail of her right hand, she began tracing three connecting lines on his palm, over and over again. "A Blood triangle has four sides, foolish boy. Like the candelabra on a Dark Altar. Remember that." Over and over until the lines began to glow white on his golden-brown palm. "Father, brother, lover. Father, brother, lover. The father came first."

"He usually does," Daemon said dryly.

She ignored him. "Father, brother, lover. The lover is the father's mirror. The brother stands between." She stopped tracing and looked up at him. It was one of those times when Tersa's eyes were clear and focused, yet she was looking at some place other than where her body stood. "How many sides does a triangle have?"

Daemon studied the three white lines on his palm. "Three."

Tersa drew in her breath, exasperated.

"Where's the fourth side?" he asked quickly, hoping to avoid hearing the question again.

Tersa snapped her thumb and forefinger nail together, then pressed the knife-sharp forefinger nail into the center of the triangle in Daemon's palm. Daemon hissed when her nail cut his skin. He jerked his hand back, but her fingers held him in a grip that hurt.

Daemon watched the blood well in the hollow of his palm. Still holding his fingers in an iron grip, Tersa slowly raised his hand toward his face. The world became fuzzy, unfocused, mist-shrouded. The only painfully clear thing Daemon could see was his hand, a white triangle, and the bright, glistening blood.

Tersa's voice was a singsong croon. "Father, brother, lover. And the center, the fourth side, the one who rules all three."

Daemon closed his eyes as Tersa raised his hand to his lips. The air was too hot, too close. Daemon's lips parted. He licked the blood from his palm.

It sizzled on his tongue, red lightning. It seared his nerves, crackled through him and gathered in his belly, gathered into a white-hot ember waiting for a breath, a single touch that would turn his kindled maleness into an inferno. His hand closed in a fist and he swayed, clenching his teeth to keep from begging for that touch.

When he opened his eyes, the oval of grass was empty. He slowly opened his hand. The lines were already fading, the small cut healed.

"Tersa?"

Her voice came back to him, distant and fading. "The lover is the father's mirror. The Priest . . . He will be your best ally or your worst enemy. But the choice will be yours."

"Tersa!"

Almost gone. "The chalice is cracking."

"Tersa!"

A surge of rage honed by terror rushed through him. Closing his hand, he swung his arm straight and shoulder-high. The shock of his fist connecting with one of the trees jarred him to his heels. Daemon leaned against the tree, eyes closed, forehead pressed to the trunk.

When he opened his eyes, his black coat was covered with gray-green ashes. Frowning, Daemon looked up. A denial caught in his throat, strangling him. He stepped back from the tree and sat down on the bench, his face hidden in his hands.

Several minutes later, he forced himself to look at the tree.

It was dead, burned from within by his fury. Standing among the green living things, its gray skeletal branches still reached for its partner. Daemon walked over to the tree and pressed his palm against the trunk. He didn't know if there was a way to probe it to see if sap still ran at its core, or if it had all been crystallized by the heat of his rage.

"I'm sorry," he whispered. Gray-green dust continued to fall from the upper branches. A few minutes ago, that dust had been living green leaves. "I'm sorry."

Taking a deep breath, Daemon followed the path back the way he'd come, hands in his pockets, head down, shoulders slumped. Just before leaving the park, he turned around and looked back. He couldn't see the tree, but he could feel it. He shook his head slowly, a grim smile on his lips. He'd buried more of the Blood than they would ever guess, and he mourned a tree.

Daemon brushed the ash from his coat. He'd have to report to Dorothea soon, tomorrow at the latest. There were two more stops he wanted to make before presenting himself at court.

6 / Terreille

"Honey, what've you been doing to yourself? You're nothing but skin and bones."

Surreal slumped against the reception desk, grimaced, and sucked in her breath. "Nothing, Deje. I'm just worn out."

"You been letting those men make a meal out of you?" Deje looked at her shrewdly. "Or is it your other business that's run you down?"

Surreal's gold-green eyes were dangerously blank. "What business is that, Deje?"

"I'm not a fool, honey," Deje said slowly. "I've always known you don't really like this business. But you're still the best there is."

"The best female," Surreal replied, wearily hooking her long black hair behind her pointed ears.

Deje put her hands on the counter and leaned toward Surreal, worried.

"Nobody paid you to dance with . . . Well, you know how fast gossip can fly, and there was talk of some trouble."

"I wasn't part of it, thank the Darkness."

Deje sighed. "I'm glad. That one's demon-born for sure."

"If he isn't, he should be."

"You know the Sadist?" Deje asked, her eyes sharp.

"We're acquainted," Surreal said reluctantly.

Deje hesitated. "Is he as good as they say?"

Surreal shuddered. "Don't ask."

Deje looked startled but quickly regained her professional manner. "No matter. None of my business anyway." Coming around the desk, she put an arm around Surreal's shoulders and led her down the hall. "A garden room, I think. You can sit out quietly in the evening, eat your meals in your room if you choose. If anyone notices you're here and makes a request for your company, I'll tell them it's your moontime and you need your rest. Most of them wouldn't know the difference."

Surreal gave Deje a shaky grin. "Well, it's the truth."

Deje shook her head and clucked her tongue in annoyance as she opened the door and led Surreal into the room. "Sometimes you've no more sense than a first-year chit, pushing yourself at a time when the Jewels will squeeze you dry if you try to tap into them." She muttered to herself as she pulled down the bedcovers and plumped the pillows. "Get into a nice comfy nightie—not one of those sleek things—and get into bed. We've got a hearty soup tonight. You'll have that. And I've got some new novels in the library, nice fluff reading. I'll bring a few of them; you can take your pick. And—"

"Deje, you should've been someone's mother," Surreal laughed.

Deje put her hands on her ample hips and tried to look offended. "A fine thing to say to someone in my business." She made a shooing motion with her hands. "Into bed and not another word from you. Honey? Honey, what's wrong?"

Surreal sank onto the bed, tears rolling silently down her cheeks. "I can't sleep, Deje. I have dreams that I'm supposed to be somewhere, do something. But I don't know where or what it is."

Deje sat on the bed and wiped the tears from Surreal's face. "They're only dreams, honey. Yes, they are. You're just worn out."

"I'm scared, Deje," Surreal whispered. "There's something really wrong with him. I can feel it. Once I started running, hoping I was going in the opposite direction, that whole damn continent wasn't big enough. I need a clean place for a while." Surreal looked at Deje, her large eyes full of ghosts. "I need time."

Deje stroked Surreal's hair. "Sure, honey, sure. You take all the time you need. Nobody's going to push you in my house. Come on now, get into bed. I'll bring you something to eat and a little something to help you sleep." She gave Surreal a quick kiss on the forehead and hurried out of the room.

Surreal put on an old, soft nightgown and climbed into bed. It was good to be back at Deje's house, good to be back in Chaillot. Now if only the Sadist would stay away, maybe she could get some sleep.

7 / Terreille

Daemon knocked on the kitchen door.

Inside, the spright little tune someone was singing stopped.

Waiting for the door to open, Daemon looked around, pleased to see that the snug little cottage was in good repair. The lawn and flower beds were neatly tended. The summer crop in the vegetable garden was almost done, but the healthy vines at one end promised a good crop of pumpkins and winter squash.

Still too early for pumpkins. Daemon sighed with regret while his mouth watered at the memory of Manny's pumpkin tarts.

At the back of the yard were two sheds. The smaller one probably contained gardening tools. The larger one was Jo's woodshop. The old man was probably tucked away in there coaxing an elegant little table out of pieces of wood, oblivious to everything except his work.

The kitchen door remained closed. The silence continued.

Concerned, Daemon opened the door enough to slip his head and shoulders inside and look around.

Manny stood by her worktable, one floury hand pressed to her bosom.

Damn. He should have realized a Warlord Prince's appearance would frighten her. He'd changed enough since he'd last seen her that she might not recognize his psychic scent.

Putting on his best smile, he said, "Darling, if you're going to pretend you're not home, the least you can do is close the windows. The smell of those nutcakes will draw the most unsavory characters."

Manny gave a cry of relief and joy, hustled around the worktable, and shuffle-ran toward the door, her floury hands waving cheerfully in front of her. "Daemon!"

Daemon stepped into the kitchen, slid one arm around the woman's thick waist, and twirled her around.

Manny laughed and flapped her arms. "Put me down. I'm getting flour all over your nice coat."

"I don't care about the coat." He kissed her cheek and set her carefully on her feet. With a bow and a flourish of his wrist, he presented her with a bouquet of flowers. "For my favorite lady."

Misty-eyed, Manny bent her head to smell the flowers. "I'll put these in some water." She bustled around the kitchen, filled a vase, and spent several minutes arranging the flowers. "You go into the parlor and I'll bring out some nutcakes and tea."

Manny and Jo had been servants in the SaDiablo court when he was growing up. Manny had taken care of him, practically raised him. And the darling was still trying.

Hiding a smile, Daemon stuffed his hands in his pockets and scuffed his gleaming black shoe against the kitchen floor. He looked at her through his long black lashes. "What'd I do?" he said in a sad, slightly pouty, little-boy voice. "What'd I do not to deserve a chair in the kitchen anymore?"

Trying to sound exasperated, Manny only laughed. "No use trying to raise you proper. Sit down, then, and behave yourself."

Daemon laughed, lighthearted and boyish, and plunked himself gracelessly into one of the kitchen chairs. Manny pulled out plates and cups. "Although why you want to stay in the kitchen is beyond me."

"The kitchen is where the food is."

"Guess there's some things boys never grow out of. Here." Manny set a glass in front of him.

Daemon looked at the glass, then looked at her.

"It's milk," she added.

"I did recognize it," he said dryly.

"Good. Then drink it." She folded her arms and tapped her foot. "No milk, no nutcakes."

"You always were a martinet," Daemon muttered. He picked up the glass, grimaced, and drank it down. He handed her the glass, giving her his best boyish smile. "Now may I have a nutcake?"

Manny laughed, shaking her head. "You're impossible." She put the kettle on for tea and began transferring the nutcakes to a platter. "What brings you here?"

"I came to see you." Daemon crossed his legs and steepled his fingers, resting them lightly on his chin.

She glanced up, gasped, and then busily rearranged the cakes.

Puzzled by the stunned look on her face, Daemon watched her rearrange everything twice. Searching for a neutral topic, he said, "The place looks good. Keeping it up isn't too much work for you?"

"The young people in the village help out," Manny said mildly.

Daemon frowned. "Aren't there sufficient funds for a handyman and cleaning woman?"

"Sure there are, but why would I want some other grown woman clumping about my house, telling me how to polish my furniture?" She grinned slyly. "Besides, the girls are willing to help with the heavy work in exchange for pocket money, a few of my special recipes, and a chance to flirt with the boys without their parents standing around watching them. And the boys are willing to help with the outside work in exchange for pocket money, food, and an excuse to strip off their shirts and show their muscles to the girls."

Daemon's laughter filled the kitchen. "Manny, you've become the village matchmaker."

Manny smiled smugly. "Jo's working on a cradle right now for one of the young couples."

"I hope there was a wedding beforehand."

"Of course," Manny said indignantly. She thumped the platter of nutcakes in front of him. "Shame on you, teasing an old woman."

"Do I still get nutcakes?" he asked contritely.

She ruffled his hair in answer and took the kettle off the stove.

Daemon stared into space. So many questions, and no answers.

"You're troubled," Manny said, filling the tea ball.

Daemon shook himself. "I'm looking for information that may be hard to find. A friend told me to beware of the Priest."

Manny slipped the tea ball into the pot to steep. "Huh. Anyone with a lick of sense takes care around the Priest."

Daemon stared at her. She knew the Priest. Were the answers really this close? "Manny, sit down for a moment."

Manny ignored him and hurriedly slid the cups onto the table, keeping out of his reach. "The tea's ready now. I'll call Jo—"

"Who is the Priest?"

"—he'll be glad to see you."

Daemon uncoiled from the chair, clamped one hand around her wrist, and pulled her into the other chair. Manny stared at his hand, at the ring finger that wore no Jeweled ring, at the long, black-tinted nails.

"Who is the Priest?"

"You mustn't talk about him. You must never talk about him."

"Who is the Priest?" His voice became dangerously soft.

"The tea," she said weakly.

Daemon poured two cups of tea. Returning to the table, he crossed his legs and steepled his fingers. "Now."

Manny lifted the cup to her lips but found the tea too hot to drink. She set the cup down again, fussing with its handle until it was exactly parallel to the edge of the table. Finally she dropped her hands in her lap and sighed.

"They never should have taken you away from him," she said quietly, looking at memories. "They never should have broken the contract. The Hourglass coven in Hayll has been failing since then, just like he said it would. No one breaks a contract with the Priest and survives.

"You were supposed to go to him for good that day, the day you got your Birthright Jewel. You were so proud that he was going to be there, even though the Birthright Ceremony was in the afternoon instead of evening like it usually is. They planned it that way, planned to make him come in the harshest light of day, when his strength would be at its lowest.

"After you had your Birthright Red Jewel and were standing with your mother and Dorothea and all of Dorothea's escorts, waiting for the okay to walk out of the ceremonial circle to where he was waiting and kneel to him in service . . . that's when that woman, that cruel, scheming woman said you belonged to the Hourglass, that paternity was denied, that he couldn't have sired you, that she'd had her guards service the Dhemlan witch afterward to ensure she was seeded. It was a warm afternoon, but it got so cold, so awfully cold. Dorothea had all the Hourglass covens there, dozens and dozens of Black Widows, watching him, waiting for him to walk into the circle and break honor with them.

"But he didn't. He turned away.

"You almost broke free. Almost reached him. You were crying, screaming for him to wait for you, fighting the two guards who were holding your arms, your fingers clenched around that Jewel. There was a flash of Red light, and the guards were flung backward. You hurled yourself forward, trying to reach the edge of the circle. He turned, waiting. One of the guards tackled you. You were only a handspan away from the edge. I think if so much as a finger had crossed that circle, he would have swept you away with him, wouldn't have worried anymore if it was good for you to live with him, or to live without your people.

"You didn't make it. You were too young, and they were too strong.

"So he left. Went to that house you keep visiting, the house you and your mother lived in, and destroyed the study. Tore the books apart, shredded the curtains, broke every piece of furniture in the room. He couldn't get the rage out. When I finally dared open the door, he was kneeling in the middle of the room, his chest heaving, trying to get some air, a crazy look in his eyes.

"He finally got up and made me promise to look after you and your mother, to do the best I could. And I promised because I cared about you and her, and because he'd always been kind to me and Jo.

"After that, he disappeared. They took your Red Jewel and put the Ring of Obedience on you that night. You wouldn't eat. They told me I had to make you eat. They had plans for you and you weren't going to waste away. They locked Jo up in a metal box, put him out where there wasn't any shade and said he'd get food and water when I got you to eat. When I got you to eat two days in a row, they'd let him out.

"For three days you wouldn't eat, no matter how I begged. I don't think you heard me at all during those days. I was desperate. At night, when I'd go out and stand as close to the box as I was allowed, I'd hear Jo whimpering, his skin all blistered from touching that hot metal. So I did something bad to you. I dragged you out one morning and made you look at that box. I told you you were killing my man out of spite, that he was being punished because you were a bad boy and wouldn't eat, and if he died I would hate you forever and ever.

"I didn't know Dorothea had run your mother off. I didn't know I was all you had left. But you knew. You felt her go.

"You did what I said. You ate when I told you, slept when I told you. You were more a ghost than a child. But they let Jo out."

Manny wiped the tears from her face with the edge of her apron. She took a sip of cold tea.

Daemon closed his eyes. Before coming here, he'd gone to that crumbling, abandoned house he'd once lived in, searching for answers as he did every time he was in this part of the Realm. Memories, so elusive and traitorous, always teased him when he walked through the rooms. But it was the wrecked study that really drew him back, the room where he could almost hear a deep, powerful voice like soft thunder, where he could almost smell a sharp, spicy, masculine scent, where he could almost feel strong arms around him, where he could almost believe he had once been safe, protected, and loved.

And now he finally knew why.

Daemon slipped his hand over Manny's and squeezed gently. "You've told me this much, tell me the rest."

Manny shook her head. "They did something so you would forget him. They said if you ever found out about him, they'd kill you." She looked at him, pleading. "I couldn't let them kill you. You were the boy Jo and I couldn't have."

A door in his mind that he'd never known existed began to open.

"I'm not a boy anymore, Manny," Daemon said quietly, "and I won't be killed that easily." He made another pot of tea, put a fresh cup in front of her, and settled back in his chair. "What was . . . is his name?"

"He has many names," Manny whispered, staring at her cup.

"Manny." Daemon fought for patience.

"They call him the Seducer. The Executioner."

He shook his head, still not understanding. But the door opened a little wider.

"He's the High Priest of the Hourglass."

A little wider.

"You're stalling," Daemon snapped, clattering the cup against the saucer. "What's my father's name? You owe me that. You know what it's been like for me being a bastard. Did he ever sign the register?"

"Oh, yes," she said hurriedly. "But they changed that page. He was so proud of you and the Eyrien boy. He didn't know, you know, about the girl being Eyrien. Luthvian, that was her name. She didn't have wings or scars where wings were removed. He didn't know until the boy was born. She wanted to cut the wings off, raise the boy as Dhemlan maybe. But he said no, in his soul the boy was Eyrien, and it would be kinder to kill him in the cradle than to cut his wings. She cried at that, scared that he really would kill the babe. I think he would have if she'd ever done anything that might have damaged the wings. He built her a snug little cottage in Askavi, took care of her and the boy. He would bring him to visit sometimes. You'd play together . . . or fight together. It was hard to tell which. Then she got scared. She told me Prythian, Askavi's High Priestess, told her he only wanted the boy for fodder, wanted a supply of fresh blood to sup on. So she gave the boy to Prythian to hide, and ran away. When she went back for him, Prythian wouldn't tell her where he was, just laughed at her, and—"

"Manny," Daemon said in a soft, cold voice. "For the last time, who is my father?"

"The Prince of the Darkness."

A little wider.

"Manny."

"The Priest is the High Lord, don't you understand?" Manny cried.

"His name."

"No."

"His name, Manny."

"To whisper the name is to summon the man."

The door blew open and the memories poured out.

Daemon stared at his hands, stared at the long, black-tinted nails.

Mother Night.

He swallowed hard and shook his head. It wasn't possible. As much as he would like to believe it, it wasn't possible. "Saetan," he said quietly. "You're telling me my father is Saetan?"

"Hush, Daemon, hush."

Daemon leaped up, knocking the chair over. "No, I will not hush. He's dead, Manny. A legend. An ancestor far removed."

"Your father."

"He's dead."

Manny licked her lips and closed her eyes. "One of the living dead. One of the ones called Guardians."

Daemon righted the chair and sat down. He felt ill. No wonder Dorothea used to beat him when he would nurse the hurt of being excluded by pretending that Saetan was his father. It hadn't been pretend after all. "Are you sure?" he asked finally.

"I'm sure."

Daemon laughed harshly. "You're mistaken, Manny. You must be. I can't imagine the High Lord of Hell bedding that bitch Hepsabah."

Manny squirmed.

Memories kept pouring over him, puzzle pieces floating into place.

"Not Hepsabah," he said slowly, feeling crushed by the magnitude of the lies that had made up his life. No, not Hepsabah. A Dhemlan witch . . . who'd been driven out of the court. "Tersa." He braced his head in his hands. "Who else could it be but Tersa."

Manny reached toward him but didn't touch him. "Now you know."

Daemon's hands shook as he lit a black cigarette. He watched the smoke curl and rise, too weary to do anything else. "Now I know." He closed his eyes and whispered, "My best ally or my worst enemy. And the choice will be mine. Sweet Darkness, why did it have to be him?"

"Daemon?"

He shook his head and tried to smile reassuringly.

He spent another hour with Manny and Jo, who had finally come in from the woodshop. He entertained them with slightly risqué stories about the Blood aristos he'd served in various courts and told them nothing about his life. It would hurt him beyond healing if Manny ever thought of him as Hayll's Whore.

When he finally left, he walked for hours. He couldn't stop shaking. The pain of a lifetime of lies grew with each step until his rage threatened to tear apart what was left of his self-restraint.

It was dawn when he caught the Red Wind and rode to Draega.

For the first time in his life, he wanted to see Dorothea.

CHAPTER FIVE

1 / Terreille

As Kartane SaDiablo walked from his suite to the audience rooms, he wondered if he'd fortified himself with one glass of brandy too many before appearing before his mother and making a formal return to her court. If not, the whole damn court was acting queer. The Blood aristos scurried through the halls, eyes darting ahead and behind them as they traveled in tight little clusters. The males in the court usually acted like that, jostling and shoving until one of them was pushed to the front and offered as the sacrifice. Being the object of Dorothea's attention, whether she was pleased with a man or angry, was always an unpleasant experience. But for the women to act that way as well . . .

When he saw a servant actually smile, he finally understood.

By then it was too late.

He felt the cold as he swung around a corner and skidded to a stop in front of Daemon. He'd stopped trying long ago to understand his feelings whenever he saw Daemon—relief, fear, anger, envy, shame. Now he simply wondered if Daemon was finally going to kill him.

Kartane retreated to the one emotional gambit he had left. He pulled his lips into a sneering smile and said, "Hello, *cousin*."

"Kartane." Daemon's toneless court voice, laced with boredom.

"So you've been called back to court. Was Aunt Hepsabah getting lonely?" That's it. Remind him of what he is.

"Was Dorothea?"

Kartane tried to keep the insolence in his voice, tried to keep the sneer, tried not to remember all the things he couldn't forget.

"I was about to report to Dorothea," Daemon said mildly, "but I can delay it for a few more minutes. If you have to see her, why don't you go ahead. She's never in the best of moods after she's seen me."

Kartane felt as if he'd been slapped. Daemon hated him, had hated him for centuries for what he'd said, for the things he'd done. But Daemon remembered, too, and because he remembered, he would still extend this much courtesy and compassion toward his younger cousin.

Not daring to speak, Kartane nodded and hurried down the hall.

He didn't go directly to the audience room where Dorothea waited. Instead, he flung himself into the first empty room he could find. Leaning against the locked door, he felt tears burn his eyes and trickle down his cheeks as he whispered, "Daemon."

Daemon was the cousin whose position within the family had never quite been explained to the child Kartane except that it was tenuous and different from his own. Kartane had been Dorothea's spoiled, privileged only child, with a handful of servants, tutors, and governesses jumping to obey his slightest whim. He had also been just another jewel for his mother, property that she preened herself with, showed off, displayed.

It wasn't Dorothea or the tutors or governesses that Kartane ran to as a child when he scraped his knee and wanted comforting, or felt lonely, or wanted to brag about his latest small adventure. Not to them. He had always run to Daemon.

Daemon, who always had time to talk and, more important, to listen. Daemon, who taught him to ride, to fence, to swim, to dance. Daemon, who patiently read the same book to him, over and over and over, because it was his favorite. Daemon, who took long, rambling walks with him. Daemon, who never once showed any displeasure at having a small boy attached to his heels. Daemon, who held him, rocked him, soothed him when he cried. Daemon, who plundered the kitchen late at night, even though it was forbidden, to bring Kartane fruit, rolls, cold joints of meat—anything to appease the insatiable hunger he always felt because he could never eat his fill under his mother's watchful eye. Daemon, who had been caught one night and beaten for it, but never told anyone the food wasn't for himself.

Daemon, whose trust he had betrayed, whose love he lost with a single word.

★　　★　　★

Kartane was still a gangly boy when Daemon was first contracted out to another court. It had hurt to lose the one person in the whole court who truly cared about him as a living, thinking being. But he also knew there was trouble in the court, trouble that swirled around Daemon, around Daemon's position in the court hierarchy. He knew Daemon served Dorothea and Hepsabah and Dorothea's coven of Black Widows, although not in the same way the consorts and other men serviced them when summoned. He knew about the Ring of Obedience and how it could control a man even if he were stronger and wore darker Jewels. He puzzled over Daemon's aversion to being touched by a woman. He puzzled over the fights between Daemon and Dorothea, shouting matches that made stone walls seem paper-thin and grew more and more vicious. More often than not, those arguments ended with Dorothea using the Ring, punishing with agonizing pain until Daemon begged for forgiveness.

Then one day Daemon refused to service one of Dorothea's coven.

Dorothea summoned the First, Second, and Third Circles of the court. With her husband, Lanzo SaDiablo, by her side—Lanzo, the drunken womanizer whose only value was in providing Dorothea with the SaDiablo name—she began the punishment.

Kartane had hidden behind a curtain, chilled with fear, as he watched Daemon fight the Ring, fight the pain, fight the guards who held him so he couldn't attack Dorothea. It took an hour of agony to bring him to his knees, sobbing from the pain. It took another half hour to make him crawl to Dorothea and beg forgiveness. When she finally stopped sending pain through the Ring, Dorothea didn't allow him to go to his room, where Manny would give him a sedative and wash his sweat-chilled body so he could sleep while the pain slowly subsided. Instead, she had him tied hand and foot to one of the pillars, had him gagged so his moans of pain would be muffled, and left him there to humiliate him and warn others by the example while she leisurely conducted the other business of the court.

The lesson was not lost on Kartane. To be Ringed was the severest form of control. If Daemon couldn't stand the pain, how could he? It became very important not to give Dorothea a reason to Ring him.

That night, after Daemon had been allowed to rest a little, he was ordered to serve the witch he'd earlier refused.

That night was the first time Daemon went cold.

Among the Blood, there were two kinds of anger. Hot anger was the anger of emotion, superficial even in its fury—the anger between friends, lovers, family, the anger of everyday life. Cold anger was the Jewel's anger—deep, untouchable, icy rage that began at a person's core. Implacable, almost always unstoppable until the fury was spent, cold anger wasn't blunted by pain or hunger or weariness. Rising from so deep within, it made the body that housed it insignificant.

That first night, no one recognized the subtle change in the air when Daemon walked by on his way to the witch's chamber.

It wasn't until the maid came in the next morning and found the windows and mirrors glazed with ice, discovered the obscenity left in the bed, that Dorothea realized she had broken something in Daemon during that punishment, had stripped away a layer of humanity.

Hekatah, the self-proclaimed High Priestess of Hell, would have recognized the look in Daemon's eyes if she had seen it, would have understood how true the bloodline ran. It took Dorothea a little longer. When she finally understood that what Daemon had inherited from his father was far darker and far more dangerous than she'd imagined, she gifted him to a pet Queen who ruled a Province in southern Hayll.

Dorothea said nothing about the killing. Among the Blood, there was no law against murder. She said little about Daemon's reaction to kneeling in service, commending his training as a pleasure slave and only adding that he could be somewhat temperamental if used too often.

Before the week ended, Daemon was gone.

Not long after, Kartane learned what Daemon's presence had spared him. Dorothea's appetite for a variety of pretty faces was no less demanding than Lanzo's, the only difference in their taste being gender, and she kept a stable of young Warlords at the court to do the pretty for her and her coven. Until then, Kartane had been nothing more than Dorothea's handsome, spoiled son.

One night she summoned Kartane to her chamber. He went to her nervously, mentally ticking off the things he'd done that day and wondering what might have displeased her. But she soothed and stroked and petted. Those caresses, which always made him uneasy, now frightened him. As she leaned toward him, she told him his father had been loyal to her and she expected him to be loyal too. Kartane was too busy trying to figure out how Lanzo's spearing a different serving girl every night could be considered loyalty to recognize the intent. It wasn't until he felt

Dorothea's tongue slide into his mouth that he understood. He pushed her away, threw himself off the couch, and crawled backward toward the door, not daring to take his eyes off her.

She was furious with his refusal. It earned him his first beating.

The welts were still sore when she summoned him again. This time he sat quietly as she stroked his arms and thighs and explained in her purring voice that a Ring could help him be more responsive. But she didn't really think that would be necessary. Did he?

No, he didn't think it would be necessary. He submitted. He did what he was told.

Lying in his own bed later that night, Kartane thought of Daemon, of how night after night, year after year Daemon had done what Kartane had been forced to do. He began to understand Daemon's aversion to touching a female unless he was forced to. And he wondered how old Daemon had been the first time Dorothea had taken him into her bed.

It didn't end with that first time. It didn't end until years later when Dorothea sent him away to a private school because he was spearing the serving girls so viciously that Lanzo and his companions complained that the girls weren't usable for days afterward.

The private school he attended, where the boys all came from the best Hayllian families, put the final polish on Kartane's taste for cruelty. He found Red Moon houses disgusting and could satisfy himself with an experienced woman only if he hurt her. After being barred from a couple of houses, he discovered that it was easy to dominate younger girls, frighten them, make them do whatever he wanted.

He began to appreciate Dorothea's pleasure in having power over someone else.

But even the youngest whore was still a witch with her Virgin Night behind her, and she was protected by the rules of the house. He didn't have, as his mother had, absolute power over whomever he mounted.

He began to look elsewhere for his pleasure, and found, quite accidentally, what he craved.

Kartane and his friends went to an inn one night to drink, to gamble, to get the nectar free. They came from the best families, families no mere innkeeper would dare approach. The others had their sport with the young women who served ale and supper, using the small private dining room, like most inns had for important guests. But Kartane had been intrigued by the innkeeper's young daughter. She had the beginning blush of womanhood, the merest hint of curves. When he dragged her toward the door of the private room, the innkeeper rushed him, bellowing with rage. Kartane raised his hand, sent a surge of power through the Jeweled ring on his finger, and knocked the man senseless. Then he dragged the girl into the room and closed the door.

Her trembling, paralyzing fear felt delicious. She had no musky smell of woman, no psychic scent of a witch come to power. He reveled in her pain, stunned by the intoxication and pleasure it gave him to drive her beyond the web of herself and break her.

When he finally left the room, feeling in control of his life for the first time in oh-so-many years, he threw a couple of gold mark notes on the bar, gathered his friends, and disappeared.

That was the beginning.

Dorothea never disapproved of his chosen game as long as he satisfied her whenever he returned to court and as long as he didn't spoil any of the witches she wanted for her court. For two hundred years Kartane played his game with non-aristo Blood. Sometimes he kept the same girl for several weeks or months, playing with her, honing her fear, becoming more depraved in his requirements, until he seeded her. Many times even a broken witch was still capable of spontaneous abortion and would choose it rather than bear the seed of a man she hated, even though she would never bear any other child. Sometimes, if the girl hadn't gone completely numb and was still amusing, he got a Healer corrupted by hunger and hard times to provide the cleansing brew. Most times he simply turned them out, let them return to their families or a Red Moon house or the gutter. It was all the same to him.

Kartane played his game for two hundred years. Then, on one of his required returns to court, he found Daemon waiting for him.

By then Kartane understood why Daemon was Sadi not SaDiablo, why that was as much of a compromise as the family was willing to make. But seeing the anger in Daemon's eyes, he knew that, unlike Dorothea, Daemon would never approve of what Kartane had done. As he listened to a blistering lecture about honor, Kartane struck out at Daemon's weak spot. He told Daemon that he, Kartane, the High Priestess's son, didn't have to listen to a bastard.

A bastard.

A bastard.

A bastard.

He never forgot the shock and pain in Daemon's eyes. Never forgot how it felt when the one person he'd loved and who had loved him gathered himself into that aloof court demeanor and apologized for speaking out of turn. Would always know that if he'd run after Daemon right then and apologized, begged to be forgiven, explained about the pain and the fear, asked for help . . . he would have had it. Daemon would have found a way to help him.

But he didn't. He let the word stand. He drove it in again and again until the wedge became a chasm and the only thing they had in common was their fury with each other.

In the end, Dorothea sent Daemon away and lost him for one hundred years. By the time he returned, he'd made the Offering to the Darkness. The rumors were that Daemon had come away from the ceremony wearing a Black Jewel, but no one knew for sure because no one had seen it.

It didn't matter to Kartane what Jewels Daemon wore. He was frightened enough by what Daemon had become. Since then, they'd done their best to avoid each other.

Kartane wiped the tears from his face and straightened his jacket. He would see Dorothea and make his escape as quickly as possible. Escape from her, from the court . . . and from Daemon.

2 / Terreille

Daemon glided through the corridors of the SaDiablo mansion until he reached his suite of rooms. Presenting himself to Dorothea had been as unpleasant as usual, but at least it had been brief. Seeing her had frayed his temper to the breaking point, and right now his self-control was tenuous at best. He needed a quiet hour before dressing for dinner and spending the evening doing the pretty for Dorothea and her coven.

He walked into his sitting room and choked back the snarl when he noticed the visitor waiting for him.

Hepsabah turned toward him, a smile flickering on her lips, her flitting hands performing an intricate dance with each other. He loathed the hunger in her eyes and the muskiness of her psychic scent, but knowing he was required to play the game, he smiled at her and closed the door.

"Mother," he said with barely disguised irony. He bent his head to kiss her cheek. As always, she turned her head at the last minute so his lips brushed against hers. Her arms wound around his neck, her tongue greedily thrusting into his mouth as she pressed herself against him. Usually he pushed her away, disgusted that his mother could want such intimacy. Now he stood passively, neither giving nor taking, simply analyzing the lies that had made up his life.

Hepsabah stepped away from him, pouting. "You're not pleased to see me," she accused.

Daemon wiped his mouth with the back of his hand. "As pleased as I usually am." There she was, dressed in an expensive silk dress while Tersa, his real mother, wore a tattered coat and slept who knew where. Despite Dorothea's and Hepsabah's efforts, Tersa had given him what love she could, in her own shattered way. Somehow he was going to make it up to her, just as he was going to repay them. "What do you want?"

"It would be *nice* if you could be a little more respectful to your mother." She smoothed her dress, running her hands over her breasts and belly, looking at him from beneath her eyelashes.

"I have a great deal of respect for my mother," he replied blandly.

Looking uneasy, she patted the air near his sleeve and said with brittle cheerfulness, "I've got your room all ready for you. Nice and comfy. Maybe after dinner we can sit and have a nice little coze, hmm?" She turned toward the door, swinging her hips provocatively.

Daemon's temper snapped. "You mean I should be more amenable to putting my face between your legs." He ignored her shocked gasp. "I won't be more amenable, *Mother*. Not tonight. Not any night. Not to you or anyone else in this court. If I'm commanded to kneel while I'm here, I promise you that what happened to Cornelia will be nothing compared to what I'll do here. If you think the Ring can stop me, you'd better think again. I'm not a boy anymore, Hepsabah, and I want you *dead*."

Hepsabah backed away from him, her eyes wide with terror. She snatched at the door handle and flung herself into the corridor.

Daemon opened a bottle of brandy, paused only long enough to probe it to be sure there were no sedatives or other nasty surprises added to the liquor, put the bottle to his mouth, and tipped his head back. It burned his throat and caught fire in his stomach, but he continued to swallow until he needed to breathe. The room swam a little but steadied quickly as his metabolism consumed the liquor as it consumed food. That was a drawback to wearing darker Jewels—it took a massive amount of alcohol to get pleasantly drunk. Daemon didn't want to get pleasantly drunk. He wanted to numb the anger and the memories. He couldn't afford a full confrontation with Dorothea now. He could break the Ring, and Dorothea with it. Over the past few years he'd become sure of that. What he wasn't sure of was how much damage she might do to him before he destroyed her, wasn't sure if he'd be permanently maimed by the time he got the Ring off, wasn't sure what other damage he might do to himself that might prevent him from ever wearing the Black again. And there was a Lady out there, somewhere, that he wanted to be whole for. Once he found her . . .

Daemon smiled coldly. The Priest owed him a favor, and two Black Jewels, even if one was Ringed, should be quite sufficient to take care of an arrogant Red-Jeweled High Priestess.

Laughing, Daemon went into his bedroom and dressed for dinner.

3 / Terreille

Chewing his lower lip, Kartane walked up to Daemon, who was studying a closed door. They hadn't been seated near each other at dinner last night, and Daemon had retired early—to everyone's relief—so this was the first time since their abrupt meeting yesterday afternoon that they were together without dozens of people to act as a buffer.

Kartane wasn't a small man, and even with his excesses he remained trim and well toned, but standing next to Daemon made him feel like he was still in a boy's body. It was more the breadth of Daemon's shoulders than the couple of inches in height, the face matured by pain rather than age that made Kartane feel slight next to him. It was also the difference between a long-lived youth and a male in his prime.

"Do you know what this is about?" Daemon asked quietly.

Kartane shook his head. "She just said our presence is required for an entertainment."

Daemon took a deep breath. "Damn." He opened the door, then stood aside for Kartane to enter.

Kartane took a couple of steps into the room and felt the air behind him chill as the door closed. He glanced at Daemon's face, at the narrowed eyes suddenly turned hard yellow, and wondered, as he surveyed the room, what had provoked Daemon's temper.

It was an austere room, furnished with several rows of chairs arranged in a semicircle in front of two posts attached to the floor. Beside the posts was a long table with a white cloth pulled over it. Under and around the posts was a thick pile of white sheets.

Daemon swore viciously under his breath. "At least as the privileged son you can rest easy that you won't be part of the entertainment. You'll only have to endure watching it."

Kartane stared at the posts. "I don't understand. What is it?"

Pity flashed in Daemon's eyes before his face became impassive and his voice took on that toneless, bored quality he always used in court. "You've never seen this?"

"It seems a bit overdone if she's going to have someone whipped," he said, trying to put a sneer into his voice to hide his growing fear.

"Not whipped," Daemon said bitterly. "Shaved."

The look in Daemon's eyes turned Kartane's guts to water.

Daemon didn't speak again until they reached the first row of chairs. "Listen, Kartane, and listen well. What happens to the poor fool Dorothea's going to tie between those posts is going to depend on how much you squirm. If you stay disinterested, she won't do any less than she's already planned but at least it will be done quicker, and you'll have to endure watching for less time. Understand?"

"Shaved?" Kartane said in a strangled voice.

"Didn't anyone ever tell you how they make eunuchs?" Daemon slipped his hands in his pockets and turned away.

"But . . ." Kartane tensed when Dorothea and her coven walked through the door. "Why this?" he whispered. "Why all these chairs?"

Daemon's eyes had a worried, faraway look in them. "Because they find it amusing, Lord Kartane. This *is* the afternoon's entertainment. And if we're both lucky, we'll only be the guests of honor."

Kartane looked quickly at Daemon and then at the posts. Dorothea wouldn't. She *couldn't*. Was that why Daemon warned him, because he wasn't sure if . . . No. Not to Daemon. Not to *Daemon*.

Kartane kicked a chair before dropping into another with his arms crossed and his legs sprawled forward, looking like a sulky child. "I have better ways to spend my afternoon," he snarled.

Daemon turned, one eyebrow raised in question. Dorothea walked toward them, her eyes flashing with annoyance at Kartane's behavior.

"Well, darling," she purred, "we'll do our best to amuse you." She settled into the chair next to Kartane's, and with a gracious gesture of her hand, indicated to Daemon that he should sit on her left.

Kartane sat up straighter, but kept a sulky look on his face. He flinched as the chairs behind him filled and female voices murmured as if they were in a theater waiting for the play to begin.

Dorothea clapped her hands, and the room became silent. Two massive, raw-looking guards bowed to Dorothea and left the room. They returned a moment later leading a slightly built man.

Daemon flicked a bored glance at the man being led to the posts, leaned away from Dorothea, and propped his chin in his hand.

Dorothea hissed quietly.

Daemon straightened in his chair, crossed his legs, and steepled his fingers. "Not that it matters," he drawled, "but what did he do?"

Dorothea put her hand on his thigh. "Curious?" she purred.

Daemon shrugged, ignoring the fingers sliding up his thigh.

Dorothea removed her hand, annoyed by the bored expression on Daemon's face. "He didn't do anything. I just felt like having him shaved." She smiled maliciously, nodded to the guards, and watched with great interest as they fastened their victim spread-eagle to the posts. "He's a Warlord but a valet by profession. Comes from a family who specializes in personal service to darker-Jeweled Blood. But after today, I doubt there'll be a male in all of Hayll who'll want him around. What do you think?"

Daemon shrugged and once more propped his chin on his hand.

When the man was securely fastened to the posts, one of the guards pulled the cloth off the table. There were appreciative murmurs from the audience as whips, nutcrushers, and various other instruments of torture were presented for view. The last things the guard picked up were the shaving knives.

Kartane felt ill and yet hopeful. If all of those things were being presented, maybe . . .

No, Daemon said on a spear thread, male to male. *She'll shave him.*

You don't know for sure.

You can't have the entertainment end too quickly.

Kartane swallowed hard. *You don't know for sure.*

You'll see.

Dorothea raised one hand. The guard went to the far end of the table and raised the first whip. "What shall it be today, Sisters?" Dorothea called out gaily. "Shall we whip him?"

"Yes, yes, yes," a number of female voices yelled.

"Or . . ."

There was applause and laughter as the guard, looking more nervous, raised the nutcrusher for their viewing.

"Or . . ." Dorothea pointed, and the guard lifted the shaving knives.

Kartane studied the floor, trying not to shake, trying not to bolt for the door. He knew he wouldn't be allowed to leave, and he wondered with a touch of bitterness how Daemon could sit there looking so bored. Maybe because Sadi didn't have any use for those organs anyway.

"Shave him, shave him, shave him!" The room thundered with the coven's voices.

Kartane had been to dogfights, cockfights, any number of spectacles where dumb animals were pitted against each other. He'd heard the roar of male voices urging their favorite to victory. But he'd never heard, in all those places, the glee he heard now as the coven urged their decision.

He jumped when Dorothea's hand squeezed his knee, her cold smile letting him know she was pleased by his fear.

Dorothea raised her hand for silence. When the room was absolutely still, she said in her most melodious purr, "Shave him." She paused a long moment, then smiled sweetly. "A full shave."

Kartane's head snapped around in disbelief, but before he could say anything, Daemon turned his head just enough to look at him. The look in Daemon's eyes was more frightening than Dorothea could ever be, so Kartane swallowed the words and slumped a little farther in his chair.

The Healer and the barber entered the room and walked slowly to the table. The barber, a cadaverous man wearing a tightly cuffed black robe, had a receding hairline, pencil-line lips, and dirty yellow eyes. He bowed to Dorothea and then bowed to the coven.

The Healer, a drab woman retained to handle the servants' ills since she wasn't well versed enough in her Craft to attend to the Blood aristos, called in a bowl of warm water and soap. She held the bowl while the barber washed his hands.

Then the barber leisurely soaped his victim's testicles.

Why? Kartane sent on a spear thread.

Makes them slippery, Daemon replied. *Harder to get a clean cut the first time.*

The barber picked up a small curved knife and held it up for them to see. He positioned himself behind the man.

So everyone can see, Daemon explained.

Kartane clenched his fists and stared at the floor.

"Watch, my dear," Dorothea purred, "or we'll have to do it again."

Kartane fixed his eyes on one of the posts just as the barber pulled the knife back. A moment later, a small dark lump lay on the swiftly reddening sheets.

The Warlord tied to the posts let out a howl of agony and then clenched his teeth to stifle the sound.

Kartane's stomach churned as a disappointed murmur swept through the room. Mother Night! They'd been hoping for a second cut!

The barber set the bloody knife on a tray and washed his hands while the Healer sealed the blood vessels. When she stepped aside, he took a straight knife and positioned himself in front of a post. He pulled the man's organ to its full length, turned to his audience, shook his head sadly, and said, "There's so little here, it will hardly make a difference."

The coven laughed and applauded. Dorothea smiled.

Kartane expected a swift severing. But when the barber laid the knife on the Warlord's organ and leisurely sawed through the flesh, each stroke of the knife accompanied by a scream, Kartane found himself mesmerized, unable to look away.

They deserved what he did. They were foul things only fit for breeding and a man's pleasure. It was right to break them young, *good* to break them young before they became things like the ones sitting here. Break them all. Destroy them all. Blood males should rule, must rule. If only he could kill her. Would Daemon help him rid Hayll of that plague carrier? All of them would have to be killed, of course. Then break all the young ones and train them to serve. It was the only way. The only way.

The silence made him blink.

Dorothea rose from her chair, furiously pointing a finger at the Healer.

"I told you to give him something to make sure he wouldn't faint on us. Look at him!" Her finger swung to the man hanging limply from the posts, his head dropped to his chest.

"I did as you asked, Priestess," the Healer stammered, wringing her hands. "I swear by the Jewels I did."

Was it his imagination, or was Daemon pleased about something?

"We'll have no more sport today because of your incompetence," Dorothea screamed. She made an impatient gesture. "Take it away." Then she swept from the room, her coven trailing behind her.

"I really did give him the potion," the Healer wailed, trailing after the barber as he left the room.

Kartane sat in his chair, too numb to move, until the guards bundled the man into the bloody sheets along with the discarded organs. Then he bolted for the nearest bathroom and was violently ill.

4 / Terreille

Dorothea slowly paced her sitting room. Her flowing gown swished with the sway of her hips, and the low-cut bodice displayed to advantage the small breasts that still rode high. She picked up a feather quill from a table as she passed. Most men's backbones turned to jelly when she picked up a quill. Daemon, however, just watched her, his cold, bored expression never changing.

She brushed her chin with the quill as she passed his chair. "You've been a naughty boy again. Perhaps I should have you whipped."

"Yes," Daemon replied amiably, "why don't you? Cornelia could tell you how effective that is in making me come around."

Dorothea staggered but continued walking. "Perhaps I should have you shaved." She waved the feather at him. "Would you enjoy being one of the brotherhood of the quill?"

"No."

She feigned surprise. "No?"

"No. I prefer being neat when I piss."

Dorothea's face twisted with anger. "You've gotten crude, Daemon."

"Must be the company I keep."

Dorothea paced rapidly, slowing down only when she noticed the cold amusement in Daemon's eyes. *Damn him,* she thought as she tapped the quill against her lips. He knew how much he upset her, and he enjoyed it. She didn't trust him, couldn't trust being able to control him anymore. Even the Ring didn't stop him when he went cold. And he just sat there, so sure of himself, so uncaring.

"Perhaps I *should* have you shaved." Her usual purr turned into a growl. She twitched the quill in the direction of his groin. "After all, it's not as if you have any use for it."

"Hardly good for business, though," Daemon said calmly. "The Queens won't pay you for my service if there's nothing to buy."

"A worthless piece of meat since you can't use it anyway!"

"Ah, but they do so enjoy looking at it."

Dorothea threw the feather down and stamped on it. "Bastard!"

"So you've told me time and time again." Daemon waved one hand in irritation. "Enough theatrics. You won't shave me, now or ever."

"Give me one reason why I shouldn't!"

In one fluid move Daemon was out of the chair, pinning her against the table. His hands tightened on her upper arms, hurting her, while his mouth clamped down on hers, bruising her lips with his teeth. He thrust his tongue into her mouth with such controlled savagery that she couldn't think of anything but the feel of him and the sudden liquid heat between her legs.

It was always like this with him. Always. It was more than just his body. Not quite the Jewels, not quite a link. She could never touch his thoughts or feelings, never reach him. Yet there was such a sense of savage, controlled power, of maleness, that flowed from him, swirled around him. His hands, his tongue . . . just channels for that flow. Sensory conductors.

When she thought she couldn't stand any more, when she thought she had to push him away or drown in the sensation, he thrust his hips forward and swayed against her. Moaning, Dorothea pushed herself against him, wanting to feel him harden, needing him to want her.

Just as she raised her arms to wrap them around his neck, Daemon stepped back, smiling, his golden eyes hot with anger, not desire.

"That's why you won't shave me, Dorothea." His silky voice roughened with disgust. "There's always a chance, isn't there, that someday I'll catch fire, that the hunger will become unbearable and I'll come crawling to you for whatever release you'll grant me."

"I'd never let you go hungry," Dorothea cried, one hand reaching for him. "By the Jewels, I swear—" Shaking with anger, Dorothea forced herself to stand up straight. Once again she'd humiliated herself by begging him.

Daemon smiled that cold, cruel smile he wore whenever he had twisted the love game to hurt the woman he was serving. It's so easy, his smile said. You're all so foolish. You can punish the body all you want, all you dare, but you can never touch *me*.

"Bastard," Dorothea whispered.

"You could always kill me," Daemon said softly. "That would solve both our problems, wouldn't it?" He took a step toward her. She immediately pushed back against the table, frightened. "Why don't you want me dead, Dorothea? What will happen on the day when I no longer walk among the living?"

"Get out," she snapped, trying not to sound as weak as she suddenly felt. Why was he saying this? What did he know? She had to get him away from Hayll, away from that *place,* and quickly. Furious, she threw herself at him, but he glided away, and she fell heavily to the floor. "Get out!" she screamed, beating the floor with her fists.

Daemon left the room, whistling a tuneless little song. As a butterball Warlord puffed his way down the hall toward Dorothea's room, Daemon turned halfway to face him. "I wouldn't go in there until she's a little calmer," he said cheerfully. Then he winked at the startled man and continued down the hall, laughing.

"Damn your soul to the bowels of Hell, hurry up with that!" Kartane screamed at the manservant assigned to him when he was at court. He threw his shirts into one trunk and fastened the straps.

When the trunks were packed, Kartane's eyes swept the room for anything he might have missed.

"Lord Kartane," the manservant panted.

"I'll take care of this. You're dismissed. Get out. Get out!"

The manservant scurried out of the room.

Kartane wrapped his arms around the bedpost. He desperately wanted to rest, but every time he closed his eyes, he saw the bloody sheets, heard the screams.

Away from here. And quickly. Before Dorothea summoned him, before he was trapped. Someplace where the witches were already being silenced. A place that stood in Hayll's shadow, where they would fawn over the Priestess's son, but not yet completely tainted with the ancient land's decay. Not quite virgin territory, but still a maid learning Hayll's desecrations.

"Chaillot," Kartane whispered, and he smiled. The other side of the Realm. Hayll had an embassy there, so no one would question his appearance. Robert Benedict was an astute protégé. And there was that wonderful place he'd helped them build in Beldon Mor, that "hospital" for young, high-strung girls from aristo Blood families, where men like Lord Benedict could partake of delicacies that no respectable Red Moon house would offer. It could take weeks for Dorothea to track him down, particularly if he impressed on the embassy staff that he was there doing research for the Priestess. They'd be too frightened of what he might say about them to report his presence.

Kartane vanished the trunks and slipped from his room to the landing web. He caught the Red Web and rode hard toward the west, toward Chaillot.

5 / Hell

Hekatah flowed into the parlor, the spidersilk gown swirling around her small body, the diamonds sewn into the high neckline glittering like stars against a bloodred sky. She'd dressed with care for this well-thought-out "chance" meeting. Despite the plebeian gallantry that made him courteous to any woman, whether she was pretty or not, Saetan did appreciate a woman who displayed herself to advantage, and even past her prime, Hekatah had never wanted for men.

But he, gutter-child bastard that he was, glanced at her over the half-moon glasses he'd begun wearing, marked the page in his book, and vanished the glasses before, finally, giving her his full attention.

"Hekatah," he said with pleasant wariness.

Biting back her fury, she strolled around the room. "It's wonderful to see the Hall refurbished," she said, her girlish voice full of the cooing warmth that had once made him cautiously open to her.

"It was time to have it done."

"Any special reason?"

"I thought of giving a demon ball," he replied dryly.

She tipped her chin down and looked up at him through her lashes, not realizing it was a parody of the sulky, sensuous young witch she'd been long centuries ago. "You didn't redo the south tower."

"There was no need. It's been emptied and cleaned. That's all."

"But the south tower has always been my apartment," she protested.

"As I said, there was no need."

She stared at the sheer ivory curtains beneath the tied-back red velvet drapes. "Well," she said, as if giving the matter slow consideration, "I suppose I could take a room in your wing."

"No."

"But, Saetan—"

"My dear, you've forgotten. You've never had an apartment in the Hall in this Realm. You haven't lived in any house I own since I divorced you, and you never will again."

Hekatah knelt beside his chair, pleased by the way the gown pooled around her, one shimmering wing of her sleeve draped across his legs. "I know we've had our differences in the past, but, Saetan, you need a woman here now." She could have shouted with triumph as his eyebrow rose in question and a definite spark of interest showed in his eyes.

He raised one hand and stroked her still-black hair, flowing long and loose down her back. "Why do I need a woman now, Hekatah?" he asked in a gentle, husky voice.

His lover's voice. The voice that always enraged her because it sounded so caring and weak. Not a man's voice. Not her father's voice. Her father would never have coaxed. *He* would never have allowed her to refuse him. But *he* had been a Hayllian Prince, one of the Hundred Families, as proud and arrogant as any Blood male, and not this . . .

Hekatah lowered her eyes, hoping Saetan hadn't seen, again, what she thought of him. All that power. They could have ruled all of Terreille, and Kaeleer too, if he'd been the least bit ambitious. Even if he'd been too lazy, *she* could have done it. Who would have *dared* challenge her with the Black backing her? He wouldn't even do that. Wouldn't even support her in Dhemlan, his own Territory. Kept her leashed to Hayll, where her family had enough influence to make her the High Priestess. All that power wasted in a *thing* that had to give himself a name because his sire didn't think the seed fit enough to claim. But Terreille would be hers yet, even if she had to use a weak little puppet like Dorothea to get it.

"Why do I need a woman now?" Saetan's voice, less gentle now, called her back.

"For the child, of course," she replied, turning her head to press a kiss into his palm.

"The child?" Saetan lifted his hand and steepled his fingers. "One of our sons has been demon-dead for fifty thousand years, and you, my dear, probably know better than anyone where the other one lies."

Hekatah drew in her breath with a hiss and exhaled with a smile. "The girl child, High Lord. Your little pet."

"I have no pets, Priestess."

Hekatah hid her clenched fists in her lap. "Everyone knows you're training a girl child to serve you. All I'm trying to point out is she needs a woman's guidance in order to fulfill your needs."

"What needs are those?"

Hekatah smacked the arm of the chair. "Don't play word games with me. If the girl has any talent, she should be trained in the Craft by her Sisters. What you do with her afterward is your concern, but at least let me train her so she won't be an embarrassment."

Saetan eased out of the chair, went to the long windows, and pulled the sheer curtains aside for a clear view of Hell's ever-twilight landscape. "This doesn't concern you, Hekatah," he said slowly, his voice whispering thunder. "It's true I've accepted a contract to tutor a young witch. I'm bored. It amuses me. If she's an embarrassment to someone, it's no concern of mine." He turned from the window to look at her. "And no concern of yours. Leave it that way. Because if you persist in making her your concern, a great many things I've overlooked in the past are going to become mine."

Saetan dropped the edge of the curtain, flicked the folds back into place, and left the room.

Using the chair for support, Hekatah got to her feet, drifted to the windows, and studied the sheer curtains. She reached up slowly.

Selfish bastard. There were ways around him. Did he think after all this time she didn't know his weak spot? It had been such good sport to watch him squirm, the great High Lord chained by his honor, as those two sons she'd helped Dorothea create were battered year after year, century after century. *They hate you now, High Lord. What bastard doesn't hate the sire who won't claim him?*

The half-breed had been a bonus. Who could have anticipated Saetan having so much fire and need left? Fine, strapping boys, and neither one capable of being a man. At least the half-breed could get it up, which was a great deal more than anyone could say for the other.

With her help, Dorothea had gotten the strong, dark SaDiablo bloodline returned to Hayll. Waiting until Daemon's Birthright Ceremony to break the contract with Saetan had been a risk, but that was the time when paternity was formally acknowledged or denied. Up to that point, a male could claim a child as his, could do everything a father might do for his offspring. But until he was formally acknowledged, he had no rights to the child. Once the acknowledgment was made, however, a male child belonged to his father.

Which had been the problem. They had wanted the bloodline, but not the man. Having watched him raise two sons, Hekatah had known from the beginning that any child who grew up under Saetan's hand could never be reshaped into a male who would give his strength for her ambitions. She had thought that, since he visited each boy for only a few hours a week, his influence would be diluted, that the mark he would leave on them wouldn't begin until they were his and he began their training in earnest.

She'd been wrong. Saetan had already planted his code of honor deep in the boys' minds, and by the time she had realized that, it was too late to lead them down another path. Without knowing why, they had fought against anything that didn't fit that code of honor until the fighting, and the pain and the punishment, had shaped them, too.

And now there was this girl child.

Five years ago, she'd sensed a strange, dark power on the *cildru dyathe's* island. Ever since then, she'd been following whispered snippets of talk, leads that faded to nothing. The tangled webs she'd created had only shown her dark power in a female body, the kind of power that, if it were molded and channeled the right way, could easily control a Realm.

It had taken five years to discover that Saetan was training the child, which infuriated her. That girl should have been hers from the start, should have been an emotionally dependent tool that would have fulfilled all of her dreams and ambitions. With that kind of power at her disposal, nothing—and no one—could have stopped her.

But, again, she was too late.

If Saetan had been willing to share the girl, she might have reconsidered. Since he wasn't willing, and she wasn't going to let that child mature to become a threat to her plans, she was going to use the most brutal weapon she had at her disposal: Daemon Sadi.

He would have no love for his father. He could be offered ten years of controlled freedom—still held by the Ring, of course, but not required to serve in a court. Ten years—no, a hundred—not to kneel for any witch. What would eliminating one child be, a stranger fawned over by the very man who had abandoned him, compared with not having to serve? And if the half-breed were thrown in for good measure? Sadi had the strength to defy even the High Lord. He had the cunning and the cruelty to ensnare a child and destroy her. But how to get him close enough for an easy strike? She'd have to think about that. Somewhere to the far west of Hayll. She had tracked the girl as far as that, and then nothing . . . except that strange, impenetrable mist on that island.

Oh, how Saetan would twist, screaming, on the hook of his honor when Sadi destroyed his little pet.

Hekatah lowered her arms and smiled at the curtains hanging in shreds from the rod. She made a moue as she pulled a bit of fabric from a snag in one of her nails and hurried out of the parlor, eager to get away from the Hall and begin her little plan.

Saetan Black-locked his sitting room door before going to the corner table that held glasses and a decanter of yarbarah. A mocking smile twisted his lips when he noticed how badly his hands shook. Ignoring the yarbarah, he pulled a bottle of brandy out of the cupboard below, filled a glass, and drank deep, gasping at the unfamiliar burn. It had been centuries since he'd drunk straight alcohol. He settled into a chair, the brandy glass cradled in his trembling hands.

Hekatah would be elated if she knew how badly she'd frightened him. If Jaenelle became twisted by Hekatah's ambition and greedy hunger to crush and rule . . . No, not Jaenelle. She must be gently, lightly chained to the Blood, must accept the leash of Protocol and Blood Law, the only things that kept them all from being constantly at each others' throats.

Because soon, too soon, she would begin walking roads none of them had ever walked before, and she would become as far removed from the Blood as they were from the landens. And the power. Mother Night! Who could stop her?

Who *would* stop her?

Saetan refilled his glass and closed his eyes. He couldn't deny what his heart knew too well. He would serve his fair-haired Lady. No matter what, he would serve.

When he had ruled Dhemlan in Kaeleer and Dhemlan in Terreille, he had never hesitated to curb Hekatah's ambition. He'd believed then, and still believed, that it was wrong to use force to rule another race. But if Jaenelle wanted to rule . . . It would cost him his honor, to say nothing of his soul, but he would drive Terreille to its knees for her pleasure.

The only way to protect the Realms was to protect Jaenelle from Hekatah and her human tools.

Whatever the price.

6 / Terreille

Daemon reached his bedroom very late that evening. The wine and brandy he'd drunk throughout the night had numbed him enough for him to hold his temper despite the onslaught of innuendoes and coy chatter he'd listened to at the dinner table, despite the bodies that "accidentally" brushed against him all evening.

But he wasn't numb enough not to sense the woman's presence in his room. Her psychic scent struck him the moment he opened his bedroom door. Snarling silently at the intrusion, Daemon lifted his hand. The candle-lights beside the bed immediately produced a dim glow.

The young Hayllian witch lay in the center of his bed, her long black hair draped seductively over the pillows, the sheet tucked demurely beneath her pointed chin. She was new to Dorothea's court, an apprentice to the Hourglass coven. She had watched him throughout the evening but hadn't approached.

She smiled at him, then opened her small, pouty mouth and ran the tip of her tongue over her upper lip. Slowly peeling off the sheet, she stretched her naked body and lazily spread her legs.

Daemon smiled.

He smiled as he picked up the clothes she'd strewn across the floor and tossed them out the open door into the hall. He smiled as he teased the sheet and bedcovers off the bed and tossed them after the clothes. He was still smiling when he lifted her off the bed and pitched her out the door with enough force that she hit the opposite wall with a bone-breaking thud. The mattress followed, missing her only because she'd slumped over on her side as she began to scream.

Following the sound of running feet, Dorothea rushed through the corridors while the mansion walls shook with barely restrained violence. She pushed her way through the pack of growling guards until she reached the abigails and other witches of the coven whose concerned twittering was drowned by screams increasing in pitch and volume.

"What in the name of Hell is going on here?" she shouted, her usual melodious purr sounding more like a cat in heat.

Daemon stepped out of his bedroom, calmly tugging his shirt cuffs into place. The hallway walls instantly glazed with ice.

Dorothea studied Daemon's face. She'd never actually seen him when he was deep in the cold rage, had seen him only when he was coming back from it, but she sensed he was in the eye of the storm and something as insignificant as the wrong inflection on a single word would be enough to set off a violent explosion that would tear the court apart.

She narrowed her eyes and tried not to shiver.

It was more than the cold rage this time. Much more.

His face looked so lifeless it could have been carved from a fine piece of wood, and yet it was so filled with *something.* He appeared unnaturally calm, but those golden eyes, as glazed as the walls, looked at her with a predator's intensity.

Something had been pushing him toward the emotional breaking point, and he had finally snapped.

Among the short-lived races, pleasure slaves became emotionally un-stable after a few years. It took decades among the long-lived races, but eventually the combination of aphrodisiacs and constant arousal without being allowed any release twisted something inside the males. After that, with careful handling, they still had their uses, but not as pleasure slaves.

Daemon had been a pleasure slave for most of his life. He'd come close to this point several times in the past, but he'd always managed to step back from the edge. This time, there was no stepping back.

Finally Daemon spoke. His voice came out flat, but there was a hint of thunder in it. "When you've gotten the stench completely out of my room, I'll be back. Don't call me until then." He glided down the hall and out of sight.

Dorothea waited, counting the seconds. Several minutes passed before the front door was slammed with such force that the mansion shook and windows shattered throughout the building.

Dorothea turned to the witch, a promising, vicious little creature now modestly covered with the sheet and bravely whimpering about her cruel treatment. She wanted to rake her nails over that pretty face.

There was no way to control Sadi, not after tonight. Pain or punishment would only enrage him further. She had to get him away from Hayll, send him somewhere expendable. The Dark Priestess had been full of suggestions when he'd been conceived and when they broke the contract in order to keep the boy for the Hayllian Hourglass. Well, the bitch could come up with a suggestion now when he was cold and possibly sliding into the Twisted Kingdom.

Straightening the collar of her dressing gown, Dorothea gave the young witch a last look. "That bitch is expelled from the Hourglass and dismissed from my court. I want her and everything to do with her out of my house within the hour."

Taking the arm of the young Warlord who'd been warming her bed before the screams began, she returned to her wing of the mansion, smiling at the wail of despair that filled the hall behind her.

7 / Terreille

Dorothea hurried up the broad path to the Sanctuary, clutching at her cloak as the wind tried to whip it from her body. The old Priestess, bent and somewhat feeble-minded, opened the heavy door for her and then fought with the wind to close it.

Dorothea gave the old woman the barest nod of acknowledgment as she rushed past her, desperate to reach the meeting place.

The inner chamber was empty except for two worn chairs and a low table placed before a blazing fire. Throwing off her cloak with one hand, she carefully placed the bottle she had held tight against her body on the table and sank into one of the chairs with a moan.

Two short days ago, she had felt insolent about asking for help from the Dark Priestess, had chafed at the offerings she had to provide from her court or Hayll's Hourglass. Now she was ready to beg.

For two days, Sadi had stalked through Draega, restlessly and relentlessly trying to blunt his rage. In that time, he'd killed a young Warlord from one of the Hundred Families—an exuberant youth who was only trying to have his pleasure with a tavern owner's daughter. The man had dared protest because his daughter was virgin and wore a Jewel. The Warlord had dealt with the father—not fatally—and was dragging the girl to a comfortable room when Sadi appeared, took exception to the girl's frightened cries, and savaged the young Warlord, shattering his Jewels and turning his brain into gray dust.

The grateful tavern owner gave Sadi a good meal and an ever-full glass. By morning the story was all over Draega, and then there were no tavern owners or innkeepers, Blood or landen, who didn't have a hot meal, a full glass, or a bed waiting for him if he walked down their street.

She wasn't sure the Ring would stop him this time, wasn't sure he wouldn't turn his fury on her if she tried to control him. And if he outlasted the pain . . .

Dorothea put her hands over her face and moaned again. She didn't hear the door open and close.

"You're troubled, Sister," said the crooning girlish voice.

Dorothea looked up, trembling with relief. She sank to her knees and bowed her head. "I need your help, Dark Priestess."

Hekatah smiled and hungrily eyed the contents of the bottle. Keeping her cloak's hood pulled well forward to hide her face, she sat in the other chair and, with a graceful turn of her hand, drew the bottle toward her. "A gift?" she asked, feigning surprised delight. "How generous of you, Sister, to remember me." With another turn of her hand, she called in a ravenglass goblet, filled it from the bottle, and drank deeply. She sighed with pleasure. "How sweet the blood. A young, strong witch. But only one voice to give so much."

Dorothea crawled back into her chair and straightened her gown. Her lips curved in a sly smile. "She insisted on being the only one, Priestess, wanting you to have her best." It was the least the little bitch could do, having caused the trouble in the first place.

"You sent for me," Hekatah said impatiently, then dropped her voice back into the soothing croon. "How can I help you, Sister?"

Dorothea jumped out of the chair and began to pace. "Sadi has gone mad. I can't control him anymore. If he stays in Hayll much longer, he'll tear us all apart."

"Can you use the half-breed to curb him?" Hekatah refilled her glass and sipped the warm blood.

Dorothea laughed bitterly. "I don't think anything will curb him."

"Hmm. Then you must send him away."

Dorothea spun around, hands clenched at her sides, lips bared to show her gritted teeth. "Where? No one will have him. Any Queen I send him to will die."

"The farther away the better," Hekatah murmured. "Pruul?"

"Zuultah has the half-breed, and you know those two can't be in the same court. Besides, Zuultah's actually been able to keep that one on a tight leash, and Prythian doesn't want to move him."

"Since when have you been concerned about what that winged sow wants?" Hekatah snapped. "Pruul is west, far west of Hayll, and mostly desert. An ideal place."

Dorothea shook her head. "Zuultah's too valuable to our plans."

"Ah."

"We're still cultivating the western Territories and don't have a strong enough influence yet."

"But you have some. Surely Hayll must have made overtures *someplace* where not *all* the Queens are so valued. Is there nowhere, Sister, where a Queen has been an impediment? Nowhere a gift like Sadi might be useful to *you*?"

Dorothea settled into her chair, her long forefinger nail tapping against her teeth. "One place," she said quietly. "That bitch Queen has opposed me at every turn. It's taken three of their generations to soften their culture enough to create an independent male counsel strong enough to remake the laws. The males we've helped rise to power will gut their own society in order to have dominance, and once they do that, the Territory will be ripe for the picking. But she keeps trying to fight them, and she's always trying to close my embassy and dilute my influence." Dorothea sat up straight, her eyes glittering. "Sadi would be a perfect gift for her."

"And if his temper gets out of control . . ." Hekatah laughed.

Dorothea laughed with her. "But how to get him there."

"Make a gift of him."

"She wouldn't accept it." She paused. "But her son-in-law is Kartane's companion and a strong leader in the counsel—through Hayll's graces. If the gesture was made to *him,* how could he refuse?"

Hekatah toyed with her glass. "This place. It's to the west?"

Dorothea smiled. "Yes. Even farther than Pruul. And backward enough to make him chafe." Dorothea reached for her cloak. "If you'll excuse me, Priestess. There are things I must attend to. The sooner we're rid of him, the better."

"Of course, Sister," Hekatah replied sweetly. "May the Darkness speed your journey."

Hekatah stared dreamily at the fire for several minutes. Emptying the bottle, she admired the dark liquid in the smoky black glass, then raised the goblet in a small salute. "The sooner you're rid of him, the better. The sooner he's in the west, the better still."

8 / Hell

"SaDiablo, there's something you should know."

Silence. "Have you seen her?"

"No." A long pause. "Saetan, Dorothea just sent Daemon Sadi to Chaillot."

PART III

CHAPTER SIX

1 / Terreille

Instantly awake, Surreal probed the dark room and the corridors beyond for whatever had disturbed her sleep.

Men's voices, women's voices, muted laughter.

No danger she could feel. Still . . .

A dark, cold ripple, coming from the east, rolled over Chaillot.

Surreal snuggled deeper into the bed, tucking the covers around her. The night was cool, the bed warm, and the sleeping draught Deje had given her gently pulled her back into the dreamless sleep she'd enjoyed for the past few nights.

Whatever it was, it wasn't looking for her.

Kartane slammed the door of his suite and locked it with a vicious snap of his hand. For an hour he paced his rooms, cursing softly.

It had been a delightful night, spent with a frightened, porcelain-faced girl who had been gratifyingly revolted by everything she'd had to do for him—and everything he had done to her. He had left that private playground relaxed and sated until Robert Benedict had stopped him at the door and told him how delighted, how *honored* his family was to receive such a gift from Lady SaDiablo. Of course, his bastard brother, Philip, performed consort duties for Lady Angelline, and she probably wouldn't put him *completely* aside for a pleasure slave, no matter how celebrated, but they were *honored*.

Kartane cursed. He'd woven his web of lies to Hayll's embassy tight enough to ensure that Dorothea, even if she found him quickly, wouldn't be able to call him back without embarrassment to herself. It also meant he couldn't bolt now without answering some difficult, and very unwanted, questions. Besides, this had become his favorite playground, and he had planned to stay a while.

He undressed and fell wearily into bed.

There was time. There was time. Daemon wasn't here.

Yet.

Cassandra stood in the Sanctuary doorway and watched the sun rise, unable to pinpoint the cause of her nervousness. Whatever it was, it was coming over the horizon with the sun.

Closing her eyes and taking a slow, deep breath, she descended to the depth of the Black, took that one mental step to the side that Black Widows were trained to take, and then she stood at the edge of the Twisted Kingdom. With eyes gauzed by the dreamscape of visions, she looked at the sun climbing above the horizon.

She stared for a long moment, then shook her head violently to clear her sight and pressed her body hard against the stone doorway, hoping for support. When she was sure she was truly out of the dreamscape, she went into the Sanctuary, keeping her back to the sun.

She stumbled to the kitchen, hurriedly pulled the curtains across the windows, and sat on the bench by the banked fire, grateful for the dark.

A Black Widow who stood on the edge of the Twisted Kingdom could see the true face behind whatever mask a person wore; she could draw memories from wood and stone to know what happened in a place; she could see warnings about things to come.

The sun, when Cassandra had looked at it through the dreamscape of visions, had been a torn, bloody orb.

Alexandra Angelline studied the room with a critical eye. The wood floor gleamed, the throw rugs were freshly washed, the windows sparkled, the bed linen was crisp and new, and the wardrobe was filled with freshly washed and pressed clothes that hung in a straight row above the polished shoes. She breathed deeply and smelled autumn air and lemon polish.

And something else.

With an angry sigh, she shook her head and turned to her housekeeper. "It's still there. Faint, but there. Clean it again."

* * *

Lucivar studied the cloudless sky. Heat waves already shimmered up from the Arava Desert in Pruul, but Lucivar shivered, chilled to the bone. His outer senses told him nothing, so he turned inward and instantly felt the cold, dark fury. Nervously licking his lips, he sent a thought on an Ebon-gray spear thread narrowed toward a single mind.

Bastard?

Whatever rode the Winds over Pruul passed him and continued west.

Bastard?

Cold silence was his only answer.

In Hell, Saetan sat behind the blackwood desk in his private study deep beneath the Hall and stared at the portrait across the room, a portrait he could barely see in the dim light. He'd been sitting there for hours, staring at Cassandra's likeness, trying to feel something—love, rage—anything that would ease the pain in his heart.

He felt nothing but bitterness and regret.

He watched Mephis open the study door and close it behind him. For a long moment he stared at his eldest son as if he were a stranger, and then turned back to the portrait.

"Prince SaDiablo," Saetan said, his voice full of soft thunder.

"High Lord?"

Saetan stared at the portrait for several minutes more. He sighed bitterly. "Send Marjong the Executioner to me."

In a private compartment on a Yellow Web Coach, Daemon Sadi sat across from two nervous Hayllian ambassadors. Behind a face that looked like a cold, beautiful, unnatural mask, his rage was contained but undiminished. He'd said nothing to his escorts throughout the journey. In fact, he'd barely moved since they left Hayll.

Now he stared at a blank wall, deaf to the men's lowered voices. His right hand continued to seek his left wrist, the fingers gently rubbing back and forth, back and forth, as if needing reassurance that the scar Tersa had gifted him with was still there.

2 / Terreille

Daemon stared out the window as the carriage rolled along the smooth road leading to the Angelline estate, aware that his escort, Prince Philip Alexander, covertly watched him. He'd been relieved when Philip had stopped defensively pointing out things of interest as they rode through Beldon Mor. He understood the man's defensiveness—Hayllian ambassadors prided themselves on their ability to subtly sneer at the cultural heritage of their host cities—but he was too intrigued by the elusive puzzle that had brushed his mind shortly after arriving in Beldon Mor to give Philip more than terse, civil replies.

A few decades ago, Beldon Mor had probably been a beautiful city. It was still lovely, but he recognized the taint of Hayll's influence. In a couple more generations, Beldon Mor would be nothing more than a smaller, younger Draega.

But there was an undercurrent beneath the familiar taint, a subtle *something* that eluded recognition. It had crept up on him during the hours he'd spent at the Hayllian embassy, like a mist one could almost feel but couldn't see. He'd never experienced anything like it and yet it felt familiar somehow.

"This is all part of the Angelline estate," Philip said, breaking the silence. "The house will be visible around the next bend."

Pushing the puzzle aside, Daemon forced himself to show some interest in the place where he would be living.

It was a large, well-proportioned manor house that gracefully fit into its natural surroundings. He hoped the interior decor was as quietly elegant as the exterior. It would be a relief to live in a place that didn't set his teeth on edge.

"It's lovely," Daemon said when they reached the house.

Philip smiled warily. "Yes, it is."

As he climbed out of the carriage and followed Philip up the steps to the door, Daemon's nerves tingled. His inner senses stretched. The moment he crossed the threshold, he slid to a stop, stunned.

The psychic scent was almost gone, but he recognized it. A dark scent. A powerful, terrifying, wonderful scent.

He breathed deeply, and the lifetime hunger in him became intense. She was here. She was *here*!

He wanted to shout in triumph, but the puzzled, wary expression in Philip's gray eyes sharpened Daemon's predatory instincts. By the time he reached Philip's side, he had thought of half a dozen ways a Gray-Jeweled Prince could quietly disappear.

Daemon smiled, pleased to see Philip's involuntary shiver.

"This way," Philip said tersely as he turned and walked toward the back of the house. "Lady Angelline is waiting."

Daemon slipped his hands into his pockets, settled his face into his bored court expression, and fell into step beside Philip with graceful indifference. As impatient as he was to meet the witches in this family and find the one he sought, it wouldn't do to make Philip too uneasy, too defensive.

They'd almost reached the door when a man came out of the room. He was fat, florid, and generally unattractive, but there were enough similarities between him and Philip to mark them as brothers.

"So," Robert Benedict said with a hearty sneer. "This is Daemon Sadi. The girls are most excited to have you here. Most excited." His eyes folded up into the fat as he gave Philip a nasty smile before turning back to Daemon. "Leland spent the whole morning dressing for the occasion. Philip's more of a steward now, so he doesn't have the time to see to the girls' comfort the way you will." He rubbed his hands together in malicious glee. "If you'll excuse me, duty calls."

Stepping aside to let Robert pass, they stood in silence until the front door closed. Philip was white beneath his summer tan, his breath whistled through his clenched teeth, and he shook with the effort of controlling some strong emotion.

"They're waiting," Daemon said quietly.

Philip's eyes were full of naked hatred. Daemon calmly returned the look. A Black-Jeweled Warlord Prince had nothing to fear from a Gray-Jeweled Prince. Philip at his worst temper wasn't equal to Daemon at his best, and they both knew it.

"In here," Philip snapped, leading Daemon into the room.

Trying not to act too eager, Daemon stepped into the sunny room that overlooked an expanse of green lawn and formal gardens, certain that he would know her the moment he saw her.

Seconds later, he swallowed a scream of rage.

There were two women and a girl about fourteen, but the one he sought wasn't there.

Alexandra Angelline, the matriarch of the Angelline family and the Queen of Chaillot, was a handsome woman with long dark hair just beginning to silver, a fine-boned oval face, and eyes the color of Purple Dusk Jewels. Her clothes were simply cut but expensive. The Blood Opal that hung from her neck was set in a simple gold design. Sitting in a high-backed chair, she held her slender body straight and proud as she studied him.

Daemon studied her in turn. Not a natural Black Widow, but there was a feel about her that suggested she had spent some time in an Hourglass coven. Though why she would begin an apprenticeship and not continue . . . Unless Dorothea had already begun her purge of Chaillot's Hourglass covens by then. Eliminating potential rivals was one of the first things Dorothea did to soften a Territory, and other Black Widows were far more dangerous rivals than the Queens because they practiced the same kind of Craft. It didn't take that many stories whispered in the dark to change a wariness of Black Widows into an active fear, and once the fear set in, the killing began. Once the killing began, the Black Widows would go into hiding, and the only ones who would be trained in their Craft were the daughters born to the Hourglass.

Since she was the sole heir to one of the largest fortunes on Chaillot and the strongest Queen the island had, her continued presence in an Hourglass coven would have been a dangerous risk for them all.

Leland Benedict, Alexandra's only daughter and Robert's wife, was a paler, frivolous version of her mother. The frothy neckline and frothy sleeves of her gown didn't suit her figure, and the hair done too elaborately for the hour of the day made her look more matronly than her mother. Daemon found her air of shy curiosity particularly irritating. The ones who began shyly curious tended to become the cruelest and most vindictive once they discovered what kind of pleasure he could provide. Still, he felt sorry for her. He could almost feel the core of her still molten, still wanting something cleaner, richer, more fulfilling than this caged freedom she had. Then she fluttered her eyelashes at him, and he wanted to strike her.

Last was the girl, Wilhelmina, the only child from Robert's first marriage. Unlike her father, who had a ruddy complexion and sandy-red hair, she was raven-haired and very fair, with a startling blush in her cheeks and blue-gray eyes. She was a beautiful girl and would become even more so when her body began to fill out and curve. In fact, that was the only flaw Daemon could see in her appearance—she was thin to the point of looking unhealthy. He wondered—as he had wondered in so many other places—if these people, Blood as he was Blood, had any idea of what they were, had any understanding of what wearing the Jewels entailed—not just the pleasures or the power that could be had but the physical and emotional hardships that were part of it too. If the girl wore Jewels darker than the other women in her family, perhaps they didn't recognize what was so apparent to him.

Anyone who wore the Jewels, especially a child, had a higher metabolism. It was possible, more for a witch because of the physical demands of her moontime than for her male counterparts, to burn up her own body in a matter of days if enough food wasn't available.

Setting the small chip of Red Jewel that was hidden beneath the rubies in his cuff links to auditory retention, Daemon let his mind drift as Alexandra told him about the household and his "duties." The Jewel chip would retain the conversation until he was ready to retrieve it. Right now, he had something more important to think about.

Where was she? *Who* was she? A relation who only visited? A guest who had stayed a few days and recently left? He couldn't ask anyone. If they didn't suspect that Witch had been in their presence, his questions, no matter how innocuous, might endanger her. Dorothea already had her cancerous tentacles embedded in Chaillot. If she became aware that this Other had touched the island . . . No. He couldn't ask. Until she returned, he would do whatever was required to keep these women satisfied and unsuspecting. But after she returned . . .

Finally he was shown to his room. It was directly below Alexandra's apartment and next to a back stairway, since he was mostly here for her pleasure, Leland needing nothing more than an escort when Robert wasn't available, and Wilhelmina being too young. It was a simple room with a chair, lamp, and writing desk as well as a single bed, a dresser with a mirror hanging above it, a wardrobe—and, Daemon noted gratefully, an adjoining modern bathroom.

As he had anticipated, the conversation at dinner was strained. Alexandra talked about the cultural activities that could be explored in Beldon Mor, and Daemon asked the polite questions expected of him. While Alexandra's conversation was painstakingly impersonal, Leland was fluttery, nervous, and far too prone to ask leading questions that made her blush no matter how delicately Daemon phrased his answers—if he answered at all. Robert, who had returned unexpectedly for dinner, looked too pleased with the arrangement, made sly comments throughout the meal, and took pains to touch Leland at every opportunity to stress his claim to her. Daemon ignored him, finding Philip's distress and growing rage at Robert far more interesting.

As dinner wore on, Daemon wished Wilhelmina were there, since she was the one he was most curious about, the one he could most easily tap for information. But she was considered too young to have late dinner and sit with the adults.

Finally free to retire but too restless to sleep, Daemon paced his room. Tomorrow he would begin searching the house. A room where she had slept would still be strong with her psychic scent, even if it had been cleaned. There wasn't time to waste, but he couldn't afford to be found prowling around in the early-morning hours his first night there, not now, not when he might finally see, hear, touch what his soul had been aching for his whole life. Blood Law was nothing to him. The Blood were nothing to him. She would be Blood and yet Other, something alien and yet kindred. She would be terrifyingly magnificent.

As he paced his room, undressing in a slow striptease for no one, Daemon tried to imagine her. Chaillot born? Quite probable. Living in Beldon Mor? That would explain the subtle *something* he'd felt. And if she never physically strayed from the island, that explained why he hadn't felt her presence anywhere else in the past few years. Wise, certainly cautious to have escaped notice for so long.

He slid into bed, turned off the light . . . and groaned as an image of a wise, skinny old crone filled his mind.

No, he begged the still night. *Sweet Darkness, heed the prayer of one of your sons. Now that she's so close, let her be young enough to want me. Let her be young enough to need me.*

The night gave him no answer, and the sky was a predawn gray before he finally slept.

3 / Terreille

For two days Daemon played the polite, considerate escort as the fluttery Leland made an endless round of calls showing off Lady SaDiablo's gift. For two nights he prowled the house, his control on his temper fraying from lack of sleep and frustration. He had toured every public room, probed every guest room, flattered and cajoled his way through the servants' quarters—and had found nothing.

Not quite nothing. He had found the library tucked away on the second floor of the nursery wing. It wasn't the library visitors saw, or the one the family used. This was the small room that contained volumes on the Craft and, like so many others he had seen in the past few decades, it had the feel of a room that was almost never used.

Almost never.

Silently closing the door, Daemon moved unerringly through the dark, cluttered room to a table in the far corner that held a shaded candle-light. He touched it, stroking downward on the crystal to dim the glow, leaned against the built-in bookcases, and tilted his head back to rest on a shelf.

The scent was strong in this room.

Daemon closed his eyes, breathed deeply, and frowned. Even though it was clean, the room had the dusty, musty smell of old books, but a physical scent wouldn't obscure a psychic one. That dark scent . . . Like the body that housed it, a witch's psychic scent had a muskiness that a Blood male could find as arousing as the body—if not more so. This dark, sweet scent was chillingly clean of that muskiness, and as he continued to breathe deeply, to open himself to that which was stronger than the body, he felt distressed to find it so.

Pushing away from the bookshelves, Daemon extinguished the candle-light and waited for his eyes to adjust to the darkness before leaving the room. So, she'd spent much of her time in that room, but she must have *stayed* somewhere. His eyes flicked toward the ceiling as he slipped among the shadows and silently climbed the stairs. The only place left to look was the nursery, the third-floor rooms where Wilhelmina and her governess, Lady Graff, spent most of their days. It was also the only place

Philip had vehemently told him to stay away from, since his services weren't required there.

Daemon glided down the corridor, his probing mind identifying the rooms as he passed: classroom, music room, playroom, Lady Graff's sitting room and adjoining bedroom (which Daemon immediately turned away from, his lips curling in a snarl, as he caught the wispy scent of erotic dreaming), bathrooms, a couple of guest rooms, Wilhelmina's bedroom. And the corner room that overlooked the back gardens.

Daemon hesitated, suddenly unwilling to further invade the privacy of children. As was his custom, he had gleaned basic facts about the family before entering service. The Hayllian ambassador, annoyed at being questioned, became quite garrulous once he noticed the cold look in Daemon's eyes, saying nothing of much interest except that there were two daughters. Daemon had met Wilhelmina.

There was only one room left.

His hand shook as he turned the doorknob and slipped into the room.

The sweet darkness washed over him, but even here it was faint, as though someone had been trying to scrub it away. Daemon pressed his back against the door and silently asked forgiveness for what he was about to do. He was male, he was intruding, and, like her, it would only take a few minutes for his own dark psychic scent to be impressed on the room for anyone to read.

Cautiously lifting one hand, he engaged a candle-light by the bed, keeping it bright enough to see by but dim enough that, he hoped, the light wouldn't be noticed beneath the bedroom door if someone walked past. Then he looked around, his brow wrinkling in puzzlement.

It was a young girl's room: white dresser and wardrobe, white canopy and counterpane decorated with little pink flowers covering the four-poster bed, gleaming wood floors with cute throw rugs scattered around.

It was totally wrong.

He opened every drawer of the dresser and found clothing suitable for a young girl, but when he touched it it was like touching a tiny spark of lightning. The bed, too, when he ran his hand lightly over the counterpane, sent a spark along his nerves. But the dolls and stuffed animals—the scent was on them only because they were in this room. If any of them had been rich with her puzzling darkness, he would have taken it back to his room to hold throughout the night. Finally he turned to the wardrobe and opened the doors.

The clothes were a child's clothes, the shoes were meant for small feet. It had been a while since they'd been worn, and the scent was faint in them, too. The wardrobe itself, however . . .

Daemon went through it piece by piece, touching everything, growing more hopeful and more frantic with each discarded item. When there was nothing left to check, his trembling fingers slid along the inside walls, his tactile sense becoming a conductor for the inner senses.

Kneeling on the floor, exhausted by disappointment, he leaned forward until his hand touched the far back corner of the wardrobe.

Lightning pulsed through him until he thought his blood would boil.

Puzzled, he cupped his hands and created a small ball of witchlight. He studied the corner, vanished the witchlight, and leaned back on his heels, even more puzzled.

There was nothing there . . . and yet there was. Nothing his physical senses could engage, but his inner senses insisted something was there.

Daemon reached forward again and shivered.

The room was suddenly, intensely cold.

His thinking was slowed by fatigue, and it took him a full minute to understand what the cold meant.

"Forgive me," he whispered as he carefully withdrew his hand. "I didn't mean to invade your private place. I swear by the Jewels it won't happen again."

With trembling hands, Daemon replaced the clothes and shoes exactly the way he'd found them, extinguished the candle-light, and silently glided back to his room. Once there, he dug out the bottle of brandy hidden in his own wardrobe and took a long swallow.

It didn't make sense. He could understand finding her psychic scent in the library. But in the child's room? Not on the toys, but on the clothes, on the bed-things an adult might handle daily if she took care of the child. When he had made an innocuous comment about there being another daughter, he'd been told, snappishly, that she wasn't at home, that she was ill.

Was his Lady assuming a Healer's duties? Had she slept in a cot in the girl's room in order to be nearby? Where was she now?

Daemon put the brandy away, undressed, and slid into bed. Tersa's warning about the chalice cracking frayed his nerves, but there was nothing he could do. He couldn't hunt for her as he had in other courts. She was nearby, and he couldn't risk being sent away.

Daemon punched his pillow and sighed. When the child returned, his Lady would return.

And he would be waiting.

4 / Terreille

Surreal tilted her head back, smiling at the sun's warmth on her face and the smell of clean sea air. Her moontime had passed; tonight she would begin working for her keep to pay Deje back for her kindness. But the day was hers, and as she meandered up the path that led to Cassandra's Altar, she enjoyed the rough landscape, the sun on her back, the crisp autumn wind teasing her long black hair.

When she rounded a bend and saw the Sanctuary, Surreal wrinkled her nose and sighed. She'd trekked all this way to see a ruin. Even though she was just beginning what might be a long, long life, she had already lived enough years to see that places where she had stayed sometimes had become crumbled piles of stone by the time she next returned. What was ancient history for so many was actual memory for her. She found the thought depressing.

Pushing her hair off her face, she stepped through an open doorway and looked around, noting the gaps in the stone walls and the holes in the roof. Sitting in the autumn sun was more appealing than wandering through chilly, barren rooms, so she turned to leave, but when she reached the doorway, she heard footsteps behind her.

The woman who stepped out from the inner chambers wore a tunic and trousers made of a shimmery, dusty black material. Her red hair, which flowed over her shoulders, was held in place by a silver circlet that fit snugly around her head. A Red Jewel hung just above her breasts. Her smile of greeting was warm but not effusive.

"How may I serve you, Sister?" she asked quietly.

The hair, faded of its vibrant color by time, and the lines on the woman's face spoke of long years, but the emerald eyes and the proud carriage said this was not a witch to trifle with.

"My apologies, Lady." Surreal met the other's steady gaze. "I came to see the Altar. I didn't know someone lived here."

"To see or to ask?"

Surreal shook her head, puzzled.

"When one seeks a Dark Altar, it's usually for help that can't be given elsewhere, or for answers to questions of the heart."

Surreal shrugged. She hadn't felt this awkward since her first client at her first Red Moon house, when she realized how little she had learned in all those dirty little back rooms. "I came to . . ." The woman's words finally penetrated. Questions of the heart. "I'd like to know who my mother's people were."

Surreal suddenly felt a whisper of something that had been there all along, a darkness, a strength she hadn't been attuned to. As she looked at the Sanctuary again, she realized that the things built around this place were insignificant. The place itself held the power.

The woman's gaze never wavered. "Everything has a price," she said quietly. "Are you willing to pay for what you ask?"

Surreal dug into her pocket and extended a handful of gold coins.

The woman shook her head. "Those who are what I am are not paid in that kind of coin." She turned back toward the doorway she'd come through. "Come. I'll make some tea and we'll talk. Perhaps we can help each other." She went down the passage, letting Surreal leave or follow, as she chose.

Surreal hesitated for a moment before dropping the coins into her pocket and following the woman. It was partly the sudden feeling of awe she had for the place, partly curiosity about what sort of price this witch would require for information, partly hope that she might finally have an answer to a question that had haunted her ever since she'd fully understood how different Titian was from everyone else. Besides, she was good with a knife and she wore the Gray. The place might hold her in awe, but the witch didn't.

The kitchen was cozy and well ordered. Surreal smiled at the contrast between the feel of this room and the rest of the Sanctuary. The woman, too, seemed more like a gentle hearth-witch than a Sanctuary Priestess as she hummed a cheery little tune while the water heated. Surreal sat in a chair, propped her elbows on the pine table, and watched in amused silence as a plate of nutcakes, a small bowl of fresh butter, and a mug for the tea were placed before her.

When the tea was ready, the woman joined her at the table, a glass of wine in her hand. Suddenly suspicious, Surreal looked pointedly at the tea, the nutcakes, and the butter.

The woman laughed. "At my age, my dietary requirements preclude such things, unfortunately. But test them if it troubles you. I won't be offended. Better you should know I mean you no ill. Else, how can we talk honestly?"

Surreal probed the food and found nothing but what should be there. Picking up a nutcake, she broke it neatly in half, buttered it, and began to eat. While she ate, the woman spoke of general things, telling her about the Dark Altars, how there were thirteen of these great dark places of power scattered throughout the Realm.

The wineglass was empty and Surreal sipped her second cup of tea before the woman said, "Now. You want to know about your mother's people. True?" She stood up and leaned toward Surreal, her hands outstretched to touch Surreal's face.

Surreal pulled back, long years of caution making her wary.

"Shh," the woman murmured soothingly, "I just want to look."

Surreal forced herself to sit quietly as the woman's hands followed the curves of her face, neck, and shoulders, lifted her long hair, and traced the curve of her ear to its delicate point. When she was done, the woman refilled her wineglass and said nothing for a while, her expression thoughtful, her eyes focused on some other place.

"I can't be certain, but I could tell you what I think."

Surreal leaned forward, trying not to appear too eager and yet holding her breath in anticipation.

The woman's gaze was disconcertingly steady. "There is, however, the matter of the price." She toyed with her wineglass. "It's customary that the price be named and agreed upon before help is given. Contracts such as these are never broken because, if they are, the price is then usually paid in blood. Do you understand, Sister?"

Surreal took a slow, steadying breath. "What's your price?"

"First, I want you to understand that I'm not asking you to endanger yourself. I'm not asking you to take any risks."

"All right."

The woman placed the stem of the wineglass between her palms and slowly rolled the glass back and forth. "A Warlord Prince has recently come to Chaillot, either into Beldon Mor or an immediate outlying village. I need to know his precise whereabouts, who he's serving."

Surreal itched to call in the stiletto, but she kept her face carefully blank. "Does this Prince have a name?"

"Daemon Sadi."

"No!" Surreal jumped up and paced the room. "Are you mad? No one toys with the Sadist if they want to stay this side of the grave." She stopped pacing and gripped the back of the chair so hard it shook from the tension. "I won't do a contract on Sadi. Forget it."

"I'm not asking you to do anything but locate him."

"So you can send someone else to do the job? Forget it. Why don't you find him yourself?"

"For reasons that are my own, I can't go into Beldon Mor."

"And you've just given me a good reason to get out."

The woman stood up and faced Surreal. "This is very important."

"Why?"

The silence grew between them, straining, draining them both. Finally the woman sighed. "Because he may have been sent here to destroy a very special child."

"You got anything to drink around here besides tea and that wine?"

The woman looked pained and amused. "Will brandy do?"

"Fine," Surreal snapped, dropping back into her chair. "Bring the bottle and a clean mug." When the bottle and mug were placed before her, she filled the mug and slugged back a third of the brandy. "Listen up, sugar," she said tartly. "Sadi may be many things, and the Darkness only knows all that he's done, but he has never, *ever* hurt a child. To suggest that—"

"What if he's forced to?" the woman said urgently.

"Forced to?" Surreal squeaked. "*Forced to?* Hell's fire, who is going to be dumb enough to force the Sadist? Do you know what he does to people who push him?" Surreal drained the mug and filled it again. "Besides, who would want to destroy this kid?"

"Dorothea SaDiablo."

Surreal swore until she could feel the words swirling around the room like smoke. She finally stopped when she noticed the woman's expression of amazed amusement. She took another drink and swore again because her anger burned up the brandy so fast she couldn't feel even a little bit mellow. Thumping the mug down on the table, she ran her hands through her hair. "Lady, you really know how to knife someone in the guts, don't you?" She glared at the woman. If the witch had returned her gaze calmly, Surreal would have knifed her, but when she saw the tears and the pain— and the fear—in those emerald eyes . . .

Titian lying on the floor with her throat slit and the walls thundering the order to run, run, run.

"Look. I owe him. He took care of my mother, and he took care of me. He didn't have to, he just did. But I'll find him. After that, we'll see." Surreal stood up. "Thanks for the tea."

The woman looked troubled. "What about your mother's people?"

Surreal met her gaze. "If I come back, we'll exchange information. But I'll give you a bit of advice for free. Don't play with the Sadist. He's got a very long memory and a wicked temper. If you give him a reason to, he'll turn you to dust. I'll see myself out."

Surreal left the Sanctuary, caught a Wind, and rode past Chaillot, chasing the setting sun far out into the ocean until she felt weary enough to return to Deje's and be civil to whomever she was supposed to bed that night.

5 / Hell

Saetan toyed with the silver-handled letter opener, keeping his back to the man who stood just inside his study door. "Is it done?"

"Forgive me, High Lord," came the ragged, whispery answer. "I could not do it."

For a flickering second before he turned to face Marjong the Executioner, Saetan wasn't sure if he felt annoyed or relieved. He leaned against his blackwood desk and studied the giant man. It was impossible to read Marjong's expressions because his head and shoulders were always covered with a black hood.

"He is in that misted city, High Lord," Marjong apologized, shifting the huge, double-headed ax from one hand to the other. "I could not reach him to carry out your request."

So. Daemon was in Beldon Mor.

"I can wait, High Lord. If he travels out of the misted city, I—"

"No." Saetan took a slow, steadying breath. "No. Do nothing more unless I specifically request it. Understood?"

Marjong bowed and left the study.

With a weary sigh, Saetan sank into his chair and slowly spun the letter opener around and around. He picked it up and studied the thin ravenglass blade and the beautifully sculpted silver handle. "An effective tool," he said quietly, balancing it on his fingertips. "Elegant, efficient. But if one isn't careful . . ." He pressed one finger against the point and watched a drop of blood well up on the finger pad. "Like you, namesake. Like you. The dance is ours now. Just between us."

6 / Terreille

Daemon's days settled into a routine. Every morning he rose early, exercised, showered, and shared breakfast with Cook in the kitchen. He liked the Angellines' cook, a brisk, warm woman who reminded him of Manny—and who had been as appalled as Manny would have been when he'd asked her consent to have the first meal of the day in the kitchen instead of in the breakfast room with the family. She'd relented when she realized he was going hungry while dancing attendance to Leland's endless stream of nervous requests. Since he joined the family for breakfast anyway, Daemon wryly noted that his breakfast in the kitchen was usually better fare than what was served in the breakfast room.

After breakfast, he met with Philip in the steward's office, where he was grudgingly handed the list of activities for the day. After that was a half hour walk through the gardens with Wilhelmina.

Alexandra had decided that Wilhelmina needed some light exercise before beginning her Craft lessons with Lady Graff, an unspeakably harsh woman whom Daemon had taken an instant dislike to—as she had to him, more because he had ignored her coquettish suggestions than for any other reason. Leland then suggested that Daemon accompany the girl, since Wilhelmina had an unreasonable fear of men and exposure to a Ringed male who couldn't be a threat to her might help relieve her fear. So when the weather permitted, he escorted Wilhelmina around the grounds.

The first few days he attempted conversation, tried to find out her interests, but she skittered away from his attempts while still trying to be a polite young lady. It struck him one morning, when a silence had stretched beyond expected comfort, that this was probably one of the rare times in the day when she had the luxury of her own thoughts. Since she spent most of her time in Graff's steely presence, she wasn't allowed to "moon about"—a phrase he'd heard Graff use one day in a tone that implied it was a usual scold. So he stopped trying to talk to her, letting her have her solitary half hour while he walked respectfully on her left, hands in his pockets, enjoying the same luxury of having time for his own thoughts.

She always had a destination, although she never seemed to reach it. No matter what paths they took through the gardens, they always ended up at a narrow path that led into a heavily overgrown alcove. Her steps would falter when she reached the place, and then she would rush past it, breathing hard, as if she'd been running for a long time. He wondered if something had happened to her there, something that frightened her, repelled her, and yet drew her back.

One morning when he was lost in thought, thoroughly absorbed with the puzzle his Lady had left him, he realized they'd stopped walking and Wilhelmina had been watching him for some time. They were standing by the narrow path.

"I want to go in there," she said defiantly, her hands clenched at her sides.

Daemon bit the inside of his lip to keep his face neutral. It was the first spark of life she'd shown, and he didn't want it squelched by a smile that might be misunderstood as condescension. "All right."

She looked surprised, obviously expecting an argument. With a timid smile, she led him down the path and through a trellis arch.

The small garden within the garden was completely surrounded by large yews that looked as if they hadn't been trimmed on this side in several years. A maple tree dominated one end, girdled by a circular iron bench that had been white once, but the paint was now peeling badly. In front of the yews were the remains of flower beds, tangled, weedy, uncared for. But the thing that made his breath catch, made his heart pound too fast, too hard, was the bed of witchblood in the far corner.

Flower or weed, witchblood was beautiful, deadly, and—so legend said—indestructible. The bloodred flowers, with their black throats and black-tipped petals, were in full bloom, as they always were from the first breath of spring to the last dying sigh of autumn.

Wilhelmina stood by the bed, hugging herself and shivering.

Daemon walked over to the bed, trying to understand the pain and hope in Wilhelmina's face. Witchblood supposedly grew only where a witch's blood had been spilled violently or where a witch who had met a violent death was buried.

Daemon stepped back, reeling.

Even with the fresh air and the other garden smells, the dark psychic scent was strong there. Sweet Darkness, it was strong there.

"My sister planted these," Wilhelmina said abruptly, her voice quivering. "One for each. As remembrance." She bit her lip, her blue eyes wide and frightened as she studied the flowers.

"It's all right," Daemon said soothingly, trying to calm the panic rising in her while fighting his own. "I know what witchblood is and what it stands for." He searched for words that might comfort them both. "This is a special place because of it."

"The gardeners won't come here. They say it's haunted. Do you think it's haunted? I hope it is."

Daemon considered his next words carefully. "Where's your sister?"

Wilhelmina began to cry. "Briarwood. They put her in Briarwood." The sobs became a brokenhearted keening.

Daemon held her gently while he stroked her hair, murmuring the "words of gentle sorrow" in the Old Tongue, the language of Witch.

After a minute, Wilhelmina pushed him away, sniffling. He handed her his handkerchief and, smiling, took it back when she stared at it, uncertain what to do with it after using it.

"She talks like that sometimes," Wilhelmina said. "We'd better get back." She left the alcove and hurried down the path.

Dazed, Daemon followed her back to the house.

Daemon stepped into the kitchen and gave Cook his best smile. "Any chance of a cup of coffee?"

Cook snapped a sharp, angry look in his direction. "If you like."

Confused by this sudden display of temper, Daemon shrugged out of his topcoat and sat at the kitchen table. As he puzzled over what he'd done to upset her, she thumped a mug of coffee on the table and said, "Miss Wilhelmina was crying when she came in from the garden."

Daemon ignored the coffee, more interested in Cook's reaction. "There was an alcove in the garden she wanted to visit."

The stern look in Cook's eyes instantly softened, saddened. "Ah, well." She cut two thick slabs of fresh bread, piled cold beef between them, and set it before him, an unspoken apology.

Daemon took a deep breath. "Cook, what is Briarwood?"

"A foul place, if you ask me, but no one here does," she snapped, then immediately gave him a small smile.

"What is it?"

With a sigh, Cook brought her own mug of coffee over to the table and sat down across from Daemon. "You're not eating," she said absently as she sipped her coffee.

Daemon obediently took a bite out of the sandwich and waited.

"It's a hospital for emotionally disturbed children," Cook said. "Seems a lot of young witches from good families become high-strung of a sudden when they start leaving childhood behind, if you understand me. But Miss Jaenelle's been in and out of that place since she was five years old for no better reason that I could ever see except that she used to make up fanciful stories about unicorns and dragons and such." She cocked her head toward the front of the house. "*They* say she's unbalanced because she's the only one in the family who doesn't wear the Jewels, that she tries to make up for not being able to do the Craft lessons by making up stories to get attention. If you ask me, the last thing Miss Jaenelle wants is attention. It's just that she's . . . different. It's a funny thing about her. Even when she says wild things, things you know can't be true, somehow . . . you start to wonder, you know?"

Daemon finished his sandwich and drained his mug. "How long has she been gone?"

"Since early spring. She put a flea in *all* their ears this last time. That's why they've left her there so long."

Daemon's lip curled in disgust. "What could a child possibly say that would make them want to lock her up like that?"

"She said . . ." Cook looked nervous and upset. "She said Lord Benedict wasn't her father. She said Prince Philip . . ."

Daemon let out an explosive sigh. Yes, from what he'd observed of the dynamics of this family, a statement like that *would* throw them all into a fury. Still . . .

Cook gave him a long, slow look and refilled the mugs. "Let me tell you about Miss Jaenelle.

"Two years ago, the Warlord my daughter was serving decided he wanted a prettier wench and turned my daughter out, along with the child she'd borne him. They came here to me, not having any other place to go, and Lady Alexandra let them stay. My girl, being poorly at the time, did some light parlor work and helped me in the kitchen. My granddaughter, Lucy—the cutest little button you ever saw—stayed in the kitchen with me mostly, although Miss Jaenelle always included her in the games whenever the girls were outside. Lucy didn't like being out on her own. She was afraid of Lord Benedict's hunting dogs, and the dog boys, knowing she was scared, teased her, getting the dogs all riled up and then slipping them off the leash so they'd chase her.

"One day it went too far. The dogs had been given short rations because they were going to be taken out and they were meaner than usual, and the boys got them too riled up. The pack leader slipped his leash, took off after Lucy, and chased her into the tackroom. She tripped, and he was on her, tearing at her arm. When we heard the screams, my daughter and I came running from the kitchen, and Andrew, one of the stable lads, a real good boy, came running too.

"Lucy was on the floor, screaming and screaming with that dog tearing at her arm, and all of a sudden, there was Miss Jaenelle. She said some strange words to the dog, and he let go of Lucy right away and slunk out of the tackroom, his tail between his legs.

"Lucy was a mess, her arm all torn up, the bone sticking up where the dog had snapped it. Miss Jaenelle told Andrew to get a bucket of water quick, and she knelt down beside Lucy and started talking to her, quiet-like, and Lucy stopped screaming. Andrew came back with the water, and Miss Jaenelle pulled out this big oval basin from somewhere, I never did notice where it came from. Andrew poured the water in the basin, and Miss Jaenelle held it for a minute, just held it, and the water started steaming like it was over a fire. Then she put Lucy's arm in the basin and took some leaves and powders out of her pocket and poured them in the water. She held Lucy's arm down, singing all the while, quiet. We just stood and watched. No point taking the girl to a Healer, even if we could have scraped up the coin to pay a good one. I knew that. That arm was too mangled. The best even a good Healer could have done was cut it off. So we watched, my daughter, Andrew, and me. Couldn't see much, the water all bloody like it was.

"After a while, Miss Jaenelle leaned back and lifted Lucy's arm out of the basin. There was a long, deep cut from her elbow to her wrist . . . and that was all. Miss Jaenelle looked each of us in the eye. She didn't have to say anything. We weren't about to tell on her. Then she handed me a jar of ointment, my daughter being too upset to do much. 'Put this ointment on three times a day, and keep it loosely bandaged for a week. If you do, there'll be no scar.'

"Then she turned to Lucy and said, 'Don't worry. I'll talk to them. They won't bother you again.'

"Prince Philip, when he found out Lucy'd gotten hurt because the dogs were chasing her, gave the dog boys a fierce tongue-lashing; but that afternoon I saw Lord Benedict pressing coins into the dog boys' hands, laughing and telling them how pleased he was they were keeping his dogs in such fine form.

"Anyway, by the next summer, my daughter married a young man from a fine, solid family. They live in a little village about thirty miles from here, and I visit whenever I can get a couple of days' leave."

Daemon looked into his empty mug. "Do you think Miss Jaenelle talked to them?"

"She must have," Cook replied absently.

"So the boys stopped teasing Lucy," Daemon pressed.

"Oh, no. They went right on with it. They weren't punished for it, were they? But the dogs . . . After that day, there was nothing those boys could do to make the dogs chase Lucy."

Late that night, unable to sleep, Daemon returned to the alcove. He lit a black cigarette and stared at the witchblood through the smoke.

She has come.

He'd spent the evening reviewing the facts he had, turning them over and over again as if that would change them. It hadn't, and he didn't like the conclusion he had reached.

My sister planted these. As remembrance.

A child. Witch was still a child.

No. He was misinterpreting something. He *had* to be. Witch wore the Black Jewels.

Maybe he'd gotten the information mixed up. Maybe Wilhelmina was the younger sister. He'd still been fighting to regain his emotional control when he'd arrived at the Hayllian embassy in Beldon Mor. It would make more sense if Jaenelle was almost old enough to make the Offering to the Darkness. She'd be on the cusp of opening herself to her mature strength, which would be the Black Jewels.

But the bedroom, the clothes. How could he reconcile those things with the power he'd felt when she'd healed his back after Cornelia tied him to the whipping posts?

She talks like that sometimes.

He could count on both hands the people still able to speak a few phrases of the Blood's true language. Who could have taught her?

He shied away from the answer to that.

It's a hospital for emotionally disturbed children.

Could a child wear a Jewel as dark as the Black without becoming mentally and emotionally unbalanced? He'd never heard of anyone being gifted with a Birthright Jewel that was darker than the Red.

The chalice is cracking.

He stopped thinking, let his mind quiet. The facts fell into place, forming the inevitable conclusion.

But it still took him a few more days before he could accept it.

7 / Terreille

After parting with Wilhelmina, Daemon changed into his riding clothes and headed for the stables. He had a free morning, the first since he'd arrived at the Angelline estate, and Alexandra had given him permission to take one of the horses out.

As he reached the stableyard, Guinness, the stable master, gave him a curt wave and continued his instructions to one of the stable lads.

"Going to hack out this morning?" Guinness said when Daemon approached, his gruff manner softened by a faint smile.

"If it's convenient," Daemon replied, smiling. Here, like most places where he'd served, he got along well with the staff. It was the witches he was supposed to serve that he couldn't tolerate.

"Ayah." Guinness's eyes slowly rode up Daemon's body, starting with his boots. "Good, straight, solid legs. Strong shoulders."

Daemon wondered if Guinness was going to check his teeth.

"How's your seat?" Guinness asked.

"I ride fairly well," Daemon replied cautiously, not certain he cared for the faint gleam in Guinness's eye.

Guinness sucked on his cheek. "Stallion hasn't been out for a few days. Andrew's the only one who can ride him, and he's got a bruised thigh. Can't let the boy go out with a weak leg. You willing to try?"

Daemon took a deep breath, still suspicious. "All right."

"Andrew! Saddle up Demon."

Daemon's eyebrows shot up practically to his hairline. "Demon?"

Guinness sucked on his cheek again, refusing to notice Daemon's outraged expression. "Name's Dark Dancer, but in the stableyard, when we're out of hearing"—he shot a look at the house—"we call him what he is."

"Hell's fire," Daemon muttered as he crossed the yard to where Andrew was saddling the big bay stallion. "Anything I should know?" he asked the young man.

Andrew looked a bit worried. Finally he shrugged. "He's got a soft mouth and a hard head. He's too smart for most riders. He'll run you into the trees if you let him. Keep to the big open field, that's best. But watch the drainage ditch at the far end. It's too wide for most horses, but he'll take it, and he doesn't care if he lands on the other side without his rider."

"Thanks," Daemon growled.

Andrew grinned crookedly and handed the reins to Daemon. "I'll hold his head while you mount."

Daemon settled into the saddle. "Let him go."

Demon left the stableyard quietly enough, mouthing the bit, considering his rider. Except for showing some irritation at being held to a walk, Demon behaved quite well—until they reached a small rise and the path curved left toward the open field.

Demon pricked his ears and lunged to the right toward a lone old oak tree, almost throwing Daemon from the saddle.

The battle began.

For some perverse reason of his own, Demon was determined to reach the oak tree. Daemon was equally determined to turn him toward the field. The horse lunged, bucked, twisted, circled, fought the reins and bit. Daemon held him in check enough not to be thrown, but, circle by hard-fought circle, the stallion made his way toward the tree.

Fifteen minutes later, the horse gave up and stood with his shaking legs spread, his head down, and his lathered sides heaving. Daemon was sweat-soaked and shivering from exhaustion, and slightly amazed that his arms were still in their sockets.

When Daemon gathered the reins once more, Demon laid back his ears, prepared for the next round. Curious about what would happen, Daemon turned them toward the tree and urged the horse onward.

Demon's ears immediately pricked forward, his neck arched, and his step became high-spirited sassy.

Daemon didn't offer any aids, letting the horse do whatever he wanted. Demon circled the tree over and over, sniffing the air, alert and listening . . . and growing more and more upset. Finally the stallion bugled angrily and launched himself toward the path and the field.

Daemon didn't try to control him until they headed for the ditch. He won that battle—barely—and when Demon finally slowed down, too tired to fight anymore, Daemon turned him toward the stable.

The stable lads stared openmouthed as Daemon rode into the yard. Andrew quickly limped up and took the reins. Guinness shook his head and strode across the yard, grasped Daemon's arm as he slid wearily from the saddle, and led him to the small office beside the tackroom.

Pulling glasses and a bottle from his desk, Guinness poured out a two-finger shot and handed it to Daemon. "Here," he said gruffly, pouring a glass for himself. "It'll put some bone back in your legs."

Daemon gratefully sipped the whiskey while rubbing the knotted muscles in his shoulder.

Guinness looked at Daemon's sweat-soaked shirt and rubbed his bristly chin with his knuckles. "Gave you a bit of a time, did he?"

"It was mutual."

"Well, at least he'll still respect you in the morning."

Daemon choked. When he could breathe again, he almost asked about the tree but thought better of it. Andrew was the one who rode Demon.

After Guinness left to check on the feed, Daemon walked across the yard to where Andrew was grooming the horse.

Andrew looked up with a respectful smile. "You stayed on him."

"I stayed on him." Daemon watched the boy's smooth, easy motions. "But I had some trouble with him by a certain tree."

Andrew looked flustered. The hand brushing the stallion stuttered a little before picking up the rhythm again.

Daemon's eyes narrowed, and his voice turned dangerously silky. "What's special about that tree, Andrew?"

"Just a tree." Andrew glanced at Daemon's eyes and flinched. He shifted his feet, uneasy. "It's on the other side of the rise, you see. The first place out of sight of the house."

"So?"

"Well . . ." Andrew looked at Daemon, pleading. "You won't tell, will you?" He jerked his head toward the house. "It could cause a whole lot of trouble up there if they found out."

Daemon fought to keep his temper reined in. "Found out what?"

"About Miss Jaenelle."

Daemon shifted position, the motion so fluid and predatory that Andrew instantly stepped back, staying close to the horse as if for protection. "What about Miss Jaenelle?" he crooned.

Andrew gnawed on his lip. "At the tree . . . we . . ."

Daemon hissed.

Andrew paled, then flushed crimson. His eyes flashed with anger, and his fists clenched. "You . . . you think I'd . . ."

"Then what *do* you do at that tree?"

Andrew took a deep breath. "We change places."

Daemon frowned. "Change places?"

"Change horses. I've got a slight build. The pony can carry me."

"And she rides . . . ?"

Andrew put a tentative hand on the stallion's neck.

Daemon exploded. "You little son of a whoring bitch, you put a young girl up on *that*?"

The stallion snorted his displeasure at this display of temper.

Common sense and dancing hooves won out over Daemon's desire to throttle the stable lad.

Caught between the stallion and the angry Warlord Prince, Andrew's lips twitched with a wry smile. "You should see her up on *that*. And he takes care of her, too."

Daemon turned away, his anger spent. "Mother Night," he muttered, shaking his head as he walked toward the house and a welcome hot shower. "Mother Night."

CHAPTER SEVEN

1 / Terreille

"I just told you," Philip snapped. "You won't be needed today."

"I heard what you—"

A muscle in Philip's jaw twitched. "You have a free day. I realize Hayllians think we're a backward people, but we have museums and art galleries and theaters. There must be *something* you could do for a day that wouldn't be beneath you."

Daemon's eyes narrowed. At breakfast Leland had been skittish and unnaturally quiet, Alexandra had been unaccountably tense, Robert had been nowhere in sight, and now Philip was displaying this erratic anger and trying to force him out of the house for the day. "Very well."

Accepting a curt dismissal, he requested a carriage to take him into the shop district of Beldon Mor and went to the kitchen to see if Cook knew what was going on. But that lady, too, was in a fine fit of temper, and he retreated before she saw him, wincing as she slammed a heavy roasting pan onto her worktable.

He spent the morning wandering in and out of bookshops, gathering a variety of novels by Chaillot authors and puzzling over what could have put everyone in the household into such a state. Whatever it was, the answers weren't in the city.

He returned to the Angelline estate by lunchtime, only to find out that the entire family had left on an errand.

Annoyed at being thwarted, Daemon stacked the books on the writing desk, changed his clothes, and went to the stables.

There, too, everyone was on edge. Guinness snapped at the stable lads while they struggled to control overwrought horses.

"I'll take the stallion out if you want," Daemon offered.

"You tired of living?" Guinness snapped. He took a deep breath and relented. "It would help to get that one out of the yard for a while."

"Things are a bit tense around here."

"Ayah."

When Guinness offered nothing more, Daemon went to the stallion's box stall and waited for Andrew to saddle him. The boy's hands shook while he checked the girth. Tired of evasiveness, Daemon took the horse out of the yard and headed for the field.

Once they were out of the yard, Demon was eager, responsive, and excited. Whatever was setting the humans on edge, the stallion felt it too, but it made that simpler mind happy.

Not interested in a fight, Daemon turned them toward the tree.

Demon stopped at the tree and watched the rise they'd just come over, patiently waiting. The horse stood that way for ten minutes before eagerness gave way to dejection. When Daemon turned the horse toward the path, there was no resistance, and the gallop was halfhearted at best.

An hour later, Daemon handed the reins to Andrew and entered the house by a back door. He felt it as soon as he stepped through the doorway, and a rush of blazing anger crested and broke over him.

Striding through the corridors, Daemon slammed into his room, hurriedly showered and dressed. If he had encountered Philip during that brief walk to his room, he would have killed him.

How dare that Gray-Jeweled fool try to keep him away? How *dare* he?

Daemon knew his eyes were glazed with fury, but he didn't care. He tore out of his room and went hunting for the family.

He spun around a corner and skidded to a halt.

Wilhelmina looked pale but relieved. Graff scowled. Leland and Alexandra stared at him, startled and tense. Philip's shoulders straightened in obvious challenge.

Daemon saw it all in an instant and ignored it. The other girl commanded his full attention.

She looked emaciated, her arms and legs little more than sticks. Her head hung down, and lank strands of gold hair hid most of her face.

"Have you forgotten your manners?" Graff's bony fingers poked the girl's shoulder.

The girl's head snapped up at Graff's sharp prod, and her eyes, those *eyes,* locked onto his for a brief moment before she lowered her gaze, made a wobbly curtsy, and murmured, "Prince."

Daemon's heart pounded and his mouth watered.

Knowing he was out of control, he bowed curtly and harshly replied, "Lady." He nodded to Philip and the others, turned on his heel, and once out of sight, bolted for the library and locked the door.

His breath came in ragged sobs, his hands shook, and may the Darkness help him, he was on fire.

No, he thought fiercely as he stormed around the room looking for some explanation, some kind of escape. NO! He was not like Kartane. He had *never* hungered for a child's flesh. He was *not* like Kartane!

Collapsing against a bookcase, Daemon forced one shaking hand to slide to the mound between his trembling legs . . . and sobbed with relief to find those inches of flesh still flaccid . . . unlike the rest of him, which was seared by a fierce hunger.

Pushing away from the bookcase, Daemon went to the window and pressed his forehead against the cold glass. *Think, damn you, think.*

He closed his eyes and pictured the girl, piece by piece. As he concentrated on remembering her body, the fire eased. Until he remembered those sapphire eyes locking onto his.

Daemon laughed hysterically as tears rolled down his face.

He had accepted that Witch was a child, but he hadn't been prepared for his reaction when he finally saw her. He could take some comfort that he didn't want the child's body, but the hunger he felt for what lived inside that body scared him. The thought of being sent to another court where he couldn't see her at all scared him even more.

But it had been decades since he'd served in a court for more than a year. How was he going to keep this dance going until she was old enough to accept his surrender?

And how was he going to survive if he didn't stay?

2 / Terreille

Early the next morning Daemon staggered to the kitchen, his eyes hot and gritty from a sleepless night, his stomach aching from hunger. After leaving the library yesterday afternoon, he'd stayed in his room, unwilling to have dinner with the family and unwilling to meet anyone if he slipped down to the kitchen for something to eat.

As he reached the kitchen, the muffled giggles immediately stopped as two very different pairs of blue eyes watched him approach. Cook, looking happier than he'd ever seen her, gave him a warm greeting and told him the coffee was almost ready.

Moving cautiously, as though approaching something young and wild, Daemon sat down at one end of the kitchen table, on Jaenelle's left. With a pang of regret, he looked at the remains of a formidable breakfast and the one nutcake left on a plate.

There was an awkward moment of silence before Jaenelle leaned over and whispered something to Wilhelmina, Wilhelmina whispered something back, and the giggling started again.

Daemon reached for the nutcake, but, without looking, Jaenelle took it. She was just about to bite into it when Cook put the mug of coffee on the table and gasped.

"Now what's the Prince going to do for a breakfast, I ask you?" she demanded, but her eyes glowed with pride at the empty plates.

Jaenelle looked at the nutcake, reluctantly put it back on the plate, and edged the plate toward Daemon.

"It's all right," Daemon said mildly, looking directly at Cook. "I'm really not hungry."

Cook opened her mouth in astonishment, closed it again with a click of her teeth, and went back to her worktable, shaking her head.

He felt a warmth in his cheeks for telling so benign a white lie while those sapphire eyes studied him, so he concentrated on his coffee, avoiding her gaze.

Jaenelle broke the nutcake in half, handing him one half in a gesture that was no less a command for being unspoken, and began to eat the other half.

"You don't want to get yourself too stuffed during the day, you know,"

Cook said pleasantly as she puttered at her worktable. "We're having leg for dinner."

Daemon looked up, startled, as the nutcake Jaenelle was holding dropped to the table. He had never seen anyone go so deathly pale. Her eyes, enormous unblinking pools, stared straight ahead. Her throat worked convulsively.

Daemon pushed his chair back, ready to grab her and get her to the sink if she was going to be sick. "Don't you like lamb, Lady?" he asked softly.

She slowly turned her head toward him. He wanted to scream as his insides twisted at the pain and horror in her eyes. She blinked, fought for control. "L–lamb?"

Daemon gently closed one hand over hers. Her grip was painfully, surprisingly strong. Her eyes didn't waver from his, and he sensed that, with the physical link between them, he was completely vulnerable. There could be no dissembling, no white lies. "Lamb," he said reassuringly.

Jaenelle released his hand and looked away, and Daemon breathed a quiet sigh of relief.

Jaenelle turned to Wilhelmina. "Do you have time for a walk in the garden before you go to Graff?"

Wilhelmina's eyes flicked toward Daemon. "Yes. I take a walk most mornings."

Jaenelle was out of her chair, into her coat, and out the door before Wilhelmina got her chair pushed back.

"I'll be along in a minute," Daemon said quietly.

Wilhelmina slipped into her coat and hurried after her sister.

Cook shook her head. "I don't understand it. Miss Jaenelle has always liked lamb."

But you didn't say lamb, you said leg, Daemon thought as he shrugged into his topcoat. What other kind of leg would they serve in that hospital that would horrify a young girl so?

"Here." Cook handed him another mug of coffee and three apples. "At least this will get you started. Put the apples in your pocket—and mind you keep one for yourself."

Daemon slipped the apples into his pocket. "You're a darling," he said as he gave Cook a quick kiss on the cheek. He turned away to hide his smile and also so she could tell herself—and believe it—that he hadn't seen how flustered and pleased he'd made her.

The girls were nowhere in sight. Unconcerned, he strolled along the garden paths, sipping his coffee. He knew where to find them.

They were in the alcove, sitting on the iron bench.

Wilhelmina was chattering as though the words couldn't tumble out fast enough and gesturing with an animation startlingly at odds with the quiet, sedate girl he was accustomed to. When he approached, the chattering stopped and two pairs of eyes studied him.

Daemon polished two apples on his coat sleeve and solemnly gave one to each of them. Then he walked to the other end of the alcove. He couldn't make himself turn his back on them, couldn't give up looking at her altogether, but he settled his face into a bland expression and began to eat the apple. After a moment, the girls began to eat too.

Two pairs of eyes. Wilhelmina's eyes held a look of uncertainty, caution, hesitation. But Jaenelle's . . . When he came into the alcove, those eyes had told him she'd already come to some decision about him. He found it unnerving that he didn't know what it was.

And her voice. He was far enough away not to catch the quiet words, but the cadence of her voice was lovely, lilting, murmuring surf on a beach at sunset. He frowned, puzzled. Then, too, there was her accent. There was a common language among the Blood, even though the Old Tongue was almost forgotten, as well as a native language among each race. So every people, even speaking the same language, had a distinctive accent—and hers was different from the general Chaillot accent. It was a swirling kind of thing, as if she'd learned various words in various places and had melded them together into a voice distinctly her own. A lovely voice. A voice that could wash over a man and heal deep wounds of the heart.

The sudden silence caught him unaware, and he turned toward them, one eyebrow raised in question. Wilhelmina was looking at Jaenelle. Jaenelle was looking intently in the direction of the house.

"Graff's looking for you," Jaenelle said. "You'd better hurry."

Wilhelmina jumped up from the bench and ran lightly down the path.

Jaenelle shifted position on the seat and studied the bed of witchblood. "Did you know that if you sing to them correctly, they'll tell you the names of the ones who are gone?" Her eyes slid from the bed to study his face.

Daemon walked up to her slowly. "No, I didn't know."

"Well, they can." A bitter smile flickered on her lips, and for a brief moment there was a savage look in her eyes. "As long as Chaillot stands above the sea, the ones they were planted for won't be forgotten. And someday the blood debt will be paid in full."

Then she was a young girl again, and Daemon told himself, insisted, that the midnight, sepulchral voice he'd just heard was the result of his own light-headedness from lack of sleep and food.

"Come," Jaenelle said, waiting for him to fall into step. They strolled up the garden paths toward the house.

"Don't you have lessons with Lady Graff too?"

Anguish and grim resignation washed the air around her. "No," she said in a carefully neutral voice. "Graff says I have no ability in the Craft and there's no point holding Wilhelmina back, since I can't seem to learn even the simpler lessons."

Daemon slid a narrow-eyed look toward her and said nothing for a moment. "Then what do you do while Wilhelmina is having lessons?"

"Oh, I . . . do other things." She stopped quickly, head cocked, listening. "Leland wants you."

Daemon made a rude noise and was rewarded with an astonished giggle. Her pale, frail-looking hand gripped his arm and pulled him forward. His heart thumped crazily as she tugged him up the path, laughing. They continued playing all the way to the house. She tugged, he protested. Finally she tugged him into the kitchen, through the kitchen, ignoring Cook's astonished gasp, and toward the doorway leading into the corridor.

Two feet from the doorway, Daemon dug in his heels. Leland could go to Hell for all he cared. He wanted to stay with Jaenelle.

She pressed her hands against his back and propelled him through the doorway.

Landing on the other side, Daemon spun around and stared at a closed door. There hadn't been time for her to close a door. Come to think of it, he didn't remember there *being* an actual door there.

Daemon stared a moment longer, his eyes molten gold, his lips fighting to break into a grin. He made another rude noise for the benefit of whoever might be listening on the other side of the door, shrugged out of his coat, and went to see what Leland wanted.

3 / Terreille

Daemon undid the silk tie and loosened his collar. After the morning walk, he'd gone shopping with Leland. Until now he hadn't cared what she wore, except to acknowledge to himself that the frilliness of her clothes and the frothiness of her personality irritated him. Today he saw her as Jaenelle's mother, and he'd coaxed and cajoled her into a blue silk dress with simple lines that suited her trim body. She'd been different after that, more at ease. Even her voice didn't scrape his nerves as it usually did.

When Leland's shopping was done, he'd had the afternoon to himself. In any other court, he would have put the time to good use reviewing the papers his man of business sent to a post box in the city.

They would be amazed, he thought with a chilly smile, if they knew how much of their little island he owned.

Gambling at business was a mental game he excelled in. With the annual income he drew in from all corners of the Realm, he could have owned every plank of wood and every nail in Beldon Mor—and that didn't count the half dozen accounts in Hayll that Dorothea knew about and plundered occasionally when her lifestyle exceeded her own income. He always kept enough in those accounts to convince her that they were his total investments. For himself . . . Without the freedom to live as he chose, his personal indulgences were clothes and books, the books being the more personal acquisition since the clothes, like his body, were used to manipulate whomever he served.

In any other court, he would have put a free afternoon to good use. Today he'd been bored, bored, bored, chafing because he was forbidden the nursery wing and whatever was going on there.

The evening had been taken up with dinner and the theater. On the spur of the moment, Robert had decided to go with them, and Daemon had found the jockeying for seats in their private box and the tension between Philip and Robert more interesting than the play.

So here he was at the end of the day, unable to stop his restless wandering. He walked past the Craft library and stopped, his attention caught by the faint light coming from beneath the door.

The moment he opened the door, the light went out.

Daemon slipped into the room and raised his hand. The candle-light in the far corner glowed dimly, but the light was sufficient.

His golden eyes shone with pleasure as he wound his way through the cluttered room until he was standing by the bookcases, looking at a golden-haired head studiously looking at the floor. Her bare feet peeked out from beneath her nightgown.

"It's late, little one." He chided himself for the purring, seductive throb in his voice, but there was nothing he could do about it. "Shouldn't you be in bed?"

Jaenelle looked up. The distrust in her eyes was a cold slap in the face. That morning he'd been her playmate. Why was he suddenly a stranger and suspect?

Trying to think of something to say, Daemon noticed a book on the top shelf that was pulled halfway out. Taking a hopeful guess about the reason for her sudden distrust, he pulled the book off the shelf and read the title, one eyebrow rising in surprise. If this was her idea of bedtime reading, it was no wonder she had no use for Graff's Craft lessons. Without a word, he gave her the book and reached up to brush the others on the top shelf. When he was done, the space where the book had been was no longer there, and anyone quickly glancing at the shelves wouldn't notice its absence.

Well? He didn't say it. He didn't send it. Still, he was asking the question and waiting for an answer.

Jaenelle's lips twitched. Beneath the wariness was amusement. Beneath that . . . perhaps the faintest glimmer of trust?

"Thank you, Prince," Jaenelle said with laughter in her voice.

"You're very welcome." He hesitated. "My name is Daemon."

"It would be impolite to call you that. You are my elder."

He snarled, frustrated.

Laughing, she gave him an impudent curtsy and left the room.

"Irritating chit," he growled as he left the library and returned to his room. But the gentle, hopeful smile wouldn't stop tugging at his lips.

Alexandra sat on her bed, her arms wrapped around her knees. A bell cord hung on either side of her bed. The one on the left would summon her maid. The one on the right—she looked at it for the sixth time in fifteen minutes—would ring in the bedroom below hers.

She rested her head on her arms and sighed.

He had looked so damned elegant in those evening clothes so perfectly cut to show off that magnificent body and beautiful face. When he'd
spoken to her, his voice had been such a sensual caress it had caused a fluttering in her stomach—a feeling no other man had ever produced. That
voice and body were maddening because he seemed completely unaware
of the effect he had. At the theater, there'd been more opera glasses focused on him than on the stage.

There was his reputation to consider. However, outside of his being
coolly civil, she had found nothing to fault him on. He answered when
summoned, performed his duties as an escort with intuition and grace,
was always courteous if never flattering—and produced so much sexual
heat that every woman who had been in the theater was going to be
looking for a consort or a lover tonight.

And that was the problem, wasn't it?

She hadn't had a steady lover since she'd asked Philip to take care of
Leland's Virgin Night. She'd always known about Philip's passionate love
for her daughter. It wouldn't have been fair to any of them to demand his
presence in her bed after that night.

While a part of her objected to keeping males solely for sexual purposes,
her body hadn't given up craving a man's touch. Most of the time, she satisfied that craving whenever she was a guest at a lower Queen's court—or
when she sneaked away to spend a night or two with a couple of Black
Widow friends and feasted on and with the males who served that coven.

Now, in the room below hers, there was a Warlord Prince who made
her pulse race, a Warlord Prince who had centuries of training in providing sexual pleasure, a Warlord Prince who was hers to command.

If she dared.

Alexandra pulled the bell cord on the right side. She waited a minute
and pulled it again. How did one act with a pleasure slave? They weren't
considered in the same category as consorts or lovers, that much she
knew. But what should she do? What should she say?

Alexandra combed her hair with her fingers. She would figure it out.
She had to. If she didn't get some relief tonight, she would go mad.

Despite her frustration, she almost gave up and turned off her light, almost felt relieved that he hadn't obeyed, when there was a quiet tap on
her door.

"Come in." She sat up, trying for a measure of dignity. Her palms were wet with nervous sweat. She flushed when he entered the room and leaned back against the door. He was still in evening dress, but his hair was slightly disheveled, and the half-unbuttoned shirt gave her a glimpse of his smooth, muscular chest.

Her body reacted to his physical presence, leaving her unable to think, unable to speak. She had resisted this since he arrived, but now she wanted to know what it felt like to have him in her bed.

For a long time, he said nothing. He did nothing. He leaned against the door and stared at her.

And something dangerous flickered in his golden eyes.

She waited, unwilling to dismiss him, too frightened to demand.

In the end, he came to the bed and showed her what a pleasure slave could do.

4 / Hell

Saetan ignored the light tap on his study door, as he had ignored everything these past few weeks. He watched the doorknob turn, but the door was Black-locked, and whoever was on the other side would stay on the other side.

The knob turned again and the door opened.

His lips curling in a snarl at this blatant intrusion, he limped around the desk and froze as Jaenelle slipped through the door and closed it behind her. She stood there, shy and uncertain.

"Jaenelle," he whispered. "Jaenelle!"

He opened his arms. She ran across the room and leaped into them, her thin arms gripping his neck in a stranglehold.

Saetan staggered as his weak leg started to give, but he got them to a chair by the fire. He buried his face in the crook of her neck, his arms tight around her. "Jaenelle," he whispered over and over as he kissed her forehead, kissed her cheeks. "Where have you been?"

After a while, Jaenelle braced her hands on his shoulders and pushed back. She studied his face and frowned. "You're limping again," she said in an aggrieved voice.

"The leg's weak," he replied curtly, dismissing it.

She unbuttoned the top of her blouse and pushed back the collar.

"No," he said firmly.

"You need the blood. You're limping again."

"No. You've been ill."

"No, I haven't," she protested sharply and then quickly looked away.

Saetan's eyes turned hard yellow, and he drew in a hissing breath. *If you haven't been ill, witch-child, then what was done to your body was done deliberately. I haven't forgotten the last time I saw you. That family of yours has much to explain.*

"Not really ill," Jaenelle amended.

It almost sounded like she was pleading with him to agree. But, Hell's fire, how could he look at her and agree?

"The blood's strong, Saetan." She definitely was pleading now. "And you need the blood."

"Not while you need every drop for yourself," Saetan snarled. He tried to shift position, but with Jaenelle straddling him, he was effectively tethered. He sighed. He knew that determined look too well. She wasn't about to let him go until he'd taken the blood.

And it occurred to him that she had her own reasons for wanting to give it beyond it being beneficial to him. She seemed more fragile—and not just physically. It was as if rejecting the blood would confirm some deep-seated fear she was trying desperately to control.

That decided him. He gently closed his mouth on her neck.

He took a long time to take very little, savoring the contact, hoping she would be fooled. When he finally lifted his head and pressed his finger against the wound to heal it, he read doubt in her eyes. Well, two could play that game.

"Where have you been, witch-child?" he asked so gently that it was a whip-crack demand.

The question effectively silenced her protest. She gave him a bland, innocent look. "Saetan, is there anything to eat?"

Stalemate, as he'd known it would be.

"Yes," he said dryly, "I think we can come up with something."

Jaenelle edged backward out of the chair and watched him struggle to his feet. Without a word, she fetched the cane leaning against the blackwood desk and handed it to him.

Saetan grimaced but took the cane. With one arm resting lightly around her shoulders, they left the study and the lower, rough-hewn corridors, traveled the upstairs labyrinth of hallways, and finally reached the double front doors. He led her around the side of the Hall to the Sanctuary that held the Dark Altar.

"There's a Dark Altar next to the Hall?" Jaenelle asked as she looked around with interest.

Saetan chuckled softly as he lit the four black candles in proper order. "Actually, witch-child, the Hall is built next to the Altar."

Her eyes widened as the stone wall behind the Altar turned to mist. "Ooohh," she whispered in a voice as close to awe as he'd ever heard from her. "Why's it doing that?"

"It's a Gate," Saetan replied, puzzled.

"A Gate?"

He pushed the words out. "A Gate between the Realms."

"Ooohh."

His mind stumbled. Since she'd been traveling between the Realms for years now, he'd always assumed she knew how to open the Gates. If she didn't even know there *were* Gates, how in the name of Hell had she been getting into Kaeleer and Hell all this time?

He couldn't ask. He wouldn't ask. If he asked, she'd tell him and then he'd have to strangle her.

He held out his hand. "Walk forward through the mist. By the time you count slowly to four, we'll be through the Gate."

Once they were on the other side, he led her back around the side of the Hall and through the front doors.

"Where are we?" Jaenelle asked as she studied the prisms made by the arched, leaded-glass window above the doors.

"SaDiablo Hall," he replied mildly.

Jaenelle turned slowly and shook her head. "This isn't the Hall."

"Oh, but it is, witch-child. We just went through a Gate, remember? This is the Hall in the Shadow Realm. We're in Kaeleer."

"So there really is a Shadow Realm," she murmured as she opened a door and peered into the room.

Certain she hadn't meant for him to hear that, he didn't answer. He simply filed it with the other troubling, unanswered questions that shrouded his fair-haired Lady. But it made him doubly relieved that he'd decided to introduce her to the Hall in Kaeleer.

Even before her long disappearance, he'd wanted to wean her away from Hell. He knew she would still visit Char and the rest of the *cildru dy-athe,* would visit Titian, but Hekatah was too much in evidence lately, stirring up mischief with the small group of demon witches she called her coven, mischief designed to distract him, draw his attention, while her smug smiles and overly contrite apologies filled him with a dread that was slowly crystallizing into icy rage. Every day he kept Jaenelle away from Hekatah was one more day of safety for them all.

Jaenelle finished her peek at the rooms off the great hall and skipped back to him, her eyes sparkling. "It's wonderful, Saetan."

He slipped his arm around her shoulders and kissed the top of her head. "And somewhere among all these corridors is a kitchen and an excellent cook named Mrs. Beale."

They both looked up at the *click-click* of shoes coming purposefully toward them from the service corridor at the end of the great hall. Saetan smiled, recognizing that distinctive *click-click*. Helene, coming to see exactly who was in "her" house. He started to tell Jaenelle who was coming, but he was too stunned to speak.

Her face was the coldest, smoothest, most malevolent mask he had ever seen. Her sapphire eyes were maelstroms. The power in her didn't spill out in an ever-widening ring as it would have with any other witch whose temper was up, acting as a warning to whoever approached. No, it was pulling inward, spiraling downward to her core, where she would then turn it outward, with devastating results. She was turning cold, cold, cold, and he was helpless to stop her, helpless to bridge the distance that was suddenly, inexplicably, between them. She twitched her shoulders from beneath his arm, and with a grace that would have made any predator envious, began to glide in front of him.

Saetan glanced up. Helene would enter the great hall at any moment—and die. He summoned the power in his Jewels, summoned all his strength. Everything was going to ride on one word.

He thrust out his right hand, the Black Jewel ablaze, stopping Jaenelle's movement. "Lady," he said in a commanding voice.

Jaenelle looked at him. He shivered but kept his hand steady. "When Protocol is being observed and a Warlord Prince makes a request of his Queen, she graciously yields to his request unless she's no longer willing to have him serve. I ask that you trust my judgment in choosing who serves us at the Hall. I ask permission to introduce you to the housekeeper, who will do her utmost to serve you well. I ask that you accompany me to the dining room for something to eat."

He had never taught her about Protocol, about the subtle checks and balances of power among the Blood. He had assumed she'd picked up the basics through day-to-day living and observation. He'd thought he would have time to teach her the fine points of interaction between Queens and dark-Jeweled males. Now it was the only leash he had. If she failed to answer . . . "Please, witch-child," he whispered just as Helene entered the great hall and stopped.

The Darkness swirled around him. Mother Night! He'd never felt anything like this!

Jaenelle studied his right hand for a long time before slowly placing her hand over it. He shuddered, unable to control it, seeing the truth for just a moment before she kindly shut him out.

"This is my housekeeper, Helene," Saetan said, never taking his eyes off Jaenelle. "Helene, this is Lady—" He hesitated, at a loss. To say "Lady Jaenelle" was too familiar.

Jaenelle turned her maelstrom eyes on Helene, who cringed but, with the instinct of a small hunted creature, didn't move. "Angelline." The word rolled out of her in a midnight whisper.

"Angelline." Saetan looked at Helene, willing her to remain calm. "My dear, would you see what Mrs. Beale might have for us today?"

Helene remembered her station and curtsied. "Of course, High Lord," she replied with dignity. Turning around, she left the great hall with a steady, measured step that Saetan silently applauded.

Jaenelle moved away from him, her head down, her shoulders slumped.

"Witch-child?" Saetan asked gently.

The eyes that met his were pained and haunted, full of a grieving that twisted his heart because he didn't know what caused it—or, perhaps, because he did.

He hadn't shuddered because, with her touch, he had found himself looking at power as far beneath him as he was to the White. He hadn't turned away from *her*. It was what he had seen there that horrified him—during those months when she'd been gone, she'd learned the one lesson he had never wanted her to learn.

She had learned to hate.

Now he had to find a way to convince her that he hadn't turned away from her because of what she was, had to bridge the distance between them, had to find a way to bring her back. He had to understand.

"Witch-child," he said in a carefully neutral voice, "why were you going to strike Helene?"

"She's a stranger."

Rocked by her cold response, Saetan's weak leg buckled. Her arms immediately wrapped around his waist, and he didn't feel the floor at all. Somewhat bemused, he looked down and tapped the floor with his shoe. He stood on air, a quarter inch above the floor. If he walked normally, it would take a keen eye to realize he wasn't walking on the floor itself. That and the lack of sound.

"It will help you," Jaenelle explained, her voice so full of apology and concern that the arm he'd been sliding around her shoulders pulled her to him in a fierce hug.

As they walked toward the dining room, Saetan used the excuse of his weak leg to move slowly, to give himself time to think. He had to understand what had brought out that ferocity in her.

Helene was a stranger, true. But he had a score of names on a sheet of paper locked in his desk drawer, and all of them had been strangers once. Because Helene was an adult? No. Cassandra was an adult. So was Titian, so was Prothvar, Andulvar, and Mephis. So was he. Because Helene was living? No, that wasn't the answer either.

In frustration, he replayed the last few minutes, forcing himself to view it from a distance. The sound of footsteps, the sudden change in Jaenelle, her predatory glide . . . in front of him.

He stopped suddenly, shocked, but got tugged along for a few more steps before Jaenelle realized he wasn't trying to walk.

He'd wondered what her reaction would be to being with him in Kaeleer, being with him outside the Realm he ruled, and now he knew. She cared for him. She was ready to protect him because, to her anyway, a weak leg might make him vulnerable against an adversary.

Saetan smiled, squeezed her shoulder, and began walking again.

Geoffrey had been right. He had a more potent leash than Protocol to keep her in check. Unfortunately, that leash worked two ways, so from now on, he was going to have to be very, very careful.

★   ★   ★

Saetan looked with growing dismay at the amount of food on the table. Along with a bowl of stew and sticks of cornbread, there were fruit, cheese, nutcakes, cold ham, cold beef, a whole roasted chicken, a platter of vegetables, fresh bread, honeybutter, and a pitcher of milk. It ended there only because he'd refused to allow the footman to bring in the last heavily laden tray. The volume would have daunted a hungry full-grown male, let alone a young girl.

Jaenelle stared at the dishes arranged in a half-circle around her place at the table.

"Eat your stew while it's hot," Saetan suggested mildly, sipping a glass of yarbarah.

Jaenelle picked up her spoon and began to eat, but after one bite she put the spoon down, once more shy and uncertain.

Saetan began to talk in a leisurely manner. Since he talked as if he had nothing else to do and nowhere else to go and was going to sit at the table for quite some time, Jaenelle picked up the spoon again. He noticed that every time he stopped talking she put the spoon down, as if she didn't want her eating to detain him. So he gossiped, telling her about Mephis, Prothvar, Andulvar, Geoffrey, and Draca, but he ran out very quickly. *The dead don't do much,* he thought dryly as he launched into a long discourse about the book he'd been reading, completely unconcerned with whether or not it was over her head.

He started feeling a bit desperate about what to say next when she finally leaned back, her hands folded over a bulging tummy, and gave him the sweet, sleepy smile of a well-fed, content child. He put his glass up to his lips to hide his smile and briefly glanced at the carnage in front of him. Perhaps he'd been too hasty in sending that last tray back to the kitchen.

"I have a surprise for you," he said, biting his cheek as she wrestled herself into a sitting position.

He led her to the second floor of his wing. The doors along the right side led into his suite of rooms. He opened a door on the left.

He had put a lot of thought into these rooms. The bedroom had the feel of a seascape with its soft, shell-colored walls, plush sandy carpets, deep sea-blue counterpane on the huge bed, warm brown furniture, and throw pillows the color of dune grass. The adjoining sitting room belonged to the earth. The rooms still required personal touches that he'd deliberately kept absent to make them feminine.

Jaenelle admired, examined, exclaimed, and shouted back to him when she saw the bathroom, "You could swim in this bathtub!"

When she finally returned to him, he asked, "Do you like them?"

She smiled at him and nodded.

"I'm glad, because they're your rooms." He ignored her delighted gasp and continued. "Of course, they'll need your personal touches and lady's paraphernalia to give them character, and I didn't put any paintings on the walls. Those are for you to choose."

"My rooms?"

"Whenever you want to use them, whether I'm here or not. A quiet place, all your own."

He watched with pleasure as she explored the rooms again, a territorial gleam in her eyes. His smile didn't fade until she tried the door on the opposite side of the bedroom. Finding it locked, she turned away, not interested enough to question it.

When Jaenelle returned to the bathroom to ponder the possibilities of the bathtub, Saetan studied the locked door.

He loved her dearly, but he was no fool. On the other side of that locked door was another suite of rooms, somewhat smaller but no less carefully decorated. Someday a consort would reside in those rooms whenever she came to visit. For now, or at least until she asked, there was no reason to tell her what was on the other side of that door or what its occupant would be for.

"Saetan?"

He came out of his dark reverie to find her beside him again, her happiness putting a little color back into her cheeks. "Do you think we could begin my lessons again?"

"Of course." He thought for a moment. "Do you know how to create witchlight?"

Jaenelle shook her head.

"Then that's a good place to begin." He paused and added casually, "How about having your lessons here?"

"Here?"

"Yes, here. That way—"

"But then I wouldn't see Andulvar and Prothvar and Mephis," Jaenelle protested.

For the briefest moment, he was honest enough to acknowledge the jealousy he felt at her wanting to see them, at her not being exclusively his. "Of course you can see them," he said mildly, trying not to grind his teeth. "There's no reason they can't come here."

"I thought demons didn't leave Hell."

"Most of the time it's more comfortable for the dead to remain among the dead, just as it's more comfortable for the living for the dead to remain among the dead. But we all lived so long ago . . ." He shrugged. "Besides, even if it's been a long time, Mephis has been here and still handles a number of my business arrangements in this Realm. I think he would enjoy an excuse to get out of the Dark Realm—as would Andulvar and Prothvar." He hoped he wasn't going to botch this by being too sly. "And when your lessons are over, you could stop in and see your friends in Kaeleer more easily."

"That's true," Jaenelle said slowly, considering. "That way, most of the time I'd only have to jump the Webs once instead of twice." Her eyes lit up and she snapped her fingers. "Or I can even use the Gates if you show me how to open them."

His mind didn't stumble. It went head over mental heels and landed in a heap. He tried to swallow, but his mouth was desert dry. "Quite so," he finally choked out. He definitely had to strangle her. Otherwise, he'd do himself an injury with the mental acrobatics required to translate the impossible into something reasonably probable. "Your lessons," he croaked, hoping, a bit hysterically, that this would be a safe subject.

Jaenelle beamed at him, and he sighed, defeated.

"When would you like to begin?"

Jaenelle thought about this. "It's getting late today. I'll be missed if I don't come to lunch." She wrinkled her nose. "I should see Lorn tomorrow. I haven't seen him in a while and he'll be worried."

He'll be worried! Saetan bit back a growl.

"The day after tomorrow? Wilhelmina has her lessons in the morning, so no one would really miss me before lunchtime."

"Done." He kissed the top of her head, led her to the front door of the Hall, and watched her vanish as she waved good-bye. He stayed long enough to make sure Helene was over any shock she might have had, left explicit instructions about conduct when Jaenelle arrived—particularly if she arrived without him—and made his way back to his private study in the Dark Realm.

Andulvar found him there a little later, pouring a very large brandy. The Eyrien's eyes narrowed when he noticed Saetan's shaking hands. "What are you doing?"

"I'm going to get very drunk," Saetan replied calmly, taking a large swallow of brandy. "Care to join me?"

"Demons don't drink straight alcohol, and for that matter, neither should Guardians. Besides," Andulvar persisted as Saetan knocked back a second glass, "why do you want to get drunk?"

"Because I'll strangle her if I don't get drunk."

"The waif's back and you didn't tell us?" Andulvar braced his fists on his hips and growled, "Why do you want to strangle her?"

Saetan carefully poured his third large brandy. Why had he given up drinking brandy? Such a delightful drink. Like pouring water on a blazing mental fire. Or was it like pouring oil? No matter. "Did you know she jumps the Webs?"

Andulvar shrugged, unimpressed. "At least half the Jeweled Blood can jump between the ranks of the Winds."

"She doesn't jump between the ranks, my darling Andulvar, she jumps between the Realms."

Andulvar gulped. "That isn't possible," he gasped, grateful that Saetan was pouring brandy into a second glass.

"That's what I always thought. And I'm not even going to think about the danger of doing it while I can still think. That's how she's been coming and going all these years, by the way. Until today, she didn't know there were Gates."

Andulvar eyed the bottle of brandy. "That's not enough to get us both drunk—assuming, of course, it's still *possible* to get drunk."

"There's more."

"Ah, well, then."

They settled in the chairs by the fire, intent upon their task.

5 / Hell

"Guardians shouldn't drink, you know," Geoffrey said, too amused to be sympathetic.

Saetan gave the other Guardian a baleful look, then closed his eyes, hoping they would just fall out so at least some part of his head didn't hurt. He cringed when Geoffrey scraped his chair along the library floor and sat down.

"Names again?" Geoffrey asked, keeping his voice low.

"A surname, Angelline, probably from Chaillot, and Wilhelmina."

"A surname and a place to start. You're too kind, Saetan."

"I wish you dead." Saetan winced at the sound of his own voice.

"Wish granted," Geoffrey replied cheerfully as he left to get the appropriate register.

The library door opened. Draca, the Keep's Seneschal, glided to the table and placed a cup in front of Saetan. "Thiss will help," she said as she turned away. "Although you don't desserve it."

Saetan sipped the steaming brew, grimaced at the taste, but got down half of it. He leaned back in the chair, his hands loosely clasped around the cup, and listened to Geoffrey considerately turn the register's pages with the least possible amount of noise. By the time he finished the brew Draca had made, the pages had stopped turning.

Geoffrey's black eyebrows formed a V below his prominent widow's peak. He pressed his sensuous bloodred lips together. "Well," he said finally, "there's a Chaillot witch named Alexandra Angelline, who is the Queen of the Territory. She wears the Blood Opal. Her daughter, Leland, wears the Rose and is married to a Yellow-Jeweled Warlord named Robert Benedict. There's no witch named Wilhelmina Angelline, but there is a Wilhelmina Benedict who is fourteen years old, Chaillot-born, and wears the Purple Dusk."

Saetan sat very still. "Any other family connections?" he asked too quietly.

Geoffrey glanced up sharply. "Only one of interest. A Gray-Jeweled Prince named Philip Alexander shares a paternal bloodline with Robert Benedict and serves Alexandra Angelline. If the bloodline wasn't formally acknowledged, it's not unusual for a bastard to take a surname that reflects the Queen he serves."

"I'm aware of that. What about Jaenelle?"

Geoffrey shook his head. "Not listed."

Saetan steepled his fingers. "She said her name was Angelline, which would indicate that she, at least, is continuing the old tradition of the distaff gender following the matriarchal bloodline. She said she could come in the mornings when Wilhelmina had her lessons. Same family?"

Geoffrey closed the book. "Probably. Terreille has become lax about registering Blood family lines. But if they registered one child, why not the other?"

"Because one child wears Purple Dusk," Saetan replied with a cold smile. "They don't realize the other child wears the Jewels at all."

"Considering the fair-haired Lady, it would be hard to miss."

Saetan shook his head. "No, it wouldn't. She's never worn the Jewels she was gifted with, and she's lousy at basic Craft. If she never mentioned the more creative ways she uses Craft, they would have no way of knowing she could do anything at all." A cold fist settled between his shoulder blades. "Unless they didn't believe her," he finished softly, remembering what Jaenelle had said about the Shadow Realm. He filed that thought for later consideration and looked at the empty cup. "This stuff tastes vile, but it is helping my head. Any chance of another cup?"

"Always a chance," Geoffrey said with a hint of laughter in his voice as he pulled the bell cord. "Especially if it tastes vile."

Saetan brushed his fingers against his chin. "Geoffrey, you've been the Keep's librarian for a long, long time and probably know more about the Blood than the rest of us put together. Have you ever heard of anyone spiraling down to reach the depth of her Jewels?"

"Spiraling?" Geoffrey thought for a moment and shook his head. "No, but that doesn't mean it can't happen. Ask Draca. Compared to her, you're still in the nursery and I'm just a stripling." He pursed his lips and frowned. "There's something I read once, a long time ago, part of a poem, I think, about the great dragons of legend. How did it go? 'They spiral down into ebony—' "

" '—catching the sstars with their tailss.' " The cup in front of Saetan vanished as Draca placed the fresh one before him.

"That's it," Geoffrey said. "Saetan was asking if it was possible for the Blood to spiral down to the core."

Draca turned her head, her slow, careful movement a testimony more to great age than to grace, and fixed her reptilian eyes on Saetan. "You wish to undersstand thiss?"

Saetan looked into those ancient eyes and reluctantly nodded.

"Remove the book," Draca said to Geoffrey. She waited until she had their complete attention. "Not the Blood."

A square tank filled with water appeared on the table, each side as long as Saetan's arm and just as high. Slowly withdrawing her hands from the long sleeves of her robe, Draca opened one loosely clenched fist over the tank. Little bangles, the kind that women sew on clothing to shimmer in the light, fell into the water and floated on the surface. The bangles were the same colors as the Jewels.

In her other hand, Draca held a smooth egg-shaped stone attached to a thin silk cord. "I will demonsstrate the wayss the Blood reach the inner web, the Sself'ss core." Slowly and smoothly she lowered the stone into the water until it was suspended an inch above the bottom of the tank. She had broken the water with such ease that there was no disturbance. The bangles floated on the still surface.

"When desscent into the abysss or asscent out of the abysss iss made sslowly," she said, pulling the stone toward the surface, "it iss a private matter, a communion with onesself. It doess not dissturb thosse around. When anger, fear, or great need requiress a fasst desscent to the core to gather the power and asscend . . ." She dropped the stone into the tank. It plunged to the full length of the cord, stopping an inch above the bottom.

Saetan and Geoffrey silently watched the ripples on the surface spread out toward the edge of the tank, watched the bangles dance on the ever-widening rings.

Draca quickly jerked her hand. The stone shot straight up out of the tank, a little jet of water coming with it. Tossed back and forth in the waves, some of the light-colored bangles sank.

Draca waited for them to absorb this. "A sspiral."

The stone moved in a circular motion above the tank. As it touched the surface, the water moved with it, circling, circling, circling as the stone leisurely made its descent. The bangles, caught in the motion, followed the stone. The spiraling descent continued until the stone was an inch from the bottom. By then all the water was in motion, all the bangles caught.

"A whirlpool," Geoffrey whispered. He glanced uneasily at Saetan, who was watching the tank, his lips pressed tight, his long nails digging into the table.

"No." Draca pulled the stone straight up. The water rose with the stone, well above the tank, and splashed down on the table. The bangles, pulled out of the tank with the water, lay on the table like tiny dead fish. "A maelsstrom."

Saetan turned away. "You said the Blood don't spiral."

Draca put her hand on his arm, forcing him to turn and look at her. "Sshe iss more than Blood. Sshe iss Witch."

"It doesn't matter if she's Witch. She's still Blood."

"Sshe iss Blood and sshe iss Other."

"No." Saetan backed away from Draca. "She's still Blood. She's still one of us. She has to be." And she was still his gentle, inquisitive Jaenelle, the daughter of his soul. Nothing anyone could say would change that.

But someone had taught her to hate.

"Sshe iss Witch," Draca said with more gentleness than he'd ever heard from her. "Sshe will almosst alwayss sspiral, High Lord. You cannot alter her nature. You cannot prevent the ssmall sspiralss, the flashess of anger. You cannot prevent her from sspiraling down to her core. All the Blood needss to desscend from time to time. But the maelsstrom . . ." Draca slipped her hands into the sleeves of her robe. "Sshield her, Ssaetan. Sshield her with your sstrength and your love and perhapss it will never happen."

"And if it does?" Saetan asked hoarsely.

"It will be the end of the Blood."

CHAPTER EIGHT

1 / Terreille

Daemon shuffled the deck of cards as Leland glanced at the clock—again. They'd been playing cards for almost two hours, and if she followed the routine, she would let him go in ten minutes or one more hand, whichever came first.

It was the third night that week that Leland had requested his company when she retired. Daemon didn't mind playing cards, but it annoyed him that she insisted on playing in her sitting room instead of the drawing room downstairs. And her coquettish remarks at breakfast about how well he'd entertained her annoyed him even more.

The first morning after they'd played cards, Robert had flushed burgundy and blustered as he listened to Leland's chatter until he noticed Philip's silent rage. After that, since a pleasure slave wasn't considered a "real" man and, therefore, wasn't a rival, Robert had gleefully patted Leland's hand and told her he was pleased that she found Sadi such good company since he had to work so many evenings.

Philip, on the other hand, became brutally terse, tossing the day's itinerary at Daemon and spitting out verbal orders. He also joined Daemon and the girls for their morning walk, putting Jaenelle and Wilhelmina on either side of him, forcing Daemon to follow behind.

Neither man's reaction pleased Daemon, and Leland's pretending to be oblivious to the mounting tension pleased him even less. She wasn't as frothy or feather-headed as he'd first thought. When they played cards alone and she concentrated on the game, he saw the quiet cunning in her, the skill at dissembling so that, superficially at least, she fit into Robert's circle of society.

None of that explained why she was using him as a tease. Philip was jealous enough of his brother's right to stretch out in Leland's bed. She didn't have to flaunt another male at him.

Daemon curbed his impatience and concentrated on the cards. Leland's reason for watching the clock was no concern of his. He had his own reasons for wanting the evening to end.

Finally dismissed, Daemon headed for the Craft library. Finding it empty, he throttled the desire to destroy the room out of frustration.

That was the most irritating part about Leland's sudden attention. Jaenelle always took a nocturnal ramble around midnight, ending in the library, where he usually found her poring over some of the old Craft books. He kept his intrusions brief, never asked why she was roaming the house at that hour, and was rewarded with equally brief, although sometimes startling, snippets of conversation.

Those snippets fascinated him. They were an unsettling blend of innocence and dark perception, ignorance and knowledge. If, during their conversation, he managed to note the book and the section she was reading, he could sometimes, if he worked at it, untangle a little of what she'd said. Other times he felt as if he were holding a handful of pieces to a jigsaw puzzle the size of Chaillot itself. It was infuriating—and it was wonderful.

Daemon had almost given up waiting when the door suddenly opened and Jaenelle popped into the room. Twitching his hips out of the way so she wouldn't brush against him below the waist—something he'd taken great care to avoid since he wasn't sure what his physical reaction would be—he put his hand on her shoulder to steady her and keep her from bolting when she realized someone was in the room.

He felt a giddy pleasure when she wasn't surprised to see him. As he closed the door and lit the shaded candle-light, her right hand fluffed her hair, something she did when thinking.

"Do you like to play cards?" she asked when they'd settled on the dark brown leather couch, a discreet distance between them.

"Yes, I do," Daemon replied cautiously. Did nothing go on in this house that she didn't know about? That idea didn't please him. If she knew about his playing cards with Leland, what did she know, or understand, about his required visits to Alexandra's room?

Jaenelle fluffed her hair. "If it rains some morning and we can't take a walk, maybe you could play a card game with Wilhelmina and me."

Daemon relaxed a little. "I'd like that very much."

"Why doesn't Leland say you were playing cards? Why does she make it sound so secrety? Does she always lose?"

"No, she doesn't always lose." Daemon tried not to squirm. Why did she ask so damn many uncomfortable questions? "I think ladies like to seem mysterious."

"Or they may know things that need to stay hidden."

For a moment, Daemon forgot how to breathe. His right hand clenched the top of the couch and he winced. Damn. He'd let it slip up on him. The snake tooth had to be milked, and he hadn't taken the time to find an easily obtainable poison that wouldn't make him ill.

Jaenelle looked intently at his hand.

Suddenly uneasy, Daemon shifted position, casually dropping that hand in his lap. He'd guarded the secret of the snake tooth for centuries, and he wasn't about to tell a twelve-year-old girl about it.

He hadn't counted on her tenacity or her strength. Her hand closed on his wrist and pulled upward. He made a fist to hide his nails and pulled back, trying to break her hold. When he couldn't, he snarled in anger. It was a sound that had made strong men back away and Queens think twice about what they had ordered him to do.

Jaenelle simply looked him in the eyes. Daemon looked away first, shaking slightly as he opened his hand for her examination.

Her touch was feather-light, gentle, and knowing. She studied each finger in turn, finding the length of his nails of particular interest, and finally focused on the ring finger for a long time.

"This one's warmer than the others," she said, half to herself. "And there's something beneath it."

Daemon jumped up, pulling her halfway to the floor before she let go of his wrist. "Leave it alone, Lady," he said tightly, carefully putting his hands in his pockets.

Out of the corner of his eye, Daemon watched her resettle on the couch and study her own hands. It seemed as if she were struggling to say something, and it struck him that she, too, was considering what might inadvertently be revealed.

Finally she said shyly, "I know some healing Craft."

"I'm not ill," Daemon replied, staring straight ahead.

"But not well." Suddenly her voice sounded years older.

"There's nothing wrong, Lady," Daemon said firmly. "I thank you for your concern, but there's nothing wrong."

"It seems ladies aren't the only ones who like to seem mysterious," Jaenelle said dryly as she headed for the door. "But there is something wrong with your finger, Prince. There is pain there."

He felt cornered. If anyone else had found out about the snake tooth, he would have been creating a quiet grave right now. But Jaenelle . . . Daemon sighed and turned to look at her. From a distance, particularly in dim light, she seemed like such a frail, plain child, friendly enough but not terribly intelligent. From a distance. When you got close enough to see those eyes change from summer-sky blue to sapphire, it was hard to remember you were talking to a child, hard not to feel a shiver of apprehension at the sharp, slightly feral intelligence just beneath the surface that was drawing its own conclusions about the world.

"I helped you once," she said quietly, daring him to deny it.

Too startled to respond, Daemon stared at her. How long had she known he was the one who had given his strength to the Priest the night she had asked for help, the night Cornelia had whipped him? When he realized the answer, he could have kicked himself for being such a fool. How long? Since the first morning in the alcove when she'd made her decision about him.

"I know," he said respectfully. "I was, and am, grateful for the healing. But this isn't a wound or an illness. It's part of what I am. There's nothing you can do."

He shivered under her intense scrutiny.

Finally she shrugged and slipped out the door.

Daemon extinguished the candle-light and stood in the musty, comforting dark for a few minutes before going to his room. His secret was in her hands now. He wouldn't protect himself against anything she might say or do.

A few minutes later, Alexandra's bell began to ring.

2 / Kaeleer

Saetan looked up from the book he was reading aloud and suppressed a shiver. Jaenelle had been intently studying the book's cover for the past half hour, with that vague look in her eyes that meant she was absorbing the lesson as he intended but was also considering the information in an entirely different way. He continued to read aloud, but his mind was no longer on the words.

A few minutes later, he gave up and put the book and his half-moon glasses on the table. Jaenelle's eyes didn't follow the book as he'd expected. She focused on his right hand, her forehead puckered in concentration while she fluffed her hair.

Ah. While it was difficult to be certain until a witch reached puberty, Jaenelle showed a strong inclination to being a natural Black Widow. It would be a few years yet before the physical evidence was apparent, but her interest demanded that the training begin now.

With one eyebrow rising in amusement, Saetan held out his right hand. "Would you care to examine it more closely, Lady?"

Jaenelle gave him a distracted smile and took his hand.

He watched her explore his hand, turning it this way and that, until her fingers finally came to rest on his ring-finger nail.

"Why do you wear your nails long?" she asked in a soft voice as she studied the black-tinted nails.

"Preference," he replied easily and waited to see how much she could detect.

Jaenelle gave him a long look. "There's something beneath this one." She lightly brushed the ring-finger nail.

"I'm a Black Widow." He turned his hand so she could see beneath the nail, flexed his finger, and watched her eyes widen as the snake tooth slid out of its sheath. "That's a snake tooth. The small venom sac it's attached to lies beneath the nail. Careful," he warned as her finger moved to touch it. "My venom may not be as strong as it used to be, but it's still potent enough."

Jaenelle considered the snake tooth for a while. "Your finger isn't hot. What does it mean if your finger gets hot?"

Saetan's amusement fled. So this wasn't idle curiosity after all. "It means trouble, witch-child. If the venom isn't used, the snake tooth has to be milked every few weeks. Otherwise the venom thickens. It can even crystallize. If it can still be forced through the snake tooth, it will be a painful procedure at best." He shrugged his shoulders unhappily. "If it can't, removal of the tooth and the sac would be the only way to stop the pain."

"Why would someone wait to milk it?"

Again Saetan shrugged. "Venom needs venom. After the venom sac fills, a Black Widow's body craves poison of some kind. But what's taken into the body must be taken with care. The wrong poison can be as deadly to a Black Widow as poison generally is to the rest of the Blood. The best poison is your own. Usually Black Widows milk the sac right before their moontime so that during those days when they must rest, their bodies, stimulated by a few drops of their own venom, will slowly refill the sac with no discomfort."

"And if it's thick?"

"No good. The body will reject it." Saetan reclaimed his hand and steepled his fingers. "Witch-child—"

"If you can't use your own venom, is there a safe poison?"

"There are some poisons that can be used," he said cautiously.

"Could I have some?"

"Why?"

"Because I know someone who needs it." Jaenelle stepped away from him, suddenly hesitant.

Saetan's rib cage clamped around his heart and lungs. He fought against a desire to sink his nails into flesh and tear it. "Male or female?" he asked silkily.

"Does it make a difference?"

"Indeed it does, witch-child. If the distillation of poisons isn't blended to take gender into account, the effects could be unpleasant."

Jaenelle studied him, her eyes troubled. "Male."

Saetan sat still for a long time. "I have something I can give you. Why don't you see what sort of snack Mrs. Beale has for you? This will take a few minutes."

As soon as Jaenelle was distracted by taste-testing Mrs. Beale's offerings, Saetan returned to his private study in the Dark Realm. He locked the door and checked the adjoining rooms before going to the secret door in the paneling beside the fireplace. His workshop was Gray-locked, a sensible precaution that kept Hekatah out but still allowed Mephis and Andulvar to reach him. He flicked a thought at the candle-lights at the end of the narrow corridor, locked the door behind him, and went into his Widow's den.

This was the place where he brewed his poisons and wove his tangled webs of dreamscapes and visions. Going to the worktable that ran the entire length of one wall, he called in a small key and opened the solid wood doors of one of the large cupboards that hung above it.

The poisons sat in neat rows, their glass containers precisely labeled in the Old Tongue. Another precaution, since Hekatah had never mastered the Blood's true language.

He removed a small stoppered jar and held the glass up to the candle-light. He opened the jar and sniffed, then dipped his finger into it and tasted. It was the distillation he used for himself. Since he wasn't born a Black Widow, his body couldn't produce the venom on its own. He replaced the stopper on the jar, looked in the cupboard again, and took out a jar of tiny, bloodred flakes.

Just a flake or two of dried witchblood added to the distillation and the pain Daemon felt now would be a sweet caress compared to the agony that would be his last experience among the living. Men had actually opened themselves with a knife and pulled their own guts out trying to relieve the pain. Or this one. A softer death but just as sure. Because he was sure now that Daemon was too close. Jaenelle was reaching out to help him, but how would Daemon repay that kindness?

Saetan hesitated. And yet . . .

When he'd walked among the living and raised his sons, Mephis and Peyton, he was one note and they were two others, harmonious but different. Lucivar, too, was a different note, more often than not a sharp. Saetan had known from the first time Lucivar hauled himself to his feet, his little wings stirring the air to help him keep his balance, that this son would be a father's plague as he threw himself at the world with that arrogant Eyrien respect for all things that belong to sky and earth.

But Daemon. From the first moment Saetan had held him, he had sensed on some deep, instinctive level that the Darkness would sing to this son in the same way it sang to him, that this son would be the father's mirror. So he'd given Daemon a legacy and a burden he'd never intended to give any of his children.

His name.

He had intended to teach Daemon about honor and the responsibility that came with wearing Jewels as devastating as the Black. But because of honor, he hadn't been there. Because he believed in the Blood Laws and Protocol, he had accepted the lie when Dorothea denied him paternity. And because he had accepted the lie, Daemon had been raised as a bastard and a slave, an outcast who had no place in Blood society.

So how could he condemn Daemon to death when it was his failure to protect the child that had helped shape the man? And how could he not make that choice when Jaenelle's life might be at risk?

Saetan replaced the dried witchblood and locked the cupboard door.

There had been many times in his long, long life when he'd been required to make hard choices, bitter choices. He used the same measuring stick to make this one.

Daemon had given his strength to help Jaenelle when she needed it.

He couldn't repay that debt with a bottle full of death.

Honor forbade it.

He returned to the Kaeleer Hall, gave the distillation to Jaenelle, and went over and over the instructions with her until he was sure she had them exactly right.

3 / Terreille

Daemon sat on the edge of his bed, his right hand cradled in his lap. His shirt clung to him, sweat-soaked from the fever and the pain.

He had tried to milk the snake tooth that morning, but the venom had thickened more quickly than he'd expected, and except for inflaming already tender flesh, he'd accomplished nothing. He'd managed to get through the day, and after dinner he had asked to be excused, claiming, truthfully, that he was unwell. Since Philip had gone to dinner elsewhere and hadn't returned and Robert was going about his usual nightly business, Alexandra and Leland had been sympathetic enough not to demand anything further from him.

Now, as midnight approached and the pain was a sharp, thin line that ran from his finger up to his elbow and slowly climbed toward his shoulder, Daemon vaguely wondered what Leland and Alexandra would do when they found him. He might lose the finger or the hand, possibly even the arm at this point. Given a choice, he would rather die within his own pain. That would be preferable to what Dorothea would do to him after learning about the snake tooth, particularly since he doubted he would be capable of protecting himself.

His bedroom door opened and closed.

Jaenelle stood in front of him, solemn and still.

"Let me see your hand," she said, holding out her own.

Daemon shook his head and closed his eyes.

Jaenelle touched his shoulder. Her fingers unerringly followed the line of pain from shoulder to elbow, elbow to wrist, wrist to finger.

Daemon slowly opened his eyes. Jaenelle held his hand, but he couldn't feel it, couldn't feel his arm at all. He tried to speak but was silenced by the dark look she gave him. Positioning the small bowl he used to milk the snake tooth beneath his hand, she slowly stroked the finger from knuckle to nail tip. He felt no pain, only a growing pressure at his fingertip.

Then a faint sound, as if a grain of salt had been dropped into the bowl. Then another, and another, and one more before she squeezed a thin, white, steady thread of thickened venom out of the tooth.

"May I recite the lesson I learned today?" Jaenelle asked quietly as she continued to stroke his finger. "It will help me remember."

"If you like," Daemon replied slowly. It was hard to think, hard to concentrate as he stared at the little coil of venom at the bottom of the bowl, at the crystallized grains that had caused so much pain.

When Jaenelle began to speak, Daemon's head cleared enough to listen and understand. She told him about the snake tooth and about venom, about how a Black Widow uses four drops of her own venom mixed with a warm drink to restore the balance of poison her body needs after milking the snake tooth, about the dangers of letting venom thicken, and on and on. In the time it took her to completely milk the thick venom from the tooth, she had told him more than he'd been able to glean from centuries of effort. The fact that what she told him contradicted most of what he'd learned didn't surprise him. Dorothea and her coven made an effort to educate their Sisters in other Territories, an education Daemon knew they themselves didn't ascribe to. It explained why so many potential rivals died in such agony.

Finally it was done.

"There," Jaenelle said with satisfaction. She plumped the pillows. "You should lie back and rest now." She frowned at his shirt.

His mind felt fuzzy. She had him half out of the shirt before he realized what she was doing and made a fumbling effort to help her. Holding the drenched material by her fingertips, she wrinkled her nose and vanished it. She disappeared into the bathroom with the bowl, returned with a towel, rubbed him dry, and pushed him back onto the pillows.

Daemon closed his eyes. He felt light, dizzy, and empty to the marrow of his bones. He also felt a craving for poison that was so fierce he almost would have welcomed the pain back.

He heard water running in the bathroom, heard it stop. He opened his eyes to find Jaenelle standing by the bed holding one of Cook's mugs. "Drink this."

Daemon clumsily took the cup in his left hand and obediently sipped. His body tingled. He drank gratefully, relieved when the craving started to disappear. "What is this?" he finally asked.

"A distillation of poisons that are safe for you to drink."

"Where did—"

"Drink." She darted back into the bathroom.

He finished the drink before she returned. She placed the clean bowl on the bedside table, took the empty cup, and vanished it. "You need to sleep now." She pulled off his shoes and reached for his belt.

"I can undress myself," he growled, ashamed of how harsh his voice sounded after she'd done so much to help him.

Jaenelle stepped back. "You're embarrassed."

Daemon studied her. She wasn't being coy. "I don't undress in front of young girls."

She gave him a strange, thoughtful look. "Very well. The snake tooth hasn't drawn back into its sheath yet, so be careful not to snag it." She turned and went to the door.

It hurt to have her use that neutral, formal voice. "Lady," he called softly. When she returned to the bed, Daemon raised her hand to his lips for a light kiss. "Thank you. If you ever want to recite another lesson to help you remember it, I'd be very pleased to listen."

She smiled at him. He was asleep before she slipped out the door.

4 / Terreille

Surreal tried to shift her hips to a more comfortable position, but the arm around her tightened and the hand resting on her arm gripped with bruising force.

Philip Alexander had arranged for this evening with her early that morning. That was the only predictable thing he'd done. There was no leisurely dinner, no conversation, no turning out the lights, no light love-making before he covered her. He took her, hard, with the candle-lights glaring at full intensity so there could be no illusion about who was under him. When he was through, he rolled off her, ate the cold dinner, drank most of the wine, and took her again. Now he stared at the canopy above the bed, grinding his fingers into her bruised arm.

She could have stopped him, Gray against Gray. Her Green Jewel had shielded her a little, but not enough to keep her from getting hurt. The Gray was her surprise weapon, and she didn't want to give up that edge until she absolutely had to. After the second time, he'd done nothing but hold her tight against him, but she felt the anger in him, watched his Jew-els flash as they absorbed the energy.

"I'd kill that bastard if I could," Philip said through clenched teeth. "He acts as if nothing's happening while she . . ."

"Who?" Surreal tried to lift her head. "Who's a bastard?" If she had *some* idea what had made him act this way, she might be able to get through the rest of the night.

"That 'gift' Dorothea SaDiablo sent to Alexandra. There's more warmth in a glacier than there is in him, and yet Leland . . ."

Surreal smelled blood. She turned her head just a little. Philip, in his rage, had bitten his lip.

She'd already guessed that Philip's attachment to the Angelline court had more to do with the daughter than the mother. Wasn't that what the completely dark room was all about, being able to pretend he was leisurely making love to Leland? Were there hurried couplings when Robert Benedict wasn't there, couplings so tainted with the fear of being found out that there was no pleasure in them? Now Sadi was there, and Leland could be physically gratified by another male under Robert's watchful and approving eye.

Surreal shivered, remembering all too well what it felt like to be grat-ified by the Sadist.

"Cold?" Philip asked, his voice a little gentler.

Surreal let him tuck the quilt up around them. Now that she knew where to look, it wouldn't be difficult to reach Sadi—if she wanted to. Still, there was that red-haired witch at Cassandra's Altar who was asking about him, and she did owe him.

Surreal pushed herself up on one elbow, fighting Philip's restraining hand. She smoothed her hair away from her face, letting it fall in a long black curtain across her back and shoulder. "Philip, why do you believe Sadi is serving Lady Benedict?"

"She publicly summons him to her room so that the whole family and most of the staff knows he's with her," Philip snarled. His anger made his gray eyes look flat and cold. "And at the breakfast table, she chatters on about how entertaining he was."

"She actually says he was entertaining?" Surreal flung herself backward and laughed. Damn. Leland was smarter than she'd thought.

Philip threw himself on her, pinning her to the bed. "You find this amusing?" he spat at her. "You think this is funny?"

"Ah, sugar," Surreal said, gulping back her laughter. "From what I know about Sadi, he can be *very* entertaining out of bed, but he's seldom entertaining *in* bed."

Philip's grip eased a little. He frowned, puzzled.

"She's not the first, you know," Surreal said with a smile.

"First what?"

"The first woman to so blatantly call attention to the use of a pleasure slave." She stifled her laughter. He still didn't get it.

"Why—"

"So that after people come to expect it and the maids aren't going to gossip about rumpled linen because the story's already stale, the slave can be dismissed quietly and the lady's lover can spend a couple of leisurely hours with her without anyone suspecting." Surreal looked him in the eye. "And Lady Benedict does have a lover, doesn't she?"

Philip stared at her for a moment. He started to smile and winced when it pulled his cut lip.

Surreal playfully pushed him away, rolled off the bed, and casually walked into the bathroom. She turned on the light and studied her reflection. There were bruises on her arms and shoulders from his hands, bruises on her neck from his teeth. She winced at the raw ache between her legs. Deje was going to lose her for a few days.

By the time she returned to the bedroom, Philip had straightened the bed and was lying back comfortably, his hands under his head. The Gray Jewel glowed softly as he pulled the covers back to let her in. He studied the bruises, brushing them gently with his fingers.

"I hurt you. I'm sorry."

"Professional hazard," Surreal replied with sweet venom. He deserved a short knife in the ribs.

Philip settled her head on his shoulder and tucked the covers around them once again. She knew he was looking for a way to get back on familiar ground, to take back the pain he'd caused. She let the silence stretch and strain, making no effort to help him. She was a whore now because it was the easiest way to get close to males, learn their habits, and make a kill. Since Philip was in only one of her two books, and unlikely to be in the other, she didn't care if he ever came back.

Sadi was a different problem. She had to find a way to meet him that wouldn't arouse suspicion. That, however, was something she would consider after some sleep.

"You didn't get anything to eat," Philip said quietly.

Surreal waited for a couple of heartbeats before accepting the peace offering. "True, and I'm ravenous." She sent an order to the kitchen for two prime ribs with the works and another bottle of wine. The hefty tab Deje was going to hand him would disconcert him, but it would also alleviate some of his guilt for hurting her.

"I wouldn't worry about Sadi," Surreal said as she slipped out of bed and wrapped a dressing gown around her slim body. "Although"—how nice to see that immediate flicker of worry in his eyes—"a lover who requires his silent participation and discretion would do well to understand that Sadi remembers courtesies just as he remembers slights."

She smiled as the obelisk on the table chimed and the two meals appeared on the table. *Let him chew on that,* she thought, as she cut into the prime rib.

5 / Terreille

Daemon glided into the breakfast room but stopped just inside the door when he saw Leland and Philip engrossed in quiet conversation. Philip's back was to the door, and as he talked, his hand moved gently up and down Leland's arm. Leland's eyes, as she listened to him, were lit with the fire of a woman in love.

She was dressed in riding clothes, her hair pulled back from her face in a simple, becoming style. Yes, underneath the frills and fripperies she wore for the society ladies beat the heart of a witch.

As Leland smiled at something Philip said, she looked over his shoulder and saw Daemon. Her eyes became chilly. Stepping away from Philip, she went to the buffet table and began to fill her plate.

Philip's eyes became hard when he noticed Daemon, but he managed a smile and a courteous greeting.

Well, well, well, Daemon thought as he filled his own plate. Something was in the wind. He was supposed to go riding with Leland that morning, but he noticed Philip was also dressed to ride.

Breakfast was over and Leland had left for the stables before Philip spoke directly to Daemon. He sounded like a polite host dealing with a not-quite-welcome guest. "There's no reason for you to go out, unless you want to, of course. Since I'd planned to ride this morning, Lady Benedict doesn't require another escort."

Or a chaperon, Daemon thought as he sipped his coffee. Overnight Philip's attitude had changed from terse and jealous to this attempt at courtesy. Why? Not that it mattered. He knew exactly what he would do with a free morning—and it would be free with Leland and Philip out of the house. Alexandra was visiting a friend and wouldn't be back until after lunch, and Robert, always so occupied with his all-consuming "business," spent as little time as possible at the estate.

In fact, as that delicious dark scent once again permeated the walls of the Angelline mansion, Robert seemed more and more uncomfortable about staying there. It had reached the point that Daemon always knew when Robert came back even if he didn't see him because, in the front hallway and on the stairs leading up to the family's living quarters, there was always the slight stink of fear.

Daemon poured another cup of coffee and shrugged in response to Philip's suggestion. "I don't mind not riding this morning," he said in his bored court voice. "Most likely you're a more enthusiastic rider and would therefore be a more suitable companion."

Philip's eyes narrowed, but there was nothing in Daemon's silky, bored voice that gave any indication of an intended double meaning.

Daemon smiled and reached for another piece of toast. "You shouldn't keep the lady waiting, Prince Alexander."

Philip hesitated at the doorway. Daemon buttered his toast with slow, sensuous strokes, knowing that Philip was watching him and uneasily imagining something other than toast beneath his hand. Well, if Philip actually believed someone like Leland could make a Black-Jeweled Warlord Prince pant, the fool deserved to sweat.

The moment Philip was gone, Daemon went to his room and swiftly changed his clothes. Wilhelmina was with Graff having her lessons; Cook was in the kitchen, sipping a cup of tea and starting to plan the lunch menu; and the servants were bustling about doing their various chores. There was only one person left.

Daemon whistled a cheery little tune as he headed for the private alcove to spend a pleasant morning with his Lady.

He had prowled the gardens, prowled the house, slipped in and out of the stableyard, checked the Craft library, and finally stood in the nursery wing feeling frustrated and concerned. He simply couldn't find her. He had even checked her room, tapping quietly on the door in case she was resting or wanted some privacy. When there'd been no answer, he had slipped into the room for a cursory look.

Daemon caught his lower lip between his teeth and listened to Graff scolding Wilhelmina. He'd wondered why that harsh and not terribly educated woman was teaching Craft to a young witch from such a powerful family until he'd learned that Robert Benedict had hired her. Since Wilhelmina wasn't directly related to Leland and Alexandra, Robert's preference had overruled their objections. Daemon conceded that Graff was a good choice if a man's intention was to have a girl's sensibilities about what she was and the power she contained mangled to such an extent that she would never find any joy in the Craft or in herself. Yes, Graff was an excellent choice to bruise a young girl's ego and make her susceptible to more intimate brutality when she got a little older.

Daemon approached the classroom to see if Jaenelle might possibly be there at the same time Graff yelled, "You're worthless this morning. Absolutely worthless. You call that Craft? Go on. The lesson's over. Go do something useless. *That* you can manage. GO!"

Wilhelmina flew out the door and barreled into him. Daemon caught her by the shoulders, planting his feet to keep them both upright. She gave him a shaky smile of thanks.

"So, you're free," Daemon said, smiling in return. "Where's—"

"Oh, good, you're here," Wilhelmina said in a loud, commanding voice. "Help me practice my duet." She turned toward the music room.

"First tell me where—"

Wilhelmina stepped back and planted her heel squarely on Daemon's toes. Hard. He grunted from the pain but said nothing because Graff was now standing in the doorway, watching them closely.

Wilhelmina stepped aside. "Oh, I'm sorry. Did I hurt you?" Without waiting for an answer, she hauled him toward the music room. "Come on, I want to practice."

Once they reached the music room, she went to the piano and started digging through the music for the duet she was learning. "You can play the bass part," she said as she placed her hands on the keys.

Daemon limped to the bench and sat down. "Miss Wil—"

Wilhelmina hit the keys, drowning him out. She continued for a few bars and then turned to him and said accusingly, "You're not playing."

It was such a perfect imitation of Graff's scolding voice that Daemon's lips curled in a snarl as he twisted around to face her, but the look on her face was a plea for understanding and her eyes were glazed with fear. Grinding his teeth, he placed his hands on the keys. "One, two, three, four." They began to play.

She was badly frightened, and it had something to do with him. As they stumbled through the duet, he noticed Graff standing in the music room doorway, listening, observing, spying. They finished the duet and started again. The longer they played and the longer Graff watched them the more Wilhelmina mangled the music until Daemon wondered if they were playing the same piece. Certainly the sheet music he was reading had nothing to do with what he was hearing, and he winced more than once at the sounds being produced.

When Wilhelmina doggedly began the duet for the third time, Graff turned away with a grimace, and Daemon felt sourly envious of her ability to leave. As soon as she left, however, Wilhelmina began to play more smoothly, more quietly.

"You must never ask about Jaenelle," she said so quietly Daemon had to lean toward her to hear. "If you can't find her, you must never ask anyone where she is."

"Why?"

Wilhelmina stared straight ahead. Her throat worked convulsively as if she were choking on the words. "Because if they find out, she might get into trouble, and I don't want her to get into trouble. I don't want her to go back to Briarwood." She stopped playing and turned toward him, her eyes misty. "Do you?"

He smoothed her hair away from her face and lightly caressed her cheek. "No, I don't want her to go back. Wilhelmina . . . Where is she?"

Wilhelmina started playing again, but quietly. "She goes for lessons in the mornings now. Sometimes she goes and sees friends."

Daemon frowned, puzzled. "If she goes for lessons, surely your father or Alexandra or Leland had arranged—"

"No."

"But a maid must accompany her and would—"

"No."

As Daemon considered this, his hands slowly closed into fists. "She goes alone?" he finally said, keeping his voice carefully neutral.

"Yes."

"And your family doesn't know she goes at all?"

"No, they mustn't know."

"And you don't know where she goes or who gives her these lessons?"

"No."

"But if your family found out about the lessons or who's giving her lessons, they might put her back in the hospital?"

Wilhelmina's chin quivered. "Yes."

"I see." Oh, yes, he did see. Beware of the Priest. She belongs to the Priest. It was careless of him to forget so formidable a rival. But she did have an innocent way of dazzling a man. He'd forgotten about the Priest. Was she with him now? What could Saetan, one of the living dead, have to offer that was preferable to what he, a living man, could offer her? But then, she wasn't ready for what a man could offer. Would Saetan try to keep her away from him? If her family ever found out about the High Lord . . .

There were too many undercurrents in this family, too many secrets. Alexandra balanced on a political knife's edge, trying to remain the ruling power of Chaillot while Robert's position in the male council that opposed her constantly undermined the trust she needed from the other Chaillot Queens. The rivalry between Robert and Philip was an open secret among the aristo Blood in Beldon Mor, and Alexandra's inability to control her own family was causing doubts about her ability to rule the Territory. Add to that the social embarrassment of having a granddaughter who had been going in and out of a hospital for emotionally disturbed children since she was five years old.

And add to that having that same child admit that the High Lord of Hell, the Prince of the Darkness, the most powerful and dangerous Warlord Prince in the history of the Blood, was teaching her Craft.

Even if they thought it was just another story, they would lock her away for good to keep her from telling anyone who might listen. But if, for once, they did believe her, what else might they do to her to end the High Lord's interest in her and keep themselves safe? And Daemon felt sure that there were things going on in Beldon Mor that Saetan wouldn't be willing to overlook or forgive.

Daemon looked up and breathed a sigh of relief.

Jaenelle stood in the doorway wearing riding clothes. Her golden hair was braided and a riding hat perched on top of her head at a rakish angle. "I'm going riding. Want to come?"

"Oh, yes!" Wilhelmina said happily. "I'm done practicing."

As he watched Wilhelmina dash out of the room, there was a bitter taste in Daemon's mouth. The ashes of dreams. After all, he was Hayll's Whore, a pleasure slave, an amusement for the ladies no matter what their age, a way to pass the time. He closed the music and made a pretense of straightening the stack. Why should he hope Jaenelle felt anything for him? Why should he hurt now like a child who's not picked for a game?

Daemon turned. Jaenelle stood by the piano, studying him, a puzzled frown wrinkling her forehead.

"Don't you ride, Prince?"

"Yes, I ride."

"Oh." She considered this. "Don't you want to come?"

Daemon blinked. He looked at her beautiful, clear sapphire eyes. It had never occurred to her to exclude him. He smiled at her and gave her braid a gentle, playful tug. "Yes, I would like to come."

She studied him again. "Don't you have any other clothes?"

Daemon choked. "I beg your pardon?"

"You're always dressed like that."

Daemon looked at his perfectly tailored black suit and white silk shirt, completely taken aback. "What's wrong with the way I dress?"

"Nothing. But if you wear those clothes, you're going to get wrinkled."

Daemon started coughing and thumped his chest to give himself time to swallow the laughter. "I have some riding clothes," he wheezed.

"Oh, good." Her eyes sparkled with amusement.

Little imp. You know why I'm choking, don't you? You're a merciless little creature to mock a man's vanity.

Jaenelle trotted to the door. "Hurry up, Prince. We'll meet you at the stable."

"My name is Daemon," he growled softly.

Jaenelle spun around, gave him an impudent curtsy, and grinned before running down the hall.

Daemon walked to his room as quickly as his still-sore toes allowed. His name was Daemon, not Prince, he growled to himself as he changed clothes. It always sounded like she was calling a damn dog even if it *was* his proper Protocol title. It wouldn't hurt to call him by name, but she wouldn't because he was her elder.

Daemon paused as he pulled on his boots. He started to laugh. If *he* was her elder, then what did she think about the Priest?

When Daemon got to the stableyard, there were two ponies saddled as well as a gray mare and Dark Dancer. Not sure which horse was intended for him, he approached Andrew. The stable lad gave Daemon a wobbly smile before ducking his head and rechecking Dancer's saddle.

"Be careful," Andrew said quietly. "He's jumpy today."

"Compared to what?" Daemon asked dryly.

Andrew hunched his shoulders.

Daemon's eyes narrowed. "Is there a reason for this jumpiness?"

The shoulders hunched a bit more.

Feeling the tension running through the yard, Daemon looked around.

Jaenelle was talking quietly to one of the ponies. Wilhelmina stood nearby, waiting for someone to help her mount. Her cheeks were prettily flushed from the crisp autumn air and the excitement of riding, but she kept glancing nervously in his direction and refused to acknowledge him. "Mother Night," he muttered and went over to Wilhelmina to give her a leg up.

After helping Wilhelmina mount, Daemon turned to give Jaenelle a hand, but she was already on her pony, grinning at him.

"We'd best be off if we're going," Andrew said nervously.

As Daemon turned to answer him, he glanced around the yard. All the stable lads stood absolutely still, watching him. They all know, he thought as he mounted Dark Dancer. She was their precious secret.

Guinness came out of his office and headed toward them, his head down and shoulders hunched as if he were walking into a heavy wind. When he reached them, he sucked his cheek for a minute, cleared his throat a couple of times, and looked in their direction without looking at any of them. He cleared his throat again. "Now, you ladies haven't been out for a while, so I want you to take a nice easy hack. No rough riding, none of them big jumps. Nothing faster than a canter. And De—Dark Dancer there hasn't been out much either"—he glanced guiltily at Daemon—"so I don't want you to let him have his head and hurt himself. Understand?"

"We understand, Guinness," Jaenelle said quietly. Her voice was serious, but her lips twitched and her eyes sparkled.

"Lady Benedict and Prince Alexander are still out riding, so you watch for them, you hear?" Guinness sucked on his cheek. He waved a hand at them and said gruffly, "Go on now."

The girls took the lead, walking their ponies sedately through the yard and down the path while Daemon and Andrew followed.

"I don't remember Guinness ever calling this horse by name before," Daemon said.

Andrew shrugged his shoulders and smiled. "Miss Jaenelle doesn't like us calling him Demon. She says it makes him unhappy."

"You know, Andrew," Daemon said in a quiet, silky voice, "if this horse breaks her neck, I'm going to break yours."

Andrew chuckled. Daemon raised one eyebrow at the response.

"Wait until you see them together. It's worth watching," Andrew said. "When we get to the tree, you can have the mare. I don't think the pony can carry you."

"Very considerate of you," Daemon said dryly.

They kept to a walk all the way to the tree. When Andrew and Daemon got there, Jaenelle was already dismounted and waiting. Daemon's heart thumped crazily at the soft, shining look in her eyes, and then felt squeezed by a taloned hand when he realized she wasn't looking at him.

The stallion nickered softly and thrust his head forward. "Hello, Dancer," Jaenelle said in a voice that was a sweet, sensuous caress.

Sweet Darkness, he would give his soul if her voice sounded like that when she talked to him, Daemon thought as he dismounted. He adjusted the stirrups for her. "Give you a leg up?"

Andrew's head whipped around as if the suggestion was totally inappropriate. Perhaps it was. Daemon had the feeling she didn't need the help, but what he wouldn't have admitted to anyone for anything was that he wanted—he needed—to be able to touch her in some innocent way, even if it was just to feel her small booted foot in his cupped hands.

Jaenelle's eyes met his and held them. He fell into those sapphire pools, and he knew she saw what he didn't want to admit.

"Thank you . . . Daemon." Her voice was a feathery caress down his spine that set him on fire and soothed him.

A little giddy, Daemon cupped his hands and bent over. For the briefest moment, she pressed her foot into his hands. Then she lifted it just slightly and propelled herself into the saddle.

Daemon stared at his empty hands and slowly straightened up. The eyes looking at him were amused, but they didn't belong to a child.

"Shall we go?" Jaenelle said quietly.

As Daemon mounted the mare, Jaenelle vanished her hat and undid her braid, letting her hair float behind her in a golden wave. They set out for the field, Jaenelle riding ahead of them, her murmuring voice floating back on the breeze.

Relieved that Philip and Leland weren't in the field, it took Daemon a moment to realize that Dark Dancer was cantering far ahead of them and stretching into a ground-eating gallop.

"They're heading for the ditch!" Just as Daemon started to urge the mare forward to cut across the field and head the stallion off, Andrew grabbed his arm.

"Watch," Andrew said.

Daemon gritted his teeth and held the mare still.

Dark Dancer came up to the ditch fast, his black tail and Jaenelle's golden hair streaming behind them like flags of glory. As they approached the ditch, he checked his speed and made a wide, easy turn back toward the center of the field where the small jumps were placed. He took the little wooden jumps as if they were brick walls, high and showy, and as he cantered toward them, Daemon heard Jaenelle's silvery, velvet-coated laugh of delight.

She turned the stallion to circle the field again. Daemon urged the mare forward and they circled at an easy pace, side by side, with Wilhelmina and Andrew following.

As they reached the beginning of the circle, Jaenelle slowed Dancer to a walk. "Isn't he wonderful?" She stroked his sweaty neck.

"He's been a little more ambitious when I've ridden him," Daemon said dryly.

Jaenelle's forehead wrinkled. "Ambitious?"

"Mm. He's wanted to teach me to fly."

She laughed. The sound sang in his blood. She turned toward him then. Beneath the high spirits her eyes were haunted and sad. "Perhaps he'd like you more if you talked to him—and listened."

Daemon wanted to say something light and cheerful to take away the look in her eyes, but there was something about the way the stallion suddenly twitched his ears and seemed to be listening to them that pricked his nerves. "People talk to him all the time. He probably knows more of the stable lads' secrets than any other living thing."

"Yes, but they don't listen to him, do they?"

Daemon kept quiet, trying to steady his breathing.

"He's Blood, Daemon, but just a little. Not enough to be kindred, but too much to be . . ." Jaenelle made a small gesture with her hand that took in the mare and the ponies.

Daemon licked his lips, but his mouth was too dry. He remembered Cook's story about the dogs. "What do you mean, kindred?"

"Blood, but not the same. Blood, but not human. Kindred is . . . like but not like."

Daemon looked up. A few fluffy clouds floated in the deep blue autumn sky, and the sun shone down with its last warmth. No, the physical day hadn't changed. That's not what made him shiver. "He's half Blood," he finally said, reluctant to know the truth. "Half Blood, half landen, forever caught in between."

"Yes."

"But you can understand him, talk to him?"

"I listen to him." Jaenelle urged Dancer into a trot.

Daemon held the mare back and watched the girl and horse circle the field. "Damn." It hurt. Dark Dancer was a Brother, and knowing that hurt worse than knowing about the human half-Bloods Daemon had seen over the years who were too strong, too driven, and too aching with an unanswered need to fit into the life of a landen village yet were still left standing on the other side of a great psychic ravine from where the weakest of the Blood stood because they weren't strong enough to cross over. But humans could at least talk to other humans. Who did this four-footed Brother have? No wonder he took such care with her.

Suddenly Jaenelle and Dancer hurtled toward Andrew as he flung himself off the pony and frantically adjusted the stirrups. Daemon put his heels into the mare and galloped over to join them.

"Andrew—"

"Hurry! Get Dancer's stirrups down!"

Daemon dropped the mare's reins and hurried over to the stallion. "Easy, Dancer," he said, stroking the horse's neck before reaching for the stirrups.

"Miss Jaenelle." Andrew grabbed her by the waist and tossed her up onto the pony. He turned in a circle, his eyes sweeping the ground. "Your hat. Damn it, your hat."

"Here." Jaenelle held the hat up and put it on her head. Her hair still flowed down her back, tangled by her ride.

Wilhelmina glanced at Jaenelle, all the color gone from her face. "Graff's going to be mad when she sees your hair."

"Graff is a bitch," Jaenelle snapped, her eyes on the path where it took a bend through some trees.

The ponies must be mares, Daemon thought as he adjusted the stirrups. All the males had flinched at the knife-edge in her voice.

"That's it," Andrew said, sliding under Dancer's neck. "Stay on the mare. There's no time to do more." He mounted, gathered the reins, and started walking forward. The stallion was furious, and showed it, but kept moving toward the path. Wilhelmina followed behind Andrew, trying to calm the nervous pony and only upsetting it more.

Daemon mounted, started forward, and then stopped. Jaenelle sat perfectly still, her eyes fixed on the bend in the path. Pain and anger filled those eyes, a hurt that went so deep he knew he had no magic to help her. Beneath the childish features was an ancient face that seared him, froze him, wrapped silk chains around his heart.

He blinked away tears, and there was Miss Jaenelle with her childish face and her not-too-intelligent summer-sky blue eyes. She gave him a little-girl smile and urged her pony to a trot just as Philip and Leland rounded the bend and stopped.

Across the field, Philip stared first at Daemon, then at Jaenelle. He said nothing when they reached the group, but he maneuvered his horse so that Jaenelle was riding beside him all the way back to the stable.

Daemon fastened the ruby cuff links onto his shirt and reached for his dinner jacket. He hadn't had a moment to himself since leaving the stable that morning. First Leland had needed an escort for an extended shopping trip on which she'd bought nothing, then Alexandra suddenly decided to visit an art gallery, and finally Philip insisted they needed to go over invitation by boring invitation all the possible social functions Daemon might have to escort Leland or Alexandra to.

Something in the field this morning had made them all nervous, something that had swirled and crackled like mist and lightning. They wanted to blame him, wanted to believe he'd done something to upset the girls, wanted to believe that the scent of the restrained violence was male and not female in origin. More than that, they wanted to believe they weren't the cause of it, and that was possible only if he was the source.

Ladies like to seem mysterious.

Not Lady Jaenelle Benedict. She didn't try to be mysterious, she simply was. She walked in full sunlight shrouded in a midnight mist that swirled around her, hiding, revealing, tantalizing, frightening. Her honesty had been blunted by punishment. Perhaps that was for the best. She was good at dissembling, had some understanding about her family's reaction if they learned some of the truths about her, and yet she couldn't dissemble enough because she cared.

How many people knew about her? Daemon wondered as he brushed his hair. How many people looked upon her as their secret?

All the stable lads as well as Guinness knew she rode Dark Dancer.

But Philip, Alexandra, Leland, Robert, and Graff didn't know.

Cook knew about her ability to heal. So did Andrew. So did a young parlor maid who'd had her lip split by the senior footman when she refused his amorous advances. Daemon had seen her that particular morning with her lip still leaking blood. An hour later she had passed him in the hallway, her lip slightly swollen but otherwise undamaged, a stunned, awed expression in her eyes. So did one of the old gardeners, who now had a salve for his aching knees. So did he.

But Philip, Alexandra, Leland, Robert, and Graff didn't know.

Wilhelmina knew her sister disappeared for hours at a time to visit unnamed friends and an unknown mentor, knew how the witchblood had come to grow in that alcove.

He knew about her midnight wandering and her secret reading of the ancient Craft texts, knew there was something terrifying and beautiful within the child cocoon that, when it came of age and finally emerged, would no longer be able to live with these people.

But Philip, Alexandra, Leland, Robert, and Graff didn't know. They saw a child who couldn't learn simple Craft, a child they considered eccentric, strange, and fanciful, a child willing to speak brutal truths that adults would never speak and didn't want to know, a child they couldn't love enough to accept, a child who was like a pin hidden in a garment that constantly scratched the skin and yet could never be found.

How many beyond Chaillot knew what she was?

But not Philip or Alexandra or Leland or Robert or Graff. Not the people who should protect her, keep her safe. They were the ones she wasn't safe from. They were the ones who had the power to harm her, to lock her away, to destroy her. They, the ones who should have kept her safe, were her enemies.

And, therefore, they were his.

Daemon studied his cold reflection one last time to make sure nothing was out of place, then joined the family for dinner.

6 / Terreille

Leland smiled nervously and glanced at the clock in her brightly lit sitting room. Instead of cards, the table held a bottle of chilled wine and two glasses. The bedroom door stood partially open, and soft light spilled out.

Daemon's stomach tightened, and he welcomed the familiar chill that began to ice his veins. "You requested my presence, Lady Benedict."

Leland's smile slipped. "Um . . . yes . . . well . . . you look tired. I mean, we've all kept you so busy these last few days and, well . . . maybe you should go to your room now and get a good night's sleep. Yes. You do look tired. Why don't you just go to your room? You *will* just go to your room, won't you? I mean . . ."

Daemon smiled.

Leland glanced at the bedroom door and blanched. "It's just . . . I'm feeling a bit off tonight. I really don't want to play cards."

"Nor do I." Daemon reached for the wine bottle and corkscrew.

"You don't have to do that!"

Daemon narrowed his eyes, studying her.

Leland scurried behind a chair.

He set the bottle and corkscrew down and slipped his hands into his pockets. "You're quite right, Lady. I am tired. With your kind permission, I'll retire now." But not to his room. Not yet.

Leland smiled weakly but stayed behind the chair.

Daemon left the room, walked down the corridor, turned the corner, and stopped. He counted to ten and then took two steps backward.

Philip stood outside Leland's door, frozen by Daemon's appearance at the end of the corridor. They stared at each other for the space of eight heartbeats before Daemon nodded in courteous greeting and stepped out of sight. He stopped and listened. After a long pause, Leland's door quietly opened, closed, and locked.

Daemon smiled. So that was their game. A pity they hadn't come to it sooner. It would have spared him all those interminable hours of playing cards with Leland. Still, he'd never been adverse to using the knowledge he gathered about the people he served, and this was just the kind of quiet leverage he needed to keep Philip out of his way. Oh, he would be a splendid silent partner in their game. He had always been a splendid partner, sympathetic and ever so helpful—unless someone crossed him. Then . . . Well, he wasn't called the Sadist for nothing.

He found it strangely flattering that she didn't look up when he slipped into the library and locked the door. She sat cross-legged on the couch, absorbed in the book tucked in her lap, her right hand fluffing her hair as she read.

He glided around the furniture, his smile becoming warmer with each step. When he reached the couch, he bowed formally. "Lady Benedict."

"Angelline," Jaenelle replied absently.

Daemon said nothing. He had discovered that if he kept his voice quiet and neutral when she was distracted with something else, she usually spoke without considering her words, responding with a simple, brutal honesty that always left him feeling as though the ground was cracking beneath his feet.

"Witch follows the matriarchal bloodline," Jaenelle said, turning a page. "Besides, Uncle Bobby isn't my father."

"Then who is your father?"

"Philip. But he won't acknowledge me." Jaenelle turned another page. "He's Wilhelmina's father too, but he was in a dream web when he sired her so he doesn't know that."

Daemon sat on the couch, so close that her arm brushed his side. "How do you know he's Wilhelmina's father?"

"Adria told me." She turned another page.

"Who's Adria?"

"Wilhelmina's mother. She told me."

Daemon considered his next words very carefully. "I had understood Wilhelmina's mother died when your sister was just an infant."

"Yes, she did."

Which meant Adria was demon-dead.

"She was a Black Widow but was broken just before she had completed her training," Jaenelle continued. "But she already knew how to weave a dream web, and she didn't want to be seeded by Bobby."

Daemon took a deep breath. When he tried to exhale, it shuddered out of him. With an effort, he dismissed what she'd just said. He wasn't here to talk about Adria. "How was your lesson this morning?"

Jaenelle became very still.

Daemon closed his eyes for a moment. He was afraid of what she might say if she answered, but he was more afraid of what might happen if she didn't. If she shut him out now . . .

"All right," she said hesitantly.

"Did you learn anything interesting?" Daemon rested his arm on the back of the couch and tried to look relaxed and lazy. Inside, he felt as if he'd swallowed shards of glass. "My own education was regrettably spotty. I envy you having such a learned mentor."

Jaenelle closed the book and stared straight ahead.

Daemon swallowed hard but pushed on. "Why don't you have your lessons here? It's customary for the tutor to come to the pupil, not the other way around." She wasn't fooled, and he knew it.

"He can't come here," she said slowly. "He mustn't come here. He mustn't find out about . . ." Jaenelle pressed her lips together.

"Why can't he come here?" Keep her talking, keep her talking. If she shut him out now, she might shut him out forever.

"His soul is of the night."

It took all of Daemon's self-control to sit still, to look relaxed and only mildly interested.

Jaenelle paused. "And I don't think he'd approve."

"You mean Philip wouldn't approve of his teaching you?"

"No. *He* wouldn't approve of Philip." She shook her head. "He wouldn't approve at all."

Nor do I, my Lady. Nor do I. As Daemon thought about the little he knew about Guardians and the stories he'd heard or read about the High Lord of Hell, he saw Jaenelle swallow, and his own throat tightened. Guardians. The living dead. They drank . . . "He doesn't hurt you, does he?" he asked harshly, instantly regretting the words.

Jaenelle twisted to face him, her eyes skimmed with icy anger.

Daemon immediately retreated, trying to find a way to soften what he'd just said. "I mean . . . does he scold you if you don't get a lesson right? The way Graff does?"

The anger left her eyes, but she was still wary. "No, he doesn't scold." She repositioned herself until she was sitting back on her heels. "Well, most of the time he doesn't. Only once, really, but that was because I scared them and it was really Prothvar's fault because I asked him to teach me and he wouldn't teach me he just laughed and said I couldn't but I knew I could so I did to show him I could but he didn't know I could and then he got scared and they got angry and that's when I got scolded. But it was really Prothvar's fault." Her eyes were full of an appeal for him to be on her side.

Daemon felt dizzied by the explanation and grasped the one thing he could pull out. "Who's Prothvar?"

"Andulvar's grandson."

Daemon was getting a headache. He'd spent too many nights getting into heated but friendly arguments with Lucivar over who was the most powerful Warlord Prince in the history of the Blood not to know who Andulvar was. Mother Night, he thought as he surreptitiously rubbed his aching temple, how many of the dead did she know? "I agree," he said decisively. "I think Prothvar was at fault."

Jaenelle blinked. She grinned. "That's what I think too." She wrinkled her nose. "Prothvar didn't think so. He still doesn't."

Daemon shrugged. "He's Eyrien. Eyriens are stubborn."

Jaenelle giggled and snuggled up next to him. Daemon slowly lowered his arm until his hand lightly caressed her shoulder, and sighed, content.

He would have to make peace with the Priest. He wouldn't step aside, but he didn't want her trapped in the middle of that kind of rivalry. Besides, the High Lord was just a rival, not an enemy. She might need him too.

"Your mentor is called the Priest, is he not?" Daemon asked in a sleepy, silky voice.

Jaenelle tensed but didn't pull away. Finally she nodded.

"When you next see him, would you tell him I send my regards?"

Jaenelle's head shot up so fast that Daemon's teeth snapped together, just missing his tongue. "You know the Priest?"

"We were briefly acquainted . . . a long time ago," Daemon said as his fingers became entangled in her hair.

Jaenelle snuggled closer, hiding a huge yawn with both hands. "I'll remember," she promised sleepily.

Daemon kissed the top of her head, reluctantly drew her to her feet, put the book back on the shelf, and led her out of the library. He pointed her toward the stairs that would take her up to her bedroom on the floor above. "Go to bed—and sleep." He tried to sound stern, but even to his own ears it came out lovingly exasperated.

"You sound like him sometimes," Jaenelle grumbled. She climbed the stairs and disappeared.

Daemon closed his eyes. Liar. Silky, court-trained liar. He didn't want to smooth away a rivalry. That wasn't why he sent the message. He wanted—secondhand and only for an instant—he wanted to force Saetan to acknowledge his son.

But what kind of message would the Priest send in return, if he cared to send any at all?

7 / Terreille

Greer stood before the two women seated by the fire, his hands clasped loosely behind his back. He was the High Priestess of Hayll's most trusted servant, her favorite assassin, her caretaker of meddlesome, messy details. This assignment was an exquisite reward for his loyalty.

"You understand what you're to do?"

Greer turned slightly toward the one called the Dark Priestess. Until tonight he had never understood why his powerful Priestess should feel so compelled to make accommodations for this mysterious "adviser." Now he understood. She had the scent of the graveyard about her, and her keen malevolence frightened and excited him. He was also aware that the "wine" she drank came from a different kind of vineyard.

"I understand and am honored that you have chosen me for this assignment." While Dorothea may have chosen who would take on the task, it quickly became apparent that the assignment had come from the other. It was something he would keep in mind for the future.

"He won't balk because you're the one explaining the terms of the agreement?" Dorothea said, glancing at his right arm. "His dislike for you is intense."

Greer gave Dorothea an oily smile and turned his attention fully on the Dark Priestess. So. Even the choice of who hadn't been made by Hayll's High Priestess. "All the more reason for him to listen—particularly if I'm not pleased to be offering such generous terms. Besides, if he chooses to lie about what he knows, I may be able to detect it far better than one of the ambassadors who"—he put his left hand over his breast in an expression of sincerity—"although most highly qualified for their usual assignments are, regrettably, reluctant to deal with Sadi except in the most perfunctory ways."

"You're not afraid of Sadi?" the Dark Priestess asked.

Her girlish voice annoyed Greer because it was at odds with her deliberately concealed face and her attitude of being a dark, powerful force. No matter. Tonight he finally understood who really controlled Hayll. "I'm not afraid of Sadi," he said with a smile, "and it will give me great pleasure to see him dirty his hands with a child's blood." Great pleasure.

"Very well. When can you leave?"

"Tomorrow. I'll allow my journey to seem casual so that it will go unremarked. While I'm there, I'll take the opportunity of looking around their quaint little city. Who knows what I might find that would be of value to you Ladies."

"Kartane's in Beldon Mor," Dorothea said as she refilled her wineglass.

"No doubt he can save you a great deal of preliminary work. Contact him while you're there."

Greer gave her another oily smile, bowed to them both, and left.

"You don't seem pleased with the choice, Sister," Hekatah said as she drained her glass and stood to leave.

Dorothea shrugged. "He was your choice. Remember that if it goes wrong." She didn't look up when Hekatah raised her hands and pulled the hood away from her face.

"Look at me," Hekatah hissed. "Remember what I am."

It always amazed Dorothea that the demon-dead didn't look any different from the living. The only distinction was the faint odor of meat beginning to spoil. "I never forget what you are," Dorothea said with a smile. Hekatah's eyes blazed with anger, but Dorothea didn't look away. "And you should remember who owns Sadi, and that it's my generosity and my influence over Prythian that's making your little game of vengeance possible."

Hekatah flipped the hood back over her face and flung out one hand. The door opened with a crash, its brass knob embedded in the stone wall. With another hiss of anger, she was gone.

Dorothea refilled her wineglass. She'd seen the slight sneer, the change in Greer's eyes after he'd met the Dark Priestess. But what was she anyway? A bag of bones that didn't know enough to fall to dust. A leech. A scheming little harpy who was still trying to get back at a man who cared for nothing in Terreille. Nothing at all. She wasn't sure she believed this story about a child the Priest was besotted with, wasn't sure what difference it made if he was. Let him have his toy. She'd thrown enough youths into the Dark Priestess's lair. Now the walking carrion wanted her to give up the use of Sadi for a hundred years, and as gratitude for Dorothea's willingness to make such an accommodation, was trying to sway her best servant, to make him untrustworthy.

Very well. Let Greer fawn. The day would come when he would realize his error—and pay for it.

Greer sat in a dark corner booth, sipping his second tankard of ale and watching the worn, weary faces of the men at the other tables. He could have gone to a tavern where he would have had a better dinner and the ale wouldn't have left an aftertaste of wash water in his mouth, but he would have had to smile and fawn over the Blood aristos that crowded a place like that. Here, because they were afraid of him, he had the table of his choice, the best cut of meat, and privacy.

He drained the tankard and raised a finger at the barmaid, who hurried to refill it for him, fending off roaming hands as she passed between the tables. Greer smiled. That, too, in this place, he could have for the asking.

When he was sure everyone else was preoccupied, he lifted his right hand and laid it on the table.

He still didn't know why Sadi had done that to him, what had provoked the Sadist to such calculated destruction. He'd been sitting quietly in a tavern not unlike this one, exploring a wench's luxuries, when Sadi had walked up to his table and held out his right hand. Since Sadi had said nothing, since there was only that blank, bored face looking down at him, Greer had extended his own right hand, thinking Sadi had come to grovel for some favor. The moment Sadi's hand had closed around his, everything changed. One moment there was only the firm pressure of a handshake; the next he felt his bones being crushed, his fingers snapping, felt himself held in a mental vise so he didn't even have the luxury of fainting to escape. When the vise finally did allow him to escape . . .

His first thought when he came to was to get to a Healer right away, get to someone who could reshape the pulp that used to be a valuable tool. But someone had already done a healing. Someone had tenderly shaped his hand into a twisted claw and healed the bones sufficiently so that a Healer would have to crush them all over again in order to straighten the hand, and even Greer knew the best a second healing could do was make the shape a little better. It could never make that twisted claw into a usable hand.

Sadi had done the healing, knowing what the result would be. Sadi, who had never failed thereafter to greet him courteously, mockingly, hatefully, whenever they were both in attendance at Dorothea's court. Sadi, who now was going to butcher a child for the illusion of freedom.

Greer drained the tankard for the last time and threw a few coins on the table. There was a Web Coach heading west in an hour's time. He had wanted to wait, wanted to seem casual, but in truth, he couldn't wait to make this offer.

CHAPTER NINE

1 / Kaeleer

Saetan sat in a comfortable chair in what had become known as the "family" room at the Kaeleer Hall, his legs crossed at the knee, his fingers steepled and resting on his chin. He watched Jaenelle happily weave bright-colored ribbons through a thin sheet of wood.

Her lessons were no longer private, and he resented having so little time alone with her, but she was a living ball of witchlight who drew the males of his family to her; and he, who understood so well what drew them, couldn't find it in himself to shut them out.

Today Prothvar and Mephis haphazardly played chess while Andulvar relaxed in a chair with his eyes half-closed. Jaenelle sat on the floor in front of Saetan's chair, brightly colored sticks, playing cards, and ribbons scattered around her.

The lessons were getting better, Saetan thought dryly as he watched Jaenelle weave another ribbon through the wood. All he had to remember was to start at the end and work back to the beginning.

The lesson was supposed to be on how to pass one physical object through another. The idea was that once a witch knew how to pass one object through another, she could eventually learn how to pass living matter through non-living matter, thus being able to pass through a door or a wall. That was the idea anyway.

He had explained it in every way he could think of, had demonstrated it over and over again. She simply didn't get it. Finally, after an hour of frustration, he'd said brusquely, "If you wanted to pass your arm through that wood, what would you do?"

Jaenelle paused for the briefest moment, thrust her arm through the wood, and wiggled her fingers on the other side. "Like this?"

Andulvar had muttered something that sounded like "Mother Night." Mephis and Prothvar had upset the game table, spilling all the chess pieces on the floor. Saetan's eyes had glazed as he studied the wiggling fingers. "Like that," he'd finally said, choking.

Working backward from what she already knew made him queasy—he had never forgotten the young Warlord who had been too cocky about the lessons and then had panicked halfway through the pass—but it had only taken a few minutes to translate from flesh and wood to ribbons and wood, and it had been so pleasing to see that spark in her eyes, to almost hear the click when she put the pieces together and understood.

So now she was happily weaving ribbons through a piece of solid wood with an ease that women at a loom would envy.

"Oh, I almost forgot," Jaenelle said as she picked up another ribbon. "The Prince asked me to send his regards."

Andulvar's eyes flew open and immediately closed again. Mephis's hand froze above the piece he was about to move. Prothvar's head whipped around and immediately whipped back. Only Saetan, who was sitting in front of her, didn't react.

"The Prince?" he asked lazily.

"Mm. We have a Hayllian Warlord Prince living with us now. He's sort of a playmate for Leland and Alexandra." She paused in her weaving, her brow puckered. "I don't think he likes it much. He doesn't seem happy when he's with them. But he doesn't mind playing with Wilhelmina and me."

"And what does he play with you and Wilhelmina?" Saetan asked softly. He noticed Andulvar's sharp look, but he ignored it. Daemon wasn't just in Beldon Mor, he was in the damn house!

Jaenelle brightened. "Lots of things. We take walks, and he rides well, and he knows lots of stories, and he plays the piano with Wilhelmina, and he reads to us, and he's not like lots of grown-ups who think our games are silly." She picked up two ribbons and braided them through the wood. "He's like you in lots of ways." She tilted her head and studied his face. "He looks like you in some ways."

Saetan's blood roared in his ears. He lowered his hands and pressed one against his stomach. "And what way is that, witch-child?"

"Oh, the way your eyes get that funny look sometimes, like you've got a tummy ache and you want to laugh but you know it would hurt." She looked at the hand, now curled into a fist, that was pressing into his stomach. "Is there something wrong with your tummy?"

"Not yet."

Andulvar suddenly found the ceiling intensely interesting. Prothvar and Mephis just stared at her back. Saetan ground his teeth.

"He's really very nice, Saetan," Jaenelle said, puzzled by the strange emotional currents. "One day when it was raining, he played cradle with Wilhelmina and me for hours and hours."

"Cradle?" he said in a strangled voice.

Jaenelle embedded the Queen of Hearts into the wood. "It's a card game. The rules are pretty tricky, and the Prince kept forgetting some of them and then he'd lose."

"Did he?" Saetan bit his cheek. Hard to believe that Daemon would find the rules to any game "tricky."

"Mm. I didn't want him to feel bad, so . . . well, I was dealing, and I helped him win a game."

The ceiling above Andulvar was *intensely* interesting. Mephis started to cough. Prothvar found the texture of the curtains riveting.

Saetan cleared his throat and pushed his fist deeper into his stomach. "Did . . . did the Prince say anything?"

Jaenelle wrinkled her nose. "He said he'd be happy to teach me poker if he didn't have to bet against me. What did he mean, Saetan?"

Mephis and Prothvar leaped toward the game board and smacked their heads together. Andulvar started to shake and held the arms of the chair as if they were the only things keeping him close to the ground.

Saetan felt sure that if he didn't laugh soon his insides were going to be pulverized by the strain. "I think . . . he meant . . . that he would have liked . . . to have won by himself."

Jaenelle considered this and shook her head. "No, I don't think that's what he meant."

There was a muffled *ack ack ack* as Prothvar desperately tried to hold in the laughter, but the sound acted like a trigger and all four of them helplessly exploded.

Saetan's body felt like jelly. He slid out of the chair, landed with a thump on the floor, pitched over on his side, and howled.

Jaenelle looked at them and smiled as if willing to join in if someone would explain the joke. After a minute, she got to her feet, smoothed down her dress with the quiet pride and dignity of a young Queen, stepped over Saetan's legs, and headed for the door.

Saetan instantly sobered. Pushing himself up on one elbow, he said, "Witch-child? Where are you going?" The other three men stayed silent, waiting for an answer.

Jaenelle turned and looked down at Saetan. "I'm going to the bathroom and then I'm going to see if Mrs. Beale has anything to eat." She walked to the door, stiff-legged. The last thing they heard her mutter before she closed the door on them was, "Males."

There was a moment's more silence before the laughter sputtered to life again, continuing until none of them could stand anymore.

"I'm glad I'm dead," Andulvar said as he wiped at his eyes.

Saetan, lying on his back, tilted his head to look at his friend. "Why?"

"Because she'd be the death of me otherwise."

"Ah, but Andulvar, what a glorious way to die."

Andulvar sobered. "What are you going to do now? He went out of his way to tell you where he is. A challenge?"

Saetan slowly got to his feet, straightened his clothes, and smoothed back his hair. "Do you think he's that careless?"

"Maybe that arrogant."

Saetan thought it over and shook his head. "No, I don't think it's arrogance, but it is a challenge." He turned to face Andulvar. "To me. He may trust my intentions as little as I trust his. Perhaps we both need to trust . . . a little."

"So what will you do?"

Saetan sighed. "Send my regards in return."

2 / Terreille

As Greer looked out the embassy windows at the city called Beldon Mor, he heard the door quietly open and close. He probed the room behind him, expecting that some hand-wringing ambassador was waiting to tell him the meeting would be delayed. Instead he felt nothing but a slight chill. The fools who served here had a decent expense account. The least they could do was heat the rooms. Perhaps the little sniveler had entered, seen him, and scurried out without speaking.

Sneering, Greer turned from the windows and took one involuntary step backward.

Daemon Sadi stood by the closed door, his hands in his trouser pockets, his face that familiar, cool, bored mask. "Lord Greer," he said in a silky croon.

"Sadi," Greer replied contemptuously. "The High Priestess sent me with an offer for you."

"Oh?" Daemon said, raising one eyebrow. "Since when does Dorothea have her favorite act as a messenger boy?"

"This wasn't my idea," Greer snapped and immediately changed tack. "I do as I'm told, the same as you. Please." He gestured with his left hand toward two chairs. "Let's at least be comfortable."

Greer stiffened as Sadi glided over to the chairs and gracefully settled into one of them. The way the man moved pricked at him. There was something feline, something not altogether human in that movement. Greer sat in the other chair, the sunlight to his back, so that he could easily observe Sadi's face.

"I have an offer for you," Greer repeated. "It doesn't please me to be the one to bring it."

"So you've said."

Greer pressed his lips together. There wasn't even a spark of interest in the bastard's face. "The offer is this: one hundred years without having to serve in a court, to live where you choose and do what you choose, to spend your time in whatever society amuses you." Greer paused for dramatic effect. "And the offer includes the same terms for the Eyrien half-breed. Excuse me—your brother."

"The Eyrien is Ringed by the High Priestess of Askavi. Dorothea has no say as to what is done with him."

That was a lie, as Sadi well knew, but it annoyed Greer that there were no questions, no subtle changes in voice or expression. Could things have changed? Did he no longer have any interest in Yaslana?

"It's a generous offer," Greer said, fighting to control his desire to lash out, to force Sadi to react.

"Beyond words."

Greer's left hand clutched the chair. He took a deep breath. *He* had wanted to do the goading.

"And what's the string attached to this generous offer?" Sadi said with a feral smile.

Greer shivered. Damn those little idiots. When he was done with them, they'd know how to heat a room! He had to make this offer just right, and it was hard to think with the room so cold. "A good friend of the High Priestess has discovered that her consort has been dallying with a young witch, is besotted with her, in fact. She would like to do something to end that activity, but because of political sensitivities is unable to do anything herself."

"Mm. I would think that if she wants her consort quietly buried, you'd be more skilled to handle it than I."

"It's not the consort she wants buried." Hell's fire, it was cold!

"Ah. I see." Sadi crossed his legs at the knee and steepled his fingers, resting his long nails on his chin. "However, as you must know, my ability to travel is severely limited by the desires of the Queen I'm serving. An unexplained jaunt would be difficult."

"And not necessary. That's why the offer is being made to you."

"Oh?"

"The High Priestess's friend has reason to believe that her nemesis is in this very city." Greer's feet were numb. He wanted to rub his hands together to warm them, but Sadi didn't seem to notice the cold, and he wasn't about to show any sign of weakness.

Sadi frowned, the first change in his face since the interview began. "And how old is this nemesis? What does she look like?"

"Hard to tell exactly. You know how hard it can be to judge these flash-in-a-day races. Young, though, at least in looks. Golden hair. That's the only definite feature. Probably has a strange aura—"

Sadi laughed, an unnerving sound. He looked highly amused, but there was something queer about the glitter in his eyes. "My dear Lord Greer, you're talking about half the females living on this clump of rock. Strange aura? Compared to what? High-strung eccentricity is a prepubescent epidemic here. You won't find an aristo family on the whole damn island that doesn't have at least one daughter with a 'strange aura.' What do you expect me to do? Approach each one while her chaperon looks on and ask her if she's screwing a Hayllian from one of the Hundred Families?" He laughed again.

Greer ground his teeth. "Then you're refusing the offer?"

"No, Greer, I'm simply telling you that without more information, the friend's consort is going to be playing with his toy for a very long time.

So unless you can tell me more than that, it isn't worth the effort." Sadi stood up and tugged his jacket sleeves down over his cuffs. "The offer is intriguing, however, and if I stumble across a golden-haired girl with a taste for Hayllians, I'll give her a very good look. Now if you'll excuse me, I'm overdue at a dressmaker's shop where my tasteful opinions are required." He bowed mockingly and left.

Greer counted to ten before leaping out of the chair and stumbling to the door on his numb feet. He clawed at the door, the knob so cold it almost stuck to his skin. He finally pulled the door open, stepped into the hallway—and sagged against the wall.

The hallway felt like an oven.

Daemon stared at the bed of witchblood in the alcove. Unable to sleep, he'd gone for a walk and had ended up here. The night air was cold and he'd forgotten his topcoat, but it felt good to be numbed by a cold that wasn't coming from within.

Dorothea was looking for Jaenelle. It didn't matter if she was looking for her own reasons or at someone else's behest. Dorothea always tried to destroy strong young witches who might one day rival her power. Once she found out who and what Jaenelle was, she would use every weapon at her disposal to destroy the girl.

Greer was sniffing around for information, which meant Dorothea wasn't certain that Jaenelle lived in Beldon Mor. But there was no reason to think that Greer's visit would be brief, and if he stayed around long enough, sooner or later he would overhear someone talking about Leland Benedict's eccentric, golden-haired daughter. And then?

Have you taught her how to kill, Priest? Can you teach her such a thing? She's so wise in her innocence, so innocent in her wisdom.

He should have killed Greer instead of just crippling the hand that had slit Titian's throat. But the timing had been wrong, and even if she had had no proof, Dorothea would have suspected him. An oversight he still couldn't correct without drawing too much attention to this house. There was no place he could hide Jaenelle that would be safe enough, not with her propensity to wander, and he wasn't willing to give her to the Priest yet, even if she would go and stay away. Not yet.

Daemon shook his head. The night was fleeing, and since he'd reached the alcove, he'd known what he had to do. If the offer had been made for him alone, there would have been no question about his answer. But it hadn't been made for him alone. He took a deep breath and sent a spear thread along the Ebon-gray.

Prick? Prick, can you hear me?

There was the sudden awareness of someone waking instantly from a light sleep. *Bastard?* A stirring, a focusing. *Bastard, what—*

Listen. There's not much time. Greer made me an offer today.

Greer? Icy wariness. *Why?*

A friend of Dorothea's wants a favor. Daemon swallowed hard and shut his eyes tight. *One hundred years out of court service . . . for both of us . . . if I kill a child.*

The next words floated into Daemon's mind, venomously sweet. *Any child? Or one in particular?*

Daemon looked down. His right hand was rubbing the scar on his left wrist. *A very special child. An extraordinary child.*

And your answer was?

I told you. The offer wasn't for me al—

Where are you?

Chaillot.

A hiss of fury. *Listen to me, you son of a whoring bitch. If you accept that offer for my sake, the first thing I'll do is kill you.*

The first thing I'd do is let you. Daemon sank to his knees, shaking with relief. *Thank you.*

What? The waves of fury rolling through the thread stopped.

Thank you. I . . . had hoped . . . that would be your answer, but I had to ask. Daemon took a deep breath. *There's something else you should—*

The bitch is up. There's no time. Take care of her, Bastard. If you have to bleed everyone else dry, do it, but take care of her.

Lucivar was gone.

Daemon slowly got to his feet. He'd taken a tremendous risk contacting Lucivar. If they were caught communicating, a whipping would be the least of the punishments. He wasn't worried for himself. He was too far away from Hayll for Dorothea to detect it through her primary controlling ring, and he was confident of his ability to slide around Alexandra, who wore the secondary controlling ring. But Zuultah wasn't Alexandra, and Lucivar didn't always walk cautiously.

Be careful, Prick, Daemon thought as he slowly walked back to the house. *Be careful.* In a few more years, Jaenelle would be of age. And then they would serve the kind of Queen they'd always dreamed of.

He could have followed the Ebon-gray spear thread back to Lucivar to find out if Zuultah had detected their communication, but he didn't because he didn't want to know for certain that Zuultah was using the Ring. He didn't want to know that Lucivar was in pain.

Daemon glanced up at the windows of the nursery wing. Not a glimmer of light. He wanted to slip up the stairs, slide into that small bed, and curl himself around her, warmed by the knowledge that she was alive and safe. Because if Lucivar was in pain . . .

Daemon let himself into the house and went to his room. He undressed quickly and got into bed. His room was crowded with shadows, and as the sky lightened with the coming dawn, he kept wondering what the sun was witnessing in Pruul.

3 / Terreille

Surreal unbuttoned her coat as she meandered down a path in the Angelline public gardens, a part of the estate that Alexandra Angelline had opened for the city's use. The gardens were one of the few places left in Beldon Mor where people could walk on grass or sit under a tree, and it seemed like all of the Blood aristos were there, enjoying one of the last warm days of autumn.

Twenty years ago, when Surreal had come to the city to lend her reputation to Deje for the opening of the Red Moon house, there had been grass and trees aplenty. Now Beldon Mor was just a newer, cleaner version of Draega, thanks to the Hayllian ambassadors' skill at prostituting the council and leeching away the strength of the Blood.

More than the landens of each race, the Blood needed to stay in touch with the land. Without that contact, it was too easy to forget that, according to their most ancient legends, they were created to be the caretakers. It was too easy to become embroiled in their own egos.

Surreal walked along the garden paths, amused by the reactions to her presence. Young men on the strut watched her with calculated interest; young men walking with the Ladies they were courting glanced at her and blushed while their companions hastily tugged them in a different direction; men who were making an obligatory public appearance with their wives stared straight ahead, while their wives looked from Surreal to their husbands' pale, tight-lipped faces and back to Surreal again. She ignored all of them, to the intense relief of her clients. Well, almost all. She did smile intimately at one Warlord who had treated a young whore very harshly a few nights ago and waggled her fingers at him in greeting before hurrying away, laughing quietly and wishing she could hear his blustering explanation.

But that was enough fun. Time for business.

Surreal continued her meandering, moving closer and closer to the wrought-iron fence that separated the private gardens from the public ones. Beneath her shirt she wore the Gray Jewel mounted in a gold setting that was an exact replica of Titian's Green Jewel. She'd been probing with the Gray since she entered the gardens, hoping she wouldn't get a flickering answer because that would mean Philip was nearby—and it wasn't Philip she was looking for.

As she neared the fence, she sent the private signal Daemon had taught her so many years ago, the signal that told him she needed him. Then she turned away and continued exploring the smaller paths nearby.

Maybe he wasn't at the house. Maybe he was but couldn't get away. Maybe he wouldn't answer the signal. She hadn't dared use it since the night she pushed him into showing her Hayll's Whore.

She felt him before she saw him, coming up a path behind her. Turning, she headed toward him, pausing now and then to admire a late-blooming flower. The path was an offshoot, with less chance of someone seeing them, but even so, Surreal didn't want anyone asking questions. As she passed him, she pretended to stumble and turn her foot.

"Damn," she said as Daemon held her arm to steady her. "Hold still a minute, would you, sugar?" She put a hand on his shoulder, leaned against him, and fiddled with her shoe. "There's someone looking for you." She felt him tense, saw the small ring of frost around his feet.

"Oh? Why?"

Still fiddling with her shoe, Surreal couldn't see his face, but she knew there would be nothing but a bored, slightly put-upon expression despite the silky chill in his voice.

"She thinks you're interested in a child here, one, apparently, of great interest to her, one that Dorothea wants out of the way. If I were you, I'd watch my back. She didn't hire me for a contract, but that doesn't mean she hasn't been interviewing others who would be willing to have a try at you." She put her foot down and wobbled her ankle as if testing it.

"Do you know who she is?"

Surreal frowned and shook her head, still studying her shoe. "A witch staying at Cassandra's Altar. No way to tell how long she's been there. There are a couple of rooms fixed up. That's about it. I've stayed in worse places."

Daemon kept his head turned away from her. "Thank you for the warning. Now if you'll ex—"

"Prince? Prince, you must come and see."

Surreal turned toward the sound of the girl's voice. It sounded like silk feels, she thought as the thin, golden-haired girl skipped around the bend and stopped in front of them, her smile warm, her eyes—eyes that seemed to shift color depending on the way the sunlight found its way through the leaves—full of high spirits and curiosity.

"Hello," the girl said as she studied Surreal's face.

"Lady," Surreal replied, trying to sound respectful and dignified, but she'd heard Sadi's exasperated sigh and wanted to laugh.

"We should be getting back," Daemon said, moving to the girl's side and trying to turn her toward the private gardens.

Surreal was about to slip away when she heard Daemon say, "Lady." The coaxing, pleading note in his voice rooted her to the path. She'd never heard him sound like that. She looked at the girl, who had planted her feet and refused to be turned.

"Jaenelle," he said a bit desperately.

Jaenelle ignored him as she studied Surreal's face and chest.

That was when Surreal realized that the Gray Jewel had slipped out from under her shirt when she bent over to examine her shoe. She looked at Daemon, silently asking what she should do.

As Daemon gently squeezed Jaenelle's shoulder to get her attention, Jaenelle said, "Are you Surreal?" When Surreal didn't answer, Jaenelle tipped her head back to look at Daemon. "Is she Surreal?"

Daemon's face had a guarded, trapped look. He took a deep breath and released it, slowly. "Yes, she's Surreal."

Jaenelle clasped her hands in front of her and smiled happily at Surreal. "I have a message for you."

Surreal blinked, totally at a loss. "A message?"

"Lady, just give her the message. We have to go," Daemon said, trying to put some strength into his words.

Jaenelle frowned at him, obviously puzzled by his lack of courtesy, but she obeyed. "Titian sends her love."

Surreal's legs buckled at the same time Daemon grabbed her. "Is this your idea of a joke?" she whispered savagely, hiding her face against his chest.

"May the Darkness help me, Surreal, this is no joke."

Surreal looked up at him. Fear, too, was something she'd never heard in his voice. She braced herself and stepped away from him. "Titian is dead," she said tightly.

Jaenelle looked even more puzzled. "Yes, I know."

"How do you know Titian?" Daemon asked quietly, but his voice vibrated with tension. He shivered, and Surreal knew it had nothing to do with the fresh little breeze that had sprung up.

"She's Queen of the Harpies. She told me her daughter's name is Surreal, and she told me what she looked like, and she told me her Jewel's setting might look like the family crest. The Dea al Mon usually wear it in silver, but the gold looks right on you." Jaenelle looked at them. She was still pleased that she'd been able to deliver the message, but their reactions made no sense.

Surreal wanted to run, wanted to escape, wanted to hold on to this child who didn't think it strange to be a bridge between the living and the dead. She tried to say something, anything, but only an inarticulate sound came out, so she looked to Daemon for help and realized he wasn't standing on solid ground either.

Finally he shook himself, slipped an arm around Jaenelle's shoulders, and led her toward the private gardens.

"Wait," Surreal called. She swayed but stayed on her feet. Tears filled her eyes, filled her voice. "If you should see Titian again, send my love in return."

The smile she saw through the blur of tears was gentle and understanding. "I will, Surreal. I won't forget."

Then they were gone.

Surreal stumbled to a tree and wrapped her arms around it, tears streaming down her cheeks. Dea al Mon. The family name? The people Titian had come from? She didn't know, but it was more than she'd ever had before. She felt torn apart inside, and yet, for the first time since she'd stumbled into that room and saw Titian lying dead, she didn't feel alone.

4 / Terreille

As Cassandra opened the cupboard where she kept the wineglasses, she felt the dark male presence at the kitchen door, that unmistakable scent of the Black. Without turning, she reached for a wineglass and said, "I didn't expect you until later."

"I'm surprised you expected me at all."

She missed the glass. Only one male's psychic scent could be mistaken for Saetan's. Buying time while she vanished the Red Jewel and called in her Black, she took two glasses from the cupboard and set them on the counter before turning around.

He leaned against the door frame, his hands in his trouser pockets.

Ah, Saetan, look what you've sired. Cassandra's heart beat in an odd little rhythm as she admired his body and the almost too beautiful face. If there had been the merest hint of seduction in the air, her ancient pulse would have been racing. But there was only a bone-chilling cold and a look in his eyes that she couldn't meet.

Think, woman, think. She was a Guardian, one of the living dead, but he didn't know that. If he damaged her body, she could instantly make the transition to demon and keep fighting. She doubted he had the knowledge or skill to destroy her completely. Black against Black. She could hold her own against him.

She glanced at his eyes and knew, with shocking certainty, that it wasn't true. He had come for the kill, and he knew exactly who and what she was.

"You disappoint me, Cassandra. Your legends paint you differently," Daemon said softly, his voice thick with malevolence.

"I'm a Priestess serving at this Altar," she said, working to keep her voice steady. "You're mistaken if you think—"

He laughed softly. She stepped back from the sound and found herself pressed against the counter.

"Do you think I can't tell the difference between a Priestess and a Queen? And the Jewels, my dear, name you for what you are."

She bent her head slightly in acknowledgment. "So I'm Cassandra. What do you want, Prince?"

He eased away from the door and stepped toward her. "More to the point, Lady"—he put a nasty edge on the word—"what do *you* want?"

"I don't understand." Training demanded she stand her ground. Instinct screamed at her to run.

He kept moving toward her, smiling as she edged around the table to keep it between them. It was a seducer's smile, soft and almost gentle, except it was carved from ice. "Who are you waiting for?" He withdrew his hands from his pockets.

Cassandra glanced at his hands. The momentary relief of not seeing a ring on his right hand was stripped away by the realization of how long he wore his nails. Mother Night, he was his father's son! She kept easing around the table. If she could get to the door . . .

Daemon changed directions, blocking her escape. "Who?"

"A friend."

He shook his head in mocking sadness.

Cassandra stopped moving. "Would you like some wine?" He was dangerous, dangerous, dangerous.

"No." He paused and studied the nails on his right hand. "You don't think I can create a grave deep enough to hold you, do you?" His voice was silky, crooning, almost sleepy. Terrifying. And familiar. Another deep voice with a slightly different cadence, but the crooning rage was the same. "For your information, just in case you've been considering it, I *know* you can't create one deep enough to hold *me.*"

Cassandra lifted her chin and looked him in the eye. She'd used that pause to put a strengthening spell on her nails, making them as strong and sharp as daggers. "Maybe not, but I'm going to try."

Daemon lifted one eyebrow. "Why?" he asked too gently.

Cassandra's temper flared. "Because you're dangerous and cruel. You're Hekatah's puppet and Dorothea's pet sent here to destroy an extraordinary witch. I won't let you. I won't. You may put me in the grave for good, but I'll give you a taste of it, too."

She flung herself at him, her hand curved and ready, the Black Jewel blazing. He caught her wrists, holding her off with an ease that made her scream. He hit the Black shields on her inner barriers hard enough to make her work to keep them intact, but they wouldn't keep him out for long. She was draining her Jewels and he hadn't tapped his yet. When her Black were drained, there would be no way to stop him from shattering her mind.

She tried to twist away from him, tried to eliminate the immediate physical danger so she could concentrate on protecting her mind. Then she froze as his snake tooth pressed into her wrist. She didn't think his venom would be deadly to a Guardian, but if he pumped his full shot into her, it would paralyze her long enough for him to pick her apart at his leisure.

She looked up at him defiantly, her teeth bared, ready to fight to the end. It was the look on his face, the change in his eyes that arrested her. There was wariness there. And hope?

"You don't like Dorothea," he said slowly, as if puzzling out a difficult problem.

"I like Hekatah even less," she snapped.

"Hekatah." Daemon released her, swearing softly as he paced the room. "Hekatah still exists? Like you?"

Cassandra sniffed. "Not like me. I'm a Guardian. She's a demon."

"I beg your pardon," he said dryly as he prowled the room.

"Are you saying you weren't sent here to kill the girl?" Cassandra rubbed her sore wrists.

Daemon stopped pacing. "I'll take some wine, if you're still offering it."

Cassandra got the glasses, a bottle of red wine, and the decanter of yarbarah. Pouring a glass of each, she handed him the wine.

Daemon tested it, sniffed it, and took a sip. One eyebrow rose. "You have excellent taste in wine, Lady."

Cassandra shrugged. "Not my taste. It was a gift." When he didn't say anything else, she prodded, "Is that why you're here?"

"Perhaps," he said slowly, thinking it over. Then he smiled wryly. "I was of the opinion that I was sent here because I had been a bit too troublesome of late and there wasn't another court that would have me, or another Queen that Dorothea was willing to sacrifice in order to blunt my temper." He sipped the wine appreciatively. "However, if what you believe is true—and recent events do seem to support that belief—it was a grave error on her part." He laughed softly, but there was a brutality to the sound that made Cassandra shiver.

"Why is it an error? If she offered you something of value to—"

"Like my freedom?" The wariness was back in his eyes. "Like a century of not having to kneel and serve?"

Cassandra pressed her lips together. This was going wrong, and if he turned against her again, he wouldn't relent a second time. "The girl means everything to us, Prince, and she means nothing to you."

"Nothing?" He smiled bitterly. "Do you think that someone like me, having lived as I've lived, being what I am, would destroy the one person he's been looking for his whole life? Do you think me such a fool I don't recognize what she is, what she'll become? She's magic, Cassandra. A single flower blooming in an endless desert."

Cassandra stared at him. "You're in love with her." Sudden anger washed over her at the next thought. "She's just a child."

"That fact hasn't eluded me," he said dryly as he refilled his wineglass. "Who is 'us'?"

"What?"

"You said 'the girl means everything to us.' Who?"

"Me . . ." Cassandra hesitated, took a deep breath. "And the Priest."

Daemon's expression was a mixture of relief and pain. He licked his lips. "Does he . . . Does *he* think I mean her harm?" He shook his head. "No matter. I've wondered the same about him."

Cassandra gasped, incensed. "How could—" She stopped herself. If they had presumed that about him, why would he not presume the same about them? She sat at the kitchen table. He hesitated and then sat across from her. "Listen to me," she said earnestly. "I can understand why you feel bitter toward him, but you don't feel half as bitter as he does. He never wanted to walk away from you, but he had no other choice. No matter what you think of him because of the way you've had to live, one thing is true: he adores her. With every breath, with every drop of his blood, he adores her."

Daemon toyed with the wineglass. "Isn't he a little old for her?"

"I'd say he was experienced," Cassandra replied tartly. "She'll be a powerful Queen and should have an older, experienced Steward."

Daemon glanced at her, amused. "Steward?"

"Of course." She studied him. "Do you have ambitions to wear the Steward's ring?"

Daemon shook his head. His lips twitched. "No, I don't have any ambitions to wear the *Steward's* ring."

"Well, then." Cassandra's eyes widened. Now that the chill was gone, now that he was a little more relaxed . . . "You really are your father's son," she said dryly and was startled by his immediate, warm laughter. Her eyes narrowed. "You thought—that's wicked!"

"Is it?" His golden eyes caressed her with disturbing warmth. "Perhaps it is."

Cassandra smiled. When the anger and cold were gone, he really was a delightful man. "What does she think of you?"

"How in the name of Hell should I know?" he growled. His eyes narrowed as she laughed at him.

"Does she try your patience to the breaking point? Exasperate you until you want to scream? Make you feel as if you can't tell from one step to the next if you're going to touch solid ground or fall into a bottomless pit?"

He looked at her with interest. "Do you feel that way?"

"Oh, no," Cassandra said lightly. "But then, I'm not male."

Daemon growled.

"That's a familiar sound." It was fun teasing him because, despite his strength, he didn't frighten her the way Saetan did. "You and the Priest might have more in common than you think where she's concerned."

He laughed, and she knew it was the idea of Saetan being as bewildered as he that amused him, consoled him, linked him to them.

Daemon finished his wine and stood up. "I'm . . . glad . . . to have met you, Cassandra. I hope it won't be the last time."

She linked her arm through his and walked with him to the outer door of the Sanctuary. "You're welcome anytime, Prince."

Daemon raised her hand to his lips and kissed it lightly.

She watched him until he was out of sight before returning to the kitchen and washing the glasses.

Now there was just the delicate little matter of explaining this meeting to his father.

5 / Terreille

There are some things the body never forgets, Saetan thought wryly as Cassandra snuggled closer to him, her hand tracing anxious little circles up and down his chest. Before tonight he'd politely refused to stay with her, wary that she might want more from him than he was willing—or able—to give. But she, too, was a Guardian, and that kind of love was no longer part of her life. There were, after all, some penalties to the half-life. Still, it pleased him to feel skin against skin, to caress the curves of a feminine body. If only she'd get to the point and stop making those damn little circles, because he remembered only too well what they meant.

He captured her hand and held it against his chest. "So?" As he turned his head and kissed her hair, he felt her frown. He pressed his lips together, annoyed. Had she forgotten how easy it was for him to read a woman's body, to pick up her subtlest moods? Was she going to deny what had screamed at him the moment he stepped into the kitchen?

"So?" She lightly, teasingly, kissed his chest.

Saetan took a deep breath. His patience frayed. "So when are you going to get around to telling me what happened this afternoon?"

She tensed. "What happened this afternoon?"

He clenched his teeth. "The walls remember, Cassandra. I'm a Black Widow, too. Do you want me to pull it out of the walls and replay it, or are you going to tell me yourself?"

"There's really not much—"

"Not much!" Saetan swore as he rolled away from her and leaned against the headboard. "Have the centuries addled your mind, woman?"

"Don't . . ."

Saetan looked into her eyes. "I frighten you," he said bitterly. "I've never harmed you, never touched you in anger, seldom even raised my voice at you. I loved you, served you well, and used my strength to keep a vow to you through all those desolate years. And I frighten you. Since the day I returned with the Black, I've frightened you." He leaned his head back and stared at the ceiling. "You're frightened of me, and yet you have the audacity to provoke *my son* into a murderous rage and try to dismiss it as if nothing happened. What I don't understand is why this place is standing at all, why I'm not trying to locate your remains, or why he wasn't standing on the threshold waiting for me. Did you tell him about me? Was I your trick card to make him hesitate long enough for you to try to smooth it over?"

"It wasn't like that!" Cassandra pulled the sheet around her.

"Then what was it like?" His voice sounded flat with the effort to keep his temper in check.

"He came here because he thought I—we—wanted to harm Jaenelle."

Saetan shook his head. "You, perhaps. Not me. He already knew about me." He looked away. He didn't want to see her confusion, didn't want to consider what might happen if that tenuous link between Daemon and himself shattered.

"Saetan . . . listen to me." Cassandra reached out to him.

He hesitated a moment before holding out his arm and letting her settle on his shoulder. He listened, without interrupting, while she told him about her meeting with Daemon, suspecting that she had blunted far too many edges, had given him the bone without any of the meat.

"You were very lucky," he said when she finally stopped talking.

"Well, I realize he wears the Black."

Saetan snorted and shook his head. "There is a range of strength within every Jewel. You know that as well as I."

"He's not really trained."

"Don't mistake ability for polish. He may not do everything he wants to with finesse, but that doesn't mean he can't do it."

She fidgeted, annoyed because he wasn't soothed by her rendition of the meeting. But there was still all that meat he hadn't gotten.

"You sound as if you're afraid of him," she said crossly.

"I am."

She gasped.

Saetan suddenly felt weary. Weary of Cassandra, weary of Hekatah, weary of all the witches he'd known who, no matter what they did or didn't feel for him as a man, all looked at his Jewels and saw the potential to achieve their own ends. Only the one with sapphire eyes saw him as Saetan. Just Saetan.

"Why?" Cassandra asked, watching his face intently.

Saetan closed his eyes. So weary. And there was another man, a far more desperate man, who had seen only seventeen centuries and was just as weary. "Because he's stronger than me, Cassandra. And not just because he's living. He's stronger than I was in my prime, and he's . . . more ruthless."

Cassandra bit her lip. "He knows about Jaenelle. I had the impression he knows where to find her."

Saetan let out a sharp laugh. "Oh, I imagine he does. It's probably not that far a walk from his room to hers."

"What?"

"He's serving her family, Cassandra. He's living in the same house." He leaned toward her, taking her chin between his fingers. "Now do you begin to understand? He knows about me because Jaenelle told him, completely ignorant, I'm sure, that it would make him climb the walls. And I know about him because he sent a message to me, through Jaenelle. A polite message, basically warning me off his territory."

"He doesn't want to be Steward of the court."

Saetan laughed, genuinely amused. "No, I wouldn't think he would. He's in his prime, virile, living, and well trained in seduction. That twelve-year-old body must be driving him out of his skin."

Cassandra hesitated. "He thought you wanted to be her Consort."

Saetan gave her a sidelong look. "What did you tell him?"

"That she needed an older, experienced Steward."

"Very kind of you."

Cassandra sighed. "You're still angry about my talking to him."

"No, I'm not. I just wish . . ." *That I could have seen him, talked to him, felt the strength of his grip, heard the sound of his voice. That we could have judged each other honestly. We're forced to trust each other because Jaenelle is asking us to, because she trusts.*

He caressed Cassandra's hair. "Promise me you'll be careful. Hekatah's searching for Jaenelle. If Dorothea is supporting the effort, he'll know best where to look for danger from that quarter. Whether or not he'll ask us for help will depend on whether or not he trusts us. I want that trust, Cassandra, and not just for Jaenelle's sake. You owe me that much."

CHAPTER TEN

1 / Terreille

Why does she ask so damn many uncomfortable questions? Daemon thought, clenching his teeth and staring straight ahead as they walked through the garden. He almost missed Wilhelmina, who was in bed with a cold. At least when her sister was present, Jaenelle didn't ask questions that made him blush.

"You're not going to answer, are you?" Jaenelle asked after a minute of teeth-grinding silence.

"No."

"Don't you know the answer?"

"Whether I know the answer or not is beside the point. It's not something a man discusses with a young girl."

"But you know the answer."

Daemon growled.

"If I were older, would you tell me?" Jaenelle persisted.

There might be a way out of this yet. "Yes, if you were older."

"How old?"

"What?"

"How old would I have to be?"

"Nineteen," he said quickly, beginning to relax. Who knew what sort of questions she might have in seven years, but at least he wouldn't have to answer this one.

"Nineteen?"

Daemon's stomach fluttered. He walked a little faster. The pleased way she said that made him distinctly uncomfortable.

"The Priest said he wouldn't tell me until I was twenty-five," Jaenelle said happily, "but you'll tell me six years sooner."

Daemon skidded to a stop. His eyes narrowed as he regarded the happy, upturned face and clear sapphire eyes. "You asked the Priest?"

Jaenelle looked a little uncomfortable, which made him feel a little better. "Well . . . yes."

Daemon imagined Saetan trying to deal with the same question and fought the urge to laugh. He cleared his throat and tried to look stern. "Do you always ask me the same questions you ask him?"

"It depends on whether or not I get an answer."

Daemon clamped his teeth together in order to keep a wonderfully pithy response from escaping. "I see," he said in a strangled voice. He started walking again.

Jaenelle skipped ahead to examine some leaves. "Sometimes I ask lots of people the same question."

His head hurt. "What do you do if you don't get the same answer?"

"Think about it."

"Mother Night," he muttered.

Jaenelle gathered some of the leaves and then frowned. "There are some questions I'm not allowed to ask again until I'm a hundred. I don't think that's fair, do you?"

Yes!

"I mean," she continued, "how am I supposed to learn anything if people won't tell me?"

"There are some questions that shouldn't be asked until a person is mature enough to appreciate the answers."

Jaenelle stuck her tongue out at him. He responded in kind.

"Just because you're a little older than me doesn't mean you have to be so bossy," she complained.

Daemon looked over his shoulder to see if anyone else was around. There wasn't, so that meant she was referring to him. When did he change from being an elder to being just a *little* older . . . and bossy?

Impertinent chit. Maddening, impossible . . . how did the Priest stand it? How . . .

Daemon put on his best smile, which was difficult since his teeth were still clenched. "Are you seeing the Priest today?"

Jaenelle frowned at him, suspicious. "Yes."

"Would you give him a message?"

Her eyes narrowed. "All right," she said cautiously.

"Come on, I've got some paper in my room."

As Jaenelle waited outside his room, Daemon penned his question and sealed the envelope. She eyed it, shrugged, and slipped it into the pocket of her coat. They parted then, he to escort Alexandra on her morning visits, and she to her lessons.

Saetan looked up from his book. "Aren't you supposed to be with Andulvar?" he asked as Jaenelle bounced into his public study. He and Andulvar had decided that, under the guise of studying Eyrien weapons, Andulvar would teach her physical self-defense while he concentrated on Craft weaponry.

"Yes, but I wanted to give you this first." She handed him a plain white envelope. "Is Prothvar going to be helping with the lesson?"

"I imagine so," Saetan replied, studying the envelope.

Jaenelle wrinkled her nose. "Boys play rough, don't they?"

He's pushing because he's afraid for you, witch-child. "Yes, I guess they do. Go on now."

She gave him a choke-hold hug. "Will I see you after?"

He kissed her cheek. "Just try to leave without seeing me."

She grinned and bounced out of the room.

Saetan turned the envelope over and over in his hands before finally, carefully, opening the flap. He took out the single sheet of paper, read it, read it again . . . and began to laugh.

When she returned and had plundered her way through the sandwich and nutcakes that were waiting for her, Saetan handed her the envelope, resealed with black wax. She stuffed it into her pocket, tactfully showing no curiosity about this exchange between himself and Daemon.

After she left, he sat in his chair, a smile tugging at his lips, and wondered what his fine young Prince would do with his answer.

Daemon was helping Alexandra into her cloak when Jaenelle popped into the hallway. He'd spent the day teetering between curiosity and apprehension, regretting his impulsiveness at sending that message. Now he and Alexandra were on their way to the theater, and it wasn't the right time or place to ask Jaenelle about the message.

"You look wonderful, Alexandra," Jaenelle said as she admired the elegant dress.

Alexandra smiled, but her brow puckered in a little frown. It always annoyed her that Jaenelle persisted in addressing everyone on a first-name basis. Except him. "Thank you, dear," she said a bit stiffly. "Shouldn't you be in bed by now?"

"I just wanted to say good night," Jaenelle said politely, but Daemon noticed the slight shift in her expression, the sadness beneath the child mask. He also noticed that she said nothing to him.

They were on their way out the door when he suddenly felt something in his jacket pocket. Slipping his fingers inside, he felt the edge of the envelope, and his throat tightened.

He spent the whole evening surreptitiously touching the envelope, wanting to find an excuse to be alone for a minute so he could pull it out. Years of self-control and discipline asserted themselves, and it wasn't until he left Alexandra drifting into a satisfied sleep and was in his own room that he allowed himself to look at it.

He stared at the black wax. The Priest had read it, then. He licked his lips, took a deep breath, and broke the seal.

The writing was strong, neat, and masculine with an archaic flourish. He read the reply, read it again . . . and began to laugh.

Daemon had written: "What do you do when she asks a question no man would give a child an answer to?"

Saetan had replied: "Hope you're obliging enough to answer it for me. However, if you're backed into a corner, refer her to me. I've become accustomed to being shocked."

Daemon grinned, shook his head, and hid the note among his private papers. That night, and for several nights after, he fell asleep smiling.

2 / Terreille

Frowning, Daemon stood beneath the maple tree in the alcove. He had seen Jaenelle come in here a few minutes ago, could sense that she was very nearby, but he couldn't find her. Where . . .

A branch shook above his head. Daemon looked up and swallowed hard to keep his heart from leaping past his teeth. He swallowed again—

hard—to keep down the tongue-lashing that was blistering his throat in its effort to escape. All that swallowing made his head hurt. As his nostrils flared in an effort to breathe and his breath puffed white in the cold air, Jaenelle let out her silvery velvet-coated laugh.

"Dragons can do that even if it isn't cold," she said gaily as she looked down at him from the lowest branch, a good eight feet above his head. She squatted on the branch with her arms around her knees and no discernible way to save herself if she overbalanced.

Daemon wasn't interested in dragons, and his heart was no longer trying to leap out—it was trying to crawl into his stomach and hide.

"Would you mind coming down from there, Lady?" he said, astounded that his voice sounded so casual. "Heights make me a bit queasy."

"Really?" Jaenelle's eyebrows lifted in surprise. She shrugged, stood up, and leaped.

Daemon jumped forward to catch her, pulled himself back in time, and was rewarded by having a muscle in his back spasm in protest. He watched, wide-eyed, as she drifted down as gracefully as the leaves dancing around her, finally settling on the grass a few feet from him.

Daemon straightened up, winced as the muscle spasmed again, and looked at the tree. *Stay calm. If you yell at her, she won't answer any questions.*

He took a deep breath, puffed it out. "How did you get up there?"

She gave him an unsure-but-game smile. "The same way I got down."

Daemon sighed and sat down on the iron bench that circled the tree. "Mother Night," he muttered as he leaned his head against the tree and closed his eyes.

There was a long silence. He knew she was watching him, fluffing her hair as she tried to puzzle out his seemingly strange behavior.

"Don't you know how to stand on air, Prince?" Jaenelle asked hesitantly, as though she was trying not to offend him.

Daemon opened his eyes a crack. He could see his knees—and her feet. He sat up slowly and studied the feet planted firmly on nothing. "It would seem I missed that lesson," he said dryly. "Could you show me?"

Jaenelle hesitated, suddenly turning shy.

"Please?" He hated the wistfulness in his voice. He hated feeling so vulnerable. She'd begun to make some excuse, but that note in his voice stopped her, made her look at him closely. He had no idea what she saw in his face. He only knew he felt raw and naked and helpless under the steady gaze of those sapphire eyes.

Jaenelle smiled shyly. "I could try." She hesitated. "I've never tried to teach a grown-up before."

"Grown-ups are just like children, only bigger," Daemon said brightly, snapping to his feet.

She sighed, her expression one of harried amusement. "Up here," she said as she stood on the iron bench.

Daemon stepped up beside her.

"Can you feel the bench under your feet?"

Indeed he could. It was a cold day that promised snow by morning, and he could feel the cold from the iron bench seeping up through his shoes. "Yes."

"You have to really *feel* the bench."

"Lady," Daemon said dryly, "I really *feel* the bench."

Jaenelle wrinkled her nose at him. "Well, all you have to do is extend the bench all the way across the alcove. You step"—she placed one foot forward and it looked as if she was stepping on something solid—"and you continue to feel the bench. Like this." She brought the other foot forward so that she was standing on the air at exactly the same height as the bench. She looked at him over her shoulder.

Daemon took a deep breath, puffed it out. "Right." He imagined the bench extending before him, put one foot out, placed it on the air, and pitched forward since there was nothing beneath him. His foot squarely hit the hard ground, jarring him from his ankle to his ears.

He brought his other foot to the ground and gingerly tested his ankle. It would be a little sore, but it was still sound. He kept his back half turned from her as he ground his teeth, waiting for the insolent giggle he'd heard in so many other courts when he'd been maneuvered into looking foolish. He was furious for failing, furious because of the sudden despair he felt that she would think him an inadequate companion.

He had forgotten that Jaenelle was Jaenelle.

"I'm sorry, Daemon," said a wavering, whispery voice behind him. "I'm sorry. Are you hurt?"

"Only my pride," Daemon said as he turned around, his lips set in a rueful smile. "Lady?" Then, alarmed. "Lady! Jaenelle, no, darling, don't cry." He gathered her into his arms while her shoulders shuddered with the effort not to make a sound. "Don't cry," Daemon crooned as he stroked her hair. "Please don't cry. I'm not hurt. Honestly I'm not." Since her face was buried against his chest, he allowed himself a pained smile as he kissed her hair. "I guess I'm too much of a grown-up to learn magic."

"No, you're not," Jaenelle said, pushing away from him and scrubbing the tears off her face with the backs of her hands. "I've just never tried to explain it to anyone before."

"Well, there you are," he said too brightly. "If you've never shown any-one—"

"Oh, I've *shown* lots of my other friends," Jaenelle said brusquely. "I've just never tried to explain it."

Daemon was puzzled. "How did you show them?"

Instantly he felt her pull away from him. Not physically—she hadn't moved—but within.

Jaenelle glanced at him nervously before ducking behind her veil of hair. "I . . . touched . . . them so they could understand."

The ember in his loins that had been warming him ever since the first time he saw her flared briefly and subsided. To touch her, mind to mind, to get beneath the shadows . . . He would never have dared suggest it, would never have dared make the first overture until she was much, much older. But now. Even to connect with her, just briefly, inside the first inner barrier—ah, to touch Jaenelle.

Daemon's mouth watered.

There was the risk, of course. Even if she initiated the touch, it might be too soon. He was what he was, and even at the first barrier there was the swirl of anger and predatory cunning that was the Warlord Prince called Daemon Sadi. And he was male, full grown. That, too, would be ev-ident.

Daemon took a deep breath. "If you're afraid of hurting me by the touch, I—"

"No," she said quickly. She closed her eyes, and he could sense her hurting. "It's just that I'm . . . different . . . and some people, when I've touched them . . ." Her voice trailed away, and he understood.

Wilhelmina. Wilhelmina, who loved her sister and was glad to have her back, had, for some reason, rejected that oh-so-personal touch.

"Just because some people think you're different—"

"No, Daemon," Jaenelle said gently, looking up at him with her ancient, wistful, haunted eyes. "*Everyone* knows I'm different. It just doesn't matter to some—and it matters a lot to others." A tear slipped down her cheek. "Why am I different?"

Daemon looked away. Oh, child. How could he explain that she was dreams made flesh? That for some of them, she made the blood in their veins sing? That she was a kind of magic the Blood hadn't seen in so very, very long? "What does the Priest say?"

Jaenelle sniffed. "He says growing up is hard work."

Daemon smiled sympathetically. "It is that."

"He says every living thing struggles to emerge from its cocoon or shell in order to be what it was meant to be. He says to dance for the glory of Witch is to celebrate life. He says it's a good thing we're *all* different or Hell would be a dreadfully boring place."

Daemon laughed, but he wasn't about to be sidetracked. "Teach me." It was an arrogant command softened only by the gentle way he said it.

She was there. Instantly. But in a way he'd never experienced before. He felt her sense his confusion, felt her cry of despair at his reaction.

"Wait," Daemon said sharply, raising one hand. "Wait."

Jaenelle was still linked to him. He felt the quick beating of her heart, the nervous breathing. Cautiously, he explored.

She wasn't inside the first barrier, where thoughts and feelings were open for perusal, and yet this was more than the simple inner communication link the Blood used. And it was more than the physical monitoring he usually did in bed. This was sharing physical experience. He felt her hair brushing against her cheek as if it were his own, felt the texture of her dress against her skin.

Oh, the possibilities of this kind of link during . . .

"Okay," he said after a while, "I think I've got the feel of it. Now what?" His face burned as she watched him warily.

At last she said, "Now we walk on air."

It was queer to feel that his legs were both long and short, and it took him a couple of tries to stand on the bench again. Amused, he just shook his head at her puzzled expression. Naturally, if all the other friends had been children, they were probably all close to the same age and the same size. And the same gender? He pushed that thought away before he had time to feel jealous.

After that, it was amazingly simple, and he reveled in it. He learned by experiencing her movements. It was similar to floating an object on air, except you did it to yourself. They practiced straight walking, parading around the alcove. Next came straight up and down. Pretending to climb stairs took longer to get the hang of, since he wanted a distance more compatible with his own legs and kept tripping on nothing.

Then the link was gone, and he was standing on air, alone, with Jaenelle watching him, her eyes shining with pride and pleasure. When he lowered himself to the ground with a graceful flourish, she clapped her hands in delight.

Daemon opened his arms. Jaenelle skated to him and wrapped her arms around his neck. He held her tightly, his face buried in her hair. "Thank you," he said hoarsely. "Thank you."

"You're welcome, Daemon." Her voice was a lovely, sensuous caress.

Holding her so close, with his lips so near her neck, he didn't want to let her go, but caution finally won over desire.

He didn't push her away. Rather, he gently held her shoulders and stepped back. "We'd better get back before someone comes looking."

Jaenelle's happy glow dimmed. She carelessly dropped to the ground. "Yes." She looked at the bed of witchblood. "Yes." She walked out of the alcove, not waiting for him.

Daemon stayed for another minute. Better not to come in together. Better not to make it obvious. To keep her safe, he had to be careful.

He glanced at the witchblood and bolted from the alcove. As he glided along the garden paths, his face settled into its familiar cold mask, the happiness he'd felt a few minutes before honing the blade of his temper so sharp he could have made the air bleed.

If you sing to them correctly, they'll tell you the names of the ones who are gone.

Everything has a price.

Whatever the price, whatever he had to do, he would make sure one of those plants wasn't for her.

3 / Terreille

Daemon pulled the bright, deep-red sweater over his head and adjusted the collar of the gold-and-white-checked shirt. Satisfied, he studied his reflection. His eyes were butter melted by humor and good spirits, his face subtly altered by the relaxed, boyish grin. The change in his appearance startled him, but after a moment he just shook his head and brushed his hair.

The difference was Jaenelle and the incalculable ways she worried, intrigued, fascinated, incensed, and delighted him. More than that, now, when he was so long past it, she was giving him—the bored, jaded Sadist—a childhood. She colored the days with magic and wonder, and all the things he'd ceased to pay attention to he saw again new.

He grinned at his reflection. He felt like a twelve-year-old. No, not twelve. He was at least a sophisticated fourteen. Still young enough to play with a girl as a friend, yet old enough to contemplate the day he might sneak his first kiss.

Daemon shrugged into his coat, went into the kitchen, pinched a couple of apples from the basket, sent Cook a broad wink, and gave himself up to a morning with Jaenelle.

The garden was buried under several inches of dry snow that puffed around his legs like flour. He followed the smaller footprints that walked, hopped, skipped, and leaped along the path. When he reached the small bend that mostly took him out of sight of anyone looking out the upper windows of the house, the footprints disappeared.

Daemon immediately checked all the surrounding trees and let out a gusty sigh of relief when she wasn't in any of them. Had she backed up in her own tracks waiting for him to pass her?

Grinning, he gathered some snow in his gloved hands, but it was too fluffy and wouldn't pack. As he straightened up, something soft hit his neck. He yowled when the clump of snow went down his back.

Daemon pivoted, his eyes narrowing even as his lips twitched. Jaenelle stood a few feet from him, her face glowing with mischief and good fun, her arm cocked to throw the second snowball. He put his fists on his hips. She lowered her arm and looked at him from beneath her lashes, trying to look solemn as she waited for the tongue-lashing.

He gave her one. "It is totally unfair," he said in his most severe voice, "to engage in a snowball fight when only one combatant can make snowballs." He waited, loving the way her eyes sparkled. "Well?"

Even without reading the thoughts beneath it, he could tell her touch was filled with laughter. Daemon bent down, gathered some snow, and learned how to make a snowball from snow too fluffy to pack. This, too, was similar to a basic lesson in Craft—creating a ball of witchlight—yet it required a subtler, more intrinsic knowledge of Craft than he'd ever known anyone to have.

"Did the Priest teach you how to do this?" he asked as he straightened up, delighted with the perfect snowball in his hand.

Jaenelle stared at him, aghast. Then she laughed. "Noooo." She quickly cocked her arm and hit him in the chest with her snowball.

The next few minutes were all-out war, each of them pelting the other as fast as they could make snowballs.

When it was over, Daemon was peppered with clumps of white. He leaned over, resting his hands on his knees. "I leave the field to you, Lady," he panted.

"As well you should," she replied tartly.

Daemon looked up, one eyebrow rising.

Jaenelle wrinkled her nose at him and ran for the alcove.

Daemon leaped forward to follow her, ran a few steps, stopped, and looked behind him. His were the only footprints. He squatted, examining the snow. Well, not quite. There *were* the merest indentations in the snow leading toward the alcove path. Daemon laughed and stood up. "Clever little witch." He raised one foot, placed it on top of the snow, and concentrated until he had the sensation of standing on solid ground. He positioned his other foot. Step, step, step. He looked back and grinned at the lack of footprints. Then he ran to the alcove.

Jaenelle was struggling to push the bottom of a snowman into the center of the alcove. Still grinning, Daemon helped her push. Then he started on the middle ball while she made the one for the head. They worked in companionable silence, he filling in the spaces while she stood on air and fashioned the head.

Jaenelle stepped back, looked at what they had fashioned, and began to laugh. Daemon stepped back, looked at it, and started to cough and groan and laugh. Even though it was crudely shaped, there was no mistaking the face above the grossly rotund body.

"You know," he choked, "if any of the groundskeepers see that and word gets back to Graff . . . we're going to be in deep trouble."

Jaenelle gave him a slant-eyed look sparking with mischief, and he didn't care how much trouble they got into.

He took the apples from his pocket and handed her one. Jaenelle took a bite, chewed thoughtfully, and sighed. "It won't last, you know," she said regretfully.

Daemon looked at her quizzically. "They never do." He looked at the sun beginning to peek out from behind the clouds. "I don't think this snow's going to last. Feels like it's warming up."

Jaenelle shook her head and took another bite. "No," she said, swallowing. "It'll go before it melts. I can't hold it very long." She frowned and fluffed her hair as she studied the snow-Graff. "Something's missing. Something I don't know about yet that would be able to hold it longer—"

That you can do it at all is beyond what most achieve, Lady.

"—would be able to weave it—"

Daemon shivered. He tossed the apple core toward the bushes for the birds to find. "Don't think of it," he said, not caring that his voice sounded harsh.

She looked at him, surprised.

"Don't think about experimenting with dream weaving without being instructed by someone who can do it well." He put his hands on her shoulders and squeezed gently. "Weaving a dream web can be very dangerous. Black Widows don't learn how to do it until the second stage of their training because it's so easy to become ensnared in the web." He held her at arm's length, searching her face. "Promise me, please, that you won't try to do this by yourself. That you'll get the very best there is to train you." *Because I couldn't bear it if there was only a blank-eyed, empty shell to love and I knew you were lost somewhere beyond reach, beyond return.*

Daemon's hands tightened on her shoulders. Her thoughtful expression frightened him.

"Yes," she said at last. "You're right, of course. If I'm going to learn, I should ask the ones who were born to it to teach me." She studied the snow-Graff. "See? Already it goes."

The snow was starting to lose its shape, to sift into a fluffy pile in the center of the alcove.

Together they air-walked to the main garden path. Dropping into the snow, Jaenelle trudged away from the house for a few feet, turned, and trudged back, kicking up the snow, leaving a very clear trail. Daemon looked back at the unmarked path, considered what the consequences would be if the others found out that Jaenelle could move about without leaving a trace, lowered himself to the ground, and trudged behind her, back to the house.

4 / Terreille

Daemon stormed into his room, slammed the door, stripped off his clothes, showered, and stormed back into the bedroom.

Bitch. Stupid, mewling *bitch*! How dare she? How *dare* she?

Leland's words burned through him. *We're having a gathering this evening, just a few of my friends. You'll be serving us, of course, so I expect you to dress appropriately.*

The cold swept over him, crusting him with glacial calm. He took a deep breath and smiled.

If the bitch wanted a whore tonight, he'd give her a whore.

Lifting one hand, Daemon called in two private trunks. Wherever he traveled, the trunks that contained his clothes and "personal" effects were always openly displayed and the contents could be examined by any Queen or Steward who chose to rummage through his things. Those were the only ones he ever acknowledged. The private trunks contained the items that were, in some way, of value to him.

One of those trunks was half empty and held personal mementos, a testimony to the paucity of his life. It also contained the locked, velvet-lined cases that held his Jewels—the Birthright Red and the cold, glorious Black. The other trunk contained several outfits that he sneeringly referred to as "whore's clothes"—costumes from a dozen different cultures, designed to titillate the female senses.

He opened the costume trunk and examined the contents. Yes, that outfit would do very nicely.

He removed a pair of black leather pants, the leather so soft and cut so well they fit like a second skin. He pulled them on, adjusting the bulge in the front to best advantage. Next came black, ankle-high leather boots with a high stacked heel. The perfectly tailored white silk shirt formed a slashing *V* from his neck to his waist, where two pearl buttons held it closed, and had billowing, tight-cuffed sleeves. Next he took out the paint pots, and with cold, cruel deliberation, applied subtle color to his cheeks,

eyes, and lips. It was done with such skill that it made him look androg-
ynous and yet more savagely male, an unsettling blend. Returning the
paint pots to the trunks, he took a small gold hoop from its box and
slipped it into his ear. He brushed his hair and used Craft to set it in a rak-
ishly disheveled style. Last was a black felt hat with a black leather band
and a large white plume. Standing before the full-length mirror, he carefully set the hat in place and inspected his reflection.

As Daemon smiled in anticipation of Leland's reaction to his dress,
someone quickly tapped on his door before it opened and closed.

He saw her in the mirror. For just a moment, shame threatened to
splinter the cold crust of rage, but he held on to it. She was, after all, female. His cruel, sensuous smile bloomed as he turned around.

Jaenelle stared at him, her eyes huge, her mouth dropping open. Daemon did nothing, said nothing. He simply waited for the inspection,
waited for the damning words.

She started at his feet, her eyes slowly traveling up his body. His breath
hitched when she reached his hips. He waited for the all-too-familiar
speculation of what hung between his legs or the quick, flushed glance
back down after hurrying past. Jaenelle didn't seem to notice. Her inspection never changed speed as she studied the shirt, the earring, the face,
and finally the hat. Then she started from the hat and went back down.

Daemon waited.

Jaenelle opened her mouth, closed it, and finally said timidly, "Do you
think, when I'm grown up, I could wear an outfit like that?"

Daemon bit his cheek. He didn't know whether to laugh or cry. Buying time, he looked down at himself. "Well," he said, giving it slow consideration, "the shirt would have to be altered somewhat to accommodate
a female figure, but I don't see why not."

Jaenelle beamed. "Daemon, it's a wonderful hat."

It took him a moment to admit it to himself, but he was miffed. He
stood in front of her, on display as it were, and the thing that fascinated
her most was his *hat*.

You do know how to bruise a man's ego, don't you, little one? he thought
dryly as he said, "Would you like to try it on?"

Jaenelle bounced to the mirror, brushing against him as she passed.

The sudden heat, the jolt of pleasure, the intense desire to hold her
against him shocked him sufficiently to make him jump out of her way.

His hands shook as he placed the hat on her head, but a moment later he was laughing as the hat rested on the tip of her nose and the only part of her face he could see was her chin.

"You'll have to grow into it, Lady," he said warmly. Using Craft, he positioned the hat above her head and locked it on the air.

He instantly regretted it.

She was going to be devastating, he realized as he stared at the face looking at his reflection, his nails biting into his palms.

In that moment he saw the face she would wear in a few years when the pointed features were finally balanced out. The eyebrows and eyelashes. Were they a soot-darkened gold or a gold-dusted black? The eyes, no longer hiding behind childish pretenses, summoned him down a darker road than he had ever known existed, one he felt desperate to follow.

For the first time in his life, Daemon felt a hungry stirring between his legs. He closed his eyes, gritted his teeth, and dug his nails deeper into his palms.

No, he pleaded silently. Not now. Not yet. He couldn't, mustn't respond yet. No one must know he *could* respond. They were lost, both of them, if anyone felt that physical response through the Ring. Please, please, please.

"Daemon?"

Daemon opened his eyes. Jaenelle the child watched him, her forehead puckered in concern. He smiled shakily as he slowly unclenched his hands and took the hat.

"Leland's guests will be arriving anytime now and I still have to dress, so scat."

There was something strange about the way she looked at him, but he couldn't figure it out. Then she was gone, and he slumped on the bed, staring at the open trunk. After a minute, he took off the shirt, pants, and boots and returned them and the hat to the trunk. He vanished both private trunks, taking the time to make sure they were safely stored, before dressing in formal evening attire.

The painted face and the earring would have to do for Leland. The clothes in that trunk would be worn for only one woman's pleasure.

5 / Terreille

Daemon woke instantly. Something was wrong, something that made his nerves quiver. He lay on his back, listening to the hard, cold rain beat against the windows. Shivering, he tossed back the covers, pulled on his robe, and pushed open the curtains to look outside.

Only the rain. And yet . . .

Taking a deep, steadying breath, he began a slow descent into the abyss, testing each rank of the Jewels, waiting for the answering quiver along his nerves.

Above the Red, nothing. The Red, nothing. The Gray, the Ebon-gray. Nothing. He reached the level of the Black and pain flooded his nerves as an eerie keening filled his mind, a dirge full of anger, pain, and sorrow. The voice that sang it was pure and strong—and familiar.

Daemon closed his eyes and leaned his head against the glass as he ascended to the Red. No one else here would be able to hear it. No one else would know.

He'd known since he met her that she was Witch—and Witch wore the Black Jewels. He'd known, but he'd been able to deceive himself into believing she'd wear the Black at maturity, not *now*. In all the Blood's long history, only a handful of witches had worn the Black, and they had been gifted with it after the Offering to the Darkness. *No one* had ever worn the Black as their Birthright.

It had been a foolish deceit, especially when the evidence was right in front of him. She could do things the rest of the Blood had never dreamed of. She had sought out the High Lord of Hell to be her mentor. There were facets of her that were breathtaking and terrifying.

Birthright Black. She wore Birthright Black. Sweet Darkness, what would become of her when she made the Offering?

Daemon opened his eyes and saw a small white figure moving slowly along the garden path. He opened his window and was instantly soaked by the cold rain, but he didn't notice. He whistled once, softly, sharply, sending it on an auditory thread directed toward the figure.

It turned toward him, resigned, and made its way to his window.

Daemon leaned over as Jaenelle floated up to him, grasped her beneath the arms, and pulled her in. He set her on the floor, closed and locked the window, pulled the curtains together. Then he looked at her, and his heart squeezed with pain.

She stood there, shivering, dripping on the rug, her eyes glazed and pain-filled. Her nightgown, bare feet, and hands were muddy.

Daemon picked her up, took her into the bathroom, and filled the tub with hot water. She'd been unnaturally quiet all day, and he'd feared she was becoming ill. Now he feared she was in shock. There were dark smudges beneath her eyes, and she didn't seem to know where she was.

She struggled when he tried to lift the nightgown over her head. "No," she said feebly as she attempted to hold the garment down.

"I know what girls look like," Daemon snapped as he pulled off the nightgown and lifted her into the tub. "Sit there." He pointed a finger at her. She stopped trying to get out of the tub.

Daemon went into the bedroom and got the brandy and glass he kept tucked in the bottom drawer of the nightstand. Returning to the bathroom, he sat on the edge of the tub, poured a healthy dose into the glass, and handed it to her.

"Drink this." He watched her take a small taste and grimace before he put the bottle to his own lips and took a long swallow. "Drink it," he said angrily when she tried to hand him the glass.

"I don't like it." It was the first time he'd ever heard her sound so young and vulnerable. He wanted to scream.

"What—" He knew. Suddenly, all too clearly, he knew. The mud, the dirge, her hands cut up from digging in the hard ground, the dirt beneath her fingernails. He knew.

Daemon took another long swallow of brandy. "Who?"

"Rose," Jaenelle replied in a hollow voice. "He killed my friend Rose." Then a savage light burned in her eyes and her lips curled in a small, bitter smile. "He slit her throat because she wouldn't lick the lollipop." Her eyes slid to his groin before drifting up to his face. "Is that what you call it, Prince?"

Daemon's throat closed. His blood pounded in him, pounded him, angry surf against rock. It was so very, very hard to breathe.

The sepulchral voice. The midnight, cavernous, ancient, raging voice that held a whisper of madness. He hadn't imagined it, that other time. Hadn't imagined it.

Birthright Black.

Witch.

She wanted to kill him because he was male. Accepting that made it easier to be calm.

"It's called a penis, Lady. I have no use for euphemisms." He paused. "Who killed her?"

Jaenelle sipped the brandy. "Uncle Bobby," she whispered. She rocked back and forth as tears slid down her cheeks. "Uncle Bobby."

Daemon took the glass from her and set it aside. It didn't matter if she killed him, didn't matter if she hated him for touching her. He lifted her out of the tub and cradled her in his arms, letting her cry until there were no tears left.

When he felt her breathing even out and knew she was falling into exhausted sleep, he wrapped her in a towel, carried her to her room, found a clean nightgown, and tucked her into bed. He watched her for a few minutes to be sure she was asleep before returning to his room.

He paced, gulping brandy, feeling the walls close in on him.

Uncle Bobby. Rose. Lollipop. How did she know? All day she must have known, must have waited for the night so she could plant her living memento mori. All day, while Robert Benedict had been so conspicuously at home.

If you sing to them correctly, they'll tell you the names of the ones who are gone.

He snarled quietly. His pacing slowed as cold rage filled him.

There was something wrong with this place. Something evil in this place. Chaillot had too many secrets. Added to that, Dorothea and Hekatah were hunting for Jaenelle, and Greer was still in Beldon Mor sniffing around.

Tersa had said the Priest would be his best ally or his worst enemy.

He would have to decide soon, before it was too late.

Finally, exhausted, he stripped off the robe and fell into bed. And dreamed of shattered crystal chalices.

CHAPTER ELEVEN

1 / Terreille

The only thing in the cell besides the overflowing slop bucket was a small table that held a plate of food and a metal pitcher of water.

Lucivar stared at the pitcher, clenching and unclenching his fists. The chains that tethered his ankles and wrists to the wall were long enough to reach one end of the table and the food, but not long enough to reach over and tear out the throat of the guard who brought it.

He needed food. He was desperate for water. These little ovens that Zuultah laughingly referred to as her "enlightenment" chambers were located in the Arava Desert, where the sun was voracious. The heat was sufficient by midday to make his own waste steam.

The first three days he'd been locked up, the guards had brought food and water and emptied the slop bucket. During the first two, he'd eaten what he was given. The third day, the food and water were laced with *safframate,* a vicious aphrodisiac that would keep a man hard and needy enough to satisfy an entire coven at one of their gatherings. It would also drive a man to the point of madness because, while it made it possible for him to be an enduring participant, it also prohibited him from physical release.

He'd sensed it before he consumed anything. A less vigilant man wouldn't have noticed, but Lucivar had experienced *safframate* before and wasn't about to experience it again for Zuultah's entertainment.

Lucivar licked his cracked lips as he stared at the pitcher of water, his tongue prodding the cracks, wetting itself with his blood.

His answer, that third day, had been to throw the plate and pitcher against the wall. The viper rats—large, venomous rodents that were able to live anywhere—scurried out of the shadowy corners and fell upon the food. He'd spent the rest of the day watching them tear each other apart in frenzied mating.

For the next two days no one came. There was no food, no water. The slop bucket filled. There was nothing but the rats and the heat.

An hour ago, a guard had come in with the food and water. Lucivar had snarled at him, his dark wings unfurling until the tips touched the walls. The guard scurried out with less dignity than the rats.

Lucivar approached the table, his legs shaking. He picked up the pitcher and licked the condensation off the outside.

It wasn't nearly enough.

He looked at the plate. The stench of the slop bucket warred with the smell of food, but his stomach twisted with hunger, and over all of it was the need for the water that was so close. So very close.

Holding the pitcher in both hands so that he wouldn't drop it, he took a mouthful of water.

The *safframate* ran through him, a fiery ice.

Lucivar's mouth twisted into a teeth-baring grin. His lips cracked wider and bled.

There was only one reason to eat, to submit to what would come, and it wasn't to stay alive. He fiercely loved life, but he was Eyrien, a hunter, a warrior. Growing up with death had dulled his fear of it, and a part of him rather relished the idea of being a demon.

There was only one reason. One sapphire-eyed reason.

Lucivar lifted the pitcher again and drank.

2 / Terreille

Lucivar clenched his teeth and squeezed his eyes shut. He hated being on his back. All Eyrien males hated being on their backs, unable to use their wings. It was the ultimate gesture of submission. But tied as he was to the "game bed," there was nothing he could do but endure.

As one of Zuultah's witches moved on him, intent on her pleasure, he silently swore the most vicious curses he could think of. His hands clenched the brass rails of the headboard, had been clenching them throughout the night with such pressure that the shape of his fingers was embedded in them.

Again and again and again, one after another. With each the pain grew worse. He hated them for the pain, for their pleasure, for their laughter, for the food and water they taunted him with, trying to make him beg.

He was Lucivar Yaslana, an Eyrien Warlord Prince. He wouldn't beg. Wouldn't beg. Wouldn't.

Lucivar opened his eyes to silence. The bed curtains were closed at the bottom of the bed and along one side, cutting off his view of the room. He tried to shift position and ease his stiff muscles, but he'd been stretched out when they tied him, and there wasn't any slack.

He licked his lips. He was so thirsty, so tired. So easy to slip away from the pain, from memories.

Male voices murmured in the hallway. Movement in the room, hidden by the closed curtains. At last, Zuultah saying, "Bring him."

The room was gray, a sweet, misty gray where the light danced through shards of glass and voices were heard under water.

The guards untied his hands and feet, retied his hands behind his back. Lucivar snarled at them, but it was a faraway sound of no importance, no importance at all.

For a moment, when he saw the marble lady, his vision cleared, and the pain made his legs buckle. The guards dragged him to the leather leg straps, forced him to his knees, and strapped him to the floor behind his knees and at his ankles. They rolled the marble cylinder, with its smoothly carved orifices, into position. When he was fitted into an orifice, they held him in place with a leather strap beneath his buttocks. There was enough slack for him to thrust but not enough for him to withdraw.

The gray. The sweet, twisting gray.

"That will be all," Zuultah said arrogantly, waving the guards out of the room with her switch and locking the door.

The floor hurt his knees. Pain. Sweet pain.

The switch hit his buttocks. Blood trickled over the leather strap. Scented silk brushed against his shoulder and face.

"Are you thirsty, Yasi?" Zuultah cooed as she swung herself up on the flat top of the marble lady. "Want some cream?" She opened her robe and spread her thighs, revealing the dark triangle of hair.

The switch hit his shoulder. "This is your reward, Yasi. This is your pleasure."

Red streaks in the gray. Red streaks and a dark triangle.

"Thrust, you bastard." The switch hitting, cutting where one wing joined his back.

Thrust, thrust, thrust into the gray. Lips against the wet. Tongue obedient. Thrust, thrust. Deeper into the pain, the wet, the dark, the dark, the dark, the pain twisting to a sweetness, shards of glass, twisting, the wet, the dark, the dark streaked with red, the hunger, the pain, the red fire boiling, rising, the Ebon-gray boiling, rising, the hunger, the hunger, teeth, pleasure, pain, moaning, moaning, teeth, pleasure, rising, boiling, pain, pleasure, moaning, hunger, teeth, moaning, teeth, screaming, screaming, screaming, red, red, hot sweet red, boiling, rushing, free.

Lucivar swayed, confused. Zuultah rolled on the floor, screaming, screaming. He tried to lick the moisture from his lips but something was in the way. He turned his head and spat.

For a long time, while guards pounded on the locked door and Zuultah screamed, he stared at the small thing his teeth had found to ease the hunger. At first he didn't understand what it was. When his flaccid organ finally slipped out of the orifice and he recognized the red for what it was, Lucivar lifted his head and let out a howling, savage laugh. ·

3 / Terreille

"You have a visitor," Philip said tersely as he tapped piles of papers into neat stacks, something he did when annoyed.

Daemon raised an eyebrow. "Oh?"

Philip glanced toward him but refused to look at him. "In the gold salon. Keep it brief, if possible. You have a full schedule today."

Daemon glided to the gold salon. The psychic scent hit him before he touched the door. He settled his face into its cold mask, locked away his heart, and opened the door.

"Lord Kartane," he said in a bored voice as he closed the door and leaned against it, his hands in his trouser pockets.

"Sadi." Kartane's eyes were filled with malicious glee. Still, he took a nervous step backward.

Daemon waited, watching Kartane pace one side of the room.

"Probably no one's thought to tell you, so I took it upon myself to bring the news," Kartane said.

"About what?"

"Yasi."

The anticipation in Kartane's eyes made Daemon's heart pound and his mouth go dry. He shrugged. "The last time I heard anything about him, he was serving the Queen of Pruul. Zuultah, isn't it?"

"Apparently he's served her better than he's ever served anyone," Kartane said maliciously.

Get to the point, you little bastard.

Kartane paced. "The story's a bit muddled, you understand, but it appears that, while under the influence of a substantial dose of *safframate,* Yasi went berserk and bit Zuultah." Kartane let out a high-pitched, nervous laugh.

Daemon sighed. Lucivar's temper in the bedroom was legendary. At the best of times, he was unpredictable and violent. Under the influence of *safframate* . . . "So he bit her. She's not the first."

Kartane laughed again. It was almost a hysterical giggle. "Well, actually, *shaved* might be a better way to describe it. Anything she mounts now won't be for *her* pleasure."

No, Lucivar, no. By the Darkness, no. "They killed him," Daemon said flatly.

"He wasn't that lucky. Zuultah wanted to, when she finally came to her senses and realized what he'd done. He also killed ten of her best guards while they were trying to subdue him." Kartane wiped nervous sweat from his forehead. "Prythian intervened as soon as she found out. For some insane reason, she still thinks she can eventually tame him and breed him. However, Zuultah wasn't going to let him get away without *some* kind of punishment." Kartane waited, but Daemon didn't rise to the bait. "She put him in the salt mines."

"Then she's killed him." Daemon opened the door. "You were right," he said too gently, turning to look at Kartane. "No one else would have dared tell me that."

He closed the door with a silence that made the whole house shake.

All the tears were gone now, and Daemon felt as dry and empty as the Arava Desert.

Lucivar was Eyrien. He would never survive in the salt mines of Pruul. In those tunnels with all the salt and the heat, no room for him to stretch his wings, no air to dry the sweat. There were a dozen different molds that could infect that membranous skin and eat it away. And without wings . . . An Eyrien warrior was nothing without his wings. Lucivar had once said he'd rather lose his balls than his wings, and he'd meant it.

Oh, Lucivar, Lucivar, his brave, arrogant, foolish brother. If he'd accepted that offer, Lucivar would be hunting in Askavi right now, gliding through the dusk, searching for prey. But they had known it might come to this. The wisest thing for Lucivar to do would be to end it quickly while his strength was intact. He would be welcome in the Dark Realm. Daemon was sure he would be.

She won't go unpunished, I promise you that. No matter how long it takes to do it properly, I'll see the debt paid in full.

"Lucivar," Daemon whispered. "Lucivar."

"They've all been looking for you."

He hadn't heard her come in, which wasn't surprising. It wasn't surprising she was there even though he'd locked the library door.

Daemon shifted on the couch. He held out one hand, watching her small fingers curl around his own. That gentle touch, so full of understanding, was agony.

"What happened to him?"

"Who?" Daemon said, fighting the grief.

"Lucivar," Jaenelle said with steely patience.

Daemon recognized that strange, unnerving something in her face and voice—Witch focusing her attention. He hesitated a moment, then took her in his arms. He needed to hold her, feel her warmth against him, needed reassurance that the sacrifice was worth it. He didn't know how or when the tears began falling again.

"He's my friend, my brother," he whispered into her shoulder. "He's dying."

"Daemon." Jaenelle gently stroked his hair. "Daemon, we have to help him. I could—"

"No!" *Don't tempt me with hope. Don't tempt me to take that kind of risk.* "You can't help him. Nothing can help him now."

Jaenelle tried to push back to look at him, but he wouldn't let her. "I know I promised him I wouldn't wander around Terreille, but—"

Daemon licked a tear. "You met him? He saw you once?"

"Once." She paused. "Daemon, I might be able to—"

"*No,*" Daemon moaned into her neck. "He wouldn't want you there, and if something happened to you, he'd never forgive me. Never."

Witch asked, "Are you sure, Prince?"

The Warlord Prince replied, "I am sure, Lady."

After a moment, Jaenelle began to sing a death song in the Old Tongue, not the angry dirge she'd sung for Rose, but a gentle witchsong of grief and love. Her voice wove through him, celebrating and acknowledging his pain and grief, tapping the deep wells he would have kept locked.

When her voice finally faded, Daemon wiped the tears from his face. He blindly allowed Jaenelle to lead him to his room, stand over him while he washed his face, and coax a glass of brandy into him. She said nothing. There was nothing she needed to say. The generous silence and the understanding in her eyes were enough.

Lucivar would have been proud to serve her, Daemon thought as he brushed his hair, preparing to face Alexandra and Philip. He would have been proud of her.

Daemon took a shuddering breath and went to find Alexandra.

Everything has a price.

CHAPTER TWELVE

1 / Terreille

Winsol approached rapidly. The most important holiday in the Blood calendar, it was held when the winter days were shortest, and it was a celebration of the Darkness, a celebration of Witch.

Daemon wandered through the empty hallways. The servants had been given a half-day off and had deserted the house to shop or begin their holiday preparations. Alexandra, Leland, and Philip were off on their own excursions. Robert, as usual, was not at home. Even Graff had gone out, leaving the girls in Cook's care. And he . . . Well, it wasn't kindness that had made them leave him behind. His temper had been too sharp, his tongue too cutting the last time he'd escorted Alexandra to a party. They'd left hastily after he'd told a simpering young aristo witch that the cut of her dress would make any woman in a Red Moon house envious, even if what she was displaying didn't.

Daemon climbed the stairs to the nursery wing. The only thing that eased the ache he'd felt since Kartane had told him about Lucivar was being with Jaenelle.

The music room door stood open. "No, Wilhelmina, not like that," Jaenelle said in that harried, amused tone.

Daemon smiled as he looked into the room. At least he wasn't the only one who made her sound like that.

The girls stood in the center of the room. Wilhelmina looked a bit grumpy while Jaenelle looked patiently exasperated. She glanced toward the door and her eyes lit up.

Daemon suppressed a sigh. He knew that look, too. He was about to get into trouble.

Jaenelle rushed over to him, grabbed his wrist, and hauled him into the room. "We're going to attend one of the Winsol balls and I've been trying to teach Wilhelmina how to waltz but I'm not explaining it well because I don't really know how to lead but you'd know how to lead because boys—"

Boys?

"—lead in dancing so you could show Wilhelmina, couldn't you?"

As though he had a choice. Daemon looked at Wilhelmina. Jaenelle stood to one side, her hands loosely clasped, smiling expectantly.

"Yes, men," he said dryly, putting a slight emphasis on that word, "do lead when dancing."

Wilhelmina blushed, instantly understanding his distinction.

Jaenelle looked baffled. She shrugged. "Men. Boys. What's the difference? They're all males."

Daemon gave her a calculating look. In a few more years, he'd be able to show her the difference. He smiled at Wilhelmina and patiently explained the steps. "Some music, Lady?" he said to Jaenelle.

She raised her hand. The crystal music sphere sparkled in the brass holder, and stately music filled the room.

As Daemon waltzed with Wilhelmina, he watched her expression change from concentration to relaxation to pleasure. The exertion brought a glow to her cheeks and a sparkle to her blue eyes. He smiled at her warmly. Dancing was the only activity he enjoyed with a woman, and he regretted that court dancing was no longer in vogue.

If you want to bed a woman, do it in the bedroom. If you want to seduce her, do it in the dance.

It was hard to imagine the Priest saying that to a small boy, but it was like so many other things that had come to him over the years in those moments between sleep and waking, and he no longer questioned whose voice seemed to whisper up from somewhere deep within him, a voice he'd always known wasn't his own.

When the music faded, Daemon released Wilhelmina and made an elegant, formal bow. He turned to Jaenelle. Her strange expression made his heart jump. The crust of civility he lived behind, all the rules and regulations, cracked beneath her gaze. Her psychic scent distracted him. His mind sharpened, turned inward, and he reveled in the keen awareness of his body, the smooth feline way he moved.

The music began again. Jaenelle raised one hand. He raised the opposite hand. Stepping toward each other, their fingertips touched, and the court dance began.

He didn't need to think about the steps. They were natural, sensual, seductive. The music caressed him, narrowing his senses to the young body that moved with him. Fingertips touched fingertips, hands touched hands, nothing more. The Black sang in him, wanting more, wanting much, much more, and yet it pleased him to have his senses teased this way, to feel so alive, so male.

When the music faded again, Jaenelle stepped back, breaking the spell. She skipped to the brass holder, changed the music sphere, and began a lively folk dance, hands on her hips, feet flying.

Daemon and Wilhelmina were applauding when Cook came in carrying a tray. "I thought you'd like some sandwiches . . ." Her words faded as Daemon, with a dazzling smile, took the tray from her, placed it on a table, and led her to the center of the room. He bowed; with a pleased smile, she curtsied. He swept her into his arms and they waltzed to a Chaillot tune he'd heard at a number of balls. As they whirled about the room, he grinned at the girls, who were whirling around with them.

Then Cook stumbled and moaned, her eyes fixed on the doorway.

"What's the meaning of this?" Graff said nastily as she stepped into the room. She nailed Cook with an icy stare. "You were entrusted to look after the girls for a few short hours, and here I return to find you engaged in questionable entertainment." Her eyes snapped to Daemon's arm, which was still around Cook's waist. She sniffed, maliciously pleased. "Perhaps, when this is reported, Lady Angelline will find someone with culinary talent."

"Nothing happened, Graff."

Daemon shivered at the chilling fury in Jaenelle's too calm voice.

Graff turned. "Well, we'll just see, missy."

"Graff." It was a thunderous, malevolent whisper.

Daemon shook. Every instinct for self-preservation screamed at him to call in the Black and shield himself.

There had been a strange swirling when Graff first appeared that had made him think he was being pulled into a spiral. He'd never felt anything like that before and hadn't realized that Jaenelle was gliding down into the abyss. Now something rose from far below him, something very angry and so very, very cold.

Graff turned slowly, her eyes staring wide and empty.

"Nothing happened, Graff," Jaenelle said in that cold whisper that shrieked through Daemon's nerves. "Wilhelmina and I were in the music room practicing some dance steps. Cook had brought some sandwiches for us and was just leaving when you arrived. You didn't see the Prince because he was in his room. Do you understand?"

Graff's eyebrows drew together. "No, I—"

"Look down, Graff. Look down. Do you see it?"

Graff whimpered.

"If you don't remember what I've told you, that's what you'll see . . . forever. Do you understand?"

"Understand," Graff whispered as spittle dribbled down her chin.

"You're dismissed, Graff. Go to your room."

When they heard a door close farther down the corridor, Daemon led Cook to a chair and eased her into it. Jaenelle said nothing more, but there was pain and sadness in her eyes as she looked at them before going to her room. Wilhelmina had wet herself. Daemon cleaned her up, cleaned up the floor, took the tray of sandwiches back to the kitchen, and dosed Cook with a liberal glass of brandy.

"She's a strange child," Cook said carefully after her second glass of brandy, "but there's more good than harm in her."

Daemon gave her calm, expected responses, allowing her to find her own way to justify what she'd felt in that room. Wilhelmina, too, although embarrassed that he'd witnessed her accident, had altered the confrontation into something she could accept. Only he, as he sat in his room staring at nothing, was unwilling to let go of the fear and the awe. Only he appreciated the terrible beauty of being able to touch without restraint. Only he felt knife-sharp desire.

2 / Terreille

Daemon sat on the edge of his bed, a pained, gentle smile tugging his lips. Even with preservation spells, the picture's colors were beginning to fade, and it was worn around the edges. Still, nothing could fade the hint of a brash smile and the ready-for-trouble gleam in Lucivar's eyes. It was the only picture Daemon had of him, taken centuries ago when Lucivar still had an aura of youthful hope, before the years and court after court had turned a handsome, youthful face into one so like the Askavi mountains he loved—beautifully brutal, holding a trace of shadow even in the brightest sunlight.

There was a shy tap on his door before Jaenelle slipped into the room. "Hello," she said, uncertain of her welcome.

Daemon slipped an arm around her waist when she got close enough. Jaenelle rested both hands on his shoulder and leaned into him. The skin beneath her eyes looked bruised, and she trembled a little.

Daemon frowned. "Are you cold?" When she shook her head, he pulled her closer. There wasn't any kind of outside heat that could thaw what chilled her, but after he'd been holding her for a while, the trembling stopped.

He wondered if she'd told Saetan about the music room incident. He looked at her again and knew the answer. She hadn't told the Priest. She hadn't gone roaming for three days. She'd been locked in her cold misery, alone, wondering if there was any living thing that wouldn't fear her. He had come to the Black as a young man, but mature and ready, and even then living that far into the Darkness had been unsettling. For a child who had never known anything else, who had been traveling strange, lonely roads since her first conscious thought, who tried so hard to reach toward other people while suppressing what she was . . . But she couldn't suppress it. She would always shatter the illusion when challenged, would always reveal what lay beneath.

Daemon intently studied the face that, in turn, studied the picture he still held. He sucked in his breath when he finally understood. He wore the Black; Jaenelle *was* the Black. But with her, the Black was not only dark, savage power, it was laughter and mischief and compassion and healing . . . and snowballs.

Daemon kissed her hair and looked at the picture. "You would have gotten along well with him. He was always ready to get into trouble." He was rewarded with a ghost of a smile.

She studied the picture. "Now he looks more like what he is." Her eyes narrowed, and then she shot an accusing look at him. "Wait a minute. You said he was your brother."

"He was." Is. Would always be.

"But he's Eyrien."

"We had different mothers."

There was a strange light in her eyes. "But the same father."

He watched her juggling the mental puzzle pieces, saw the moment when they all clicked.

"That explains a lot," she murmured, fluffing her hair. "He isn't dead, you know. The Ebon-gray is still in Terreille."

Daemon blinked. "How—" He sputtered. "How do you know that?"

"I looked. I didn't go anywhere," she added hurriedly. "I didn't break my promise."

"Then how—" Daemon shook his head. "Forget I said that."

"It's not like trying to sort through Opals or Red from a distance to find a particular person." Jaenelle had that harried, amused look. "Daemon, the only other Ebon-gray is Andulvar, and he doesn't live in Terreille anymore. Who else can it be?"

Daemon sighed. He didn't understand, but he was relieved to know.

"May I have a copy of that picture?"

"Why?" Jaenelle gave him a look that made him wince. "All right."

"And one of you, too?"

"I don't have one of me."

"We could get one."

"Why—never mind. Is there a reason for this?"

"Of course."

"I don't suppose you'd tell me what it is?"

Jaenelle raised one eyebrow. It was such a perfect imitation, Daemon choked back a laugh. *Serves me right,* he thought wryly. "All right," he said, ruefully shaking his head.

"Soon?"

"Yes, Lady, soon."

Jaenelle skipped away, turned, gave him a feather-light kiss on the cheek, and was gone.

Raising one eyebrow, Daemon looked at the closed door. He looked at the picture. "You stupid Prick," he said fondly. "Ah, Lucivar, you would have had such fun with her."

3 / Hell

Saetan leaned back in his chair, steepling his fingers. "Why?"

"Because I'd like one."

"You said that before. Why?"

Jaenelle loosely clasped her hands, looked at the ceiling, and said in a prim, authoritative voice, " 'Tis not the season for questions."

Saetan choked. When he could breathe again, he said, "Very well, witch-child. You'll have a picture."

"Two?"

Saetan gave her a long, hard look. She gave him her unsure-but-game smile. He sighed. There was one unshakable truth about Jaenelle: Sometimes it was better not to know. "Two."

She pulled a chair up to the blackwood desk. Resting her elbows on the gleaming surface, her chin propped in her hands, she said solemnly, "I want to buy two frames, but I don't know where to buy them."

"What kind do you want?"

Jaenelle perked up. "Nice ones, the kind that open like a book."

"Swivel frames?"

She shrugged. "Something that will hold two pictures."

"I'll get them for you. Anything else?"

She was solemn again. "I want to buy them myself, but I don't know how much they cost."

"Witch-child, that's not a problem—"

Jaenelle reached into her pocket and pulled something out. Resting her loosely closed fist on the desk, she opened her hand. "Do you think if you sold this, it would buy the frames?"

Saetan gulped, but his hand was steady when he picked up the stone and held it up to the light. "Where did you get this, witch-child?" he asked calmly, almost absently.

Jaenelle put her hands in her lap, her eyes focused on the desk. "Well . . . you see . . . I was with a friend and we were going through this village and some rocks had fallen by the road and a little girl had her foot caught under one of the rocks." She scrunched her shoulders. "It was hurt, the foot I mean, because of the rock, and I . . . healed it, and her father gave me that to say thank you." She added hurriedly, "But he didn't say I had to keep it." She hesitated. "Do you think it would buy two frames?"

Saetan held the stone between thumb and forefinger. "Oh, yes," he said dryly. "I think it will be more than adequate for what you want."

Jaenelle smiled at him, puzzled.

Saetan struggled to keep his voice calm. "Tell me, witch-child, have you received other such gifts from grateful parents?"

"Uh-huh. Draca's keeping them for me because I didn't know what to do with them." She brightened. "She's given me a room at the Keep, just like you gave me one at the Hall."

"Yes, she told me she was going to." He smiled at her obvious relief that he wasn't offended. "I'll have the pictures and frames for you by the end of the week. Will that be satisfactory?"

Jaenelle bounced around the desk, strangled him, and kissed his cheek. "Thank you, Saetan."

"You're welcome, witch-child. Off with you."

Jaenelle bumped into Mephis on her way out. "Hello, Mephis," she said as she headed wherever she was headed.

Even Mephis. Saetan smiled at the bemused, tender expression on his staid, ever-so-formal eldest son's face.

"Come look at this," Saetan said, "and tell me what you think."

Mephis held the diamond up to the light and whistled softly. "Where did you get this?"

"It was a gift, to Jaenelle, from a grateful parent."

Mephis groped for the chair. He stared at the diamond in disbelief. "You're joking."

Saetan retrieved the diamond, holding it between thumb and forefinger. "No, Mephis, I'm not joking. Apparently, a little girl got her foot caught under a rock and hurt it. Jaenelle healed it, and the grateful father presented her with this. And, apparently, this is not the first such gift that's been bestowed upon her for such service." He studied the large, flawless gem.

"But . . . how?" Mephis sputtered.

"She's a natural Healer. It's instinctive."

"Yes, but—"

"But the real question is, what really happened?" Saetan's golden eyes narrowed.

"What do you mean?" Mephis said, puzzled.

"I mean," Saetan said slowly, "the way Jaenelle told the story, it didn't sound like much. But how severe an injury by how large a rock, when healed, would make a father grateful enough to give up this?"

4 / Kaeleer

"Witch-child, since a list of your friends would be as long as you are tall, you can't possibly give each of them a Winsol gift. It's not expected. You don't expect gifts from all of them, do you?"

"Of course not," Jaenelle replied hotly. She slumped in the chair. "But they're my friends, Saetan."

And you are the best gift they could have in a hundred lifetimes.

"Winsol is the celebration of Witch, the Blood's remembrance of what we are. Gifts are condiments for the meat, and that's all."

Jaenelle eyed him skeptically—and well she should. How many times over the past few days had he caught himself daydreaming of what it would be like to celebrate Winsol with her? To be with her at sunset when the gifts were opened? To share a tiny cup of hot blooded rum with her? To dance, as the Blood danced at no other time of the year, for the glory of Witch? The daydreams were bittersweet. As he walked through the corridors of the Kaeleer Hall watching the staff decorate the rooms, laughing and whispering secrets; as he and Mephis prepared the benefaction list for the staff and all the villagers whose work directly or indirectly served the Hall; as he did all the things a good Prince did for the people who served him, a thought rubbed at him, rubbed and rubbed: She would be spending that special day with her family in Terreille, away from those who were truly her own.

The one small drop of comfort was that she would also be with Daemon.

"What should I do?"

Jaenelle's question brought him back to the present. He lightly rubbed his steepled fingers against his lips. "I think you should select one or two of your friends who, for whatever reason, might be left out of the celebrations and festivities and give gifts to them. A small gesture to one who otherwise will have nothing will be worth a great deal more than another gift among many."

Jaenelle fluffed her hair and then smiled. "Yes," she said softly, "I know exactly the ones who need it most."

"It's settled, then." A paper-wrapped parcel lifted from the corner of his desk and came to rest in front of Jaenelle. "As you requested."

Jaenelle's smile widened as she took the parcel and carefully unwrapped it. The soft glow in her eyes melted century upon century of loneliness. "You look splendid, Saetan."

He smiled tenderly. "I do my best to serve, Lady." He shifted in his chair. "By the way, the stone you gave me to sell—"

"Was it enough?" Jaenelle asked anxiously. "If it wasn't—"

"More than enough, witch-child." Remembering the expression on the jeweler's face when he brought it in, it was hard not to laugh at her concern. "There were, in fact, a good number of gold marks left over. I took the liberty of opening an account in your name with the remainder. So anytime you want to purchase something in Kaeleer, you need only sign for it, have the store's proprietor send the bill to me at the Hall, and I'll deduct it from your account. Fair enough?"

Jaenelle's grin made Saetan wish he'd bitten his tongue. The Darkness only knew what she might think to purchase. Ah, well. It was going to be just as much of a headache for the merchants as it was going to be for him—and he found the idea too amusing to really mind.

"I suppose if you *did* want to get an unusual gift, you could always get a couple of salt licks for the unicorns," he teased.

He was stunned by the instant, haunted look in her eyes.

"No," Jaenelle whispered, all the color draining from her face. "No, not salt."

He sat for a long time after she left him, staring at nothing, wondering what it was about salt that could distress her so much.

5 / Kaeleer

Draca stepped aside to let Saetan enter. "What do you think?"

Saetan whistled softly. Like all the rooms in the Keep, the huge bedroom was cut out of the living mountain. But unlike the other rooms, including the suite Cassandra had once had, the walls of this room had been worked and smoothed to shine like ravenglass. A wood floor peeked out from beneath immense, thick, red-and-cream patterned rugs that could only have come from Dharo, the Kaeleer Territory renowned for its cloth and weaving. The four-poster blackwood bed could comfortably sleep four people. The rest of the furniture—tables, nightstands, bookcases, storage cupboard—was also blackwood. There was a dressing room with wardrobes and storage cupboards of cedar, and a private bath with a sunken marble tub—black veined with red—a large shower stall, double sinks, and a commode enclosed in its own little room. On the other side of the bedroom was a door leading into a sitting room.

"It's magnificent, Draca," Saetan said as his eyes drank in the odds and ends scattered on the tables—a young girl's treasures. Fingering the lid of a box that had an intricate design created from a number of rare woods, he opened it and shook his head, partly amused and partly stunned. One finger idly stirred the contents of the box, stirred the little seashells that had obviously come from widely distant beaches, stirred the diamonds, rubies, emeralds, and sapphires that were no more than pretty stones to a child. He closed the box and turned, one eyebrow rising in amusement.

Draca lifted her shoulders in the merest hint of a shrug. "Would you have it otherwisse?"

"No." He looked around. "This room will please her. It's truly a dark sanctuary, something she'll need more and more as the years pass."

"Not all ssanctuariess are dark, High Lord. The room you gave her pleasess her, too." For the first time in all the years he'd known her, Draca smiled. "Sshall I desscribe it to you? I have heard about it often enough."

Saetan looked away, not wanting her to see how pleased he was.

"I wanted to sshow you the Winssol gift I have for her." Draca retreated into the dressing room and returned holding a wisp of black. She spread it out on the bed's satin coverlet. "What do you think?"

Saetan stared at the full-length dress. There was a lump in his throat he couldn't swallow around, and the room was suddenly misty. He fingered the black spidersilk. "Her first Widow's weeds," he said huskily. "This is what she should wear for Winsol." He let the silk slip through his fingers as he turned away. "She should be with us."

"Yess, sshe sshould be with her family."

"She will be with her family," Saetan said bitterly. He laughed, but that was bitter, too. "She'll be with her grandmother and mother . . . and her father."

"No," Draca said gently. "Not with her father. Now, finally, doess sshe have a father."

Saetan took a deep breath. "I used to be the coldest bastard to ever have walked the Realms. What happened?"

"You fell in love . . . with the daughter of your ssoul." Draca made a little sound that might have been a laugh. "And you were never sso cold, Ssaetan, never sso cold ass you pretended to be."

"You might spare my pride by allowing me my illusions."

"For what purposse? Doess sshe allow you to be cold?"

"At least she allows me my illusions," Saetan said, warming to the gentle argument. "However," he added wryly, "she doesn't let me get away with much else." He sighed, his expression one of pained amusement. "I must go. I have to talk to some distressed merchants."

Draca escorted him out. "It hass been a long time ssince you celebrated Winssol. Thiss year, when the black candless are lit, you will drink the blooded rum and dance for the glory of Witch."

"Yes," he said softly, thinking of the spidersilk dress, "this year I will dance."

6 / Hell

Saetan settled his cape around his shoulders. On the floor of his private study were six boxes filled with the many brightly wrapped gifts he had purchased for the *cildru dyathe*. Since the children were so skittish of adults, it was impossible to know how many were on the island. The best he could do was fill a box for each age group and leave it to Char to distribute the gifts. There were books and toys, games and puzzles, from as many Kaeleer Territories as he had access to. If he had been overly indulgent this year, it was to fill the hole in his heart, to make up for the gifts he wanted to give Jaenelle and couldn't. There could be no trace of him in Beldon Mor, no gift that might provoke questions. Knowledge was the only thing he could give her that she could take back to Terreille.

He vanished the boxes one by one, left his study, and caught the Black Wind to the *cildru dyathe*'s island.

Even for Hell, it was a bleak place made of rocks, sand, and barren fields. A place where even Hell's native flora and fauna couldn't thrive. He'd always wondered why Char had chosen that place instead of one of the many others that wouldn't have been so stark. And then Jaenelle had unthinkingly given him the answer: The island, in its starkness, in its unyielding bleakness, held no deceptions, no illusions. Poisons weren't sugarcoated, brutality wasn't masked by silk and lace. There was nowhere for cruelty to hide.

He took his time reaching that rocky place that was as close to a shelter as the children would condone. As he reached the final bend in the twisting path and mentally prepared himself to watch them flee from him, he heard laughter—innocent, delighted laughter. He wrapped his cape tightly around him, hoping to blend into the rocks and remain unnoticed for a moment. To hear them laugh that way . . .

Saetan eased around the last rock and gasped.

In the center of their open "council" area stood a magnificent evergreen, its color undimmed by Hell's forever-twilight. Throughout the branches, little points of color winked in and out like a rainbow of fireflies performing a merry dance. Char and the other children were hanging icicles—real icicles—from the branches. Little silver and gold bells tinkled as they brushed against the branches. There was laughter and purpose, an animation and sparkle in their young faces that he'd never seen before.

Then they saw him and froze, small animals caught in the light. In another moment, they would have run, but Char turned at that instant, his eyes bright. He stepped toward Saetan, holding out his hands in an ancient gesture of welcome.

"High Lord." Char's voice rang with pride. "Come see our tree."

Saetan came forward slowly and placed his hands over Char's. He studied the tree. A single tear slipped down his cheek, and his lips trembled. "Ah, children," he said huskily, "it's truly a magnificent tree. And your decorations are *wonderful.*"

They smiled at him, shyly, tentatively.

Without thinking, Saetan put his arm around Char's shoulders and hugged him close. The boy jerked back, caught himself, and then hesitantly put his arms around Saetan and hugged him in return.

"You know who gave us the tree, don't you?" Char whispered.

"Yes, I know."

"I've never . . . most of us have never . . ."

"I know, Char." Saetan squeezed Char's shoulder once more. He cleared his throat. "They seem a bit . . . dull . . . compared with this, but there are gifts for you to put beneath the tree."

Char rubbed his hand across his face. "She said it would only last the thirteen days of Winsol, but that's all they ever last, isn't it?"

"Yes, that's all they ever last."

"High Lord." Char hesitated. "How?"

Saetan smiled tenderly at the boy. "I don't know. She's magic. I'm only a Warlord Prince. You can't expect me to explain magic."

Char smiled in return, a smile from one man to another.

Saetan called in the six boxes. "I'll leave these in your keeping." One finger gently stroked Char's burned, blackened cheek. "Happy Winsol, Warlord." He turned and glided quickly toward the path. As he passed the first bend, a sound came from a smattering of voices. When it was repeated, it was a full chorus.

"Happy Winsol, High Lord."

Saetan choked back a sob and hurried back to the Hall.

7 / Hell

"You did tell me to give a Winsol gift to someone who might not get one, so . . . well . . ." Jaenelle nervously brushed her fingers along the edge of Saetan's blackwood desk.

"Come here, witch-child." Saetan gently hugged her. Putting his lips close to her ear, he whispered, "That was the finest piece of magic I've ever seen. I'm so very proud of you."

"Truly?" Jaenelle whispered back.

"Truly." He held her at arm's length so he could see her face. "Would you share the secret?" he asked, keeping his voice lightly teasing. "Would you tell an old Warlord Prince how you did it?"

Jaenelle's eyes focused on his Red Birthright Jewel hanging from its gold chain. "I promised the Prince, you see."

"See what?" he asked calmly as his stomach flip-flopped.

"I promised that if I was going to do any dream weaving I'd learn from the best who could teach me."

And you didn't come to me? "So who taught you, witch-child?"

She licked her lips. "The Arachnians," she said in a small voice.

The room blurred and spun. When it stopped revolving, Saetan gratefully realized he was still sitting in his chair. "Arachna is a closed Territory," he said through clenched teeth.

Jaenelle frowned. "I know. But so are a lot of places where I have friends. They don't mind, Saetan. Truly."

Saetan released her and locked his hands together. Arachna. She'd gone to Arachna. Beware the golden spider that spins a tangled web. There wasn't a Black Widow in all the history of the Blood who could spin dream webs like the Arachnians. The whole shore of their island was littered with tangled webs that could pull in unsuspecting—and even well-trained—minds, leaving the flesh shell to be devoured. For her to blithely walk through their defenses . . .

"The Arachnian Queen," Saetan said, fighting the urge to yell at her. "Whom did she assign to teach you?"

Jaenelle gave him a worried little smile. "She taught me. We started with the straight, simple webs, everyday weaving. After that . . ." Jaenelle shrugged.

Saetan cleared his throat. "Just out of curiosity, how large is the Arachnian Queen?"

"Um . . . her body's about like that." Jaenelle pointed at his fist.

The room tilted. Very little was known about Arachna—with good reason, since very few who had ever ventured there had returned intact—but one thing was known: the larger the spider, the more powerful and deadly were the webs.

"Did the Prince suggest you go to Arachna?" Saetan asked, desperately trying to keep the snarl out of his voice.

Jaenelle blinked and had the grace to blush. "No. I don't think he'd be too happy if I told him."

Saetan closed his eyes. What was done was done. "You will remember courtesy and Protocol when you visit them, won't you?"

"Yes, High Lord," Jaenelle said, her voice suspiciously submissive.

Saetan opened his eyes to a narrow slit. Jaenelle's sapphire eyes sparkled back at him. He snarled, defeated. Hell's fire, if he was so outmaneuvered by a twelve-year-old girl, what in the name of Darkness was he going to do when she was full grown?

"Saetan?"

"Jaenelle."

She held out a brightly though clumsily wrapped package with a slightly mangled bow. "Happy Winsol, Saetan."

His hand shook a little as he took the package and laid it gently on the desk. "Witch-child, I—"

Jaenelle threw her arms around his neck and squeezed. "Draca said it was all right to open your gift before Winsol because I should only wear it at the Keep. Oh, thank you, Saetan. Thank you. It's the most wonderful dress. And it's *black*." She studied his face. "Wasn't I supposed to tell you I already opened it?"

Saetan hugged her fiercely. *You, too, Draca. You, too, are not as cold as you pretend to be.* "I'm glad it pleases you, witch-child. Now." He turned to her package.

"No," Jaenelle said nervously. "You should wait for Winsol."

"You didn't," he gently teased. "Besides, you won't be here for Winsol, so . . ."

"No, Saetan. Please?"

It piqued his curiosity that she would give him something and not want to be there when he opened it. However, tomorrow was Winsol, and he didn't want her leaving him feeling heartsore. Adeptly turning the conversation to the mounds of food being prepared at the Kaeleer Hall and broadly hinting that Helene and Mrs. Beale just might be willing to parcel some out before the next day, he sent her on her way and leaned back in his chair with a sigh.

The package beckoned.

Saetan Black-locked the study door before carefully unwrapping the package. His heart did a queer little jig as he stared at the back of one of the swivel frames he had purchased for her. Taking a deep breath, he opened the frame.

In the left side was a copy of an old picture of a young man with a hint of a brash smile and a ready-for-trouble gleam in his eyes. The face would have changed by now, hardened, matured. Even so.

"Lucivar," he whispered, blinking away tears and shaking his head. "You had that look in your eyes when you were five years old. It would seem there are some things the years can't change. Where are you now, my Eyrien Prince."

He turned to the picture on the right, immediately set the frame on the desk, leaned back in his chair and covered his eyes. "No wonder," he whispered. "By all the Jewels and the Darkness, no wonder." If Lucivar was a summer afternoon, Daemon was winter's coldest night. Sliding his hands from his face, Saetan forced himself to study the picture of his namesake, his true heir.

It was a formal picture taken in front of a red-velvet background. On the surface, this son of his was not a mirror—he far exceeded his father's chiseled, handsome features—but beneath the surface was the recognizable, chilling darkness, and a ruthlessness Saetan instinctively knew had been honed by years of cruelty.

"Dorothea, you have re-created me at my worst."

And yet . . .

Saetan leaned forward and studied the golden eyes so like his own, eyes that seemed to look straight at him. He smiled in thanks and relief. Nothing would ever undo what Dorothea had done to Daemon, what she had turned him into, but in those golden eyes was a swirling expression of resignation, amusement, irritation, and delight—a cacophony of emotions he was all too familiar with. It could only mean one thing: Jaenelle had maneuvered Daemon into this and had gone with him to make sure it was done to her satisfaction.

"Well, namesake," Saetan said quietly as he positioned the frame on the corner of his desk, "if you've accepted the leash she's holding, there's hope for you yet."

8 / Terreille

For Daemon, Winsol was the bitterest day of the year, a cruel reminder of what it had been like to grow up in Dorothea's court, of what had been required of him after the dancing had fired Dorothea's and Hepsabah's blood.

His stomach tightened. The stone he sharpened his already honed temper on was the knowledge that the one witch he wanted to dance with, the only one he would gladly surrender to and indulge, was too young for him—for any man.

He celebrated Winsol because it was expected of him. Each year he sent a basket of delicacies to Surreal. Each year he sent gifts to Manny and Jo—and to Tersa whenever he could find her. Each year there were the expected, expensive gifts for the witches he served. Each year he got nothing in return, not even the words "thank you."

But this year was different. This year he'd been caught up in a whirl-wind called Jaenelle Angelline—as impossible to deflect as she was to stop—and he had become an accomplice in all sorts of schemes that, even in their innocence, had been thrilling. When he had dug in his heels and balked at one of her adventures, he'd been dragged along like a toy so well loved it didn't have much of its stuffing left. With his defenses breached, with his temper dulled and battered by love and his coldness trampled by mischief, he had briefly thought to appeal to the Priest for help until, with amused dismay, he realized the High Lord of Hell was probably faring no better than he.

Now, however, as he thought of the kinds of adventures Alexandra and Leland and their friends would require of him, the cold once more whis-pered through his veins and his temper cut with every breath.

After a light meal that would hold off hunger until the night's huge feast, they gathered in the drawing room to unwrap the Winsol gifts. Flushed from her dizzying work in the kitchen, Cook carried in the tray with the silver bowl filled with the traditional hot blooded rum. The small silver cups were filled to be shared.

Robert shared his cup with Leland, who tried not to look at Philip. Philip shared his with Wilhelmina. Graff sneeringly shared hers with Cook. And he, because he had no choice, shared his with Alexandra.

Jaenelle stood alone, with no one to share her cup.

Daemon's heart twisted. He remembered too many Winsols when he had been the one standing alone, the outcast, the unwanted. He would have damned the tradition that said only one cup was shared, but he saw that strange, unnerving light flicker in her eyes for just a moment before she lifted her cup in a salute and drank.

There was a moment of nervous silence before Wilhelmina jumped in with a brittle smile and asked, "Can we open the gifts now?"

As the cups were put back on the tray, Daemon maneuvered to Jaenelle's side. "Lady—"

"It's fitting, don't you think, that I should drink alone?" she said in a midnight whisper. Her eyes were full of awful pain. "After all, I am kin-dred but not kind."

You're my Queen, he thought fiercely. His body ached. She was his

Queen. But with her family surrounding them, watching, there was nothing he could say or do to help her.

During the next hour, Jaenelle played her expected role of the slightly befuddled child, fawning over gifts so at odds with what she was that it made Daemon want to paint the walls in blood. No one else noticed she was fighting harder and harder to draw breath with each gift she unwrapped until it seemed the bright paper and bows were fists pounding her small body. When he opened her gift of handkerchiefs, she flinched and went deathly pale. With a gasp, she leaped to her feet and ran from the room while Alexandra and Leland sternly called for her to come back.

Not caring what they thought, Daemon left the room, cold fury rolling off him, and went to the library. Jaenelle was there, gasping for breath, feebly trying to open a window. Daemon locked the door, strode across the room, viciously twisted the lock on the sash, and snapped the window open with wall-shaking force.

Jaenelle leaned over the narrow window seat, gulping in the winter air. "It hurts so much to live here, Daemon," she whimpered as he cradled her in his arms. "Sometimes it hurts so much."

"Shh." He stroked her hair. "Shh."

As soon as her breathing slowed to normal, Daemon closed and locked the window. He leaned against the wall, one leg stretched out along the window seat, and drew her forward until she was pressed against him. Then he hooked his other foot under his leg, effectively capturing her in a tight triangle.

It was insane to have her pushed up against him that way. Insane to take such pleasure in her hands resting on his thighs. Insane not to stop the slow uncurling of those psychic tendrils of seduction.

"I'm sorry I couldn't share the cup with you."

"It doesn't matter," Jaenelle whispered.

"It does to me," he replied sharply, his deep, silky voice having more of a husky edge than usual.

Jaenelle's eyes were getting confused and smoky. He pulled the tendrils back a little.

"Daemon," Jaenelle said hesitantly. "Your gift . . ."

There was a rumbling in Daemon's throat—his bedroom laugh, except there was fire in it instead of ice, and his eyes were molten gold. "That was no more your choice than the paint set was truly mine." He raised one eyebrow. "I had considered getting you a saddle that would fit both you and Dark Dancer—"

Jaenelle's eyes widened and she laughed.

"—but that wouldn't have been practical." One long-nailed finger idly stroked her arm. He knew he should walk away from this—now—when he had amused her, but her pain had twisted something inside him, and he wasn't going to let her believe she was alone here. It made him wonder about something else. "Jaenelle," he said cautiously as he watched his finger, "did the Priest . . ." If Saetan hadn't given her a Winsol gift, would his asking hurt her more?

"Oh, Daemon, it's so wonderful. I can't wear it here, of course."

He started to untwist. "Wear what?"

"My dress." She squirmed in his tight triangle and almost sent him through the wall. "It's floor-length and it's made of spidersilk and it's black, Daemon, *black*."

Daemon concentrated on breathing. When he was sure his heart remembered its proper rhythm, he reached into his inner jacket pocket and took out a small square box. "Then this, I think, would be a proper accessory."

"What is it?" Jaenelle asked, hesitantly taking the box.

"Your Winsol gift. Your *real* Winsol gift."

Smiling shyly, Jaenelle unwrapped the box, opened it, and gasped.

Daemon's throat tightened. It was an inappropriate gift for a man like him to give a young girl, but he didn't care about that, didn't care about anything except whether or not it pleased her.

"Oh, Daemon," Jaenelle whispered. She took the hammered silver cuff bracelet from the box and placed it on her left wrist. "It will be perfect with my dress." She reached up to hug him and froze.

He watched her emotions swirl in her eyes, too fast for him to identify. Instead of hugging him, she lowered her hands to his shoulders, leaned forward, and kissed him lightly on the mouth, a girl child testing the waters of womanhood. His hands closed on her arms with just enough pressure to keep her close to him. When she pulled back, he saw in her eyes a whisper of the woman she would become.

Seeing that, he couldn't let it finish there.

Gently cupping her face in his hands, Daemon leaned forward and returned her kiss. His kiss was as light and close-lipped as hers had been, but it wasn't innocent and it wasn't chaste. When he finally raised his head, he knew he was playing a dangerous game.

Jaenelle swayed, bracing her hands on his thighs for support. She licked her lips and looked at him with slightly glazed eyes. "Do . . . do all boys kiss like that?"

"Boys don't kiss like that at all, Lady," he said quietly, seriously. "Neither do most men. But I'm not like most men." He slowly pulled in his seduction tendrils. He had done more than he should have already tonight; anything else would harm her. Tomorrow he would be the companion he'd been yesterday, and the day before that. But she would remember that kiss and compare every kiss from every weak-willed Chaillot boy against it.

He didn't care how many boys kissed her. They were, after all, boys. But the bed . . . When the time came, the bed would be *his*.

He removed the bracelet from her wrist and put it back in its box. "Vanish that," he said quietly while he disposed of the ribbon and paper. When the box was gone, he unwound his legs and led her back to the drawing room, where Graff immediately hurried the girls off to bed.

Philip glared at him. Robert smirked. Leland was fluttery and pale. It was Alexandra's jealous, accusing look that unsheathed his temper. She rose to confront him, but at that moment the guests began arriving for the night-long festivities.

That night Daemon didn't wait for Alexandra to "ask" him to accommodate a female guest. He seduced every woman in the house—beginning with Leland—teasing them into climaxes while he danced with them, watching them shudder while they bit their lips until they bled, trying not to cry out with so many people crowded around them. Or slipping away with one of the women to a little alcove, and after the first ice-fire kiss, standing primly against the wall, his hands in his trouser pockets, while his phantom touch played mercilessly with her body until she was sprawled on the floor, pleading for the caress of a real hand—and then his merest touch, the tickling slide of his nails along her inner thigh, the briefest touch to the undergarments in the right place, and she would be glutted—and starved.

Still, Daemon wasn't done.

He had deliberately avoided Alexandra, taunting her with his open seduction of all the other women, frustrating her beyond endurance. Before the door shut on the last guest, he swept her into his arms, climbed the stairs, and locked them into her bedroom. He made up for everything. He showed her the kind of pleasure he could give a woman when inspired. He showed her why he was called the Sadist.

When he stumbled into his own room long after dawn, the first thing he noticed was that his bed had been fussed with. One swift, angry probe located the package beneath his pillow. Cautiously pulling back the covers and tossing the pillow aside, Daemon looked at the clumsily wrapped package and the folded note tucked under the ribbon. He smiled tenderly, sinking gratefully onto the bed.

She must have put it there as soon as he'd left the room.

The note said: "I couldn't give you the gift I wanted to because the others wouldn't understand. Happy Winsol, Daemon. Love, Jaenelle."

Daemon unwrapped the package and opened the swivel frame. The left side was empty, waiting for Lucivar's picture. On the right . . .

"It's funny," Daemon said quietly to the picture. "I'd always thought you'd look more formal, more . . . distant. But for all your splendor, all your Craft and power, you really wouldn't mind putting your feet up and downing a tankard of ale, would you? I'd never guessed how much of you is in Lucivar. Or how much of you is in me. Ah, Priest." Daemon gently closed the frame. "Happy Winsol, Father."

CHAPTER THIRTEEN

1 / Terreille

"We should have brought the others," Cassandra said as she clenched Saetan's arm.

He laid his hand over hers and gave it a gentle squeeze. "He didn't ask to see the others. He asked to see me."

"He didn't ask," Cassandra snapped. She glanced nervously at the Sanctuary and lowered her voice. "He didn't ask, High Lord, he *demanded* to see you."

"And I'm here."

"Yes," she said with an undercurrent of anger, "you're here."

Sometimes you make it hard for me to remember why I loved you so much for so long. "He's my son, Cassandra." He smiled grimly. "Are you offended by his manners on my behalf or because your vanity's pricked that he wasn't sufficiently obsequious?"

Cassandra snatched her hand from his arm. "He's charming when he wants to be," she said nastily. "And I've no doubt his bedroom manners are flawless, since he's had so much practice perfecting . . ." Her words faded when she noticed Saetan's glacial stare.

"If his manners leave something to be desired, Lady, I'll thank you to remember whose court trained him."

Cassandra lifted her chin. "You blame me, don't you?"

"No," Saetan said softly, bitterly. "I knew the price for what I became. The responsibility for him rests solely with me. But I'll allow no one, *no one,* to condemn him for what he's become because of it." Saetan breathed deeply, trying to gather his frayed temper. "Why don't you go to your room? It's better that I meet him alone."

"No," Cassandra said quickly. "We both wear the Black. Together we can—"

"I didn't come here to fight him."

"But he's come to fight you!"

"You don't know that."

"You weren't the one he pinned to the wall while he made his demands!"

"I'll give him a slap. Will that appease you?" Saetan snarled as he marched into the ruins of the Sanctuary, heading toward the kitchen and another confrontation.

Halfway to the kitchen, Saetan slowed down. He'd kept his promise to Draca. On Winsol he had danced for the glory of Witch. Thanks to the blood Jaenelle insisted on giving him, he no longer needed a cane or walked with a limp, but the dancing had stiffened his bad leg, had shortened his fluid stride. He regretted that he might appear old or infirm for this first meeting with Daemon after so many, many years.

Fury poured out the kitchen doorway as Saetan approached. So. Cassandra hadn't exaggerated about that. At least the rage was hot. They might still be able to talk.

Daemon prowled the kitchen with panther grace, his hands in his trouser pockets, his body coiled with barely restrained rage. When he sent a dagger glance toward the doorway and noticed Saetan, he didn't alter his stride; he simply pivoted on the ball of his foot and came straight toward the High Lord.

That picture told only half the truth, Saetan thought as he watched Daemon's swift approach and waited to see if blood would be drawn.

Daemon stopped an arm's length away, nostrils flaring, eyes stabbing, silent.

"Prince," Saetan said calmly. He watched Daemon fight for control, fight the searing rage in order to return the greeting.

"High Lord," Daemon said through clenched teeth.

Slowly approaching the table, aware of Daemon watching his every move, Saetan took off his cape, laying it across a chair. "Let's have a glass of wine, and then we'll talk."

"I don't want any wine."

"I do." Saetan got the wine and glasses. Settling into a chair, he opened the wine, poured two glasses, and waited.

Daemon stepped forward, carefully placing his hands on the table.

Dorothea was blind not to know what Daemon was, Saetan thought as he sipped the wine. Having expected to see them, Saetan found Daemon's long nails less disconcerting than his ringless fingers. If he could be this formidable without wearing a Jewel to help focus his strength . . .

No wonder Cassandra had been terrified. Black Jewels or no, she was no match for this son of his.

"Do you know where she is?" Daemon asked, obviously straining not to scream.

Saetan's eyes narrowed. Fear. All that fury was covering an avalanche of fear. "Who?"

Daemon sprang away from the table, swearing.

When the torrent of expletives showed no sign of abating, Saetan said dryly, "Namesake, do you realize you're making this room quite uninhabitable?"

"What?" Daemon pivoted and sprang back to the table.

"Leash your rage, Prince," Saetan said quietly. "You sent for me, and I'm here." He looked over his shoulder toward the window. "However, the dawn is a few short hours away, and you can't afford to be here beyond that, can you?"

As Daemon dropped into the chair across from him, Saetan handed him a glass of wine. Daemon drained it. Saetan refilled it. After refilling it for the third time, he said dryly, "From experience I can tell you that getting drunk doesn't lessen the fear. However, the agony of the hangover can do wonders for a man's perception."

There was dismayed amusement in Daemon's eyes.

"Bluntly put, my fine young Prince, this is obviously the first time our fair-haired Lady has scared the shit out of you."

Daemon frowned at the empty wine bottle, found a full one in the cupboard, and refilled both glasses. "Not the first time," he growled.

Saetan chuckled. "But it is a matter of degree, yes?"

There was a hint of warmth in Daemon's reluctant smile. "Yes."

"And this time is bad."

Daemon closed his eyes. "Yes."

Saetan sighed. "Start at the beginning and let's see if we can untangle this."

"She's not at her family's estate."

"It *is* the Winsol season. Could her . . . family"—Saetan choked on the word—"have left her with friends to visit?"

Daemon shook his head. "*Something's* there, but it isn't Jaenelle. It looks like her, talks like her, plays the obedient daughter." Daemon looked at Saetan, his eyes haunted. "But what makes Jaenelle Jaenelle isn't there." He laughed scornfully. "Her family has been most gratified that she's been behaving so well and not embarrassing them when the girls are presented to guests." He played with his wineglass. "I'm afraid something has happened to her."

"Unlikely." Fascinated, Saetan watched the anger melt from Daemon's face. He liked the man he saw beneath it.

"How can you be sure?" Daemon asked hopefully. "Have you seen something like that before?"

"Not quite like that, no."

"Then how—"

"Because, namesake, what you're describing is called a shadow, but there's no one in any of the Realms, including me, who has the Craft to create a shadow that's so lifelike—except Jaenelle."

Daemon sipped his wine and brooded for a minute. "What, exactly, is a shadow?"

"Basically, a shadow is an illusion, a re-creation of an object's physical form." Saetan looked pointedly at Daemon, who shrank in his chair just a little. "Some children have been known to create a shadow in order to appear to be asleep in their beds while they are really off having adventures that, if discovered, would prevent them from comfortably sitting down for a week." He saw the briefest flicker of memory in Daemon's eyes and the beginning of a wry smile. "That's a first-stage shadow and is stationary. A second-stage shadow can move around, but it has to be manipulated like a puppet. That kind of shadow looks solid but can't be felt, doesn't have tactile capabilities. The third-stage shadow, which is the strongest I've ever heard of being achieved, has one-way tactile ability. It can touch but can't be touched. However, it, too, must be manipulated."

Daemon thought this over and shook his head. "This is more."

"Yes, this is much, much more. This is a shadow so skillfully created that it can act independently through expected routines. I don't imagine the conversation's stimulating"—that made Daemon snort—"but it does mean the originator can be doing something entirely different."

"Ah," Saetan said as he refilled their glasses, "*that* is the interesting question."

Daemon's eyes flashed with relieved anger. "Why would she create one?"

"As I said, *that* is the interesting question."

"Is that it? We just wait?"

"For now. But whoever gets to her first gets to go up one side of her and down the other. Twice."

A slow smile curled Daemon's lips. "You're worried."

"You're damn right I'm worried," Saetan snapped. Now that he didn't have to rein in Daemon's temper, he felt free to unleash his own. "Who in the name of Hell knows what she's up to this time?" He slumped in his chair, snarling.

Daemon leaned back in his chair and laughed.

"Don't be so amused, boy. *You* deserve a good kick in the ass."

Daemon blinked. *"Me?"*

Saetan leaned forward. "You. The next time you suggest she get proper instruction before trying something, you'd damn well better remember to add that I'm the one to give the proper instruction."

"What—"

"Dream weaving. Do you remember dream weaving, namesake?"

Daemon paled. "I remember. But I—"

"Told her to be instructed by the best. Which she did."

"Then what—"

"Have you ever heard of Arachna?"

Daemon got paler. "That's a legend," he whispered.

"Most of Kaeleer's a legend, boy," Saetan roared. "That hasn't stopped her from meeting some *very* interesting individuals."

They glared at one another. Finally Daemon said with menacing quiet, "Like you?"

Damn, this boy was fun! Saetan took a deep breath and sighed dramatically. "I used to be interesting," he said mournfully. "I used to be respected, even feared. My study was a private sanctuary no one willingly entered. But I've gotten long in the tooth"—Daemon flicked a startled glance at his mouth—"and now I have demons pounding on my door, some upset because she hasn't visited with them, some upset because she has. My cook backs me into corners, wanting to know if the Lady will be

coming today so her favorite meat pie can be prepared. And I have merchants cluttering up my doorstep, cringingly seeking an audience, actually
relieved to be in my presence while they wring their hands and pour out
their tales of woe."

Daemon, who had become more and more amused, frowned slightly.
"The demons and the cook I understand. Why the merchants?"

Saetan let out another dramatic sigh, but his eyes glowed with dark
amusement. "I opened a blanket account for her in Kaeleer."

Daemon sucked in his breath. "You mean . . ."

"Yes."

"Mother Night."

"That's the kindest thing that's been said to me on that score." Enjoying the drama, Saetan continued, "And it's going to get worse. You do realize that?"

"Worse?" Daemon said suspiciously. "Why will it get worse?"

"She's only twelve, namesake."

"I know," Daemon almost moaned.

"Just consider what sort of mischief she'll have the capacity to get into
when she's seventeen and has her own court."

Daemon groaned, but there was a sharp, hopeful look in his eyes. "She
can have her own court at seventeen? And fill it?"

Ah, namesake. Saetan sat quietly for a moment, thinking of a politic
way to explain. "Most positions can be filled then." Daemon's instant bitterness stunned him.

"Of course you'll want better for her than a whore who's serviced almost every Queen in Terreille," Daemon said, refilling his wineglass.

"That isn't what I meant," Saetan said, despairing that any explanation
now might seem a poor bone.

"Then what did you mean?" Daemon snapped.

"What if, at seventeen, she isn't ready for a consort?" Saetan countered
softly. "What if it takes a few more years before she's ready for the bed?
Will you hold an empty office, becoming comfortable and familiar while
lesser men intrigue her because they're strangers? Time has great magic,
namesake, if you know how to play the game."

"You talk as though it's decided," Daemon said quietly, with only an
aftertaste of bitterness.

"It is . . . as far as I'm concerned."

Daemon's naked, grateful look was agony.

They sat quietly, companionably, for a few minutes. Then Daemon said, "Why do you keep calling me namesake?"

"Because you are." Saetan looked away, uncomfortable. "I never intended to give any of my sons that name. I knew what I was. It was difficult enough for them to have me as a father. But the first time I held you, I knew no other name would suit you. So I named you Saetan Daemon SaDiablo."

Daemon's eyes were tear bright. "Then you really did acknowledge paternity? Manny said the Blood register in Hayll had been changed, but I had wondered."

"I'm not responsible for Dorothea's lies, Prince," Saetan said bitterly. "Or for what the Hayllian register does or doesn't say. But in the register kept at Ebon Askavi, you—and Lucivar—are named and acknowledged."

"So you called me Daemon?"

Saetan knew there was much, much more Daemon would have liked to ask, but he was grateful his son chose to step back, to try for lighter conversation in the short time left to them.

"No," Saetan said dryly, "*I* never called you anything but Saetan. It was Manny and Tersa"—he hesitated, wondering if Daemon knew about Tersa, but there was no surprise—"who called you Daemon. Manny informed me one day, when I pointed out her error, that if I thought she was going to stand at the back door bellowing that name to get a boy to come in for supper I had better think again."

Daemon laughed. "Come now, Manny's a sweetheart."

"To *you*." Saetan chuckled. "Personally I always thought she just wanted to avoid having both of us answer that summons."

"Would you have?" Daemon asked warmly.

"Considering the tone of voice used, I wouldn't have dared not to."

They both laughed.

The parting was awkward. Saetan wanted to embrace him, but Daemon became tense, almost skittish. Saetan wondered if, after all those years in Dorothea's court, Daemon had an aversion to being touched.

And there was Lucivar. He had wanted to ask about Lucivar, but Daemon's haunted expression at the mention of his brother's name eliminated that possibility. Since he wanted to know his sons, he would have to have the patience to let them approach when they were ready.

2 / Terreille

Jaenelle returned a teeth-grinding day and a half later.

After a hectic afternoon of social calls with Alexandra, Daemon was prowling the corridors, too restless to lie down and get some badly needed rest, when he saw the girls come in from a walk in the garden.

"But you must remember how funny it was," Wilhelmina said as he approached. She looked bewildered. "It only happened yesterday."

"Did it?" Jaenelle replied absently. "Oh, yes, I remember now."

Daemon gave them an exaggerated bow. "Ladies."

Wilhelmina giggled. Jaenelle raised her eyes to meet his.

He didn't like the weariness in her face, didn't like how ancient her eyes looked even though they were the dissembling summer-sky blue, but he met her steady gaze. "Lady, may I have a word with you?"

"As you wish," Jaenelle said, barely suppressing a sigh.

They waited until Wilhelmina climbed the stairs to the nursery before going to the library. Daemon locked the door. Before he could decide what to say, Jaenelle grumbled, "Don't be scoldy, Prince."

Hackles rising, Daemon slipped his hands into his pockets and leisurely walked toward her. "I haven't said a word."

Jaenelle removed her coat and hat, dropping them on the couch. She slumped beside them. "I've already had one scolding today."

So the Priest had gotten to her first. Just as well. All Daemon wanted to do was hug her. He settled beside her, perversely wanting to take the sting out of the very scolding he had wanted to administer. "Was the scolding very bad?" he asked gently.

Jaenelle scowled at him. "He wouldn't have scolded at all if you hadn't told him. Why'd you tell him?"

"I was scared. I thought something had happened to you."

"Oh," Jaenelle said, immediately chastened. "But I worked so hard to create that shadow so no one would worry, so there wouldn't be any difference. No one else noticed the difference."

They noticed, my Lady. They were grateful for the difference. It amused him—a little—that she was more concerned that her Craft hadn't been as effective as she'd thought than she was about the worry she'd caused. "It took the Black to notice the difference, and even I wasn't sure until a whole day had gone by."

"Really?" Jaenelle perked up.

"Really." Daemon tried to smile but couldn't quite do it. "Don't you think I'm entitled to an explanation?"

Jaenelle ducked her face behind her golden veil of hair. "I was going to tell you. I promised I'd tell you. And I had to tell the Priest because he has to arrange some things."

Daemon frowned. "Promised who?"

"Tersa."

Daemon counted to ten. "How do you know Tersa?"

"It was time, Daemon," Jaenelle said, ignoring his question.

Daemon counted to ten again. "Tersa's very special to me."

"I know," Jaenelle said quietly. "But you're grown up now, Daemon. You don't really need her anymore. And it was time for her to leave the Twisted Kingdom . . . but she'd been there so long, she couldn't find her way back by herself."

The room was so cold—not the cold of anger, the cold of fear. Daemon held Jaenelle's hands between his own, taking small comfort from their warmth. He didn't want to understand. He truly did not want to understand. But he did. "You went into the Twisted Kingdom, didn't you?" he said, trying desperately to keep his voice calm. "You walked the roads of madness to find her and led her back to sanity—at least as far as she can come."

"Yes."

"Didn't you think—" His voice broke from the strain. "Didn't it occur to you it might be dangerous?"

Jaenelle looked puzzled. "Dangerous?" She shook her head. "No. It's just a different way of seeing, Daemon."

Daemon closed his eyes. Did she fear nothing? Not even madness?

"Besides, I've traveled that far before, so I knew the way back."

Daemon tasted blood where his teeth had nicked his tongue.

"But it took a while to find her, and it took a while to convince her it was time to go, that she didn't need to stay inside the visions all the time." Jaenelle gave his hands a little squeeze. "The Priest is going to buy a cottage for her in a little village near the Hall in Kaeleer. She'll have people there who will look after her, and a garden to work in, and Black Widow Sisters to talk to."

Daemon pulled her into his arms and held her tight. "You convinced her to live there?" he whispered into her hair. "She'll really be in a decent house with decent clothes and good food and people who will understand?" Her head moved up and down. He sighed. "Then it was worth the worry. A hundred times that would have been worth it."

"That's what the Priest said—after the scolding."

Daemon smiled against her hair. "Did he say anything else?"

"Lots of things," Jaenelle grumbled. "Something about sitting down comfortably, but I didn't understand him and he wouldn't repeat it."

Daemon coughed. Jaenelle raised her head, eyeing him suspiciously. He tried for a bland expression. She looked more suspicious.

Passing footsteps in the corridor made him turn, his body tensed, his eyes fixed on the door.

"You'd better join your sister." He handed her the coat and hat. Before he opened the door, Daemon paused. "Thank you." It was far from adequate, but it was all he could think of to say.

Jaenelle nodded and slipped out the door.

3 / Terreille

Daemon had just finished brushing his hair, ready for another day of Winsol activity, when Jaenelle tapped lightly on his door and bounced into the room. He wasn't sure when his room had become mutual territory, but he was much less casual about the way he dressed—and undressed—than he had been.

Jaenelle bounced up beside him, her eyes fixed on his face. Daemon smiled. "Do I meet with your approval?"

She reached up, brushed her fingers against his cheek, and frowned. "Your face is smooth."

One eyebrow rising, Daemon turned back to the mirror to check his collar. "Hayllian men don't have facial hair." He paused. "Neither do Dhemlans or Eyriens, for that matter."

Jaenelle still frowned. "I don't understand."

Daemon shrugged. "Differences in race is all."

"No." Jaenelle shook her head. "If you don't have to take the hair off the way Philip does, why did Graff say you might serve better if you were shaved? Philip does it hims—"

Daemon's fist hit the top of the dresser, splitting the wood from end to end. He gripped the edges while he fought for control. The bitch. The *bitch,* to make such a suggestion!

"It means something else, doesn't it?" Jaenelle said in her midnight voice.

"It's nothing," Daemon growled through clenched teeth.

"What does it mean, Daemon?"

"Leave it alone, Jaenelle."

"Prince."

Daemon's fist smashed the dresser again. "If you're so curious, ask your damn mentor!" He turned away, struggling to regain control. After a moment, he turned again, saying, "Jaenelle, I'm sorry."

She was already gone.

4 / Hell

Saetan and Andulvar sat around the blackwood desk, drinking yarbarah while waiting for Jaenelle. Saetan had returned to the private study beneath the Hall in order to have some private, concentrated time with Jaenelle for her lessons after discovering that *all* of the Kaeleer staff seemed to make their way into his public study on some pretense or other just to say hello to her.

"What's the lesson to be today?" Andulvar asked.

"How should I know?" Saetan replied dryly.

"You're the one in charge."

"I'm delighted that someone thinks so."

"Ah." Andulvar refilled his glass and warmed the blood wine. "You're still annoyed about Tersa?"

Saetan studied his silver goblet. "Annoyed? No." He rested his head against the back of his chair. "But Hell's fire, Andulvar, trying to keep up with these leaps she makes . . . the enormity of the raw strength it must take to do some of these things. I want her to have a childhood. I want her to do all the silly things young girls do, whatever they are. I want her to be young and carefree."

"She'll never have a normal childhood, SaDiablo. She knows us, the *cildru dyathe,* Geoffrey and Draca—and Lorn, whatever and wherever he may be. She's seen more of Kaeleer than anyone else in thousands of years. How can you hope for a normal childhood?"

"Those things *are* normal, Andulvar," Saetan said wearily, ignoring Andulvar's grunt of denial. "Do you wish you'd never met her? Don't scowl at me that way; I know the answer." He leaned forward, resting his folded hands on the desk. "The point is, a child plays with the unicorns in Sceval. A child visits friends in Scelt and Philan and Glacia and Dharo and Narkhava and Dea al Mon—and in Hell—and who knows how many other places. I've listened to her stories, the innocent, albeit nerve-racking, adventures of young, strong witches growing up and learning their Craft. No matter where she is when she's doing those things, she's a child."

"Then what's the problem?"

"The only place she never mentions, the only place that doesn't figure into these adventures of hers, is Beldon Mor. She says nothing about her family."

Andulvar thought about this. "SaDiablo, you're jealous enough as it is. Would you really want to know that the people who have more claim to her adore her as much as you? Would a child as sensitive to others' moods as she is be willing to tell you?"

"Jealous?" Saetan hissed. "You think it's jealousy that makes me want to tear them apart?"

Andulvar eyed his friend before saying cautiously, "Yes, I do."

Saetan snapped away from his desk, rose halfway out of his chair, then reconsidered. "Not jealousy," he said, closing his eyes. "Fear. I keep wondering what happens when she leaves here. I keep wondering about some of the things she's asked me to teach her, wondering why a child wants to know about some things, wondering why I sometimes hear desperation in her voice or, worse, a chilling anger." He looked at Andulvar. "We survived brutal childhoods and stayed true to the Blood because that's what we are. Blood. But she . . . Oh, Andulvar, in a few short years she'll make the Offering, and when she does, she'll be beyond reach. If she feels isolated from us . . . Do you really want to see Jaenelle in her full, dark glory ruling from the Twisted Kingdom?"

"No," Andulvar said quietly, a faint tremor in his voice. "No, I don't want to see our waif in the Twisted Kingdom."

"Then—" There was a quiet knock on the door. Saetan and Andulvar exchanged a look. Andulvar's face settled into a frown. Saetan's became neutral. "Come."

Both men tensed when Jaenelle walked into the room, the set of her shoulders all the warning they needed.

"High Lord," she said, giving him a regal nod. "Prince Yaslana."

"A bit formal, aren't you, waif?" Andulvar said with good-humored gruffness.

Saetan pressed his lips together, gratefully dismayed. Trust an Eyrien to push a battle into the open. What made him wary was Jaenelle's lack of response.

She turned to Saetan, her sapphire eyes pinning him to the chair. "High Lord, I want to ask a question, and I don't want to be told I'm too young for the answer."

Saetan could see Andulvar become very still, gathering his strength in case it was needed. "Your question, Lady?"

"What does being shaved mean?"

Andulvar stifled a gasp. Saetan felt as if he were falling down a bottomless chasm. He licked his lips and said quietly, "It means to remove a man's genitals."

For a brief moment the room felt the way a sky full of lightning looks. Saetan didn't dare take his eyes off Jaenelle's, didn't dare miss whatever he might read in them.

It made him ill.

After the flash of anger, he could see her considering, weighing, deciding something. Even though he knew what she was going to say, he dreaded hearing the words.

"Teach me."

"Wait a minute, waif!"

Jaenelle raised her hand. Not even the Demon Prince would challenge that imperious order for silence. "High Lord?"

This was how it must feel to be a dried-out husk. "There are two ways," Saetan said stiffly. "The easiest way requires skill with a knife. It also requires physical contact. The other way is subtler but requires knowledge of male anatomy to be effective. Which would you prefer to learn?"

"Both."

Saetan looked away. "May I have until tomorrow to prepare?"

Jaenelle nodded. "High Lord. Prince Yaslana."

They watched her leave. For a while they said nothing, neither willing to meet the other's eyes.

Finally Andulvar said tensely, "You're going to do it, aren't you?"

Saetan leaned back in his chair and closed his eyes, rubbing his temples to ease a searing headache. "Yes, I am."

"You're mad!" Andulvar roared, leaping from his chair. "She's only twelve, Saetan. How can she understand what it means to a man to be shaved?"

Saetan slowly opened his eyes. "You didn't see her eyes. She already appreciates the ramifications of shaving a man. That's why she wants to learn how to do it."

"And who is to be the first victim?" Andulvar snarled.

Saetan shook his head. "The question, my friend, is *why* is there going to be a victim? And where?"

5 / Terreille

When Surreal realized what sort of party this was going to be, she almost told her escort she wanted to leave, but she'd extracted his promise to take her to a Winsol party under the most distracting—and persuasive—circumstances and didn't want to give him an excuse to bolt. At another time, it would have been amusing to watch his flustered cockiness as he tried to seem nonchalant about the woman he'd brought, a woman whose name would never be mentioned in any family of good repute—at least not while the women were in hearing. But this . . . Surreal itched to call in the stiletto and slip it between a few ribs.

It was the children's party, the girls' party. And the uncles were there in force, almost drooling as they eyed the prospects.

Even worse, Sadi was present, looking bored as usual, but the sleepy look in his eyes and the lazy way he moved around the room made her uneasy. As she sipped sparkling wine and stroked her escort's arm in a way that made his ears burn, she watched Sadi, finally realizing that he, too, was keeping an unobtrusive, continuous watch over someone. Her eyes slid around the room, catching and holding men's glances for an uncomfortable heartbeat before passing by them, until they came back to the group of girls clustered in a corner, whispering and giggling.

Except one.

For a moment, Surreal was caught by those wary sapphire eyes. When she was allowed to look away, she found Sadi studying her.

"I need some air," Surreal said to her young Warlord, slipping away from him to find a terrace, an open window, anything.

The terrace was deserted. Surreal called in a heavy shawl and wrapped it around her shoulders. It was foolish to stand out here, but the lust stench in the crowded rooms was unbearable.

"Surreal."

Surreal tensed. She hadn't heard him come out, hadn't heard even the softest scrape of shoe on stone. She stared at the unlit garden, seeing nothing, waiting.

"Cigarette?" Daemon said, holding his gold case out to her.

Surreal took one and waited for him to create the little tongue of witchfire to light it. They smoked in silence for a while.

"Your escort doesn't quite know what to do with himself this evening," Daemon said with a touch of dry amusement.

"He's an ass." Surreal flicked the cigarette into the garden. "Besides, if I'd known what kind of party this was going to be, I wouldn't have come."

"And what kind is that?"

Surreal let out an unladylike snort. "With Briarwood's esteemed here? What kind of party do you think it's going to be?"

The night was still and cold. Now it was filled with something more still—and colder.

"What do you know about Briarwood, Surreal?" Daemon crooned.

Surreal flinched when he stepped toward her. "Nothing more than everyone who works in a Red Moon house knows," she said defensively.

"And what is that?"

"Why?" she said sharply, wishing for her knife and not daring to call it in. "Have you become an uncle, Sadi?"

Daemon's voice was too soft, too sleepy. "And what is an uncle?"

She'd been looking into his eyes, frozen by what she saw in them, and didn't feel his hand close around her wrist until it was too late.

Anger. Anger was the only defense.

"An uncle is a man who likes to play with little girls," she said with sweet venom.

Daemon's expression didn't change. "What does that have to do with Briarwood?"

"Kartane helped build the place," she snapped. "Does that answer your question?" She jerked her wrist out of his hand, half surprised that he didn't break it instead of letting go. "No respectable Red Moon house would sell a girl that young or allow her to be . . ." She rubbed her wrist. "The Chaillot whores call it the breaking ground. The 'emotionally un-stable' girls from good families are eventually sent home, married off. The other ones . . . The lower-class Red Moon houses are filled with girls who got too old to be amusing."

"It explains so much," Daemon whispered, shaking. "It explains so very much."

Surreal put a tentative hand on his arm. "Sadi?"

He pulled her into his arms. She struggled, frightened to be this close to him with no way to gauge what he might do. His arms tightened around her. "Surreal," he whispered in her ear. "Let me hold you. Please. Just for a moment."

Surreal forced herself to relax. Once she did, his hold loosened a lit-tle, making it possible to breathe. Resting her head on his shoulder, she tried to think. Why was he so upset about Briarwood? It wasn't the first place Kartane had helped build for that purpose. Did he know someone who was in Briarwood? Or had been in . . .

"No." Surreal shook her head fiercely, wanting to deny what she'd seen but hadn't understood in those wary sapphire eyes. "No." She pushed far enough away from Daemon to wrap her hands in his jacket's lapels. "Not that one." She continued to shake her head. "Not her."

"In and out since she was five," Daemon said in a trembling voice.

"No," Surreal wailed, hiding her face against his chest, grateful for his arms around her. Suddenly she pushed away from him, brushing the tears off her cheeks, her eyes gold-green chips of stone. "You have to get her out of here. You have to keep her away from them."

"I know," Daemon said, straightening his jacket. "I know. Come on, I'll take you back in."

"Don't you realize what they'll do to her? What—" Surreal ran her hands through her hair, never noticing the combs that fell and broke on the stone terrace. "They can't have taken her all the way yet. She doesn't act like she's been broken yet." She grabbed Daemon's arms and tried to shake him. It was like trying to shake the building. "You've got to get her away from here. She's special, Sadi. She's—"

"Shh," Daemon said, brushing his fingers over her lips. His hands ran through her hair, coaxing it back into some semblance of the style she was wearing. "Calm yourself, Surreal."

"How—"

"Calm yourself."

She hadn't known him this long without knowing an order when she heard it. Calm. Yes. Outsiders weren't supposed to know about the extra little party that was going to take place.

Daemon led her back to the main hall, his hand lightly resting on her shoulder. "Tell your escort you have a headache. Too much heat, too much sparkling wine. Whatever."

"That won't be hard." From the doorway, Surreal scanned the crowd in the ballroom, searching for the young Warlord. Instead she saw a Hayllian Warlord standing with a group of men, quietly discussing something while they watched some of the girls having their first dance with selected partners. "Who's that?" she asked, tilting her chin in the Hayllian's direction. Daemon's hand tightened on her shoulder.

"That, my dear Surreal, is Kartane SaDiablo."

Her knife was in her hand before he'd finished speaking. Kartane! Finally to see Kartane.

Surreal tried to step forward, intending to slip through the crowd until she was close enough to be sure of the kill, but she couldn't shake off Daemon's vise grip.

"No, Surreal," Daemon said quietly.

"He owes me for Titian," she hissed through clenched teeth.

"Not here. Not in Beldon Mor."

"He owes me, Sadi."

The pain in her shoulder got worse.

"If you kill him now, Dorothea will start asking questions. I don't want anyone asking any more questions. Do you understand?"

Surreal vanished the knife. It didn't please her, but she understood. However, that didn't mean she couldn't study her quarry.

"Go now, Surreal."

"I think I'll—"

"Go." Once again, it was an order.

Surreal left, aware that Daemon watched her. She didn't see her War-lord escort. No matter. He was probably too drunk by now to know what he fell into bed with.

Chaillot had too many secrets, Daemon thought as he watched the party. And this particular secret was a twisted, vicious one.

Why hadn't Saetan done something about Briarwood? Why had he left Jaenelle in such danger?

Daemon froze. Jaenelle's words, the first time he'd mentioned the Priest, spun through his mind. *He mustn't come here. He mustn't find out about . . .*

Saetan didn't know about Briarwood.

Which also explained why Cassandra had never come to Beldon Mor. Jaenelle had done something to keep them out, to keep Saetan from learning about Briarwood.

Why? *Why?* Did she think Saetan would shun her for *that?* Or did she fear his vengeance on her family if he found out they had knowingly put a child in such a place?

No. Alexandra couldn't know about Briarwood. Nor Philip or Leland. Robert?

Rose. Lollipop. *Uncle* Bobby.

Yes, Robert Benedict knew about Briarwood and, knowing, put his daughter into that place.

He had to talk to Alexandra. If she knew the truth about Jaenelle, and Briarwood, she would help protect her granddaughter. She was struggling to keep her people out of Hayll's snare. She would understand and value a Queen who could stand against Dorothea.

Daemon saw Alexandra near a curtained archway, talking with several women. He slipped past them, doubled back and was just about to step out from behind the curtain when he heard Alexandra say, "Witch is only a symbol of the Blood, an ideal we celebrate, a myth."

"But Witch did rule the Realms once, a long time ago," said another voice, one Daemon didn't recognize. "I remember hearing stories about Cassandra, who was a Black-Jeweled Queen. They called her Witch."

"I remember hearing stories, too," Alexandra said. "But that's all they are:

stories that have been dimmed by time and softened by romantic notions about a woman who probably didn't live at all. But if she did, do you really believe that, with that much power, she was a generous and benevolent Queen? Not likely. She would have been more of a monster than Dorothea SaDiablo."

"Brrr," said another woman as she indulged in a theatrical shudder.

"But what if Witch really did appear?" the first woman persisted.

Alexandra's next words cut him. Cut him again and again and again. "Then I would hope, for all our sakes, that someone would have the courage to strangle it in the cradle."

Daemon went back to the terrace, grateful for the cold air he gulped to keep down the scream of rage and despair. Why had he tried to fool himself into thinking she would help?

Because there was no one else. He was Ringed and could be incapacitated. It would take time, but not that long. Even if he did slip the Ring he would be declared rogue, and there would be no place fit for a young girl to live where they'd be safe. The only way was to get Jaenelle to Saetan and then convince her not to come back.

First he had to get her away from here.

His chance came when Jaenelle left the ballroom and headed down the hall toward a bathroom. Wrapping himself in a sight shield, he followed close behind her, waiting impatiently outside the door while she took care of her private needs. When she opened the door to leave, he pushed her back inside, locked the door, and dropped the shield.

Jaenelle lifted one eyebrow, striving for amusement.

Daemon knelt in front of her, holding her hands. "Listen to me, Jaenelle. You're in danger here, great danger."

"I've always been in danger here, Daemon," Jaenelle said quietly in her Witch voice.

"More so now. You don't understand what's going to happen here."

"Don't I?" Her voice was whispery thunder.

"Jaenelle . . ." Daemon closed his eyes and leaned forward until his head rested against her small, too thin, fragile chest. He felt her heart beating. It made him desperate. He would do anything now to keep that heart beating. "Jaenelle, please. The Priest . . . The Priest would let you stay with him, wouldn't he? I mean, you wouldn't have to live in the Dark Realm. He'd find another place, like he found for Tersa, wouldn't he? Jaenelle . . . sweetheart . . . you can't stay here anymore."

"I have to, Daemon," Jaenelle said gently. Her fingers stroked his head, tangling in his hair.

"Why?" Daemon cried. He raised his head, his eyes pleading. "I know you care for your family—"

"Family?" Jaenelle let out a small, bitter laugh. "My family lives in Hell, Prince."

"Then why won't you go? If you don't think the Priest will take you, at least go to Cassandra. A Sanctuary offers some protection."

"No."

"Why?"

Jaenelle backed away from him, troubled. "Saetan asked me to live with him, and I promised him I would, but I can't yet."

Daemon leaned back on his heels. This was brutal, and it was blackmail, but she wasn't leaving him any choice. "I know about Briarwood."

Jaenelle shuddered. "Then you know why I can't go yet."

Daemon grabbed her with bruising force and shook her. "No, I don't know why. If I tell him—"

Jaenelle looked at him, her eyes huge and horrified. "Please don't tell him, Daemon," she whispered. "Please."

"Why?" he snapped. "He won't turn on you because of what's been done. Do you really think he'll stop caring for you if he finds out?"

"He might."

Daemon leaned back, stunned. Since it made no difference to him, except that it made him want to protect her more, he'd assumed Saetan would feel the same. *Would* it make a difference?

"Daemon," Jaenelle pleaded, "if he finds out I've been . . . sick . . . if he thinks I'm not good enough to teach the Craft to . . ."

"What do you mean, 'sick'?" But he knew. A hospital for "emotionally disturbed" children. A child who told stories about unicorns and dragons, who visited friends no one else saw because, wherever they existed, it wasn't in Terreille. A child whose sense of reality had been twisted in Briarwood for so many years she didn't know what to believe or whom she could trust.

Daemon held her close, stroking her hair. He felt her tears on his neck and his heart bled. She was only twelve. For all her Craft, for all her magic, for all her strength, she was still only twelve. She believed all the lies they'd told her. Even though she struggled against them, even though she tried to doubt the words they'd pounded into her for so many years, she believed their lies. And because she believed, she was more afraid of losing her mentor and friend than she was of losing her life.

He kissed her cheek. "If I promise not to tell, will you promise to go—and not come back?"

"I can't," Jaenelle whispered.

"Why?" Daemon said angrily. He was losing patience. They were losing precious time.

Jaenelle leaned back and looked at him with her ancient, haunted eyes. "Wilhelmina," she said in a flat voice. "Wilhelmina's strong, Daemon, stronger than she knows, strong enough to wear the Sapphire if she isn't broken. I have to help her until she makes the Offering. Then she'll be stronger than most of the males here, and they won't be able to break her. Then I'll go live with the Priest."

Daemon looked away. It would be at least four years before Wilhelmina could make the Offering. Jaenelle, if she stayed in Beldon Mor, would be long dead by then.

A sharp rap on the door startled them. A woman called out, "You all right in there, missy? Hurry up, now. The girls are selecting partners for the dance."

Daemon slowly got to his feet. He felt old, beaten. But if he could keep her safe until tomorrow, Saetan might have more persuasive weapons at his disposal. Wrapping the sight shield around himself, he opened the door and slipped out behind Jaenelle. The woman, impatiently waiting outside, took a firm hold of Jaenelle's arm and steered her back into the ballroom.

Daemon slipped along the edge of the room silently, invisibly. It was such a small thing to stop a heart, to reach in and nick an artery. Was there any man here who wasn't expendable, including himself? No, not when the ice whispered in his veins, not when the double-edged sword was unsheathed. He slipped up behind his cousin and heard Kartane say, "That one? She's a whey-faced little bitch. The sister's prettier."

Daemon smiled. Still wrapped in the sight shield, his right hand reached out toward Kartane's shoulder. For a moment, before his hand tightened in a malevolent grip, he felt Kartane lean against him, enjoying the sensuous, shivery caress of the long nails. Daemon enjoyed feeling the sensuous shiver change to shivery fear as his nails pierced Kartane's jacket and shirt.

"Cousin," Daemon whispered in his ear. "Come out to the terrace with me, cousin."

"Get away from me," Kartane growled out of the corner of his mouth as he tried to shrug off Daemon's hand. "I've business here."

Daemon continued to smile. Foolish of the boy to try to bluff when he could smell the fear. "You've business with me first." He pivoted slowly, pulling Kartane with him.

"Bastard," Kartane said softly, walking toward the terrace to keep from being dragged there.

"By birth and by temperament," Daemon agreed with amiable coldness.

When they were out on the terrace, Daemon dropped the sight shield. Compared to the fiery cold he felt inside himself, the air seemed balmy. While he waited for Kartane to stop looking at the garden and face him, he absently brushed the branches of a small potted bush. He smiled as ice instantly coated them. He kept stroking the bush until the whole thing was coated. Then, with a shrug, he took his gold case from his pocket, lit a cigarette, and waited. He was between Kartane and the door. His cousin wasn't going to leave before he was ready to let him.

Shivering violently, Kartane turned.

"The whey-faced little bitch," Daemon crooned while the cigarette smoke ringed his head.

"What about her?" Kartane asked nervously.

"Stay away from her."

"Why?" Kartane said sneeringly. "Do you want her?"

"Yes."

Daemon watched Kartane stagger back and grip the terrace railing for support. Finally, the truth. He wanted her. Already, in ways Kartane and his kind would never understand, he was her lover.

"There are prettier ones if you want a taste," Kartane coaxed.

"Flesh is irrelevant," Daemon replied. "My hunger goes deeper." He pitched the cigarette, watching it sail past Kartane's cheek before falling into the garden. "But, cousin, if you should ever mention my . . . lapse . . . or my choice . . ."

The unspoken threat hung in the air.

"You'd kill me?" Kartane laughed in disbelief. "Kill *me*? Dorothea's son?"

Daemon smiled. "Killing your body is the least of what I'd do to you. Remember Cornelia? When the time came, she was actually grateful for what I did to the flesh." It took only a moment for Daemon to slip beneath Kartane's inner barriers and, with the delicacy of a snowflake, drop into his mind the memory of what Cornelia's room had looked like just before Daemon left. He waited patiently for Kartane to finish heaving. "Now—"

A shriek of rage and the sound of breaking glass in one of the rooms above the ballroom cut him off.

Daemon swayed. Why was the ground—not the ground—why was *he* spinning this way, spiraling toward something that made him shiver?

Spiraling.

The last time he'd felt something like that was when . . .

Daemon ran through the ballroom, through the hallway, and raced up the stairs. He hesitated when he saw Alexandra, Philip, Leland, and Robert standing with a group of people outside one of the doors, but another crash and a scream pulled him forward. He hit the door running and exploded into the room.

The only light in the room came from the open door. The lamps were shattered. A small brass bed, conspicuous because it didn't belong in a sitting room, was twisted almost beyond recognition. Broken vases crunched under him. A group of men, pressed together in the center of the room, stared, deathly pale, at something in the corner.

Daemon turned toward that corner of the room.

Wilhelmina huddled in the corner, shaking, whimpering. Her dress, partially undone, had slipped down, revealing one round young shoulder.

Jaenelle stood in front of her sister, holding the neck of a broken wine bottle with an ease that spoke of long familiarity with a knife. Her blazing sapphire eyes were fixed on the group of men.

Daemon moved toward her slowly, careful not to break her line of vision. He stopped an arm's length from her. If she lunged, she could gut him. It didn't occur to him to be frightened of her. That shadowy voice he could finally put a name to whispered up from the depths of his own being: Protocol. Protocol. Protocol.

Jaenelle spoke.

Daemon glanced at the men, at Philip and Alexandra and the others who were creeping in through the doorway. They looked shocked by the wreckage. He wondered how many of them would have been shocked by what was supposed to have happened here. Philip and Alexandra stared at Jaenelle, and he knew they were hearing unintelligible nonsense. Even he didn't know the Old Tongue well enough to translate all of her beautiful, deadly words.

"Dr. Carvay?" Philip said, his eyes still on Jaenelle.

Dr. Carvay, the head of Briarwood, stepped away from the group of men, glanced at Jaenelle, and shook his head. "I'm afraid the child has become unstrung by all the excitement," he said solicitously.

★Lady.★ Daemon sent his thoughts along a Black thread. Protocol. ★Lady, they can't understand you.★

Jaenelle stopped speaking. As Philip and Alexandra conferred with Dr. Carvay, she struggled to find the common language.

Dr. Carvay walked toward Jaenelle. "Jaenelle," he said in a too smooth voice that made Daemon turn squarely to face him, "come with Dr. Carvay now, dear. You're upset. You need some of your medicine."

"Stay aware from her," Daemon growled. An instant later he felt a tightening pain between his legs. He stared at Alexandra, who looked frightened but determined. She was using the Ring against him. Now, when Jaenelle needed him, she was threatening to bring him to his knees. He clenched his teeth against the pain and waited.

"Come, Jaenelle," Dr. Carvay said again.

"You can't have my sister," Jaenelle finally said, her voice husky with rage. "Not ever."

Every man in the room shuddered at the sound of her voice.

"We don't want your sister. We want to make you bet—"

"I'll send you into the bowels of Hell," Jaenelle said, her voice rising with her rage. "I'll feed you to the Harpies you helped create. I'll shave you if you ever touch my sister. I'll shave you all!"

"JAENELLE!" Alexandra stepped forward, eyes flashing. "You disgrace your family with this behavior. Put that down." She pointed at the broken bottle.

Daemon watched, heartsick, as Jaenelle, rage and confusion warring in her eyes, lowered her arm and dropped the bottle.

Alexandra grabbed Jaenelle by the shoulder to lead her from the room. When Daemon moved to follow, Alexandra swung around and pointed a finger at him. "You," she said venomously, "stay with Prince Alexander and see to Leland and Wilhelmina."

Bitch, Daemon thought. She was doing this out of jealousy. He started to argue with her to take both girls home now, but another surge of pain through the Ring made him suck in his breath. Arguing now would only make things worse.

Daemon watched Jaenelle leave the room, escorted by Alexandra, Dr. Carvay, and Robert Benedict. She looked so frail, so vulnerable. He would talk to her again once Wilhelmina was home, take her by force to Cassandra's Altar if that's what he had to do. Saetan had to have enough influence over her to keep her away from Chaillot.

Saetan. Once he got her away from Beldon Mor, at least he would have some help protecting her.

By the time the pain from the Ring subsided enough for Daemon to move, Philip had already gotten Wilhelmina to her feet and was tugging ineffectually at her dress. With a low snarl, Daemon turned her around, settled the dress back over her shoulders, and deftly buttoned up the back. Her eyes had a glazed, drugged look, and she was shaking, more from fear than cold.

"Wilhelmina," Philip said, taking hold of her arm.

Wilhelmina screamed, flailing her arms at him as she stumbled back into the corner.

Pushing Philip aside, Daemon stood in front of Wilhelmina and snapped his fingers twice in quick succession. Once her eyes focused on his hand, he raised it slowly until it was level with his face. Then he lowered his hand and held it out to her. "Come, Lady Benedict," he said in a respectful, formal voice. "Prince Alexander and I will escort you home." He held his hand steady, giving her time to decide whether or not to accept it. When she finally did, she threw herself against him, locking her other arm around his waist.

In the end, despite Philip's glaring at him, he untangled himself from her grasp and carried her downstairs to the waiting carriage and home, where, he fervently hoped, there would be someone who would take care of her.

CHAPTER FOURTEEN

1 / Terreille

As she paced around her bedroom, Alexandra nervously twisted the secondary controlling ring she wore on her right hand. She had done what she had to do. The girl was obviously out of control. Dr. Carvay said Jaenelle had probably been under undue strain for a while, but this last episode—threatening members of Chaillot's council with a broken bottle and speaking gibberish!

Alexandra knew where to place the blame. She hadn't wanted to believe Robert's hints, hadn't wanted to believe Sadi's interest in the girls was less than innocent, hadn't wanted to believe he might actually have . . . with Jaenelle! With all the perverse things Sadi was capable of doing, was it any wonder that Jaenelle had mistaken the intent of the men who had taken Wilhelmina upstairs so she could rest a bit after overindulging in her first taste of sparkling wine? But to threaten the council, to put them all at risk while Lord Kartane was there and would no doubt send this tale winging back to Hayll! Of course Hayll's High Priestess would be only too happy to send additional assistance, until Chaillot became a mere puppet dancing while Dorothea held the strings.

Sadi. She would have to send him back to—

Alexandra's bedroom door clicked as the lock slipped back into place. She whirled, her right hand raised, but before she could use the controlling ring she lay sprawled on the floor, one side of her face ablaze from the blow of a phantom hand.

Pushing herself into a sitting position, Alexandra stared at Daemon, leaning so casually against the door.

"My dear," he said in a gentle voice so full of murderous rage it terrified her worse than the most violent shout, "if you ever use the Ring on me again, I'll decorate the walls with your brains."

"If I use the Ring—"

Daemon laughed. It was an eerie sound—hollow, malevolent, cold. "I can survive a great deal of pain. Can you?" He smiled a brutal smile. "Shall we put it to the test? Your strength against mine? Your ability to withstand what I'll do to your body—not to mention your mind—while you try to hold me off with that pathetic piece of metal?" He walked toward her. "The trust women have in the Ring is so misplaced. Haven't you learned that much from the stories you've heard about me?"

"What do you want?" Alexandra tried to scoot backward, but Daemon stepped on her dressing gown, pinning her to the floor.

"What I've wanted since I came here. What I've always wanted. And you're going to get her back for me. Tonight."

"I don't know what—"

"You put her back in that . . . place, didn't you, Alexandra? You put her back in that nightmare."

"She's ill!" Alexandra protested. "She's—"

"She isn't ill," Daemon snarled. "She was never ill. And you know it. Now you're going to get her out of there." He smiled. "If you don't get her back, I will. But if I have to do it, I'll flood the streets of Beldon Mor with blood before I'm through, and you, my dear, will be one of the corpses washed into the sewer. Get her out of Briarwood, Alexandra. After that, you won't have to trouble yourself with her. I'll take care of her."

"Take care of her?" Alexandra spat. "You mean twist her, use her for your own perverse needs. Is that why you walk with her in the farthest parts of the garden? So you can fondle . . ." Alexandra choked, but the words kept tumbling out. "No wonder you can't act like a man around a real woman. You need to force children—"

"Before you begin accusing me, look to your own house, Lady." Daemon pulled her to her feet, one hand holding her wrists behind her back while the other tangled in her hair, pulling her head up.

"Get her out, Alexandra," he said too softly. "Get her out before the sun rises."

"I can't!" Alexandra cried. "Dr. Carvay is the head of Briarwood. He'll have to sign the release papers. So will Robert."

"You put her in there."

"With Robert! Besides, she was so distraught, she was heavily sedated and shouldn't be moved."

"How long?" Daemon snapped, letting her fall to the floor.

"What?" She felt weak and helpless with him towering over her.

"How long before you can bring her back here?"

Time. She needed a little time. "Tomorrow afternoon."

When he was silent for so long, she dared to look up, but quickly looked away. She flinched when he squatted beside her.

"Listen to me, Alexandra, and listen well. If Jaenelle isn't back here, unharmed, by tomorrow afternoon, you, my dear, will live long enough to regret betraying me."

Alexandra sank full length on the floor, covering her head with her hands. She couldn't stop seeing that look in his eyes, and she would go mad if she couldn't stop seeing that look in his eyes. Even when she heard him cross the room, heard the door open and quietly click shut, she was still too frightened to move.

It was so dark.

Alexandra woke, slowly opening her eyes. She was lying on her back in a lumpy, chilly, damp bed.

Something tickled her forehead.

As Alexandra raised her arm to brush the hair from her face, her hand hit something solid a few inches above her head.

Dirt trickled down, hitting her neck and shoulders.

Her other hand pressed against the bed—and found dirt.

She flung her arms out with bruising force—and found dirt.

Her toes, when she stretched her legs a little, found dirt.

No, she thought, fighting the panic, this was a dream. A bad dream. She couldn't be . . . buried. Couldn't be.

Shutting her eyes to keep the dirt out, she blindly explored.

It was a neatly cut rectangle. A well-made grave. If it was a grave, the earth above would be loose. Whoever did this would have had to dig down to put her there.

Half sobbing, half gasping, Alexandra clawed at the dirt above her face. When her hand hit tree roots, she stopped, stunned.

That wasn't right. Someone would have had to dig around the roots.

Scooting down a little, she began clawing at the dirt again. It was packed solid, frozen.

Think. *Think.* A witch could pass through solid objects. It was dangerous, yes, but she could do it if she didn't panic.

Alexandra forced herself to breathe slowly and steadily as she concentrated. Raising one hand, she slowly passed it through the dirt, moving upward, upward, slowly, slowly. She raised her other hand.

Her hands were moving through the dirt, moving upward to freedom. Alexandra let out a small laugh of relief.

Then her hands hit something more solid than the earth.

Her fingers poked, prodded. She felt nothing, and yet *something* was there.

Concentrating her energy on making the pass, she pushed against that nothingness while her Opal Jewel glowed with her effort, drawing on her reserves, focusing her strength. She sent the force of the Jewel into her hands and pushed.

A dark, crackling, overwhelming energy snaked down her fingers into her arms. Alexandra shot backward, hitting her head against a dirt wall.

Her strength was gone. The Jewel hung around her neck, dark and empty. If she'd pushed against that energy another moment longer, her Jewel would have broken, and her mind would probably have shattered with it.

"No," Alexandra moaned. She beat her hands against the floor of her dirt coffin. "No." She felt dizzy. The air. There was no more air. Gathering her legs beneath her as best she could, Alexandra sprang upward, trying to break free of the earth.

"No!"

Alexandra's chin hit the end of her bed.

She lay on her stomach, gasping, shivering.

A dream. It was, after all, a dream.

A soft, icy laugh filled her mind. ★Not a dream, my dear.★ Daemon's voice rolled through her mind, sentient thunder. ★A taste. I'm a *very* good, *very* discreet gravedigger. I've had centuries of practice. Just remember, Alexandra. If Jaenelle isn't back, unharmed, by tomorrow afternoon, you will feed the worms.★

He was gone.

Alexandra rolled onto her back. It was a trick, a dream. He *couldn't* have.

She raised a shaking hand, closing her eyes against the weak glow of the candle-light.

A dream. An evil dream.

Alexandra pushed herself up on one elbow—and stared at her hands.

Her nails were broken, her hands laced with scratches. Her nightgown was torn and dirt-smeared. A sudden, wet warmth flooded down her legs. She stared at the spreading dampness for a full minute before she understood she had wet herself.

It was almost an hour before she dragged herself off the bed, washed herself, and dressed in a clean nightgown. Then she huddled in a chair with a quilt wrapped around her, staring out the window, desperately waiting for the dawn.

2 / Terreille

Kartane inserted a key into a small, inset door hidden by a row of shrubs. The parents who came to Briarwood during visiting hours didn't know about that entrance—unless a parent was also a select member. They didn't know about these softly lit corridors, thickly carpeted to muffle sounds. They didn't know about the gaming room or the sitting room or the little soundproofed cubicles that were just big enough to hold a chair, a bed, and other amusing necessities. They didn't know about the tears and screams and pain. They didn't know about the special "medicines."

They didn't know about many things.

Kartane strolled through the corridors to the "playpen," hungry for some amusement. He was furious with Sadi and that little bitch for spoiling the game tonight. It was hard enough to bring girls in. Oh, they could buy lower-class Blood—the right kind of drink during the right kind of game and a pretty girl became a marker on the card table. But it was the aristos, the girls gently brought up with delicate sensibilities, that were the most fun—and the hardest to procure. It usually took enticing the father in order to get the child . . . except during Winsol, when a little *safframate* could be slipped into the sparkling wine. Then the girl could be broken and cleaned up before being brought back to her naive parents. The day after, when the hysteria started, Dr. Carvay would just happen to call and explain to the distraught parents about this prepubescent hysteria that was claiming a number of aristo girls of the Blood. The girl would be tenderly led away for a stay at Briarwood, and in a month or two—or a year or two—she would be returned to the bosom of her family, and eventually married off to spend the rest of her life with that slightly glazed look in her eyes, never understanding her husband's disappointment in her, never remembering what a fine little playmate she'd once been.

Of course, a few genuinely disturbed girls were also admitted. That little tart Rose had been one. And Sadi's whey-faced bitch.

Kartane shivered as he stepped into the "playpen," that guarded room where the girls selected for that evening waited in their lacy nighties for the uncles. The girls didn't seem to notice the cold, but the attendant had his shoulders hunched and kept rubbing his hands to warm them. It was like this sometimes. Not always, but sometimes.

Kartane's perusal of the girls stopped when he met a glazed, unblinking sapphire stare.

The attendant followed Kartane's gaze, shivered, and looked away. "They topped that one up after bringing her in, but something went queer. She oughtta be panting and rubbing against anything that'll come near her, but she just got real quiet." He shrugged.

She was nothing to look at, Kartane thought. What was it about her that intrigued Sadi? What was so special about this one that he would risk Dorothea's vengeance?

Kartane lifted his chin in Jaenelle's direction. "Have her in my room in ten minutes."

The attendant flinched but nodded his head.

While he waited, Kartane fortified himself with brandy. He was curious, that was all. If Daemon had taught the girl bedplay, she must know a few amusing tricks. Not that he would actually play with her after Sadi had warned him off. People could disappear so mysteriously after being around the Sadist. And Cornelia's room . . .

The brandy churned in Kartane's stomach. No, he was just curious. He wanted a few minutes alone with her to see if he could understand Daemon's interest, and he wouldn't do anything that would provoke the Sadist's temper.

The finger locks on the cubicles were set high in the wall both in the corridor and in the room itself. That kept anxious little girls from escaping at inconvenient moments. Kartane let himself into the room. Once inside, however, he couldn't stop shivering.

She was sitting on the bed, staring at the wall like a stiff doll someone had tried to arrange in a realistic pose. Kartane sat on the chair. After studying her for several minutes, he said sharply, "Look at me."

Jaenelle's head turned slowly until her eyes locked onto his face.

Kartane licked his lips. "I understand Sadi is your friend."

No answer.

"Did he show you how to be a good girl?"

No answer.

Kartane frowned. Had they given her something besides *safframate*? He'd had the shyest, most distraught girls crawling all over him, whimpering and begging, doing anything he wanted when they were dosed with that aphrodisiac. She shouldn't be able to sit on the bed like that. She shouldn't be able to sit still.

Kartane's frown smoothed into a smile. He had decided not to touch her body, but that didn't mean he couldn't touch her at all. He wore a Red Jewel. She wore nothing.

He sent a probing link to her mind, intending to at least force open the first barrier and find out what it was Sadi found so intriguing. The first barrier opened almost before he touched it, and he found . . .

Nothing.

Nothing but a black mist filled with lightning. Kartane had the sensation of standing on the edge of a deep chasm, not sure if stepping forward or back would plunge him into the abyss. He hung there, uncertain, while the mist coiled around him, slithering along the psychic link toward his mind.

The mist wasn't empty.

Far, far below him, he sensed something dark, something terrifying and savage slowly turning toward him, drawn by his presence. He was caught in a beast's lair, blind and uncertain whether the attack would come from in front of him or behind. Whatever it was, it was slowly spiraling up out of the mist. If he actually saw it, he'd . . .

Kartane broke the link. His hands were in front of him, trying to hold an invisible something at bay. His shirt was soaked with sweat. Drawing in ragged breaths, he forced himself to lower his hands.

Jaenelle smiled.

Kartane leaped from the chair and pressed his back against the wall, too frightened to remember how to unlock the door.

"You're one of us," Jaenelle said in a hollow, pleased voice. "That's why you hate us so. You're one of us."

"I'm not!" He couldn't unlock the door without turning around, and he didn't dare turn around.

"You do to us what was done to you. She lets you be her tool. Even now, though you hate her as much as you fear her, you serve Dorothea."

"No!"

"Her blood is the only blood that can pay that debt. But your debt is greater. You owe so many. In the end, you'll pay them all."

"What are you?" Kartane screamed.

Jaenelle stared at him for a long moment. "What I am," she said quietly in a voice that sang of the Darkness.

The locked door slid open.

Kartane bolted into the corridor.

The door slid shut.

Kartane leaned against the wall, shaking. Evil little bitch. Sadi's little whore. Whatever she was, if she joined with the Sadist . . .

Kartane straightened his clothes and smiled. *He* wouldn't soil himself with teaching that little bitch her rightful place. But Greer. Greer had found his visit to Briarwood most gratifying, and he had asked Kartane if he'd noticed any unusual girls.

This one should be unusual enough for his taste.

3 / Terreille

Surreal knelt beside a tree at the back edge of Briarwood's snow-covered lawn. She had watched Kartane disappear behind some bushes and not come out, so she felt sure there must be a private entrance there.

Surreal frowned. The wide expanse of lawn offered no cover, and if someone came around the building instead of through that door, she might be discovered too soon. To the right of the lawn were the remains of a very large vegetable garden, but that, too, offered no cover. She could use a sight shield, but she wasn't that adept at creating one and holding it while moving. Surreal shivered, pulling her coat tighter around her as the night wind gusted for a moment.

Something gently brushed her shoulder.

Twisting around, she probed the shrub garden behind her. Finding nothing, she glanced at the tree before focusing her attention once more on the hidden door.

The tree had a perfect branch. With all these girls locked away here, the uncles could at least put up a swing.

The wind died. In the still night air, Surreal heard the click of a door being closed, and tensed. There was enough moonlight to see Kartane leaning against the side of the building for a moment before hurrying away.

More than anything, she wanted to pursue him, find him in some shadowy corner, and watch the blood pump from his throat. Sadi was being unreasonable. He . . .

The air crackled. The lawn and building looked gauzy. Surreal felt a queer kind of spinning.

Something brushed her shoulder.

Surreal glanced up, stared, then clamped her hand over her mouth.

The girl swinging from the noose tied to the tree's perfect branch stared back from empty sockets. She and the rope were transparent, ghostly, yet Surreal didn't doubt she was there, didn't doubt the dark bloodstains that ran down the girl's cheeks, didn't doubt the dark stains on the dress.

"Hello, Surreal," said a whispery midnight voice. "That's Marjane. She told an uncle once she couldn't stand the sight of him, so they smeared honey on her eyes and hung her there. She wasn't supposed to die, but she struggled so much when the crows came and pecked out her eyes, the knot slipped and the noose killed her."

"Can't . . . can't you get her down?" Surreal whispered, still not willing to turn around and face whatever was behind her.

"Oh, her body's been gone years and years. Marjane's just a ghost now. Even so, when I'm here, she still has some strength. Girls are safe around this tree. Uncles don't like being kicked."

Surreal turned and stifled a scream.

"Hush," Jaenelle said with a savagely sweet smile. She was as transparent as Marjane, and the lacy nighty she wore didn't move when the wind gusted. Only the sapphire eyes seemed alive.

Surreal looked away. She felt drawn by those eyes, and she knew instinctively that anything drawn into those eyes now would never come back.

"The debt's not yours to pay, Surreal," Jaenelle said in her midnight whisper. "He doesn't owe his blood to you."

"But the ones he owes can't call in the debt!" Surreal hissed, keeping her voice low.

Jaenelle laughed. It was like hearing the winter wind laugh. "You think not? There is dead and there is dead, Surreal."

"He owes me for Titian," Surreal insisted.

"He owes Titian for Titian. When the time comes, he'll pay the debt to her."

"He killed her."

"No, he broke her, seeded her. A man named Greer, Dorothea's hound, killed her."

Surreal brushed at the tears spilling down her cheeks. "You're dead, aren't you?" she said wearily.

"No. My body's still there." Jaenelle pointed toward Briarwood and frowned. "They gave me some of their special 'medicine,' the one that's supposed to make girls behave, but something went wrong. I'm still connected to my body. I can't break the link and leave it, but this misty place is very nice. Do you see the mist, Surreal?"

Surreal shook her head.

"When I'm in the mist, I can see them all." Jaenelle smiled and held out a transparent hand. "Come, Surreal. Let me show you Briarwood."

Surreal stood up, brushing the snow from her knees. Jaenelle laughed softly. It was the most haunting, terrifying sound Surreal had ever heard.

"Briarwood is the pretty poison," Jaenelle said softly. "There is no cure for Briarwood. Beware the golden spider who spins a tangled web." Her hand touched Surreal's arm, drawing her toward the garden. "Rose said I should build a trap, something that will snap shut if my blood is spilled. So I did. If they spring the trap . . . dying is what they'll wish for, but their wish will be long in coming."

"You'll still be dead," Surreal said hoarsely. As she saw the shadows in the garden beginning to take shape, she tried to stop, tried to turn and run, but her legs wouldn't obey her.

Jaenelle shrugged. "I've walked among the *cildru dyathe*. Hell doesn't frighten me."

"She's too old to be one of us," said a voice Surreal knew had come, at one time, from a poorer section of Beldon Mor.

Surreal turned. A few minutes ago, seeing a girl walking toward her in a bloody dress with her throat slit would have been a shock. Now it was something her numbed mind cataloged as simply part of Briarwood.

"This is Rose," Jaenelle said to Surreal. "She's demon-dead."

"It's not so bad," Rose said, shrugging. "Except I can only cause trouble now after the sun goes down." She laughed. It was a ghastly sound. "And when I tickle a lollipop, it makes them feel *so* queer."

Jaenelle plucked at Surreal's sleeve. Her smile was sweetly vicious. "Come. Let me introduce you to some of my friends."

Surreal followed Jaenelle to the garden, grateful that Rose had disappeared.

Jaenelle's giggle held the echo of madness. "This is the carrot patch. This is where they bury the redheads."

Two redheaded girls sat side by side in blood-soaked dresses.

"They don't have any hands," Surreal said quietly. She felt feverish and slightly dizzy.

"Myrol wasn't behaving for an uncle and he hurt her. Rebecca hit him to make him stop hurting Myrol, and when he hit Rebecca, Myrol started hitting him, too." Jaenelle was silent for a moment. "No one even tried to stop the bleeding. They'd been bought from a poor family, you see. Their parents never expected them back, so it didn't make any difference." Jaenelle gestured toward the whole garden filled with misty shapes. "None of them were asked about. They 'ran away' or 'disappeared.' "

They walked to the end of the garden.

Surreal frowned. "Why are some of them easy to see and others so misty?"

"It depends on how long they've been here, how strong they were when they died. Rose was the only one strong enough to become *cildru dyathe* who wanted to stay. The other *cildru dyathe* have gone to the Dark Realm. Char will look after them. These girls have always been ghosts, too strong to slip into the ever-night but not strong enough to move away from where their bodies lay." Jaenelle nodded to the girl at the end of the garden. To Surreal's eyes, she looked more vivid, more "real" than Jaenelle. "This is Dannie." Jaenelle's voice quivered with pain. "They served her leg for dinner one night."

Surreal ran for the nearby bushes and retched. When she turned around, the garden was empty. A low wind swept over the snow, wiping away her footprints. When it was done, there was only the building, the empty lawn, and the garden with its secrets.

4 / Terreille

Daemon Sadi watched the sun rise.

All through the long, long night, he'd listened along the Black threads of a psychic web he'd created around Beldon Mor for any disturbance, any indication that Jaenelle might be in danger. Without using the Black Jewels to aid him, it was a strain to keep the web functioning, but like a determined spider, he stayed in the center, aware of the most minute vibration along every strand.

It had been a reluctant gamble to leave her in Briarwood. He didn't trust Alexandra, but if Jaenelle had been drugged, especially with something like *safframate,* it was safer for her to come out of it in the same surroundings. He'd seen too many young witches flee into the Twisted Kingdom when their minds couldn't understand the change in their surroundings, couldn't comprehend that they were safe. The thought of Jaenelle lost in madness was unbearable, so he could only hope the drugged sleep would make her uninteresting prey. If it didn't . . .

There was no reason for him to stay among the living without Jaenelle, but if he did go to the Dark Realm, he promised himself he wouldn't be the only new subject kneeling before the High Lord.

Daemon stripped off his clothes, showered, dressed in riding clothes, and quietly slipped down to the kitchen. He put a kettle on for coffee and made breakfast. When Jaenelle returned, they would have to leave quickly, not giving Philip or Alexandra any additional time to present obstacles. There would be no time for good-byes. He'd seldom had time for good-byes. Besides, there hadn't been that many people in his life who'd regretted seeing him go. But there was one here who deserved to know the Lady would be gone forever.

By the time he'd washed his breakfast dishes and was drinking his second cup of coffee, Cook stumbled into the kitchen, sinking heavily into one of the kitchen chairs. She looked at him sadly as Daemon set a cup of coffee in front of her.

"She's back in that hospital, isn't she?" Cook dabbed at her eyes.

Daemon sat beside her. "Yes," he said quietly. He held her hands and rubbed gently. "But not for long. She'll be out this afternoon."

"Do you think so?" She gave him a grateful, trembling smile. "In that case, I can—"

"No." Daemon squeezed her hands. "She'll be out of Briarwood, but she won't be coming back."

Cook withdrew her hands. Her lips quivered. "You're taking her away, aren't you?"

Daemon tried to be gentle. "There's a place she can live where she'll be cared for and she'll be safe."

"She's cared for here," Cook protested sharply.

It hurt to watch her eyes fill with tears. "But not safe. If this continues, she'll break under the strain or die." He wiped the tears from her cheeks. "I promise you, she'll be in a safe place, and no one will ever lock her away again."

Cook dabbed her eyes with her apron. "They're good people, these folk you found for her? They won't be . . . critical . . . of her odd ways?"

"They don't think her ways are odd." Daemon sipped his coffee. This, too, was a gamble. "However, I would appreciate your not mentioning any of this until we're gone. There are some here who want to harm her, who would use whatever means they could to stop us if they realized I'm going to take her out of their reach."

Cook thought about this, nodded, sniffed, and rose briskly from the table. "You'll be needing some breakfast, then."

"I've eaten, thanks." Daemon set his cup on the counter. Putting his hands on her shoulders, he turned her around, and kissed her lightly on the mouth. "You're a sweetheart," he said huskily. Then he was out the back door, heading for the stables.

Even this early in the morning, the stables were in an uproar. The stable lads scowled at him as he entered. Guinness stood in the center of the square, a bottle tucked in the crook of his arm, snarling orders and swearing under his breath. When he saw Daemon, his heavy eyebrows formed a fierce line over bleary eyes.

"And what would the high and mighty want at this hour of the morning?" Guinness snapped. He put the bottle to his lips and took a long swallow.

They knew, Daemon thought as he took the bottle from Guinness and helped himself. Whatever it was Jaenelle brought to this place was already fading, and they knew. Handing the bottle back to Guinness, he said quietly, "Saddle Dark Dancer."

"Have ya been kicked in the head recently?" Guinness shouted, glaring at Daemon. "That one kicked down half his stall last night and tried to turn Andrew into pulp. You won't get a brisk morning gallop out of him if that's what you're thinking."

Daemon looked over his shoulder. Andrew leaned against the door of Dark Dancer's stall, favoring one leg. "I'll saddle him." Daemon brushed past the stable lads, ignoring Guinness's dark muttering.

When Daemon pulled the latch to open the top half of the door, Andrew thrust out a shaking hand to stop him. "He wants to kill something," Andrew whispered.

Daemon looked at the sunken eyes in the pale, frightened face. "So do I." He opened the door.

The stallion lunged toward the opening.

"Hush, Brother, hush," Daemon said softly. "We must talk, you and I." Daemon opened the bottom half of the door. The horse trembled. Daemon ran his hand along Dancer's neck, regretting having washed Jaenelle's scent from his skin when the horse turned its head toward him, looking for reassurance. Daemon kept his movements slow. When Dancer was saddled, Daemon led him into the square and mounted.

They went to the tree.

Daemon dismounted and leaned against the tree, staring in the direction of the house. The stallion jiggled the bit, reminding him he wasn't alone.

"I wanted to say good-bye," Daemon said quietly. For the first time, he truly saw the intelligence—and loneliness—in the horse's eyes. After that, he couldn't keep his voice from breaking as he tried to explain why Jaenelle was never going to come to the tree again, why there would be no more rides, no more caresses, no more talks. For a moment, something rippled in his mind. He had the odd sensation he was the one being talked to, explained to, and his words, echoing back, lacerated his heart. To be alone again. To never again see those arms held out in welcome. To never hear that voice say his name. To . . .

Daemon gasped as Dark Dancer jerked the reins free and raced down the path toward the field. Tears of grief pricked Daemon's eyes. The horse might have a simpler mind, but the heart was just as big.

Daemon walked to the field, staring at its emptiness for a long moment before slowly making his way to the wide ditch at the far end.

Would it have been better not to have told him? To have left him waiting through the lonely days and weeks and months that would have followed? Or worse, to have promised to come back for him and not have been able to keep that promise?

No, Daemon thought as he reached the ditch. Jaenelle was Dancer's Queen. He deserved the truth. He deserved the right to make a choice.

Daemon slid down the side of the deep, wide ditch. Dancer lay at the bottom, twisted and dying. Daemon sat beside him, gently putting the horse's head in his lap. He stroked Dancer's neck, murmuring words of sorrow in the Old Tongue.

Finish the kill. Dancer's strength was ebbing. One narrow, searing probe into the horse's mind would finish it. Daemon took a deep breath . . . and couldn't do it.

If Hell was where the Blood's dead walked when the body died but the Self was still too powerful to fade into the ever-night, did the kindred Jaenelle spoke of go there too? Was there a herd of demon-dead horses racing over a desolate landscape?

"Ah, Dancer," Daemon murmured as he continued to stroke the horse's neck. A mind link now wouldn't help, but . . .

Daemon looked at his wrist. Blood. According to the legends, the demon-dead maintained their strength with blood from the living. That's why blood offerings were made when someone petitioned the Dark Realm for help.

Daemon shifted slightly. Pushing up his right sleeve, he positioned his wrist over Dancer's mouth. Gathering himself so that what he offered was the strongest he had to give, he nicked a vein with a long nail and watched his blood flow into Dancer's mouth. Daemon counted to four before pressing his thumb to the wound and healing it with Craft.

All he could do now was wait with his four-footed Brother.

For a long time, while Dancer's eyes glazed, nothing happened. Then something pricked at Daemon, made the land shift and shimmer. He no longer saw the ditch, no longer felt the cold and wet of the snow-covered ground. In front of him was a huge wrought-iron gate. Beyond it was lightning-filled mist. As he watched, the gate slowly opened with chilling silence. A faint sound came then, muffled, but drawing closer to the gate. Daemon watched Dancer race toward the gate, head high, mane and tail streaming out behind him. A moment later, the stallion was lost in the mist, and the gate swung shut.

Daemon looked down at the unblinking eyes. Gently setting the head on the ground, he climbed out of the ditch and wearily made his way back to the stable.

They all came running when he walked in alone. Daemon looked at Andrew, and only Andrew, when he finally got his voice under control enough to say, "He's in the ditch." Not trusting himself to say anything more, Daemon turned abruptly and went back to the house.

5 / Terreille

"I understand your difficulty, Lady Angelline, but you must realize that neither the ambassador nor I has the authority to remove Sadi from service without the High Priestess's consent." Greer leaned against the desk, trying to look sympathetic. "Perhaps if you exerted more effort to discipline him," he suggested.

"Haven't you been listening to me?" Alexandra said angrily. "He threatened to kill me last night. He's out of control."

"The controlling ring—"

"Doesn't work," Alexandra snapped.

Greer studied her face. She was pale, and there were dark smudges under her eyes. Sadi had frightened her badly. After so many months of quiet, when Sadi had been almost too accommodating, what had she done to provoke this explosion? "The controlling ring does work, Lady Angelline, if it's used forcefully enough and soon enough. Even he can't dismiss the pain of a Ring of Obedience."

"Is that why so many of the Queens he has served have died?" Alexandra said sharply. She rubbed her temples with her fingertips. "It's not just me. He's perverted, twisted."

Oh? "You shouldn't allow him to perform any service not to your liking, Lady," Greer said with sneering sternness.

Alexandra glared at him. "And how do I keep him from performing services on my granddaughters that are not to my liking?"

"But they're just children," Greer protested.

"Yes," Alexandra choked, "children." There was an edge in her voice that made Greer fight to hide a smile. "He's all right with the eldest one, but the other . . ."

Frowning as if this was a difficult decision, Greer said slowly, "I'll send a message to the High Priestess requesting permission to remove Sadi from Chaillot as soon as possible. It's the best I can do." He held up his good hand to cut off Alexandra's protest. "However, I realize how difficult it may be for you to keep him at your estate, especially if he should, by chance, discover you've been to see us. Therefore, I, with an armed escort, will collect him this afternoon and hold him at the embassy until we have the High Priestess's consent to return him to Hayll." He held out his hand, smiling. "I will, of course, need your controlling ring to disable him quickly and assure your safety."

Greer held his breath while Alexandra hesitated. Finally she pulled the secondary controlling ring off her finger and dropped it into his hand. Greer nodded to the ambassador who had been hovering near the door. The man hurried forward and escorted Alexandra out, muttering soothing lies.

Greer waited until the door closed behind them before fumbling to slip the ring over his little finger. He held his left hand out, admiring the gold circle.

Bastard, Greer thought gleefully. *I have you now, bastard.* First there was Kartane, almost frightened out of his skin, inviting Greer to partake in a "special party" at Briarwood, and now there was this Queen bleating about Sadi's interest in her granddaughters. And all the time Greer had been searching for the Dark Priestess's prey, the Sadist was playing with the little hussy while the half-breed sweated and bled in Pruul. *If we told him about the offer you sneeringly declined and then stretched you between two posts and handed him a whip, how much of your skin would be left before he became too tired to complete a stroke? And what part of your anatomy might be lacking when he was through?*

Greer mentally shook himself. Those tantalizing prospects would have to wait. Here was the chance he'd waited for, the chance to cut Sadi to the core and please the Dark Priestess in the bargain.

Alexandra was a fool to relinquish her only defense against the Sadist. If she'd used the controlling ring with the same brutality he intended to use, she could have brought Sadi to his knees, drained him sufficiently to reduce the threat. And the threat had to be reduced.

He didn't want Daemon Sadi in any condition to go anywhere tonight.

6 / Terreille

Daemon gave his room a cursory glance. His trunks were packed and vanished so they would travel with him. He'd even slipped into the nursery wing and packed a small suitcase for Jaenelle. It troubled him that he might have left behind something she valued. That cold corner in her wardrobe probably contained her most private possessions, but he didn't have the time or energy to spare to try to unravel whatever lock she might have on it. He hoped that, once she was safely out of Beldon Mor, he and Saetan could retrieve them for her.

Daemon opened his door, startling Cook, who stood with her hand raised as if she were about to knock.

"You're wanted in the front hall," she said worriedly.

Daemon's eyes narrowed. Why send Cook with the message? "Is Jaenelle back?"

"Don't know. Lady Angelline was gone for a while this morning, but after she came back, she and Lady Benedict stayed in the nursery with Miss Wilhelmina and Graff. I don't think Lord Benedict's home, and Prince Alexander has been in the steward's office all day."

Daemon opened his mind to the psychic scents around him. Worry. Fear. That was to be expected. Relief? His golden eyes hardened as he brushed past Cook and glided toward the front hallway. If Alexandra was playing some game . . .

He entered the main hallway and saw Greer with twenty armed Hayllian guards. A moment later, the pain from the Ring almost made his legs buckle. He fought to stay on his feet as he flicked a dagger glance at Alexandra, who stood to one side with Leland and Philip.

"No, Sadi," Greer said in his oily voice, "you answer to me now." He raised his good hand so that the gold controlling ring caught the light.

"Bitch," Daemon said softly, never taking his eyes off Greer. "I made you a promise, Lady Angelline, and I always keep my promises."

"Not this time," Greer said. He closed his hand and thrust it forward. The controlling ring flashed.

Daemon staggered backward, grabbing the wall for support as the pain from the Ring increased.

"Not this time," Greer said again, walking toward Daemon.

The cold. The sweet cold.

Daemon counted to three, thrust his right hand toward Greer, and unleashed a wide band of dark energy. Philip, wearing the Gray Jewel, thrust his hand forward at the same time. The two forces met, exploding the chandelier, snapping the furniture to kindling. Three of the guards fell to the floor, twitching. Greer shrieked with rage. Leland and Alexandra screamed. Philip continued to channel his strength through the Gray Jewel, trying to break Daemon's thrust, but the Black leached around the Gray, and where it did, the walls scorched and cracked.

Daemon braced himself against the wall. Greer continued channeling power into the Ring, intensifying the pain. Dying would be better than surrendering to Greer, but there was one chance—if he could get there intact enough to do what he had to do.

Unleashing a large ball of witchfire, Daemon made a last thrust against the Gray, counting on Philip to meet the attack. When the witchfire met the Gray shield, it exploded into a wall of fire.

Daemon pushed off from the wall and ran toward the back of the house. The pain got worse as he ran through the corridors to the kitchen. Too late he saw the young housemaid on her knees and the puddle of soapy water. He leaped, missing the girl, but his foot landed at the edge of the puddle, and he slip-skidded until his hips hit the kitchen table, pitching him forward.

The pain in his groin was agony.

Daemon clenched his teeth, drawing on his anger because he didn't dare draw on the Jewels. Not yet.

Two pairs of arms grabbed his shoulders and waist. Snarling, he tried to twist free, but Cook's "Hurry up, now" cleared his head sufficiently to realize she and Wilhelmina were trying to help him. The young housemaid, tight-lipped and pale, ran ahead of them and opened the door.

"I'm all right," Daemon gasped as he grabbed the doorway. "I'm all right. Get out of here. All of you."

"Hurry," Cook said. She gave him a shove that almost knocked his feet from under him. As he stumbled and half turned, the last thing he saw before the kitchen door closed was Cook grabbing the pail of soapy water and flinging it across the kitchen floor.

Another burst of pain from the Ring forced him to his knees. He stifled a scream, jerked himself to his feet, and stumbled forward until the momentum pushed him into a run toward the stables and the path that would lead to the field.

The pain. The pain.

Each step was a knife in Daemon's groin as Greer continued to channel his power through the controlling ring into the Ring of Obedience.

Daemon ran along the bridle path past the stables, vaguely aware of Guinness and the stable lads pouring out of the yard to form an angry, solid wall at his back. He ran down the snowy path until another burst of pain from the Ring pulled his legs out from under him. He flew through the air as his momentum carried him forward before hitting the ground with a bone-jarring thud.

Daemon sobbed as he tried to get to his knees. Behind him was a faint, muffled sound. He turned his head, trying to see through tears of pain. There was nothing there, but the sound kept coming toward him, finally stopped beside him. Daemon flung out an arm to get his balance.

His hand hit a leg.

He saw nothing, but he could feel . . .

"Dancer?" Daemon whispered as his hand traveled upward.

A moist warmth blew in his face.

Clenching his teeth, Daemon got to his feet. He was running out of time. His hands found the phantom back. Daemon propelled himself onto the demon stallion's back, gasping as he pulled his leg around. With his head bent low over Dancer's neck and his hands twisted in the mane for balance, Daemon tightened his knees, urging Dancer forward.

"To the tree, Brother," Daemon groaned. "As fast as you can fly, get me to the tree."

Daemon almost fell when Dancer surged forward, but he hung on, grimly determined to reach the one escape left to him.

When they reached their destination, Daemon slid from the horse's back, remembering in time what Jaenelle had taught him about air walking. For a moment, he lay on his side in the air, his knees curled to his chest, fighting the pain and gathering his strength.

Deep beneath this tree was a neatly cut rectangle already protected by a Black shield that would keep the others out just as much as it had kept Alexandra in.

Daemon looked back. Apparently demons didn't leave tracks. And he, fortunately, hadn't left any telltale marks in the snow. All he needed was a few uninterrupted moments to make the pass.

Fighting for patience, Daemon waited for the next burst of pain from the Ring. Once it passed, he could slip down into the earth. Behind him were shouts, sounds of fighting. He waited, feeling his strength seeping out of him as the cold and pain seeped in.

Just as Daemon decided not to wait, the pain hit again. He twisted and rolled, trying to escape it. This time, however, there was no letup. Greer was sending a steady pulse through the controlling ring into the Ring of Obedience.

Daemon crawled on air until he was over the proper place. There was no more time. With his hands clenched so hard his nails broke his skin, he took a deep, shuddering breath, closed his eyes, and plunged downward into the earth.

The moment he felt emptiness instead of earth, he pulled his feet forward so they wouldn't be locked in the frozen ground and stop the pass. He felt his pant legs catch in the earth above him, felt the skin on his knees tear as they ripped through the last crust of earth. Landing squarely on his back, it took him a moment to get his breath.

A moment was all he had. They might not be able to reach him physically, but the pain still pulsed through the Ring. Not even the Black shield could protect him from that.

With shaking hands, Daemon undid his belt, unzipped his trousers, and reached down to close his right hand on his organ and the Ring of Obedience. He screamed when his fingers accidentally touched his balls. Taking sobbing, gasping breaths, Daemon kept his hand steady and called in the Black Jewels.

It had been so very long since he'd felt a Jewel around his neck or on his finger. They pulsed with his heartbeat as he drew on their stored energy. It was a risk. He'd always known it was a risk. But there was something at stake now more important than his body. Taking a deep breath, Daemon turned inward and plunged toward the Black.

It was an oiled high dive speeding him into the Darkness, faster and faster as he hurtled toward the shimmering dark web that was himself, gaining speed as he unleashed his rage. He continued to plunge downward as his web seemed to rush upward to meet him. There was no time to check his descent. If he missed the turn and shattered the web, the least he would do was break himself, stripping himself of the ability to wear the Black or, possibly, even his Birthright Red. If he couldn't stop his descent and continued falling into the abyss, he would die or go mad.

Daemon pushed faster, watching for the moment when he could make the turn and draw the most from himself. A long way away, he could feel the tight agony in his heels and the corded muscles in his neck as they supported the arched, pain-racked body. Still he plunged downward. At the last moment he turned, tight to the web, drew all the reserve power out of his Black Jewels and hurtled upward, a tidal wave of cold black rage, a dark arrow speeding toward the center of a gold circle.

All the way up, Daemon kept his strength tight and rapier-thin, but the moment he pierced the center of the circle, he unleashed all of his Black strength. It exploded outward, forcing the circle to expand with him until it shattered under the strain.

Daemon slowly opened his eyes. He shook from exhaustion, shivered from cold. The smallest movement, even breathing, brought excruciating pain. Reaching down with his left hand, Daemon felt for the Ring of Obedience. When he drew his hands toward his chest, each hand held half a Ring.

He was free.

Since his Black Jewels were completely drained, he vanished them and called in his Birthright Red in order to do one last thing.

If Dorothea or Greer had escaped the shattering of the Ring, they could still use one of the controlling rings to trace the pieces to his hiding place.

Daemon closed his eyes, concentrated on a spot he knew well, and vanished the two pieces of the Ring of Obedience.

In a small alcove, the two halves of the Ring hovered in the air for a moment before dropping into the snowy bed of witchblood.

Daemon's last conscious thought was to call in a blanket, charge it with a warming spell, and wrap it around himself as best he could. The psychic web he'd created was gone. There was no way to tell if Jaenelle was still unharmed. There was nothing he could do for her right now. There was nothing more he could do for himself. Until his body had some rest, he didn't have the strength to get out of his grave.

7 / Terreille

Cassandra paced.

The mist around Beldon Mor kept Guardians and the demon-dead out. It didn't keep things in.

Thankfully, she'd been wearing the Black Jewel instead of her Birthright Red when the rippling aftershock of Sadi hurtling toward the Darkness hit her. Even with that much protection, her body had vibrated from the intensity of the dive.

As she'd picked herself up off the floor, she'd wondered how many of the Blood, not trained well enough to know that one must ride with those psychic waves instead of trying to shield against them, had been shattered, or at least broken back to their Birthright Jewel.

And what about Jaenelle? Had he turned against her? Was she fighting against him for her life?

Cassandra shook her head and continued pacing. No, he loved the girl. Then why the descent? She feared him now as much as she feared his father, but didn't he realize she would stand with him, fight with him to protect Jaenelle?

Descending slowly to the Black, she closed her eyes and opened her mind, sending a probing shaft westward on a Black thread. The probe hit the mist, penetrating just a little for just a moment before fading away.

It was enough.

She spent the next hour cleaning the Altar, polishing the four-branched candelabra, digging out the stubs of the old black candles and replacing them with new candles. When she was done, the Altar was once again ready to be what it was, what it had not been for centuries.

A Gate.

She bathed in hot scented water, washed and dressed her hair. She slipped on a simple gown of black spidersilk that molded itself to her body. Her Black Jewel in its ancient setting filled the dress's open neckline. The Black-Jeweled ring, in its deceptively feminine setting, slipped easily onto her finger. Two silver cuff bracelets with chips of her Red Jewel embedded in the center of an hourglass pattern fit over the tight sleeves of her dress. Last came the black slippers, made by forgotten craftsmen, which never betrayed a footfall.

She was ready. Whatever storm the night would bring, she was ready.

With a listening, thoughtful expression on her face and a faraway look in her emerald eyes, Cassandra settled down to wait.

8 / Terreille

As the slaves were brought up from the salt mines of Pruul, Lucivar turned toward the west. The salt sweat stung the new cuts on his back. The heavy chains that manacled his wrists to his waist pulled at his already aching arms. Still he stood quietly, breathing the clean evening air, watching the last sliver of sun sink beneath the horizon.

He'd ridden the dark aftershocks that hit Pruul with a lover's passion, using his Ebon-gray strength to fortify those waves and keep them rolling east a little longer. His only regret was not joining Sadi in the bloodletting. Not that the Sadist needed his help. Not that it would be safe to be in the same city with a man that deeply enraged.

As a frightened guard shook his whip at the slaves to begin leading them to their dark, stinking cells, Lucivar smiled and whispered, "Send them to Hell, Bastard. Send them *all* to Hell."

9 / Terreille

Philip Alexander sat at his desk, his head braced in his hands, staring at the shattered Gray Jewel.

It had taken—what—a minute? A bare minute to produce so much destruction? Some of the guards had felt it first, a shuddery feeling, like trying to stand against a strong wind that kept growing stronger. Then Leland. Then Alexandra. He'd been puzzled, in those moments, wondering why they had become so pale and still, why they all were straining to hear something. When it hurtled past the Gray, heading downward, he'd had a moment, just a moment, to realize what it was, a moment to throw his arms around Leland and Alexandra, pulling them to the floor, a moment to try to form a Gray shield around the three of them. A moment.

Then his world exploded.

He had held on for less than a minute before that titanic explosion of Black strength shattered the Gray and swept him along like driftwood caught in a wave before the wave smashes it into the sand. He'd felt Alexandra try to hold him before she, too, was swept away.

A minute.

When it was over, when his head finally cleared . . .

Of the Hayllian guards who had remained in the hall, all but two were dead or had their minds burned away. Leland and Alexandra, shielded from the first impact, were shaken but all right. He'd been broken back to the Green, his Birthright Jewel.

Still in shock, the three of them had staggered from the hall. They had found Graff in the nursery wing, staring empty-eyed at the ceiling, her body twisted and torn almost beyond recognition.

Most of the staff had come away from the psychic explosion frightened but intact. They'd found them huddled in the kitchen where Cook, with shaking hands, liberally filled cups with brandy.

Wilhelmina had frightened them. She had sat quietly in the kitchen chair, cheeks glowing with color, eyes flashing. When Philip had asked if she was all right, she had smiled at him and said, "She said to ride it, so I did. She said to ride it."

In that moment before the world exploded, he had heard a young, commanding female voice shouting "Ride it, ride it," but he hadn't understood—and still didn't. What was more frightening, Wilhelmina now wore a Sapphire Jewel. Somehow, in that chaos, she had made her Offering to the Darkness, too young. Now that inexperienced girl was stronger than any of them.

Worst of all was the betrayal of Guinness and the stable lads, particularly Andrew. They had fought against the Hayllian guards, holding them up. If they hadn't interfered, Sadi might have been caught and Beldon Mor . . . Well, he had dismissed Guinness and Andrew and the others who'd survived. There was no reason to keep traitors, especially traitors who said . . . who called him . . . That they would side with Sadi against her *family*!

Philip closed his eyes, rubbed his aching temples. Who would have thought one man could destroy so much in a minute? Half the Blood in Beldon Mor were dead, mad, or broken.

Philip let out a sighing sob. His body was almost too weak to wear the Green, but he would recover. That much he would recover.

Half the Blood. If Sadi had struck again . . .

But after the ripples had finally passed, there had been no sign of Daemon Sadi.

And no one knew what had become of Greer.

10 / Terreille

Surreal sat with her back against the headboard, sipping from the whiskey bottle she hugged to her chest.

She and Deje had spent the past few hours looking after the other girls, sedating those who needed it, letting the rest get blistering drunk. Deje, her face gray with the strain, had gratefully let Surreal take care of the bodies. Fortunately there weren't many, the day after the Winsol holidays always being a slow time for Red Moon houses. Even so, she'd had to bundle them up in blankets before even the brawniest of Deje's male staff would enter the rooms and lug the bodies out.

Everyone, including herself, stank of fear.

But he was, after all, the Sadist.

It would have been worse, she told herself as she continued to sip the whiskey. It would have been much, much worse, if Jaenelle hadn't shouted that warning to ride it out. Funny. Every witch in Deje's house who wore a Jewel heard that warning and knew on some instinctive level what it meant. The men . . . There wasn't time for Jaenelle to be selective. Some heard her, some didn't. That's all there was to it. Those who didn't were dead.

What had happened to send him into such a rage? What sort of danger could have provoked that kind of unleashing?

Maybe the question to ask was, *who* was in danger?

Calmed by her own rising anger, Surreal set the whiskey bottle on the nightstand and called in a small leather rectangle. As soon as she was done, she'd get a little sleep. It was unlikely that anything would happen before tonight. The Sadist had seen to that, whether he'd meant to or not.

With her lips curved in the slightest of smiles, Surreal hummed softly as she slipped the whetstone out of its leather pouch and began sharpening her knives.

11 / Terreille

Dorothea watched the flames in the fireplace dance. Any moment now, the Dark Priestess would arrive at the old Sanctuary. Then she could give the bitch the message and return home.

Who would have thought he could break a Ring of Obedience? Who would have thought, with him being on the other side of the Realm, shattering the Ring could . . .

How very fortunate that she'd started letting each of the young witches in her coven wear the primary controlling ring for a day, letting them "get the feel" of handling a powerful male, even if he was so far away they couldn't really feel anything at all. How very unfortunate her favorite witch, her little prize who had shown *so* much potential, had been the one wearing it today.

Since the body, although empty of the witch herself, still lived, she would have to keep it around for a little while so the others wouldn't realize how disposable they really were. A month or two would be enough. The witch would, of course, be buried with dignity, with full honors commensurate with her Jewels and social rank.

Dorothea shuddered. Sadi was out there, somewhere, with no leash to hold him. They could try to use the Eyrien half-breed as bait to draw him back, but Yasi was so nicely tucked into Pruul's salt mines, and it would be a shame to pull him out before he was sufficiently broken in body and spirit. Besides, she doubted that even the Eyrien would be sufficient bait this time.

The sitting room door opened for the hooded figure.

"You sent for me, Sister?" Hekatah said, making no attempt to keep her annoyance out of her voice. She looked pointedly at the small table, empty of her expected carafe of blood. "It must be important to have made you forget such a paltry thing as refreshment."

"Yes, it is." *You bag of bones. You parasite. All Hayll is in danger now. I am in danger now!* Careful not to let her thoughts become apparent, Dorothea held up a note, slipping it in and out of her fingers. "From Greer."

"Ah," Hekatah said with barely suppressed excitement. "He has some news?"

"Better than that," Dorothea answered slowly. "He says he has found a way to take care of your little problem."

12 / Terreille

Greer sat on the white-sheeted bed in one of Briarwood's private rooms, cradling what was left of his good hand.

It could have been worse. If that limping stable brat hadn't slashed at him with a knife, slicing through his little finger so it only hung by a thread of skin, he never would have gotten the secondary controlling ring off in time when Sadi broke the Ring of Obedience. In that moment when he'd felt the Black explode, he'd ripped the finger off and flung it away from him. A guard, seeing something hurled toward him, grabbed instinctively, his hand closing around the ring.

Foolish man. Foolish, foolish man.

With the Ring of Obedience broken and with no way to know if Sadi had been hurt by the effort, Greer had run to Briarwood, where the healing would be done without questions. It was also the only place the Sadist wouldn't strike at blindly. Here they had some leverage—at least for a few hours more. After that he would be gone, speeding back to Hayll to melt away among the many, encircled by Dorothea's court. Briarwood and its patrons would still be here to quench Sadi's thirst for vengeance.

Greer lay down on the bed, letting the painkillers lull him into much-needed rest. In a few short hours, the Dark Priestess's little problem would be no more, and Sadi . . .

Let the bastard scream.

13 / Hell

Saetan made another erratic circuit around his private study.

He stared at Cassandra's portrait.

He stared at the tangled web he'd finished a short time ago, at the warning that may have come too late.

He shook his head slowly, denying what the vision in the tangled web had shown him.

An inner web still intact. A shattered crystal chalice. And blood. So much blood.

He had never invaded Jaenelle's privacy. Against his better judgment, against all his instincts, he had never invaded her privacy. But now . . .

"No," he said with soft malevolence. "You will not take my Queen from me. You will not take my daughter."

There was only one place from which he could penetrate the mist. Only one place he could use to amplify his strength to reach across the Realm. Only one witch who had the knowledge to help him do it.

Throwing his cape over his shoulders, he flicked a glance at the door, tearing it off the hinges. Gliding through the deep corridors of the Hall, his rage glazing the rough stones with ice, he brushed past Mephis and Prothvar, seeing no one, seeing nothing but that web.

"Where are you going, SaDiablo?" Andulvar called, striding to intercept him.

Saetan snarled softly.

The Hall trembled.

Andulvar hesitated for only a moment before setting himself squarely in the path of the High Lord of Hell.

"Yaslana." The rage had become very quiet, very still.

This was what they feared in him.

"You can tell me where you're going, or you can go through me," Andulvar said calmly. Only a tiny muscle tic in his jaw betrayed him.

Saetan smiled, raising his right hand in a lover's caress. Remembering in time that this man was his friend and also loved Jaenelle, he sheathed the snake tooth, and the hand gently squeezed Andulvar's shoulder.

"To Ebon Askavi," he whispered as he caught the Black Wind and vanished.

CHAPTER FIFTEEN

1 / Terreille

Surreal dreamed.

She and Titian were walking through a woods. Titian was trying to warn her about something, but Surreal couldn't hear her. The woods, Titian, everything, was silenced by the loud, steady pounding of a drum.

As they reached the edge of the woods, Surreal noticed a tree with a perfect branch, a tree sweating dark red sap.

Titian walked past the tree across a lawn filled with tall, silvery flowers. As she picked a flower here and there, it turned into a knife, sharp and shining. Smiling, she offered the bouquet to Surreal.

The drum beat louder, harder.

Someone was screaming.

Titian continued walking toward a large, mist-filled rectangle, pointing here and there. Every time she pointed, the mist drew away. Two redheads. A girl with no eyes. A girl with a slit throat whose eyes blazed with impotent fury. A girl with one leg.

At the far end of the rectangle was a mound of freshly dug earth.

The drum beat faster.

Someone was shrieking, enraged and in pain.

Surreal approached the mound, drawn by something lying over the dirt. As she approached, witchblood began to sprout and bloom, forming a crown around a length of golden hair.

"No!" Surreal yelled, flinging herself out of the bed.

The heartbeat drum pounded against her ribs.

The screaming in her head didn't stop.

2 / Hell

"You're going to help me," Saetan said, turning to face Draca.

"To do what, High Lord?" Draca asked. Her unblinking reptilian eyes revealed nothing.

"Penetrate the mist around Beldon Mor." His golden eyes locked with Draca's, willing her to yield.

Draca studied him for a long time. "There iss danger?"

"I believe so."

"You break faith with her."

"I'd rather have her hate me than have her lost to all of us," Saetan replied sharply.

Draca considered this. "Even the Black iss not sso far-reaching. At leasst not the Black you wear, High Lord. The help I can offer will only let you know what iss beyond the misst, to ssee but not to act. To act, you would need to link with another, sspear to sspear."

Saetan licked his lips, took a deep breath. "There is one there who may help, who may let me use him."

"Come." Draca led him through the corridors of Ebon Askavi toward a large stairwell that descended into the heart of the mountain.

As they reached the stairwell, hurrying footsteps made Saetan swing around in challenge.

Geoffrey appeared around the corner, followed by Andulvar, Prothvar, and Mephis. Andulvar and Prothvar were dressed for battle. Mephis's anger blazed from his Gray Jewel.

Saetan flicked a dagger glance at each of them before his eyes and his anger settled on Andulvar. "Why are you here, Yaslana?" Saetan asked in his soft, dangerous croon.

Andulvar clenched his hands. "That web in your study."

"Ah, so now you possess the ability to read the Hourglass's webs."

"I could snap you like kindling!"

"You'd have to reach me first."

A slow grin bared Andulvar's teeth. Then the grin faded. "The waif's in trouble, isn't she? That's what the web warned you about."

"It's not your concern."

"She doesn't belong just to you, High Lord!" Andulvar roared.

Saetan closed his eyes. *Sweet Darkness, give me the strength.* "No," he agreed, letting Andulvar see his pain, "she doesn't belong just to me. But I'm the only one strong enough to do what has to be done, and"—he raised a hand to stop their protests, his eyes never leaving Andulvar's face—"if someone has to stand responsible for what's going to happen, if someone is going to earn her hatred, let it be only one of us so the others can still cherish her—and serve her."

"Saetan," Andulvar said, his voice husky. "Ah, Saetan. Is there nothing we can do?"

Saetan blinked rapidly. "Wish me well."

"Come," Draca said urgently. "The Darknesss . . . We musst hurry."

Saetan followed her down the stairwell to the locked door at the bottom. Pulling a large key from her sleeve, Draca unlocked the door and pushed it open.

Etched in the floor of the enormous cavern was a huge web lined with silver. In the center where all the tether lines met was an iridescent Jewel the size of Saetan's hand, a Jewel that blended the colors of all the other Jewels. At the end of each silver tether line was an iridescent Jewel chip the size of his thumbnail.

As Saetan and Draca walked along the edge of the web, the Jewels began to glow. A low hum rose from the web, rising up and up until the cavern throbbed with the sound.

"Draca, what is this place?" Saetan whispered.

"It iss nowhere and everywhere." Draca pointed at his feet. "Your feet must be bare. Flessh musst touch the web." When Saetan had stripped off his shoes and socks, Draca pointed to a tether line. "Begin here. Walk sslowly to the center, letting the web draw you into itsself. When you reach the center, possition yoursself behind the Jewel sso you are facing the tether line closesst to Beldon Mor."

"And then?"

Draca studied Saetan, her thoughts hidden. "And the Blood sshall ssing to the Blood. Your blood, darkened by your sstrength, will feed the web. You will direct the power from thiss offering sso it iss channeled to the one tether line you need. You musst not break contact with the web once you begin."

"And then?"

"And then you will ssee what you have come here to ssee."

Saetan tapped into the reserve strength in his Black Jewels and stepped on the tether line. The power in the web stabbed into his heel like a needle. He sucked in his breath and began walking.

Each step drove the power of the web upward. By the time he reached the center, his whole body vibrated with the hum. Keeping one foot in contact with the web, Saetan positioned himself behind the Jewel, his eyes and will focused on that one tether line.

He held out his right wrist and opened his vein.

His blood hissed when it hit the Jewel in the center of the web, formed a red mist. The mist twisted into a fine thread and began to inch its way along the tether line.

Drop by drop, the thread moved toward Chaillot, toward Beldon Mor.

For a moment it stopped, a finger-length away from the Jewel chip, blocked. Then it crept upward, a red vine climbing an invisible wall, until a handspan above the floor, it was over, flowing back along the tether line.

He had breached Jaenelle's mist. The moment the blood thread touched the Jewel chip, he would be able to probe Beldon Mor.

The thread touched the Jewel chip.

Saetan's eyes widened. "Hell's fire, what—"

"Don't move!" Draca's voice seemed so far away.

What had Daemon done? Saetan thought as he picked up the after-taste of rage. Sinking beneath the cacophony of the lesser Jewels, Saetan searched the Black, the too-still Black. There should have been three minds within his probing reach. There was only one, the one farthest out, the one at the Dark Altar.

Keeping his eyes locked on the Jewel chip, Saetan sent a thought along the thread, spear to spear. *Namesake?*

His answer was a brief, annoyed flicker.

Saetan tried again, spear to distaff. *Witch-child?*

For a moment, nothing.

Saetan heard Draca gasp as light flickered around him. Out of the corner of his eye, he saw all the Jewel chips begin to glow, all the silver strands of the web blaze with a fiery cold light.

Something sped toward him. Not a thought. More like a soap bubble cocooned in mist. Faster and faster it sped toward the web.

The sudden light from the Jewel at his feet blinded him. He threw his arm up over his eyes.

The bubble reached the Jewel chip and burst, and the cavern . . .
The cavern vibrated with the sound of a child screaming.

3 / Terreille

The screaming stopped.

Surreal raced across Briarwood's empty lawn toward the hidden door. The Gray Jewel around her neck blazed with her anger. Tonight there wasn't a lock anywhere in Beldon Mor strong enough to keep her out. Once inside, however, she had no idea how to find the one she sought.

A few strides away from the door, someone shouted at her, "Hurry! This way. Hurry!" Swinging to the right, she saw Rose gesturing frantically.

"They're too strong," Rose said, grabbing Surreal's arm. "Kartane and Uncle Bobby are letting him draw on their strength. He's got the room shielded so I can't get through."

"Where?" There was a stitch in Surreal's side from running, and the cold night air burned her lungs. It made her angrier.

Rose pointed at the wall. "Can you make the pass?"

Surreal stared at the wall, probing. Pain and confusion. Rage and despair. And courage. "Why isn't she fighting back?"

"Too many medicines. She's in the misty place and she can't get out." Rose tugged on Surreal's sleeve. "Please help her. We don't want her to die. We don't want her to be like us!"

Her lips pressed into a tight, angry line, Surreal reached for the knife sheathed against her right thigh, but her hand swung across her body and pulled out the knife from the left sheath.

Titian's knife.

A slow smile curled Surreal's lips. Never taking her eyes away from the wall, she held out her other hand to Rose. "Come with me," she said as she stepped forward and melted into the wall.

Briarwood's outer walls were thick. Surreal didn't notice.

This time . . . This time she would wash the walls in blood.

The shield was there, braided by the strength of two. Fools. Two Reds might have slowed her down if they were aware of her presence. But Kartane and Uncle Bobby? Never. *Never.*

Surreal unleashed one short blast of power from her Gray Jewel. The shield around the room shattered.

Surreal leaped. Landing in the small room, she whirled to face the man on the bed. Even as he thrust into the too-still body under him, he raised his head, his face twisted with hatred and lust.

Lunging forward, Surreal grabbed his hair with one hand and slashed Titian's knife across his throat.

The blood sang as the white walls turned red.

Still pushing forward and up, Surreal drove the knife into his heart, lifting him off the bed with the strength of her rage.

He fell to the floor, Titian's knife still in his heart while his maimed hands groped feebly for one heartbeat, two.

Finish the kill.

Squatting over the still body, Surreal pulled out her other knife to drive it through his brain, intending to use the steel as a channel for the Gray to break and destroy what the husk still contained. As she raised her arm for the final strike, Rose's low moan made her glance at the bed.

There was a pool of blood between Jaenelle's legs. Too much blood.

Surreal leaned over the bed. Her stomach rolled.

Jaenelle stared at the ceiling, her unblinking eyes never changing when Surreal passed her hand in front of them. Her body was a mass of bruises; a cut on her lip leaked blood.

Surreal glanced back at the Warlord and noticed scratches on his face and shoulders. So. She had fought for a while.

Surreal felt for a pulse and found one. Weak and growing weaker.

Something hit the locked door.

"Greer!" someone shouted. "Greer, what's going on?"

"Damn!" The word exploded out with her breath as she quickly Gray-locked the door. Pulling Titian's knife from Greer's heart, Surreal hesitated for just a moment, then shook her head. She didn't have the minute it would take. She cut the cords that bound Jaenelle's ankles and wrists to the bed, wrapped the girl in the bloody sheet, lifted the bundle against her, and, Gray shielding herself and her precious burden, made the pass through the walls.

Once outside, Surreal ran. When they finally broke the Gray lock and found Greer, they would be pouring out of the doors in pursuit. And following the blood scent, they would be able to trace her.

There was only one place to go, and once there, she would need help. Putting her heart into it, Surreal sent a summons along the Gray.

Sadi!

No answer.

Sadi!

4 / Hell

"No!"

Saetan's roar thundered through the cavern, drowning out the sound of feet racing down the stairs.

"SaDiablo!" Andulvar yelled as he leaped into the cavern. "We heard a scream. What's—"

Saetan pivoted, teeth bared, spearing Draca with eyes filled with cold rage. "And now?" he said too softly.

"We'll ride the Winds," Prothvar said, pulling out his knife.

"No time," Mephis countered. "It'll be too late."

"Draca," Geoffrey said.

Draca never blinked, never flinched from Saetan's glazed stare.

"Saetan—" Andulvar began.

Draca closed her eyes.

A voice filled their minds, a rumble as if the Keep itself sighed.

A male voice.

Sspear to sspear, High Lord. That iss the only way now. Her blood runss. If sshe diess now—

"She'll walk among the *cildru dyathe*."

So much sorrow in that voice. *Dreamss made flessh do not become cildru dyathe, High Lord. Sshe will be losst to uss.*

"Who are you to say this to me?" Saetan snarled.

Lorn.

Saetan's heart stopped for a beat.

You have the courage, High Lord, to do what you musst do. The other male will be your insstrument.

The sighing rumble faded.

The cavern was very still.

Turning carefully, Saetan once more faced the red-misted tether line.

And the Blood shall sing to the Blood.

Don't think. Be an instrument.

Everything has a price.

Locked in his cold, still rage, Saetan slowly drew on the power in the web, the power in his Jewels, and the power in himself until he had formed a three-edged psychic spear. With his eyes and will fixed on the Jewel chip, he sent a single, thundering summons.

SADI!

5 / Terreille

Sadi!

Sadi!

SADI!

Daemon jerked awake, head pounding, heart pounding, body throbbing. Groaning, he rubbed his fist back and forth across his forehead.

And remembered.

Sadi, please.

Daemon frowned. Even that movement hurt. *Surreal?*

A gasping sob. *Hurry. To the Altar.*

Surreal, what—

She's bleeding!

He didn't remember making the pass. One moment he was cramped in the underground rectangle, the next he was braced against the tree, eyes closed, waiting for the world to stop spinning. *Surreal, get to the Altar. Now.*

The uncles will be coming after us.

The Sadist bared his teeth in a vicious smile. *Let them come.*

The link broke. Surreal was already riding the Winds to Cassandra's Altar.

Daemon clung to the tree. His body could give him nothing. The Black Jewels were still drained and could give him nothing. Needing strength, he greedily drained the reserve power in his Birthright Red.

SADI!

The power behind that thundering voice hit his Red strength and absorbed it as easily as a lake absorbs a pail of water.

Daemon clamped his hands over his head and fell to his knees. That power was tightening like a band of iron inside his head, threatening to smash his inner barriers. Snarling, he lashed back with the little strength he had left.

Daemon.

Glacial rage waited for him just outside the first barrier, but now he recognized the voice.

Priest? Daemon let out a gasp of relief. *Father, pull back a little. I can't . . . It's too strong.*

The power pulled back—a little.

You are my instrument.

No.

The psychic band tightened.

I serve no one but Witch. Not even you, Priest, Daemon snarled.

The band loosened, became a caress. *I, too, serve her, Prince. That's why I need you. Her blood runs.*

Daemon fought to stand up, fought to breathe. *I know. She's being taken to Cassandra's Altar.* He hurt. Hell's fire, how he hurt.

Let me in, namesake. I won't harm you.

Daemon hesitated, then opened himself fully. He clenched his teeth to keep from screaming as the icy rage swept into his mind. His vision doubled. He felt the tree against his back. He also felt cold stone beneath bare feet.

The stone faded, but not completely. He slowly opened and closed his hand. It felt as though he were wearing a glove beneath his skin. Then that too faded, but not completely.

You're controlling my body, Daemon said with a trace of bitterness.

Not controlling. By joining this way, my strength will be a well for you to tap and, in turn, I will be able to see and understand what we must do to help her.

Daemon pushed himself away from the tree. He swayed, but another pair of legs held firm. Taking a deep breath, he caught the Black Wind and hurled himself toward Cassandra's Altar.

Daemon hurried through the ruins of the Sanctuary's outer rooms. The footsteps he'd heard a moment ago stopped. Now an angry Gray wall blocked the corridor that led into the labyrinth of inner rooms.

"Surreal?" Daemon called softly.

A sob answered him. The Gray wall dropped.

Daemon ran toward her. Surreal waited for him, tears streaming down her face.

"I wasn't in time," she sobbed as Daemon took the sheet-wrapped bundle from her shaking arms and held it close to his chest. "I wasn't in time."

Daemon turned back the way he'd come. "Cassandra must have a room here somewh—"

Go to the Altar, namesake.

She needs—

The Altar.

Daemon turned again, racing toward the Altar that lay in the center of the Sanctuary. Surreal ran ahead to push open the Altar room's stiff wrought-iron gate. Daemon rushed in and carefully laid Jaenelle on the Altar.

"We need some light," he said, desperation making his voice harsh.

Witchlight bloomed overhead.

Cassandra stood behind the Altar. Her Black Jewels glowed. Her emerald eyes stabbed at him.

Daemon looked down and saw the blood on his shirt.

Courage, namesake.

"So," Cassandra said quietly, her eyes never leaving Daemon's face, "you're both here."

Daemon nodded as he swiftly unwrapped the sheet.

Cassandra clamped a hand over her mouth, stifling a scream.

Blood gushed between Jaenelle's legs. Daemon's hands were slick with it as his fingers rested at the junction of her thighs and became a channel for a delicate tendril of power and the little healing Craft he knew. He searched, probed.

Witches bled more on their Virgin Night than other women, and dark-Jeweled witches most of all. They paid for their strength with moments of fragility, moments when the balance of power shifted to the male's advantage and left them vulnerable.

But even that didn't explain this much blood.

Searching, probing.

Icy shock ran through him when he found the answer. Glacial rage followed.

"They used something to tear her open. The bastards *tore her open.*" He slid his hands over her torso, over the cuts and bruises. *How much healing Craft do you know?* he snapped at Saetan.

I have a great deal of knowledge, but even less of the healing gift than you. It's not enough, Daemon.

*Then who *has* enough?*

Jaenelle's blank eyes stared at him.

Daemon reached to cup her face in his hands.

"No," Cassandra said, coming around the Altar. "Let me. A Sister won't be a threat."

Daemon hated her for saying it. Hated her even more because, right now, it was true.

Let her try, namesake, Saetan said, forcing Daemon to step back.

Cassandra pressed her fingers against Jaenelle's temples and stared into the unblinking eyes. After a minute, she stepped back and wrapped her arms around herself, as if needing comfort. Her lips quivered. "She's out of reach," she said in a hoarse, defeated whisper.

It didn't mean anything. Jaenelle was stronger than the rest of them. She could descend further. It didn't mean anything.

But Tersa's vision of the shattered crystal chalice mocked him. *You know,* it said. *You know why she doesn't answer.*

"No." Daemon wasn't sure if the denial was his or Saetan's.

Surreal stepped forward. Her face was ashen, but her gold-green eyes flashed with determination. "The girl Rose said they'd given her too much medicine and she couldn't get out of the misty place. Probably a vile mixture of *safframate* and a sedative."

Saetan's voice sounded tightly calm. *I can't sense a link between her body and her Self. It's either very faint or she's severed it completely. If we don't draw her back now, we'll lose her.*

You mean I'll lose her, Daemon snapped at him. *If her body dies, *you'll* still have her, won't you?*

He felt heart-tearing pain come through the link.

No, Saetan whispered. *I was told by one who would know that dreams made flesh don't become *cildru dyathe.**

Daemon closed his eyes and took a deep breath. *How deep is your well, Priest?*

I don't know.

Then let's find out. Daemon turned to Surreal. *Go out. Keep watch. Those sons of whoring bitches will be coming soon. Buy us some time, Surreal."

Surreal glanced at the Altar. "I'll keep them out until I hear from you." She slipped through the wrought-iron gate and disappeared into the labyrinth of dark corridors.

"Go with her," Daemon said to Cassandra. "This is private."

Before she could protest, Saetan said, *Go, Lady.*

Daemon waited until he was sure she was gone. Then he stretched out on the Altar and took Jaenelle in his arms.

The power from Saetan flowed into him, wrapped around him.

Keep the descent at a steady pace, Saetan warned.

So easy to slip into that abandoned body, so easy to glide down through all that emptiness until he reached the depth of his own inner web. He held there, trying to probe farther down.

Far, far, far below him, a flash of lightning lit up a swirling black mist.

Jaenelle! Daemon shouted. *Jaenelle!*

No answer.

Spinning out the link to make it thinner and longer, Daemon eased past the depth of his inner web.

Daemon! Saetan's worry vibrated through the link.

A little deeper. A little deeper.

He felt the pressure now, but kept spinning out the link.

Down down down.

Like diving too deep in water, the abyss pressed against him, pressed against his mind. That inner core of Self could go only so deep. Any deeper and the very power that made the Blood the Blood would try to pour into a vessel too small to hold it, crushing the spirit, shattering the mind.

Down down down. Gliding through the emptiness, spinning out the link between him and Saetan thinner and thinner.

Daemon! Saetan's voice was a hoarse, distant thunder. *You're too deep. Pull up, Daemon. Pull up!*

A tiny psychic feather rose out of the mist that was still far below him, brushed against him and withdrew, startled and puzzled.

Jaenelle! Daemon shouted. When he got no answer, he sent on a spear thread. *I felt her, Priest! I felt her!*

He also felt agony through the link and realized he was being pulled upward.

No! he yelled, fighting the upward pull. *NO!*

The link snapped.

No longer tied to the power Saetan was channeling, he became an empty vessel that the power in the abyss rushed to fill. Too much. Too fast. Too strong.

He screamed as his mind ripped, tore, shattered.

Shattering and shattering, he fell, screaming, and disappeared into the lightning-streaked black mist.

Surreal put the finishing touches on the spell she was weaving across a corridor that led to the inner rooms and toyed with the idea of shoving Cassandra into it just to see what would happen. She didn't have anything against the woman personally, but that sulky temper and the dagger glances Cassandra kept throwing back toward the Altar room were fraying nerves already stretched a little too thin.

She stepped back and rubbed her hands against her trouser seat. Calling in a black cigarette, she lit it with a little tongue of witchfire, took a puff, and then offered it to Cassandra, who just shook her head and glared.

"What are they trying to do that it has to be private?" Cassandra said for the tenth time in the past few minutes.

"Back off, sugar," Surreal snapped. "That smart-ass remark about her trusting you more than him was enough reason for him to toss you out the door."

"It's true," Cassandra said angrily. "A Sister—"

"Sister, shit. And I don't hear you bitching about the other one I caught a whiff of."

"I trust the Priest."

Surreal puffed on the cigarette. So that was the Priest. Not a male she'd care to tangle with. Then again, Sadi wasn't a male she cared to tangle with either.

She snubbed out the cigarette and vanished it. "Come on, sugar. Let's create a few more surprises for Briarwood's darling uncles."

Cassandra eyed the corridor. "What is it?"

"A death spell." A vicious gleam filled Surreal's eyes. "First one who walks through that—it'll burst his heart, burst his balls, and finish the kill with a blast of the Gray. The spell gets sucked into the body so there's nothing anyone can trace. I usually add a timing spell to it, but we want to hit them fast and dirty."

Cassandra looked shocked. "Where did you learn to build something like that?"

Surreal shook her head and headed for another corridor to set another trap. This wasn't the time to tell Cassandra that Sadi had taught her that particular little spell. Especially when she kept wishing he'd taught it to Jaenelle.

Daemon slowly opened his eyes.

He knew he was lying on his back. He knew he couldn't move. He also knew he was naked. Why was he naked?

Mist swirled around him, teasing him, offering him no landmarks. Not that he expected to find anything familiar, but even the mind had landmarks. Except this was Jaenelle's mind, not his, in a place too deep for the rest of the Blood to reach.

He remembered feeling a hint of her as he probed the abyss, remembered diving, falling. Shattering.

Something moved in the mist. He heard a quiet *clink clink,* like glass tapping glass.

He turned his head toward the sound, feeling as if it took all of his strength to do so little.

Don't move, said a lilting, lyrical voice that also contained caverns and midnight skies.

The mist drew back enough for him to see her standing next to slabs of stone piled up to form a makeshift altar.

Shock rippled through him. The crystal shards on the altar rattled in response.

Don't move, she said, sounding testy as she carefully fitted another shard of the shattered chalice into place.

It was Jaenelle's voice, but . . .

She was medium height, slender, and fair-skinned. Her gold mane—not quite hair and not quite fur—was brushed up and back from her exotic face and didn't hide the delicately pointed ears. In the center of her forehead was a tiny, spiral horn. A narrow strip of gold fur traced her spine, ending in a small gold and white fawn tail that flicked over her bare buttocks. The legs were human and shapely but changed below the calf. Instead of feet, she had dainty horse's hooves. Her human hands had sheathed claws like a cat's. As she shifted position to slip another shard into place, he saw the small, round breasts, the feminine curve of waist and hips, the dark-gold triangle of hair between her legs.

Who . . . ?

But he knew. Even before she walked over and looked at him, even before he saw the feral intelligence in those ancient, haunted sapphire eyes, he knew.

Terrifying and beautiful. Human and Other. Gentle and violent. Innocent and wise.

I am Witch, she said, a small, defiant quiver in her voice.

I know. His voice had a seductive throb in it, a hunger he couldn't control or mask.

She looked at him curiously, then shrugged and returned to the altar. *You shattered the chalice. That's why you can't move yet.*

He tried to raise his head and blacked out. By the time he could focus again, she had enough of the chalice pieced together for him to realize it wasn't the same one Tersa had shown him.

That's not your chalice, he shouted happily, too relieved to care that he'd startled her until she bared her teeth and snarled at him.

*No, you silly stubborn male, it's *yours.**

That sobered him a little, but her response sounded so much like Jaenelle the child, he didn't care about that either.

Taking it slow, he propped himself up on one elbow. *Then your chalice didn't shatter.*

She selected another piece, fit it into place. Her eyes filled with desperation and her voice became too quiet. *It shattered.*

Daemon lay down and closed his eyes. It took him a long moment to gather the courage to ask, *Can you repair it?*

She didn't answer.

He drifted after that. Minutes, years, what did it matter? Images swirled behind his closed eyes. Bodies of flesh and bone and blood. Webs that marked the inner boundaries. Crystal chalices that held the mind. Jewels for power. The images swirled and shifted, over and over. When they finally came to rest, they formed the Blood's four-sided triangle. Three sides—body, chalice, and Jewels—surrounding the fourth side, the Self, the spirit that binds the other three.

The images swirled again, became mist. He felt something settle into place inside him as the mist re-formed into a crystal chalice, its shattered pieces carefully fitted together. Black mist filled in the cracks between each piece, as well as the places where tiny pieces were missing.

He felt brittle, fragile.

A finger tapped his chest.

A thin skin of black mist coated the chalice, inside and out, forming a delicate shield around it.

The finger tapped again. Harder.

He ignored it.

The next tap had an unsheathed nail at the end of it.

Cursing, he shot up onto his elbows. He forgot what he'd intended to say because she was straddling his thighs and he could have sworn he saw little flashes of lightning deep in her sapphire eyes.

Snarly male, she said, tapping his chest again. *The chalice is back together, but it's very fragile. It will be strong again if you keep it protected long enough for it to mend. You must take your body to a safe place until the chalice heals.*

I'm not leaving without you.

She shook her head. *The misty place is too dark, too deep for you. You can't stay here.*

Daemon bared his teeth. *I'm not leaving without you.*

Stubborn snarly male!

I can be as stubborn and as snarly as you.

She stuck her tongue out at him.

He responded in kind.

She blinked, huffed, and then began to laugh.

That silvery, velvet-coated laugh made his heart ache and tremble.

Before, he'd seen Witch beneath the child Jaenelle. Now he saw Jaenelle beneath Witch. Now he saw the difference—and no difference.

She looked at him, her eyes full of gentle sadness. *You have to go back, Daemon.*

So do you, he said quietly.

She shook her head. *The body's dying.*

You could heal it.

She shook her head more violently. *Let it die. Let them have the body. I don't want the body. This is my place now. I can see them all when I stand in this place. All the dreams.*

What dreams?

The dreams in the Light. The dreams in the Darkness and the Shadow. All the dreams. She hesitated, looked confused. *You're one of the dreams in the Light. A good dream.*

Daemon swallowed hard. Was that how she saw them? As dreams? She was the living myth, dreams made flesh.

Made flesh.

I'm not a dream, Lady. I'm real.

Her eyes flashed. *What is real?* she demanded. *I see beautiful things, I hear them, I touch them with the body's hand, and they say bad girl to make up stories, those things are not real. I see bad things, cruel things, a twisted darkness that taints the land, a darkness that isn't the Darkness, and they say bad girl to make up stories, bad girl to tell lies. The uncles say no one will believe a sick-mind girl and they laugh and hurt the body so I go away to the misty place to see the gentle ones, the beautiful ones and leave them ice that hurts them when they touch it.* She hugged herself and rocked back and forth. *They don't want me. They don't want *me*. They don't love *me*.*

Daemon wrapped his arms around her and held her close, rocking with her as words kept tumbling out. He listened to the loneliness and confusion. He listened to the horrors of Briarwood. He listened to bits of stories about friends who seemed real but weren't real. He listened and understood what she didn't, what she couldn't.

If she didn't repair her shattered mind, if she didn't link with the body again, if she didn't re-form the four-sided triangle, she would be trapped here, becoming lost and entangled in the shards of herself until she could never find a way to reach what she loved most.

No, he said gently when her words finally stopped, *they don't want you. They don't love you, can't love you. But I *do* love you. The Priest loves you. The beautiful ones, the gentle ones—*they* love you. We've waited so long for you to come. We need you with us. We need you to walk among us.*

I don't want the body, she whimpered. *It hurts.*

Not always, sweetheart. Not always. Without the body, how will you hear a bird's song? How will you feel a warm summer rain on your skin? How will you taste nutcakes? How will you walk on a beach at sunset and feel the sand and surf under your . . . hooves?

He felt her mood lighten before he heard the sniffled giggle. As she raised her head to look at him, her thighs shifted where they straddled him.

A fire sparked in his loins and he stirred.

She leaned back and watched him swell and rise.

He saw innocence in her face, a kitten's curiosity. He saw a female shape that, if not fully mature, was also not a child.

He clenched his teeth and swore silently when she began stroking him lightly.

Stroke. Observe the reaction as if she'd never seen a man become aroused. Stroke. Observe.

He wanted to push her away. He wanted to pull her down on top of him. It was killing him. It was wonderful.

As he reached for her hand to stop her, she said in a quiet, wondering voice, *Your maleness has no spines.*

Rage froze him. The shards of the chalice rattled as he leashed the fury that had no outlet here. For a moment he tried very, very hard to believe she was comparing him to another species of male, but he knew too much about the twisted males who enjoyed breaking a young, strong witch on her Virgin Night.

Mother Night! No wonder she didn't want to go back.

She studied him, puzzled. *Does the body's maleness have spines?*

Daemon swallowed the rage. The Sadist transformed it into deadly silk. *No,* he crooned. *My maleness has no spines.*

Soft, she said as she stroked and explored.

His hands whispered over her thighs, over her hips. *It could give you pleasure,* he crooned softly.

Pleasure? Her eyes lit up with curiosity and anticipation.

The childlike trust stabbed him in the heart.

She must have sensed some change in him. Before he could stop her, she exploded, kicking his thigh as she leaped away from him. Out of reach, she hugged herself and glared at him.

*You want to mate with the body. Like the others. You want me to make her well so you can put your maleness inside *her.**

Rage washed through him. *Who is *her*?* he asked too softly.

Jaenelle.

You're Jaenelle.

I AM WITCH!

He trembled with the effort not to attack her. *Jaenelle is Witch and Witch is Jaenelle.*

They never want me. She thumped her chest with her fist. *Not me. They don't want me inside the body. They want to mate with Jaenelle, not Witch.*

He felt her fragment more and more.

This is Witch, she screamed at him. *This is who lived inside the body. Do you want to mate with Witch?*

Anger made him lash out. *No, I don't want to mate with you. I want to make love to you.*

Whatever she was about to say went unsaid. She stared at him as if he were something unknown. She took a hesitant step toward him.

She'll take the bait, the Sadist whispered inside him. She'll take the bait and step into the pretty trap.

Another step.

Deadly, deadly silk.

Another.

A sweet trap spun from love and lies . . . and truth.

I've waited seven hundred years for you, he crooned. *For you.* His lips curved in a seducer's smile. *I was born to be your lover.*

Lover?

Almost within reach.

Without his body, the seduction tendrils weren't as potent, but he saw the change in her eyes when they reached her.

Still, she hovered out of reach. *Then why do you want the body?*

Because that body can sheathe me so that I can give you pleasure. He watched her think about this. *Do you like my body?*

It's beautiful, she said reluctantly, and then added hurriedly, *but you look the same here. And Witch can sheathe your maleness.*

The Sadist held out his hand. *Why don't we find out?*

She took his hand and gracefully settled over him, straddling his thighs. Then she looked at him expectantly.

He smiled at her while his hands explored her, soothing and arousing. When his fingers tickled the underside of her fawn tail, she squeaked and jumped. He resettled her tighter against him, wrapped one arm around her hips to keep her still while his other hand slid through the gold mane and cupped her head. Then he kissed her. A soft kiss. A melting kiss. She sighed when he caressed her breasts. She trembled when he licked the tiny spiral horn.

When he was sure she'd taken the bait, he whispered, ★Sweetheart, you're right. This place is too dark for me. The chalice is too fragile and I . . . I hurt.★

She looked at him regretfully but nodded.

★Wait,★ he said when she tried to move away. ★Can you come up with me? Up to my inner web?★ He licked her ear. His voice became a throbbing purr. ★We'd still be safe there.★

He leashed the urgency he felt and waited for her answer. There was no way to tell how much time had passed at the Altar, no way to know if their bodies were still there, no way to know if hers still lived, no way to know if those monsters from Briarwood had reached the Sanctuary. No way to know what his body was doing.

He pushed the thought away. He didn't have a link now; the Priest did. Whatever he was doing, it was Saetan's problem.

The rushing ascent caught him by surprise. He grabbed her at the same moment she wrapped her legs around him.

★Lover,★ she said, smiling at him. Then she giggled.

He wondered if, with a lifetime of wandering in that strange blend of innocence and formidable knowledge, she knew what the word meant.

Doesn't matter, the Sadist whispered. *She took the bait.*

They rose until they were high in the Black, comfortably above his inner web.

★Better?★ she asked shyly.

★Much better,★ he answered, fitting his mouth to hers.

He kissed her until she relaxed, and then he sighed again.

Hurry, the Sadist whispered.

He leaned his forehead against hers and yelped when the tiny spiral horn jabbed him.

She giggled and kissed his forehead. ★Kisses make it better?★

Revulsion swamped him for a moment. That was a child's voice. A *young* child's voice.

He looked over her shoulder, trying to reconcile the female shape wrapped around him with that voice, and saw fragments of shattered crystal floating through the Black.

Pieces of her. Pieces and pieces of her. Part of her was still intact. Had to be. The part that held the knowledge of the Craft. How could she have put him together otherwise? But if she kept slipping in and out of those fragments . . .

Like Tersa. Worse than Tersa.

Daemon?

The midnight voice, with a deadly edge to it.

Remember this side of her, the Sadist warned. *Ignore the rest.*

Daemon smiled at her. *Lover,* he said, nipping her lower lip. Then he used every trick he'd ever learned to sweeten the bait.

But he wouldn't let her raise her hips to sheathe him.

Still too dark, he gasped when she began to whimper and snarl. *Let's go to the Red. It's my Birthright.*

She tried to shake off the seduction tendrils he'd woven around her, but he'd spun his trap well.

We can have a bed there, he coaxed.

She shuddered. Whimpered. There was no pleasure in the sound.

An image appeared. A bed just big enough for the game. A bed with straps attached to the ends to tie down wrists and ankles.

He dismissed the image and replaced it with his own. A large room with deep, soft carpets. A huge bed, its canopy made of gauze and velvet. Silk sheets and downy covers. Mounds of pillows. The only light came from a slow-burning fire and dozens of scented candles.

Blinded by romance, she sighed and melted against him.

He held the image, teasing, tantalizing as they rose to the Red.

As they settled among the silk and pillows, he tried to reach for some link—his body, the Priest, anything—and choked on frustration. So close. So close and there was nothing for him to tap into to finish it—except the power Jaenelle had shaped around his chalice to hold the pieces together.

Caressing and soothing, loving and lying, he kept her focused on the pleasure while he cautiously sipped the power forming the skin inside the chalice.

The skin shrank. The top fragments wobbled but held.

Enough.

He reached for Saetan. Found exhaustion and a killing fury.

He struck first. *Hush, Priest.* He waited a moment, tapped a little more of the power holding the chalice together. *Use whatever you can now to form a tether. And prepare for a fight. I'm bringing her back.*

He reached for his body next. It was still stretched out on the Altar, next to Jaenelle. He strengthened the connection enough so that his body imitated his movements.

Smiling, Daemon slowly rolled on top of her. Gently pinned her hands on either side of her head.

He kissed her, nuzzled her as they rose and rose and rose.

She rubbed against him. *Lover,* she whimpered.

Soon, he lied. *Soon.*

Up and up.

He was moments away from slipping back into his body when her eyes widened and she felt the trap spring around her.

No! she screamed.

Baring his teeth, he slammed both of them back into their bodies.

Her screams filled the Altar room. Blood gushed between her legs.

"Heal the body, Jaenelle!" Daemon shouted, fighting to keep her connected to her body while she tried to throw him off. *"Heal it!"*

Her fear pounded against his mind.

You lied to me. You LIED!

*I would have said anything, *done* anything to get you back,* he roared, his nails digging in to hold her. *Heal it!*

Letmego letmego letmego.

Bodies fought. Selves fought. As they tangled furiously, he felt Saetan slip the tether around her leg.

One flick of the power within her would tear him apart, would set her free. Instead she begged, pleaded.

*Daemon, please. You're my friend. *Please.**

It hurt to hear her beg.

Witch-child. Saetan's voice, cracked and trembling.

Jaenelle stopped fighting. *Saetan?*

We don't want to lose you, witch-child.

You won't lose me. I can see you all in the misty place.

Saetan's words came slowly, as if each one pained him. *No, Jaenelle. You won't see us in the misty place. If you don't heal your body, Daemon and I will be destroyed.*

Daemon's breath hissed through his teeth. The Sadist wasn't the only one who could spin a deadly trap.

Her wail filled their minds, filled his ears as the child body echoed the sound.

He felt a tidal wave of dark power rush up out of the abyss, felt it fill the young body he held in his arms, felt it mend torn flesh.

Her body relaxed, went limp.

Daemon raised a shaking hand to stroke her golden hair.

"I'm sick," Jaenelle said, her voice muffled against his chest.

"No, sweetheart," he corrected gently. "You're hurt. That's different. But we'll get you to a safe place and—"

The Sanctuary shook as someone unleashed a dark Jewel.

An angry male voice changed to a terrified shriek.

Jaenelle screamed.

Daemon dove into the abyss a second before she did, catching her at the Red as she tried to flee the body.

Sucking the power from the chalice, he held on to her.

Pieces wobbled.

No, Daemon, Jaenelle shrieked. *You can't. You *can't.** Suddenly she collapsed against his chest. *I healed the body. It's still hurt, but it will mend. Let me go. Please, let me go. You can have the body. You can use the body.*

Daemon pressed her back against his chest. He rested his cheek against her gold mane. *No, sweetheart. No one's going to use your body but you.* He closed his eyes and held her tight. *Listen, my Lady Witch. I lied to you, and I'm sorry. So very sorry. But I lied because I love you. I hope you'll understand that one day.*

She sagged against him, saying nothing.

Listen to me, he said softly. *We're going to take your body away from here. We'll keep it safe. Is there some landmark in the misty place that you can always find?*

She nodded wearily.

There's a tether around your leg. Take it off and tie it around that landmark. That way, when you're ready, it'll show you the way back. It took him a moment to say the rest. *Please, Jaenelle, please repair the chalice. Find the shards and put it back together. Return to the body when the Priest tells you it's safe. Grow up and have a rich life. We need you,

Lady. Come back and walk among those who love you, those who have longed for you.★

He let her go.

She hesitated a moment before leaping away from him. When there was enough distance between them, she turned around.

Daemon swallowed hard. ★Try to remember that I love you. And if you can, please forgive me.★

He felt her lightly touch his mind, felt her dark power re-form the thin skin that held him together.

She closed her sapphire eyes.

He watched her shape change.

When she opened her eyes, Jaenelle stood before him, not quite a woman but no longer a child. ★Daemon,★ she said, her voice a soft, sighing caress.

Then she dove into the abyss, and his heart shattered.

He made the ascent for the last time and tumbled into his body.

He heard angry male voices coming from the outer rooms. He heard shrieks of pain. Heard stone exploding. Heard the sizzle of power meeting power.

He didn't move. Didn't try. He laid his head on Jaenelle's chest and wept silently, bitterly.

★Daemon.★ Saetan brushed against his mind and pulled back. ★Daemon, what have you done?★

★I let her go,★ Daemon cried. ★I told her you'd tell her when it was safe to come back. I told her about the tether. I let her go, Priest. Sweet Darkness, I let her go.★

★What have you done to yourself?★

★I shattered the chalice. I lied to her. I seduced her into trusting me and *I lied to her.*★

A brief touch, gentle and hesitant. ★She'll understand, namesake. In time, she'll understand.★ Saetan faded, came back. ★I can't hold the link anymore. Cassandra will open the Gate and take you—★

Saetan was gone.

Daemon wiped his face with his sleeve. A little longer. He had to hold on a little longer. But he felt so empty, so terribly alone.

The sounds of fighting got closer. Closer.

Cassandra burst into the room. "There's no time left."

Daemon slid from the Altar and collapsed.

Ignoring him, Cassandra rushed over to the Altar and brushed her hand over Jaenelle's head. "You didn't bring her back."

Her anger sliced through the thin skin of power holding the chalice together, leaving weak spots.

"The body is healing," Daemon said hoarsely. "If you keep it safe, it will mend. And—"

Cassandra made a sharp, dismissive gesture.

Daemon cringed. The Altar room blurred. Sounds became muffled. He struggled to focus. Struggled to stand up.

By the time he was braced against the Altar, the bloody sheet was lying on the floor, Jaenelle was wrapped in a clean blanket, the black candles were lit, and the wall behind the Altar was turning to mist.

"How much time do you need?" Daemon asked.

Cassandra cradled Jaenelle in her arms and glanced at the mist. "Aren't you coming through the Gate?"

He wanted to go with them. Sweet Darkness, how he needed to go with them. But there was Surreal, who would keep fighting until he gave her a signal or she was destroyed.

And there was Lucivar.

Daemon shook his head. "Go," he whispered as tears filled his eyes. "Go."

"Count to ten," Cassandra said. "Then get rid of the candles. They won't be able to open the Gate without them." Holding Jaenelle tightly, she stepped into the mist and disappeared.

A male voice shouted, "There's a light!"

Surreal rushed into the Altar room. "I threw up a couple of shields to slow them down, but nothing short of blowing this place apart is going to hold them."

. . . four, five, six . . .

The Sanctuary rocked as the combined power of several Jewels blasted through one of the shields.

"Sadi, where . . ."

Another blast of power.

"Damn," Surreal hissed, pulling her knife from its sheath.

The angry voices came closer.

. . . eight, nine, ten.

Daemon tried to vanish the black candles. Not even that much power left. "Vanish the candles, Surreal. Hurry."

Surreal vanished the candles, grabbed Daemon's wrist, and hauled him through the stone wall just as Briarwood's uncles reached the Altar room's wrought-iron gate.

He wasn't prepared for a long pass through stone walls, and Surreal's attempt to shield him wasn't quite enough. By the time they finally got through the outside wall, his clothes were shredded and most of his skin was scraped raw.

"Shit, Sadi," Surreal said, grabbing him when his legs buckled. Using Craft to keep him upright, she studied his face. "Is she safe?"

Safe? He desperately needed to believe she was safe, that she would come back.

He started to cry.

Surreal wrapped her arms around him. "Come on, Daemon. I'll take you to Deje's. They'll never think to look for you in a Chaillot Red Moon house."

Before he could say anything, she caught the Green Web, taking him with her, first heading toward Pruul, then doubling back on other Webs, and finally heading for Chaillot and Deje's Red Moon house.

Daemon clung to Surreal as she flew along the Winds, too weak to argue, too spent to care. His heart, however . . . His heart held on fiercely to Jaenelle's soft, sighing caress of his name.

Everything has a price.

About the Author

Anne Bishop is a winner of the William L. Crawford Memorial Fantasy Award for *The Black Jewels Trilogy*. She lives in upstate New York. Visit her Web site at www.annebishop.com.